BLOCKADE RUNNER

RONALD A. ZEITZ

INFINITY
PUBLISHING.COM

ISBN 0-7414-5158-1

Front and back cover design by Alex Campuzano.

Published by:

INFINITY
PUBLISHING.COM

*1094 New DeHaven Street, Suite 100
West Conshohocken, PA 19428-2713
Info@buybooksontheweb.com
www.buybooksontheweb.com
Toll-free (877) BUY BOOK
Local Phone (610) 941-9999
Fax (610) 941-9959*

Printed in the United States of America

Printed on Recycled Paper

Published March 2009

Dedication

To my wonderful children,
Whitney, Victoria and Jonathan who are everything a father
could wish for; to my grandchildren, Jackson, Collin and
Nicolas, and especially to Alice, who was instrumental
in getting this book out the door.

Introduction

This is an historical novel. *The Great Eastern* was a real ship; she came into service in 1858. The scene aboard the ship in Annapolis where the owners of the ship entertain U.S. President James Buchanan was an actual event and formed the basis for the plot of this story.

As Dr. Stephen Wise noted in his introduction to his book *Lifeline of the Confederacy, Blockade Running During the Civil War,* "Blockade Running not only brought to the South the supplies needed to sustain the nation, but also caused a revolution in ship building. …goods coming into the Confederacy were carried on fast, light-drafted steel- and iron-hulled steamers." *The Great Eastern,* while not a shallow draft vessel, could certainly have performed these duties admirably, as she does in the book.

The Civil War spawned the expansion of many techno-logical developments; the telegraph, railroads, and advanced weaponry. The hot air balloon as an observation point was first introduced in the Civil War as were the first iron warships.

All of the factual characters, including President Abraham Lincoln, his Secretary of the Navy Gideon Welles, his Secretary of State William Seward and other members of his cabinet as well as Captain Farragut and Captain Du Pont acted and performed their duties much as history has recorded them.

John Beauregard and Susannah Eddings as well as many others are figments of my imagination, as is Agent George Percy. Agent Allan Pinkerton, however, is not.

BLOCKADE RUNNER
BOOK ONE

The Great Eastern

Her colossal size almost eclipsed her astonishing reputation.

She was the largest iron steamship built in the nineteenth century. Designed to carry 4,000 passengers, her capacity was twice that of vessels built 70 years later.

She had two sets of engines, five smokestacks, ten boilers and six masts, built to handle the 6,500 yards of sail. Each mast was named after a day in the week, in sequence, so the largely illiterate deckhands could easily identify the correct mast. The list of the ship's features went on and on; the largest grand saloon afloat; the first true double hull for safety in case she struck something; gas lighting; bathtubs with hot and cold running seawater in many of the staterooms and a pair of satellite steamers lashed to her sides, to shuttle passengers back and forth when she was in port.

Walt Whitman wrote of her sailing up Lower New York Bay:

"Nor I forgot to sing of the wonder, the ship as she swam up my bay,

Well shaped and stately the Great Eastern swam up my bay, she was 600 feet long, (sic)

Her moving swiftly surrounded by myriads of small craft I forgot not to sing."

She carried enough coal to send her to India and back. Fully loaded, she displaced 27,000 tons. Most vessels of her time displaced only one-tenth that weight.

But she was jinxed even before she was launched. At least six workers died during her construction; she killed and injured several more during the five months it took just to launch her into the Thames River.

She even managed the death of her builder, the famous British engineer Isambard K. Brunel, who died in sorrow after hearing that one of her funnels blew up during her maiden voyage. The same explosion also killed a number of her firemen.

Her first master also died, not by her hand directly, but by a sudden squall that capsized his gig as he was going ashore.

She bankrupt three separate sets of owners and consumed millions of British pounds before she carried her first paying passenger.

It would be hard to believe how such a blatant symbol of bad luck could become the focus of the salvation of an entire country.

1.

The tall thin man dressed in a black wool suit seemed out of place on the Annapolis waterfront. After all, this was a hot August day in 1860 and nearly everyone else was dressed for the heat and their dockside occupations.

The man walked slowly into the ship chandler's shop where the ship's carpenters and others bought the myriad of ropes, pulleys and stays needed to keep the enormously complicated sailing ship rigging in top operating shape.

"Anyone know when *The Great Eastern* is dropping anchor out in the Bay?" the stranger asked.

One of the store's clerk suddenly appeared from behind a stack of barrels. "We heard sometime early this afternoon," the clerk said, "but that's really up to the whims of the wind and the Lord," he added, invoking the name of the Almighty, as if He was in control of the gigantic iron steamship.

"Thanks." The man turned and walked back out onto the dock. He took his bowler off his head and wiped the perspiration from his brow with his handkerchief. As he put his hat back on, he turned and looked down the bay. George Percy, one of Allan Pinkerton's most effective spies, saw a huge cloud of black smoke spewing from an equally large ship's black hull.

The ship could already be seen, even though she was several miles down the Chesapeake Bay. As she drew closer, her size became better defined from the frothy green water stirred up by her sidewheels and propeller. Likewise, the size of the bow wave created by her speed helped put her monstrous size in better perspective.

By now, people from all over town were rushing towards the harbor piers, anxious to get a closer look at the 680-foot British iron steamship. Everything about her overshadowed the port city.

Her masts were nearly as tall as the just-finished, 121-foot Maryland Statehouse and could be seen from virtually any spot in the city. Her hull occupied so much space that it nearly blocked traffic from arriving or leaving the port.

But George Percy's reason for watching the ship weigh anchor went far beyond casual curiosity. As a Union espionage agent, his boss had sent him down from Washington to learn as much as he could about the ship and where she was going. There were rumors that the South was exploring a long-term charter with the owners.

The Great Eastern had come to Maryland's capital city to pay her respects to the United States and its President, James Buchanan. That was the stated purpose. But the ship's owners were simply shopping the vessel's role as a cargo ship, here to try and persuade the President to charter the vessel to carry cotton to England. And there was a subtle warning inherent in the request.

Already on board, the President was escorted to the ship's grand saloon. Over an elegant lunch, Daniel Gooch, one of the ship's directors, put the proposition directly in front of the President.

"Mr. President," he began, "what would be the possibility of the United States chartering the *Great Eastern* to carry the south's cotton crop to the mills in Great Britain? She could probably carry the entire crop in four or five voyages." The Director leaned back in his chair, awaiting the President's reaction.

The President "thought well of it," according to a later entry in Gooch's diary. But the shrewd ship company's officer saved his *coup d' grace* for last. Leaning forward and speaking in a low voice he added, "Don't you think it would be a wise move to charter the ship to keep her out of the South's hands in the event of war? If you decide to blockade the southern ports, what chance do your wooden naval vessels have against the 27,000 tons of iron that make up the ship's hull?"

In spite of the seemingly dire consequences inherent in Gooch's warning, Buchanan, true to his tradition, did nothing. The nation seemed destined for conflict; the President either unwilling or unable to do anything to prevent the South from seceding from the Union.

And George Percy, intent on the mission he was sent to do, watched the ship's smaller satellite steamers start to make their way back to the Annapolis dock with the presidential party on board. He began to plot how he was going to get on board the ship while she was still in port.

2.

Upstairs, on the main deck, newly-minted Ensign John Beauregard looked down the expanse of the vessel. He had joined the ship during its stay in Annapolis harbor and was thinking how lucky he was to be serving his apprenticeship aboard the most modern ship in the world. The appointment came through after his graduation from Annapolis last June. He would apprentice aboard *The Great Eastern* as a guest of the British government. He was told he had been selected because he had excelled in the steam propulsion courses at the Academy while most of his classmates, not believing sailing vessels would become obsolete, managed only average grades in these new technology courses.

He was excited by the prospect of traveling to London, his first foray into the world outside the South. But he was also excited about having met Susannah Eddings. He remembered the night she first kissed him.

He had been attending a party in Beaufort for Cousin Charles. John had danced with every lady who was there to honor Charles, just about the whole population of Beaufort. But it was Susannah Eddings who most interested him. Unfortunately, she was engaged to his childhood friend Peter Jenkins.

In appearance, Susannah was the quintessential Southern Belle. Her green-brown eyes and petite face were framed by shoulder-length hair that had been done up in a chignon. Her well-proportioned breasts, highlighted by the peach-colored low cut gown that she had worn, completed her perfect figure.

But her engagement to his friend stopped him from going any further than asking her to dance. Chasing after Susannah would likely result in her refusing his advances—ending his friendship with Peter.

Still, he remembered, there was that sudden kiss she gave him out on the garden walk where they had gone to cool off after a lively

Virginia Reel. They sat down on one of the cast-iron benches and were making polite conversation.

He subtly glanced at her breasts, perpetuating the ages-old male fixation and fascination. He wanted to touch her neck but knew that the gesture would be misunderstood. Instead he took Susannah's hand. "How about a short walk in the garden? Would Peter miss you for a few moments?"

"No, he's not the jealous type. Besides you're one of his best friends," she added, her eyes penetrating intensely into his clear, blue-green eyes. "Why should he mind?"

They stood up and walked out to the edge of the garden, and sat down on the low brick wall. John gently put his arm around Susannah's shoulder, noticing how the whiteness of the moonlight made her skin almost appear luminescent. She moved closer to him and he touched the glowing shoulder with his hand. She turned her head to face his, neither of them speaking a word. Her eyes showed excitement and anticipation. Suddenly her full red lips were pressed against his mouth, fulfilling his thoughts but catching him completely by surprise.

What had seemed so forbidden just moments before had become a reality, and was a delicious interlude for both of them. He knew she had been thinking the same thing.

They separated and Susannah self-consciously turned her head away. She spoke first.

"That was very impulsive of me. I'm sorry if I embarrassed you. But I trust you and want you to be my friend."

She turned her head towards him. The usually sparkling green-brown eyes were sad and moist. "John, I want you to promise me you will never repeat what I'm going to tell you."

The young ensign had no idea what was coming next. But then he had no idea she was going to kiss him either. "I promise," he replied.

"Oh John I—I love Peter, but I don't love him." She seemed to hesitate, to be unsure of what she wanted to say. "There's something missing. I just don't feel like I want to be with him, here on the Islands the rest of my life. Last spring in Charleston I found out something about myself. I want to do something that's important and means something." A big tear slowly made its way down her cheek. "I can't do that here, where people will expect me to be the quiet, devoted plantation owner's wife, always socially right. The people of Charleston seemed so alive, so vibrant, so concerned with what's happening around them. They talk about values, the South and its destiny; how passionately Governor Calhoun felt about states' rights before he died. I found myself able to relate and learn."

By now Susannah was sobbing, her unhappiness and ambition overwhelming her. The tears were rolling down the high cheekbones, glistening in the moonlight like tiny liquid diamonds. John reached in his pocket and handed her his handkerchief. "Am I so terrible? Should I break my engagement? What should I do John?" She dabbed gently at her face.

They stood up and began to walk back to the house, where the strains of "Turkey in the Straw" wafted out over the lawn.

She stopped and turned to him. "Please, please don't mention a word of this to anyone, John. I've got to get it out of my system somehow. Peter is such a good person and his family loves me. I'd never have to worry about anything. I just have to think this through."

They reached the stairs to the veranda and stopped. John gently grabbed Susannah's hand and pulled her around to face him.

"It's a sacred secret with me. I'm glad I was there when you needed to talk to someone. Say no more."

He dropped her hand and they walked up the stairs towards the music.

How much had happened between them since that first kiss! Their letters back and forth; her meeting him in Charleston when he was on leave; her mentioning that she was thinking of breaking of her engagement to Peter. John began to wonder where this was going.

3.

The reception being held on December 26, 1860 at the Trenholm mansion in Charleston was billed as a celebration of South Carolina's secession from the Union. It was a moment of great importance to George Trenholm, who headed an international trading firm known as Fraser Trenholm that had offices in London and Charleston. Fraser Trenholm handled much of the growing business that stemmed from cotton sales to the British mills.

In a little more than 100 years, Great Britain had gone from being the adversary, to becoming a very active trading partner with the United States. American cotton was in great demand for the English mills, so much so that Great Britain had become the biggest consumer of Southern cotton. And Fraser Trenholm was in an excellent position to capitalize on this need.

But George Trenholm was also the chairman of the local chapter of the Committee and thus his business acumen often meshed with the South's political issues as well.

The tall, distinguished international trader had invited Susannah Eddings to the reception to offer her a proposition. They were standing alone in a corner of the living room. "You can be of great use to the Committee and serve the Cause well if you could see your way clear to live in Washington for awhile, Susannah."

The statement caught Susannah off guard but she managed to retain her composure. She took a sip of her champagne and looked up at her host. "Mr. Trenholm, I am flattered that you think I could be of some useful service to our Committee and the Cause. But I am engaged to Peter Jenkins whose family owns a large plantation on Fripp Island. I love Peter. His family looks forward to me becoming part of them and having children."

The trader had expected Susannah to offer some resistance to such a radical proposal. So he decided to play his next card. He moved closer to her and spoke in a low voice. "I'm asking you to become a confidant of a well-known wealthy Washington socialite, Rose Greenhow. She has made many friends in the government and military, and entertains them frequently. Mrs. Greenhow has been extremely successful at obtaining important information about the government's intentions and plans. She plays an important role in our efforts to find out what the Union is going to do. You would be in a pivotal position to learn what is going on and so advising the Committee. It's a very important role to play. Would you consider postponing your marriage?"

The request surprised Susannah. She put down her champagne glass on a side table. The idea of socializing in Washington while gathering clandestine information was exciting and intriguing. It also appealed to her Southern loyalty and patriotism. So did the idea that she would be put in a very influential position.

But it was the thought of not having to address marrying Peter immediately, something she was already thinking about, that made the proposition more interesting. "When do you need an answer, Mr. Trenholm? I'd like the opportunity to discuss it with Peter and his family as well as my mother." A servant had refilled Susannah's glass. She picked it up and took another sip.

"Rose Greenhow is an old friend of mine," George Trenholm continued. "You will be in the company of many of the country's most famous people. Your upbringing and schooling in Connecticut have prepared you well for this role. You have the grace and grooming to move easily among these people."

It was the last sentence that brought a smile to Susannah's face.

4.

Susannah broke the news of postponing her wedding with Peter after a New Year's dinner party hosted by Peter's parents. Her reason seemed logical to her; she wanted to learn more about how the political system works and what better place to learn than Washington D.C.?

Susannah's decision made no one happy. Her mother, having spent the money to send her to finishing school in Connecticut to prepare her for a life as a plantation owner's wife, denounced the move as irresponsible.

Peter Jenkins was crushed. The woman he had wooed and made plans to marry and settle down with had now announced her plans to move several hundred miles away. Worse yet, Susannah did not say when she would return; only that she would write him after she had become settled in Washington.

But once in Washington, all the unhappiness she had created was in the past. She eagerly took to the social whirlwind that was a staple of Rose Greenhow; the wealthy socialite hosted grand parties for most of the elite society that made up the Capitol's population. And that included many young, handsome, single military officers.

5.

His snoring woke her up. Susannah Eddings rolled slowly over on her side, a half smile on her face. She nervously bit her lower lip—a habit she had developed when she was plotting. Slowly she pushed her long silken chestnut locks from her face as she glanced at the still-sleeping Jordan, the handsome young military attaché' whom she had met the night before at a social gathering in Rose Greenhow's Washington mansion. Susannah had gotten lost in his steely gray-blue eyes, as he responded to her own intense brown-green eyes.

She had continued to flirt with Jordan, moving around the room, letting his eyes follow her from one group of people to another, and returning his glances with an intensity that left little room for interpretation. Jordan had no suspicions of her motives, thinking it was his good looks that had attracted her attention. As he skillfully guided Susannah upstairs to one of the widowed socialite's bedrooms, the tall, mustached officer heard Susannah ask, "Why Jordan, Rose was telling me you were going to Fort Moultrie. How brave you are! Are you going by yourself?"

He turned around at the top landing of the elegant staircase to answer her. "No, I'm leading a small company of 19 men." He smiled at her and gently grasped her hand as they took the last few steps to the top of the stairs.

Oh," she said, feigning disappointment, "I guess you won't be back by the end of the week. I was going to ask you to have tea with me at Rose's on Friday afternoon. Will you be back by then?" she had asked coquettishly. She was getting very skillful at extracting sensitive information, especially when her target was such an energetic good-looking 20 year-old like herself.

He put his arm around her shoulder, drawing her closer to him. She gazed seductively into his eyes. "How thoughtful of you to invite me!" he said, somewhat surprised, squeezing her shoulder as they entered the bedroom. "I'm afraid I'll be gone for about a week." He gently closed the bedroom door, pulling her very close to him. Their eyes met again. In a voice laced with lust he muttered, "But I'll certainly look forward to seeing you when I return."

His lovemaking had gone on and on, although it seemed like it had only been a moment.

Jordan was stirring now, rolling over on his side. He was half awake and caressing the small of her back under the down comforter. She slowly slid out of his grasp, as if she herself were still asleep. After a while the hand slid off her body and the slow steady snoring resumed. She waited a few moments, and then moved silently out of the fourposter. Quickly slipping into her dressing gown, she tiptoed out of the room, grabbing her crinoline, shoes and the dress she had worn last night.

The door to Rose Greenhow's own bedroom, across the hall, was open, a sure sign that the Washington socialite had not entertained anyone last night. Susannah found her sitting in a rocking chair, working on one of her well-known tapestry bookmarks containing secret information that she passed along to Confederate officers. Rose looked up from her needlepoint and motioned for Susannah to close the door. Susannah then made her way to the washstand in the corner and poured warm water into the bowl.

In a very faint whisper, the socialite spoke. "He's very good looking. Was his information useful?" Rose Greenhow's large brown eyes had a friendly yet mischievous twinkle to them.

Susannah was dabbing the wash water from her face. She turned and crossed the room to Rose's rocking chair. She bent over and whispered "Oh yes. I've got to get it to the Committee. They need it to prepare Charleston's defense. And you? What did you learn from Breckinridge last night?"

Rose flashed her famous coquettish smile. "Well, we're making progress."

"Just what does that mean?" Susannah had raised her whisper to a low murmur.

Quickly raising her finger to her lips and whispering "sshh!", Rose Greenhow said, "He's going to introduce me to some people in the planning department. That ought to be good. I'll be getting the information before the Generals in the field. Isn't that a hoot?"

Across the hall, sounds of movement came from the bedroom Susannah had just left. The two women looked at each other. Rose Greenhow motioned to the door in her room that led to a back stairway.

In a very quiet whisper, Susannah spoke. "Would you mind telling Jordan when he gets up that I'm going to see a sick relative and had to leave town suddenly?" She was pulling on the dress she had worn last night. Hastily, she got into her coat.

Rose Greenhow nodded as Susannah tiptoed across the room and out the doorway.

6.

After the inauguration of Abraham Lincoln as President of the United States, the Government was already positioning itself for a conflict with the South.

Gideon Welles, newly appointed Secretary of the Navy and former newspaperman from Connecticut, was on his feet in the President's office, his intense stare rivaling that of his superior.

"Blockade? How the hell do you ever expect me to enforce a blockade of the entire Southern coast of the United States, Mr. President?"

Abraham Lincoln leaned back in his chair, cooly watching the reaction to his proclamation to the other cabinet member present, Secretary of State William Seward.

"It's the only way we can strangle the insurrection, the *only* way: economic deprivation." Seward leaned forward in his chair, couching his remark in a condescending tone and emphasizing his point with an index finger directed at Welles.

The President sat up abruptly, as if to seal the argument. "I have every confidence that we will restore unity to this country as quickly as possible. I see no possibility of a permanent separation of North and South. But I must take steps to limit the effectiveness of the South's military. Depriving their economy of military supplies is that first step."

Welles realized he was in no position to challenge the President. So he turned to his archrival Seward, who had a reputation for meddling in military affairs.

"Do you realize how the rest of the world will view us blockading our own ports? Why we'll be laughed at from London to St. Petersburg, and every major capital in between. What kind of diplomacy expert are you anyway? Where you study international law? In some brothel?"

"Mr. Welles! I insist you temper your remarks." The President rarely raised his voice. He didn't have to. The tone was enough to dominate. Backing that up was Lincoln's glare from his deep-seated eyes. Welles slowly eased himself back into his chair, his eyes still fixed on the Secretary of State.

"I'm sorry Mr. President, but I'm not sure Mr. Seward is aware that he has just given the South the status of a belligerent rather than just an insurrectionist. That gives them all kinds of rights, not to mention that of nations trading with them."

The President stood up and turned to gaze out the window. "I have made up my mind. We will impose the most effective blockade we can on the major ports of the South. Mr. Welles, I want you to draw up a list of those ports with your aides and submit it to me by tomorrow evening."

Abraham Lincoln sat down at his desk, a signal the meeting was over. Welles and Seward stood up and walked out of the President's office.

But the day itself was by no means over.

A messenger arrived with the news of the fall of Norfolk to the Confederates. The Union's prized Navy Yard at Gosport had been overrun, in spite of efforts to burn the drydock and machining facilities. Altogether, ten ships were destroyed and the Virginia militia seized 1,200 heavy duty cannon and 2,800 barrels of gunpowder.

7.

Susannah quickly closed the heavy glass door of the Greenhow mansion behind her. Outside, she pulled her shawl tightly about her shoulders before the chilly, late-March midmorning air.

She found an empty cab on Pennsylvania Avenue and directed its driver to take her to the railroad station, located on Capitol Hill, next to Constitution Avenue.

Alighting at the front of the station, she passed through the doors and went directly to the ticket counter. As she was counting out the train fare money, a harsh grip on her left arm startled her. The voice had a definite menace to it and Susannah Eddings was terrified.

The voice was low but she could hear it quite well over the waiting room din.

"We'll just stroll on out to the train platform Miss Eddings." His hand was hurting the soft part of her upper arm. "I want to talk privately with you."

She turned suddenly to see who the menacing stranger was. "Who are you? You know I could scream right now and have you arrested."

"In your best interest, I wouldn't do that. I could have *you* arrested by the Provost Marshall as a spy against the Federal government. We have enough on you and Rose Greenhow to have you both thrown in jail."

The bearded man pushed the door to the platform open and they walked out. A train had just pulled in. Their presence went unnoticed in the confusion and noise of passengers getting on and off the cars. The chuffing and hissing of the steam engine added to the chaos. The stranger guided Susannah to the front of the train, near the engine. He tightened his grip on her arm.

"You're really hurting me!"

"You'll be hurt much more if you don't do what I'm about to tell you. I don't know what you're taking back to Charleston, but whatever it is, it's probably not going to do the United States of America any good. Now listen and listen carefully. I want you to try and contact your Navy friend—the one you've been writing to in England. We know he's been stationed in Charleston for the winter."

He relaxed his grip.

"And then what?" Susannah then knew she was in grave danger.

"We want to know what he knows about British ships. Specifically *The Great Eastern*. Armament, speed, effectiveness of the crew, cargo capacity, even her destinations."

She eased out of his grip.

"Look, whoever you are...." she said defiantly...

"Name's Percy. That's all you need to know because that's all I'm going to tell you."

"...and what am I supposed to do with the information, assuming I can get it?" she said angrily.

"You can contact me at this address when you find out something." He handed her a piece of paper with an address unknown to her. "Don't worry, that house is way up in Northwest near Pierce Mill. It's along Rock Creek. No one will see you. If I don't hear from you in two weeks, I'll assume you want me to disclose your identity to the proper authorities, which I will do."

His stare became menacing. "They'll arrest you the next time you set foot in Washington."

"That's simple blackmail! I won't compromise and spy for you!" Susannah's voice was incredulous.

"You don't understand, young lady. You're already compromised by us knowing what you're doing. You have no choice."

The locomotive let go with a long mournful whistle, signaling imminent departure.

Susannah was staring at the intricate flashing motion of the engine's driving rods as the lumbering steam engine began to move. Percy gripped her arm firmly again, as if to seal the agreement.

He leaned close to her ear. "You know what happens to spies? They get hung. I would hate to see that beautiful neck snapped by the hangman's noose. Do you know what it feels like to be strangled to death?"

The train's coaches rumbled noisily by. Susannah turned her head to face the bearded agent.

"This time and this time *only*. Then I'm going to find out who *you* are and do something about it." She had regained enough of her composure to put some force in the word "you."

Percy let go of her arm and turned to walk away. "Two weeks," was all he said.

He disappeared back into the station.

8.

Gideon Welles was right.

The imposition of a naval blockade on the entire southern half of the United States coastline was a lot more complicated than simply issuing an edict.

Nevertheless, the word was getting out. It was easier to start in the larger coastal cities where a telegraphic notice could be sent from the United States Department of the Navy and be posted in conspicuous places around the harbor. The larger port cities would most likely have naval vessels nearby, ready to enforce the action.

Captain Joseph Fripp had just been promoted, the result of years of successfully braving storms, fighting the wind and ocean currents and trying to keep a crew together while delivering his cargo on time. His little schooner, one of the hundreds that plied the coast, would become the focus of the blockade, for it was these vessels that were able to sail in and out of the shallow channels and estuaries to pick up and deliver cargo. And it was his intimate knowledge of not just the wind and current's vicissitudes but also of the many channels and inlets that were part of the estuary of Port Royal Sound that made him effective.

He wondered how these Union blockaders, unfamiliar with the coastline, would fare chasing ships like his, led by men, who like himself, knew the territory. He was confident he could out sail, if not outrun, the Federal gunboats.

"Ready to cast off, Captain!" The voice from his ship's deck was his first mate, Ashby Wyatt.

"Give the order to cast off, Mr. Wyatt."

"Aye, aye, Sir."

The deckhands unloosened the lines from the pilings. Others pushed poles against the wharf to separate the ship from its berth.

Part of his cargo was several dozen barrels of gunpowder and boxes of cartridges, along with fifty bales of cotton, loaded in Beaufort. The ammunition was his first contraband cargo and would clearly be a violation of the new Federal order. But the offer of a bonus to carry it was hard to refuse. The ship rapidly cleared Fort Sumter and headed into the Atlantic. A fresh breeze from the southeast heeled the *Port Royal* to port. The wind had cleared out the fog, but an early morning drizzle remained.

"Course zero one zero, Mr. Scott. Hold that course." His destination would be the military dock at Georgetown. From there his forbidden cargo would make its way inland to the supply depots.

"Aye, aye, Sir. . ." The helmsman's acknowledgment was abruptly cut off.

"Warship astern sir, looks like about two thousand yards." The alarm came from First Mate Wyatt, who had been scanning the sea behind the ship with his spyglass. "Union ship, Sir, and a big one!"

"Change course to zero zero zero. That'll head us toward the North Edisto River. We should be able to outrun her in shallower water."

He ducked into his small aft cabin, which also served as the charthouse. In the dim early morning light, aided by the charthouse's single lantern, he peered at the chart and tried to calculate how far he was from the inlet. It looked to be about an hour's sail, provided the fresh breeze kept up.

The charthouse door opened suddenly. He looked up from the chart table at Ashby Wyatt's troubled face.

"It's the *Niagara,* Sir! I recognize her by her twin funnels," he yelled. "Largest and fastest the Navy's got. Over 5,000 tons. At least 31 guns. Coming straight for us. She'll make better than 14 knots."

They both ran to the fantail. Although Fripp couldn't identify just which warship it was, there was no doubt she was headed directly for the *Port Royal*. The size of her bow wave told him she was under full steam. From time to time the wind and current swung the ship to port. He could see the open gun ports in her huge black hull, menacing and threatening. For all her size and bulk she was surprisingly graceful and even majestic, her bowsprit proudly piercing the morning drizzle. But the thick black smoke that was streaming from her two funnels said that today she was in pursuit of his ship.

He decided to make another course change to a run for the South Edisto River, a direct line west from his present course. Although the navigable part of the river didn't go very far inland, it was far enough to prevent the *Niagara* from getting within effective gun range. He could also count on the dunes to help protect his ship from destruction.

"Mr. Wyatt, we're going to make a run for the South Edisto River. Tell Mr. Scott to change to course two four five and rouse the next watch now to help with the sails."

Fripp raised his spyglass to take a closer look at his pursuer but stopped. The enormous frigate was gaining on the smaller vessel so rapidly that he could clearly see that a crew was preparing to fire the bow gun at the *Port Royal*.

The *Niagara* was coming bow-on but as Joseph Fripp watched, her course changed slightly towards the shoreline, allowing it to block Fripp's escape route.

A puff of smoke, followed by an explosion, signaled the first salvo. It whistled overhead and plopped into the ocean, about forty yards to the starboard side of the schooner.

The sails were luffing, as the course change was occurring faster than the crew scurrying through the rigging could adjust the sails. Fripp could see the *Niagara* had run up signal flags, showing a "hove-to and prepare to be boarded" order. But the captain of the *Port Royal* wasn't giving up yet.

The *Niagara* fired again. This time no one even heard the whistling sound; instead a horrible crash of splintering wood, combined with a loud tearing noise, filled the deck of the ship. Pieces of the yardarms came crashing down on the crew, who ran forward to avoid the flying debris. The exploding shell rained metal shards everywhere.

First Mate Wyatt saw the impending chaos and ran out on deck, shouting an order.

"Back on station! Get that mess cleaned up fast!"

"Mr. Wyatt, what's the damage?" Fripp turned as he asked the question to see the immense black hull of the man-o-war coming closer to his little ship. He also heard the sound of flapping canvas and more debris falling through the rigging, hopelessly entangling the remaining sails on the aft mast.

Without warning, the *Port Royal* suddenly changed course again and Joseph Fripp saw why. A piece of the yardarm had struck the helmsman and he lay on the deck unconscious. Deftly jumping over the tangle of wood, ripped canvas and rope, Fripp got to the ship's wheel and swung her into the wind, knowing his schooner could probably change direction faster than the big frigate.

For a time, the maneuver worked. The 5,000 ton vessel's captain realized too late that he was going to overrun the smaller ship's position as he drew abreast of the schooner and watched helplessly as the beleaguered sloop fell astern. Unsure of their target's direction, the starboard gun crews aboard the *Niagara* withheld their fire. That, too, was a mistake, as they now had missed a clear broadside shot. As the frigate passed ahead of the smaller vessel, Joseph Fripp could hear shouted orders from the deck of his pursuer.

Ashby Wyatt appeared before the helm. "Sir, we still have the forward mast intact. The rear mast is nearly gone and two of the crew were killed by the falling debris. Do you want to rig for the single sail?"

"Yes. Stand down the clean-up crew and rig the forward sail for running. Can we get something to catch the wind on the rear mast?" Everyone had to shout over the noise and chaos.

The *Port Royal's* captain took his eyes off the course of his vessel and the *Niagara* to look up at the tangled mess of rigging and torn sails overhead, perilously swinging back and forth in the wind.

Three deckhands were ordered up into the rigging to untangle and hopefully salvage something that could serve as a sail.

Joseph Fripp now pointed the ship directly for the shoreline, hopeful that he could beach the vessel before the *Niagara* destroyed her and killed him and his crew. Crippled by having only one sail, the little ship nevertheless slowly began to pick up speed, even as the frigate, now about 300 yards astern, tried to turn towards the shore.

Using sabers and bowie knives, the aft mast crew cut through the mess and, in time, had jury-rigged a sail that slowly began to fill out.

"Mr. Wyatt," Fripp shouted, "have the lookout give me a fix on the shoreline and get someone back here to man the helm."

Visibility had improved somewhat, and the lookout shouted that they were about 1200 yards offshore. Unfortunately, Joseph Fripp saw that the captain of the *Niagara*, rather than trying to sink the *Port Royal* with cannon fire and cut off his escape route, now pointed the bow of the frigate directly at the hull of the schooner. Fripp knew that if he could get to within less than a thousand yards of the beach, the bigger vessel would have to turn back to avoid a grounding.

It would be close. Another cannonball whistled overhead, barely missing the intact forward mast. It raised a plume of water in the ocean almost half as tall as the *Port Royal's* remaining mast.

Suddenly, the wind died, creating the dreaded flapping sound in the canvas overhead. The huge black hull was less than 100 yards away. Joseph Fripp decided he and his crew would fare better in the water than on the deck of the doomed ship.

"Mr. Wyatt, abandon ship!" he shouted, "and tell the men to make it to shore. I'll follow shortly."

"Aye, aye, Sir."

The remaining sailors lost no time in going overboard, even though the water temperature was less than 60 degrees. It was just in time.

An explosion just behind the forward mast threw Joseph Fripp onto the deck. Mercifully, the smoke from the ensuing fire prevented him from seeing the terrifying sight of the *Niagara*'s bow, easily twenty feet taller than the deck of the *Port Royal*, coming directly at the ship and crashing through the side of the merchantman. He leaped to his feet, running the few yards to the fantail and jumping over to join his crew in the cold seawater.

Behind him, the destruction of the coastal schooner became complete as the momentum of the steam frigate caused her to slice clear through the schooner's hull, as if the warship's hull were a sharp knife cutting a block of lard. The captain of the *Niagara* immediately ordered a course correction to port, taking him away from the dangerously shallow water, and leaving the crew of the *Port Royal* floundering in the Atlantic Ocean.

9.

The thick bluish tobacco smoke hung in the humid June evening air, at times obscuring the customers and even the lamps that illuminated the tavern. Maybe it was just as well; most of the people crowding the bar and tiny tables didn't especially want to be seen, other than by their own company.

Gadsby's Tavern was more than four blocks from the Alexandria waterfront. But it still attracted its share of unsavory waterfront characters: drunken sailors spoiling for a fight, boatswains forcibly conscripting unsuspecting hands to make up crew shortages and the usual pimps and prostitutes.

In a dark corner of the taproom, two men were talking quietly. The shorter of the two was powerfully built and had a round face that looked like it was permanently etched in a frown. Perhaps it only appeared that way because the eyes were unusually close together, the nose forming an almost perfect triangle with the narrow bridge at the top of the triangle, blending into the bushy eyebrows.

The other man was taller, thinner, with long gangly arms and hands that had large bony fingers capped with dirty fingernails. His sunken cheeks underscored large blue eyes that had a perpetual look of sadness about them. Both wore bowlers, their brims shielding the two from casual identification. The tumblers on the rough wooden table were empty and the bottle of bourbon was almost as full as when they had sat down almost an hour ago.

Allan Pinkerton, the shorter man, had asked his most reliable associate, George Percy, to meet him down near the waterfront because he didn't want any of official or social Washington to see or hear him talking with his most trustworthy spy.

Pinkerton reached for the bottle, pulled out the cork and refilled his associate's tumbler.

"How's the Eddings girl taking her new assignment? Has she given you any information yet?"

The unshaven spy sipped from his glass. "No. Not yet. She's a feisty one. Keeps threatening to tell some rebel officer that I've stolen jewelry from her if I don't leave her alone. I reminded her of just how much trouble she's already in."

The man who had been responsible for establishing Abraham Lincoln's first Secret Service put his hands down slowly and deliberately, turning his eyes directly on his associate's. "Anything yet about *The Great Eastern*?"

"Nope. Said she didn't know what I was talking about. She told me she has to go to London to hold some meetings this spring. Something about raising money for the war. Meantime, I told her to try and find out more from her ensign friend. He's stationed in Charleston for the winter."

Allan Pinkerton suddenly perked up. What appeared to be a stalled situation had become an opportunity to get information on the ship faster.

"Good! She can sail on *The Great Eastern*. I'll go along as Major E. J. Allen. I'll have her introduce me to her ensign friend personally."

Percy's sad eyes suddenly narrowed. "What's so important about that ship?"

Pinkerton lowered his already quiet tone. "We don't know. There've been some rumors about some group chartering her." He leaned forward, his voice low. His tone became menacing, his perpetual frown deepening. "Imagine that huge iron hulk as a warship, Percy." He picked up his half-chewed, half-smoked cigar and turned to the candle on the table to light it.

"Imagine her in service against the Union fleet. Iron against wood. Her 27,000 tons against our *Hartford*'s 2,900. Fifteen knots of speed to our frigate's twelve." The cigar end began to glow bright orange as Pinkerton drew on it.

He blew out a puff of smoke. *"That's* why there's all this interest. And Susannah Eddings is the perfect foil to get us the information from her ensign about the charter."

Pinkerton leaned back in the hardwood chair. The cigar began to glow again. "With my being on board I can look the ship over for myself and also find out any arrangements being made. I'll make sure she's giving us the right information."

Percy looked at his Scottish boss, the sad eyes now showing apprehension, the eyebrows raised, the thin lips set in a line. "Mr. Pinkerton, I've heard that ship is jinxed. She ain't never sailed with a full load of passengers and she's already blown up once. I think you're taking a big chance. . ."

Another sudden puff of cigar smoke from Pinkerton cut off the rest of Percy's sentence.

". . .Percy, she's a threat to the Union. We've got to find out everything about her. Secretary Welles and the President are counting on us. . ."

Some shouting over by the bar drowned out the rest of his sentence. A couple of petty officers, their tunics unbuttoned, hats cocked to the sides of their heads, were subduing a drunken dockhand. As he struggled to escape from becoming forced labor aboard some ship, one of the officers sealed his fate with a large wooden club. His limp body collapsed on the floor. The two men picked him up and carried him out of the tavern.

10.

Susannah was hurrying along Meeting Street, already late for her encounter with the Committee. A brisk, late-afternoon breeze made the walk somewhat chilly. In her haste Susannah had left her woolen shawl at her friend Martha Peyton's house. She always stayed there when she was in Charleston.

Martha Peyton had met Susannah at one of the many social events hosted by the Trenholms. The two became best friends almost immediately and Martha recruited Susannah into the Committee in Charleston. At first Susannah naively believed that the Committee's stated mission was one of education. But like much else that was going on in Charleston, appearances were not necessarily everything they seemed. After Susannah had started working with Rose Greenhow in Washington she began to put two and two together. Soon the Committee began giving Susannah assignments to try and get specific information.

The brick building that housed Fraser Trenholm's Charleston offices and that of the Committee was already a center of activity that afternoon. There were at least three carriages parked in front of the door with as many horses tied up to the hitching post. Susannah became somewhat apprehensive.

She opened the door and hurried upstairs to the Committee's office. Inside were three people: Martha, and two men Susannah had never met. She shut the door and sat down next to the single desk that occupied the small office.

"I'm sorry I'm late. Time just seemed to get away after I arrived from Washington last night," she smiled apologetically to the two gentlemen.

Martha spoke. "Susannah Eddings, I'd like you to meet a couple of friends of the Committee, Sergeant James Cabell and Lt. Donald Stevens, both of the South Carolina militia. Because of our work, I invited them here to hear what you found out in

Washington. I also asked them not to come here in uniform for obvious reasons."

The younger of the two spoke first. "You said you just arrived from Washington last night Miss Eddings?"

"Yes, I arrived about midnight. It's almost four days on the train."

Her voice showed the fatigue of travel. "I was asked to find out just how many troops are going to be sent down here to fortify Forts Moultrie and Sumter and when they were coming and how many to each location."

She paused and crossed her legs. "Well, at first nobody would tell me anything. It turns out with the new administration in place, nobody seemed to know just how many troops would be sent."

She directed her gaze at the two men. "I finally was able to talk to someone who was a holdover from Buchanan's administration. There's only a group of soldiers to accompany the Kentuckian who's being sent to replace old General Gardner. There's no threat to the city."

This time there was an even longer pause. The lieutenant turned slowly in his chair to the sergeant, several years older than himself. The older man spoke.

"How reliable is your information, ma'am? I mean, I know you can't name your sources. . ."

Susannah cut off his sentence curtly. "Sergeant, let's just say it comes from a reliable and impeccable source. One that's been used and tested before. I'm frankly. . ."

Lt. Stevens turned to face Susannah and leaned forward, gently laying a hand on her arm. "The sergeant didn't mean no insult ma'am," he said, trying to calm her obvious impatience. "You understand, we have to pass this on to our superiors, and if all we can say is that we got it from the Committee, well, that's just not going to set well. If you could just give us an indication of what part of the government or wherever it came from, that'll help a lot."

Susannah, furious but attempting to disguise it, uncrossed her legs, slumped slightly in her chair and put her head in her hands. Her voice cracked slightly. "Forgive my outburst. I'm really tired. The man I spoke to is an attaché in Scott's office. He has direct access to the General as well as his boss, Secretary Floyd. My acquaintance in Washington, who Martha knows, can vouch for this man's integrity."

The confrontation had passed. The soldiers thanked the two ladies and quickly left the Committee office, cautiously elated at the outcome of the meeting and the information they now felt sure was correct.

Martha stood up and spoke to Susannah. "You <u>look</u> tired. Let's go back to the house. I'll have Beulah fix us some warm soup. Oh, by the way, there's a letter for you. I guess you missed it last night when you got in."

The two women left the office and hurried back to Martha's house. Outside, it had become dark and the chilly sea breeze was now uncomfortable. Once back at the small Georgian-styled house, they hurried into the parlor, where Beulah had started a fire in the fireplace. The pungent smell of wood smoke permeated the entire dwelling.

Susannah saw the letter on the entryway table and picked it up. It was from John, and had a local return address on it. She tore open the envelope. Martha watched her face for signs of emotion.

A big smile broke out as Susannah read the letter, and her eyes danced. "He's been reassigned to Charleston until the end of this month. His ship's been laid up for the winter in London. He'd like to come by and see me tomorrow. Oh. . .!"

"It's been since last fall that you saw him, right? I haven't seen you this happy in months. And how did he know you were here?"

"I don't know, I don't know. I told him I was staying both in Washington and here. Maybe he just guessed."

"You may want to think twice about seeing him. Does he know about the Committee's work? Its *real* purpose?"

"No, and I don't intend to tell him." Susannah was careful the way she phrased the sentence. Martha must not know about Percy and Allan Pinkerton and why she had to see John. So she decided to act like she was smitten.

"I am <u>dying</u> to see him. He's so handsome, so intelligent, so forceful and yet so gentle."

"Sounds like my kind of man. When do I get to meet him?"

"Can we have him for dinner tomorrow? I need time to get my clothes washed and pressed. And some sleep!"

"I'll tell Beulah to send someone with an invitation tonight."

Susannah barely heard her as she had gone into the study to write John a note.

11.

They made love all afternoon and in their afterglow the delicious haze of desire was almost fulfilled. They both lay still, expended, saying nothing for a while. Susannah spoke first. "I missed you so much darling." She was now lying supine, her left arm still curled around John's neck, and feeling very content.

"I know I've missed you. And I'm glad to be back in Charleston. Somehow the bunks on board *The Great Eastern* don't have the comfort or delight of this one, especially with you here."

John Beauregard was looking dreamily at her chestnut-brown hair spread randomly across the pillow.

At the mention of the ship she raised her eyes to his and asked in a low-keyed voice, "Tell me about the ship. Are the British good sailors? I'm really curious."

"Since when have you become interested in ships?" His question was somewhat mocking her, yet he was curious why she was interested in *The Great Eastern*. His face looked puzzled.

She noted this as she coquettishly said, "Since I think I've fallen in love with someone who sails on them."

He started to tell her about Captain Hall, about the size of the ship, how powerful *The Great Eastern* was, and how many men it took to run her. The carriage clock on the mantle interrupted his monologue by striking four o'clock.

She took her hand and put it gently to his mouth. "Martha will be back soon and we should clean up and get dressed for dinner. I understand we're having roast pheasant, in your honor. You can tell me about the ship before dinner."

She sat up suddenly as her eyes flirted with him. "You didn't react when I said I was falling in love. Did you think I meant someone else?" He was standing in front of her, pulling on his long underwear.

He stopped, and took her hand. "Susannah, I'm crazy about you. Not a day went by when I was on the ship that I didn't think about you. If I thought you'd say yes, I would ask you to marry me, while I'm here in Charleston."

She looked up at him, smiling. After a brief moment gazing into each other's eyes, she got off the bed and began putting on her clothes. "After I broke my engagement with Peter I felt so bad that I told myself I'd never get involved with anyone again. He was crushed. He told me he wanted me for his wife; how he wanted to have children with me. I told him I could never stay long on the plantation, that I loved the excitement and cosmopolitan atmosphere here. He said he'd try and understand; I think we parted as friends. Since that time, outside attending a few social affairs in Washington, I've not seen or even thought about anyone." She carefully left out her encounters with Jordan and the other army officer she'd slept with to get the information she needed. To her, that was Southern loyalty.

"Well, I want you to think about it. I could ask to be stationed permanently here in Charleston. You could continue your work for the Committee. The way things are, we're going to war and they're going to need my experience. Did you know we hardly have any warships stationed down here?"

They were both standing. He put his arms around her as hers encircled his neck. They kissed, not the passionate deep kisses of just a few moments ago; just warm loving caresses. They parted and she looked up into his deep-set maddenly green-blue eyes.

"You make me very happy, John. I will think about it. I do love you but I don't know if I've gotten rid of all the wanderlust yet."

Her role as a double agent would now include a role as a multiple lover. She wondered how long she could keep it all from John.

12.

Back in the officer's billet after dinner with Susannah, John Beauregard tried to avoid thinking about his intense lovemaking with Susannah; there would be nothing but frustration in that. He thought of what it was that attracted him to her besides the physical beauty and remembered his intuitive feelings that there was more than just beauty behind her demeanor. She seemed to have no master but herself. It was like some unknown force, recognizable to her and no one else seemed to drive her, yet make her restless. When they were together, she often seemed preoccupied, his role reduced to simply a companion or lover.

He did not mind this passive role she wordlessly asked him to play by her gestures. He had often brought up how he felt as a Southerner at Annapolis, with all the transparent Northerners who had no sense of tradition or value. He was surprised to find out how passionately Susannah also felt about the traditions of the South, in spite of her rejection of marriage to a plantation farmer. He knew it was important for her to feel independent and if that included being the quiet one from time to time, then so be it.

He wondered about her work on the Committee. When pressed for detail, she changed the subject, or, if they were alone, she would start a lovemaking session. It worked; he would forget about the conversation, so intense was the physical attraction and need for her. He liked that part of their relationship particularly well; when she wanted him, she often took the initiative, not waiting for an overture from him.

But it still troubled him that she spent so much time in Washington, meeting with members of the military. And who was this Rose Greenhow she mentioned? What was she doing with those people?

While those questions went unanswered, a senseless beating of a deckhand he had witnessed while still on the ship continued to bother him. He needed to talk to someone about his feelings; about what he had been brought up to believe and what he perceived to be a brutal practice inflicted on a helpless individual.

He decided to write his parents a letter. Their last letter to him had been full of news; the cotton planting would be doubled for the year; his friend Peter Jennings had enlisted in the local militia and was expected to serve under his uncle. Except for Peter's and other young men's enlistments, the war seemed very far away indeed to them.

But he needed to tell his mother and father about his troubled feelings regarding the treatment of the conscripted deckhands. He swung his feet off the bunk and sat down on the floor in front of his footlocker and began to write:

Dear Mother and Father,

I hope everyone is well and that the spring planting is proceeding smoothly. I have been lucky and have not contracted some of the awful maladies that go along with sea duty such as seasickness and something called the Virginia quickstep that has one continually running to the head. It is usually because of the food given to us.

But The Great Eastern *has a fine officers mess. Since we are usually not at sea for more than two weeks and always docking in big cities, the food stays pretty fresh. Our British cooks do a pretty fair job with most everything but beef. God how they can turn a steak into a piece of leather! They know how to cook lamb, though. Since this is such a large ship, we have our own herds of sheep and cattle on board which are slaughtered as needed.*

I saw something the other day that has troubled me very much and I wanted to tell you about it. There is a practice used by the officers on most sailing ships (and even steamships like The Great Eastern*) that calls for the bosuns to canvass all the dockside bars and flophouses for vagrants when the ship is in port. Once found, they beat these poor souls into unconsciousness and bring them aboard ship, locking them up until the ship is underway. They are then forced to perform the most basic labor involved in the running of the ship, including the very dangerous work atop the spars necessary to set the ship's sails properly.*

While another American officer and I were on deck the other day, one of these seaman was dragged out next to the mast, lashed to it, and flogged by the bosun until the poor man was unconscious. There was blood everywhere and he was left out in the sun without food or water for the whole day. Nobody tended to his wounds. He had apparently disobeyed an order and that was what the punishment was for.

It was the most inhuman thing I ever saw. It reminded me of the line from the Robert Burns poem Man was Made to Mourn *where he says "Man's inhumanity to man makes countless thousands mourn." I thought to myself, where is the decency, the respect for another man's body? In the next breath, I saw some of our servants in the same light. Is it right to force another man to do one's will against that man's right to freedom?*

I know Abraham Lincoln doesn't think so but that is not what you both taught me. Our servants are our property; as such they do what we tell them to do and for that we take care of them. But is it right that they too should be beaten when they have disobeyed? What gives us the right to <u>force</u> these men to do things?

I also know that you paid good money to get the best servants you could, as cotton farming is hot and dirty work. So they are our property. But does that give us the undeniable right to treat them badly when they don't do what they're told? Are we being as inhuman as the bosuns on this ship?

I'm sorry for bringing this up but it has deeply disturbed me and I wanted to see how you both felt about it. You have always taught me to be a gentleman in both word and deed. Now I find that not everyone is the same as I. There are people whose goal in life seems to be to hurt other people. That's not being a gentleman; it's being a tyrant. Everyone should be entitled to have their own good feelings about themselves.

Enough on that. Susannah Eddings and I are planning to get married after the war. We both believe that the Union is not just out to defeat us in battle; they plan to do away with the whole way of life we enjoy in South Carolina. We are both committed to supporting our army in the fight to win. I am in a good position to do all I can and am very pleased that I can contribute directly to our side's winning. Susannah, for her part, is helping to raise money and sympathy towards our cause.

I love you both very much and keep you in my thoughts often. But, as you can see, I am being presented with some very difficult choices; one's that don't match what you have always taught me.

Love, John

He reread the letter. It was certainly a lot longer than many he had written before. But he felt better putting his thoughts on paper, especially knowing that those that it is addressed to, have only his best interest at heart.

13.

The long dinner was almost over. Although it was early in May, Susannah Eddings was warm and could feel the perspiration trickling everywhere underneath her dress and petticoat. She reached back and bunched up her silken chestnut-brown shoulder-length hair, lifting it off her neck to allow some relief. Letting it hang back loose, she shook her head back and forth to let the air circulate around her neck. The gesture helped little.

It had been a relatively mild winter. Temperatures frequently climbed into the high 70s. Consequently, spring had come early to the Islands. The oppressive heat and humidity that would come in June hadn't arrived yet, but it had gotten warm since Susannah journeyed down from Charleston. She loved the beauty of the water, the graceful Spanish moss hanging from the trees and the lush vegetation in St. Helena ever since she was a child.

Her mother sent her a note while she was in Washington, inviting her to visit her before it got too hot. ". . .get away from all those blustering politicians and all of that intrigue nonsense. . ." was the way she had expressed it in the letter.

To keep peace with her mother, whom she loved dearly but thought a bit crazy and overly protective, Susannah decided to visit her before journeying back to Washington.

Susannah saw no harm in what she was doing. She smiled to herself, thinking of the grand parties she'd been to and the constant courting and attention from the men. Everyone was always talking about the war: how this general had failed to stop an advance; how that general was destined to head the Army of the Potomac because of his strategic and tactical brilliance. Sometimes the anecdotes were funny: the half-deaf old "Fuss and Feathers" General Winfield Scott passing wind loudly at one of Lincoln's cabinet meetings; another well-known officer who had contracted syphilis from his mistress and was trying desperately to keep his wife from finding out.

She mused to herself again, thinking her mother would be shocked if she saw the life she was leading. At these parties men always stared at her. Weaving her way effortlessly around the room, she portrayed a lovely gracious hostess with her carefully picked words and phrases and stunning attire. It was a very gratifying role. After years of playing the part of a passive daughter, she was now no longer just a fixture. As a child her mother had constantly chided her about her tendency to speak out at the dinner table. She hated it when the men retired to her father's study after dinner to discuss things she was not allowed to hear.

She knew that now men listened to her, her observations, her opinions and her advice. She had become a confidant to many of these officers, some of them separated from their wives and families for long periods of time.

Caroline Eddings, a once-beautiful and trim redhead whose beauty remained in spite of a rather buxom figure, came through the double doors from the butler's pantry and sat down at the end of the long table. The dinner guests had excused themselves after she had gone to check on the dessert course in the summer kitchen. She smiled at her daughter, seated at the other end of the table. Susannah could only manage a weak smile in response. Her mother was worried about Susannah. She knew about the Committee; it was very active all over South Carolina. Every edition of the *Charleston Mercury* had some mention of its progress in fundraising for the Confederacy. She had an odd feeling that there was another side to the Committee.

And now there was the broken engagement to the son of one of the most successful plantation owners in the Sea Islands. The goal of every southern lady: marriage into a prosperous, well-respected family and the main reason for sending Susannah to a finishing school, had now been summarily terminated by her daughter's penchant for independence.

Caroline's face clouded over. It was all part of a long developing pattern. When Joseph Eddings left her, Caroline told Susannah he had been killed in a shipwreck. Susannah had just turned seven and had become rebellious, resisting her mother's guidance into womanhood. First it was about what to wear, then what to eat, finally emerging into arguments about every request her mother made of her.

In a last desperate attempt to regain control, Caroline Eddings decided that sending her daughter away to the school where she could learn how to be a lady might instill some sense and discipline into her personality and give her another perspective. Most of all, she wanted Susannah to acquire the social graces that would prepare her for courtship, marriage and community leadership, befitting the wife of a prominent plantation owner.

After Joseph had deserted her, the plantation began to fall into disrepair and Caroline had to practically beg, borrow and steal from her brother Stephen to survive and keep Susannah in school. She tried to hide this from Susannah, but Susannah noticed that there never seemed to be enough money for vacations anymore or trips to Charleston to buy new clothes. Instead, Caroline had been making most of her clothes. Susannah began to tire of the dullness of the social life in the islands, always happy to return to the Wetherington Ladies School in Connecticut.

Here, among the young ladies of prominent merchant and banking families from New York and New England, Susannah became exposed to another way of life. There seemed to be no preplanned destiny for marriage among her peers. They were able to do almost what they wanted, even going out unchaperoned on occasion. She saw and heard things that the cloistered life of the Sea Islands had hidden from her. What especially fascinated her was the way her classmates were outspoken about political matters—a forbidden subject for Susannah at the Eddings dinner table.

Susannah took a long sip from the crystal glass filled with ice water. Over the lip of the glass she could see her mother's face showing the tiny lines of a frown beginning to form, a sure sign there was something unpleasant coming.

"Darling, I can't hide my concern for you any more." Caroline Eddings spoke very slowly. "Peter has been by here for dinner, asking me why you broke the engagement. Have you found someone else in Charleston or Washington?" The question was very direct.

Susannah crossed her arms and began to bite her lower lip. Her answer was very matter-of-fact.

41

"Mother, I've outgrown Peter. He wants to stay down here in this terrible heat and raise cotton. He'd like me to have his children and live the quiet and dutiful life of a plantation wife. I'd almost rather **die** than spend the rest of my life like that!" Her tone was firm but she avoided raising her voice. The blunt remark almost seemed a damnation of Island life and society. Caroline Eddings folded her napkin, drew in a deep breath and raised her eyes to her daughter's.

"You could do worse than Peter Jenkins. He's a fine young man and comes from one of the best families around, and you'd never want for anything. . ."

". . except civilized society, excitement and doing and saying what I want!" Susannah broke off her mother's familiar argument. "I want more than that. **You** sent me to finishing school to learn how to become a dignified lady. Well, I learned there's more to life than getting ready to spend it with someone I don't even love and living on a farm and having children. I **hate** it here! Ever since Daddy died . ."

Her voice trailed off, replaced by uncontrolled sobbing.

Reminded of the desertion and shame when her husband left her, as well as the story she had made up to protect Susannah about why he was gone, Caroline Eddings took another deep breath and decided to disclose this to Susannah.

"Your father did not die in a shipwreck as I once told you. He left us and I still don't know where he went. I do know he left with another woman. . ."

Susannah turned suddenly and faced her mother. This disclosure of something unknown, hidden from her to cushion her from such a heartbreaking betrayal, made her furious. She could feel her face getting hot and her heart was pounding. She was astonished that her mother had lied to her.

"You never told me that!" Susannah stammered. "All these years you lied to me. Why didn't you tell me?" Her voice was hysterical. "I hate him!" She stood up suddenly, almost knocking over her chair. "Is that why we never had any money? Why we never took vacations or ever went to Charleston?" She started to leave the room, nearly upsetting the crystal water glass with her hand.

Caroline Eddings turned away from her daughter, attempting unsuccessfully to hide her tears. Her voice was very quiet. "I only meant to try and make things easier for you because you loved him so," she sobbed. "Susannah, please don't judge me harshly; I did it only for you." Her voice quavered.

Susannah stopped at the end of the long table, pulled out one of the guest's chairs and sat down, punctuating her movement with a deep sigh. Her face still felt hot.

For a while, no one spoke. The startling disclosure and Susannah's reaction settled on both of them like some sudden blast of cold air. Her mother composed herself first and attempted to regain control of herself and Susannah. She went back to her question. "You haven't answered me about breaking the engagement. Have you found someone else?"

Susannah regained some of her composure. "Mother, I'm hot, tired, and now, very upset. I would like to go upstairs and freshen up." Susannah could feel more tears forming, as she imagined her father telling her mother he was leaving for good. Carefully dabbing her face to remove the tears and perspiration, she stood up. A servant suddenly appeared and hurried over to pull her chair back.

Her mother's tone softened. "Susannah, I'm sorry. I didn't mean to hurt you. When you have children, you'll understand." Gently, she rephrased the question.

"If you are seeing someone, I'd still like to know something about him."

The sobbing had stopped. The sorrow had turned to anger and now, deviousness. She began biting her lip again. Her mother must know nothing of Rose Greenhow, Percy, or her feelings and relationship with John Beauregard. At least not until the right moment. She'd invent a new acquaintance. Susannah turned to face her mother.

"You're right. I'm just tired and irritable. I just wished you'd told me the truth about Dad sooner. I feel so alone and deserted." She walked towards the dining room chair where her mother was sitting. Caroline Eddings rose, and they embraced.

Susannah was now smiling. "Mother, I've been out with the most wonderful naval attaché. He's responsible for establishing defenses for Charleston and knows *everybody*. He gets invitations to all the socials and has introduced me to the Trenholms." At the mention of the well-known trader's name, Caroline Eddings knew her daughter was at least mixing with the right people.

"Well, what's his name dear? Why don't you invite him down here this summer? Maybe he'd like to get away from the chaos for awhile."

The two women separated. "His name is Lieutenant Henry Bowes. He's so busy and has such an important position that I doubt if he can get away. But I'll ask him when I get back to Charleston."

The story would hold unless her mother came to Charleston and wanted to meet him. She silently breathed a sigh of relief herself for thinking so quickly.

"After you freshen up why don't you join us on the veranda for dessert, darling? I'll have Mammy open all the shutters in your bedroom, now that the sun is setting. Maybe there'll be a breeze off the river."

Susannah walked through the arch that separated the dining room from the foyer. Feeling drained from the combination of her emotional outburst and the fabrication of deception, she drew in a deep breath.

"If you don't mind Mother, I think I'll go to bed after dessert. I'm really tired."

Later, unable to sleep, she thought about Washington. The work for the Committee was beginning to trouble her. Some of the leaders were pressing her to increase her contacts in the military, pointedly asking her to find out specific information regarding the movements of men and supplies. She felt uneasy about this, but the stimulation from being near apparent danger was fascinating.

She disliked the fact that she was often not told why the information she had gotten was important. It reminded her of the humiliation she felt when she was not allowed to join her father in his study after dinner.

But it was her double life with John Beauregard on one hand and the young military officers she seduced on the other, and her other double life with Rose Greenhow and the Committee on one side and Allan Pinkerton and his dreadful agent Percy on the other that troubled her the most.

She drifted off into a fitful sleep. After awhile, it seemed as though she was in someplace very warm; someplace dripping with humidity. The perspiration clung to her and ran down her face in little rivulets. It was noisy; she could hear some rhythmic poundings alternating with the sounds of steam escaping. Several dark forms moved in and out of her vision in front of her. She seemed to be standing on some metal walkway, suspended in space.

Suddenly, she recognized John Beauregard's erect figure as one of the dark forms. As he turned to walk toward her, she recognized his profile. She tried to call out to him but it was if she had no voice or breath to talk.

She could see that he was perspiring also. Another dark form appeared; this must be someone who worked for the young ensign, as he was listening carefully as John Beauregard was explaining something to him. His right arm was pointing in the direction he had just come from. The seaman nodded vigorously and turned and headed in that direction.

He doesn't see me, she thought to herself. Poor dear! Here I am worrying about myself when he is working his heart out in that hellhole. She wanted to run up to him, give him an encouraging hug and tell him how proud she was of him.

But he had already turned and was backing down a ladder to a lower level. Slowly, his body disappeared, then his arms, finally his head. He was gone. Susannah felt feverish with guilt.

She woke up suddenly, dripping wet with perspiration. Had she been aboard the ship with him? Or did she just dream that she saw him? She was uncomfortable; she and the bedclothes were soaked, her nightgown clinging to her clammy skin. She wearily sat up, pulled off the nightgown and laid back down on the damp mattress. Her naked body soon dried off and she drifted back to sleep.

Meanwhile, the Union continued relentlessly to build up a fleet of ships to tighten the blockade along the entire East Coast.

14.

Spring was slower in coming to New York City, but orders to again report aboard *The Great Eastern* had arrived in February, compelling John Beauregard to travel to the East's most important port and the only major port on the east coast that had a deep enough harbor for *The Great Eastern.*

Stepping off the ferry, onto the Bank Street wharf where the ship was due to arrive in two days, he looked about the bustling wharf for a carriage to carry him to his hotel. His father had given him $100 in gold pieces to tide him over until such time as he received his first pay from the U.S. Navy. He had decided to avoid the flophouses that lined the street across from the wharf. They catered to deckhands and petty officers and were often owned by unscrupulous landlords who frequently turned over their drunken patrons to ship captains to make up crew shortages.

Instead, he had written to the Astor House on Broadway for a room for two nights. He had heard the hotel had a good dining room and was a relatively safe place, in the tumultuous atmosphere that permeated the New York City streets. Besides, he had told Susannah where he was staying and she made plans to secretly steal away from the plantation, also making the tortuous train trip to New York City to be with him. He was expecting her to arrive that evening.

He traveled across town to the hotel, checked in at the front desk, and went to his room, leaving a note with the clerk for Susannah to have a bellboy come to his room and tell him she was in the lobby. That way no one would raise their eyebrows if she had gone to his room directly. After a note from the bellboy announcing her arrival came to his room, he joined her in the lobby. They had dinner in the hotel dining room, stealing glances at each other, passions in each other slowly simmering, like the soup course as it was served by the waiter.

Later, they sneaked up a back stairway to his room, where the chambermaid had lit a fire in the fireplace. He closed the door behind him, turned the lock. She was in his arms in a flash, their mouths pressed hungrily together. "Darling, I don't know what I will do while you're at sea," Susannah was unbuttoning his tunic, punctuating its removal with a deep kiss. "I will miss you terribly, Susannah," John Beauregard said, "but the ship does travel back and forth fairly regularly and no doubt we'll be able to see each other while she's in port." He slid her undergarments down over her hips, the clothes dropping in a heap on the carpet.

In no time they had undressed each other completely, each garment's removal prompting a series of passionate kisses. The glow of the fire and the soft candlelight from the wall sconces cast a warm, golden tone over the small room. They lay down on the feather comforter and touched each other everywhere. He remembered her beautiful body in the firelight, her breasts heaving under him as he entered her. He had run his hands up and down her round hips as they began to move in harmony. The movement was virtually effortless, her wetness smoothing the movement and increasing his pleasure. They climaxed together, in a spasm of joy and ecstasy. She lay in his arms for a long while, feeling his regular breathing as he gradually fell asleep.

BLOCKADE RUNNER
BOOK 2

1.

The reports about Fort Sumter reached England on April 13, 1861, just one day after the assault by Confederate forces. News that would have normally taken as much as several weeks to reach Great Britain by ship, arrived in a matter of minutes by the new transatlantic telegraph cable. The value of such swift communications in wartime was only beginning to be understood.

George Trenholm was jubilant at hearing the news. He had been anticipating this moment and planning accordingly. Trade with England and Fraser Trenholm would most certainly intensify.

Commerce would go both ways. British military arms and supplies, needed by the Confederate army, would be shipped west to the United States, just as Southern cotton, needed by the English cotton mills, would be shipped east to England, on the return trip.

The announcement of a Union blockade raised the issue of how to keep trade going in both directions. The logistics challenged the newly-minted Confederate government and James Bulloch, the agent appointed to buy war materiel for the South. Bulloch had earned the trust of President Davis after the honorable act of returning a Union ship to the Union after the war began. The agent now found himself alighting from a hansom cab in front of the Fraser Trenholm office in the spring London drizzle.

Bulloch had been dispatched to England with letters of introduction from the President to act as agent for the Confederacy in obtaining military supplies and weapons. While enroute, he pored over war plans generated by Secretary Mallory and President Davis to try and grasp how supplies would be delivered. He concluded that the tons of clothing, ammunition, rifles and cannon that the armies needed would have to be shipped to a neutral port and somehow run through the enemy blockade.

Were there enough ships available to do this? He doubted it; if all the steam-powered ships exceeding three thousand tons and now crossing the Atlantic were made available for the war effort, the total would probably not exceed twenty.

Faced with this dilemma, he suddenly had a brainstorm. What about *The Great Eastern*? What about using one large ship, already in service, instead of trying to build numerous small ones in time to deliver the needed supplies? He wondered if George Trenholm would share his enthusiasm for his radical proposal.

The Confederate agent hurried across the cobblestones, eager to get out of the drizzle. Inside, he removed his coat and turned as a door opened. The air was tainted with the odor of burning soft coal.

George Trenholm entered the reception room, a broad smile on his handsome face. He was the epitome of Southern gentility and honor, tall and patrician in bearing. Like Bulloch, he enjoyed the highest respect and trust of President Davis. The two men embraced each other as Trenholm spoke.

"How was your journey Mr. Bulloch?"

A brief sigh preceded the agent's answer. "Mr. Trenholm, after the war we should design our railroads to function as efficiently as those here in Great Britain."

Trenholm laughed. "Well, you know that the railroad builder Isambard Brunel is to be given much of the credit for engineering the system," the trader remarked. "He's an absolute genius at those things." Bulloch smiled to himself at the irony of invoking the name of *The Great Eastern's* builder.

They walked past two offices where accounting clerks, perched on their high stools were bent over their desks, busy reconciling the firm's shipping activities. Their number would soon be increased dramatically if Bulloch's soon-to-be-disclosed idea could be implemented. Once in Trenholm's office, the tall Southern trader closed the door and motioned for Bulloch to sit down.

The agent slowly put on his glasses. "Mr. Trenholm, I won't beat around the bush, as the English say. I have an idea that is so right, so perfect, that I am certain it will give our nation an overwhelming advantage over the North and help in the South's victory. And I think you're the one to explore its feasibility through your connections here in the Mother country."

He continued. "One of our biggest problems in fighting this war is getting enough supplies to our forces. If we can lay our hands on enough arms, ammunition, provisions and clothing, *and the means to deliver them to our armies,* I think we can beat the Yankees at their own game!"

Trenholm sat down at his desk. He stared intently at Bulloch's large brown eyes, now dancing animatedly. The agent leaned forward in his chair.

"There aren't enough ships on the entire European coastline to provision our army. I know you are acutely aware of that and have been thinking of ways to get around that problem. I'm talking about an army of five hundred thousand, not the one hundred thousand we have now. That's what Beauregard and the other generals think it will take to defeat Scott and McClellan. President Davis concurs, and has asked me if I could have the supply line up and operating within six months."

There was a moment of silence, broken only by a hot coal that fell hissing from the fireplace grate. George Trenholm leaned back and crossed his legs.

"Mr. Bulloch, right now we are building at least a dozen blockade-runners that I know of to deliver those supplies. What's your idea—charter *The Great Eastern*?" The remark was meant to be one of jest. But judging from the startled look on his countryman's face, it was anything but a joke.

The agent's faced relaxed and a wry smile formed his mouth. "I knew you were a successful businessman and a shrewd bargainer, Mr. Trenholm, but I never knew you had clairvoyant powers as well. That's exactly what I want to propose."

Bulloch outlined his proposition to Trenholm. Here, *in one vessel,* was the means to deliver several thousand tons of goods in one trip and return to England, her hull full of Southern cotton. On the surface, the idea seemed somewhat unrealistic, given the protectionist attitude the British had about their white elephant ship. But as Bulloch's idea unfolded, with a seemingly something-

51

for-everyone logic, Trenholm began to see the genius in the idea. He also saw the difficulties involved. He stood up and gazed out the window at the dreary April fog.

"This will take a great deal of planning, power, politics, pampering, and persuasion Mr. Bulloch. You know the Queen is expected to make a formal declaration of neutrality very shortly. I will attempt to get around that by using the economic issue of supplying cotton to the mills, but it's not going to be easy."

He turned and faced Bulloch's chair. "I will use every contact at my disposal here in London and also in Washington and Charleston to make this happen. I think you may have hit on the best strategic idea in warfare since Hannibal crossed the Alps on elephants. I will arrange a meeting with the ship's owners as soon as possible."

Bulloch stood up. "Excellent. I must return to America to talk with the cotton growers and insure that they will continue to plant their crops so that we may keep our end of the economic bargain. When can I expect to hear from you?"

The two men walked back to the reception area. George Trenholm turned and faced his countryman. "I need some time to think out a strategy with respect to dealing with the Queen. I will ask for help from some old friends who can get me an audience with Her Majesty and Lord Palmerston. You know how difficult he can be. I'm certain we'll need their endorsement. I should have a plan by the end of the week."

"I look forward to hearing from you. Goodbye." James Bulloch closed the door and stepped out into the London drizzle.

2.

Almost everyone in New York City knew she was in town. Her 6 masts and 5 smokestacks could be seen from Harlem, the Bowery, even from parts of Brooklyn, nearly 3 miles away. She dwarfed everything in the harbor and on Manhattan Island, save the Trinity Church steeple, just south of her Bank street wharf. *The Great Eastern* was preparing to return to England, taking on passengers and cargo.

After the ship had docked earlier in the week, the mail was delivered to the captain. Along with all the official correspondence was a letter to John Beauregard from his father. But there was nothing from Susannah.

John Beauregard took the letter back to his cabin and sat down on the edge of his bunk to read it.

Dear John,

So glad to hear that you're well and that The Great Eastern*'s food is to your liking. It sounds like life aboard the steamship agrees with you.*

The news from here is that the Union has tightened the blockade around Charleston harbor. We hear that there is constant activity with the Fort Moultrie artillery, probably some of the Union Navy's frigates testing the defense. None of this has halted the trading as ships seem to still be able to slip in and out of the harbor, although we've read of one or two that didn't make it.

Your mother has had a touch of the gout and when it flares up it is very painful. But with the hot weather now at hand, it seems to have subsided. I have the normal aches and pains that come with getting older, but they don't bother me that much.

The crop is in the ground and, with enough rain, we should almost double what we harvested last year. Good thing; we'll need it to survive, if in fact the war ever reaches this part of the South.

Now to your feelings about the servants. Your mother and I have been careful to instill the thought in you that the servants are our wards and as such we must take care of them, which we have been doing. They have their own quarters, and, for the most part, we try not to split up their families, although sometimes it is hard to tell where one family begins and another one ends, what with the way they live and all. I try to give them fresh meat from the herds about once a month and even let them keep some of it in our icehouse during the summer. They're allowed to keep a few chickens. Together with the vegetable gardens that most of them cultivate, they're probably much better off than if they had to fend for themselves.

You've known Sam, my overseer, since you were a little boy. He's one of the most reliable Negroes I've known and keeps the work force organized and productive. We don't have many instances where he has to discipline any of the servants. If one persists in disobedience, I take steps to sell or trade him for someone who is willing to work hard and do what he is told to do.

I consider our servants as members of our family and, within the bounds of their rank, treat them as such. When they need medical care, I get it for them. I discourage them from using their own remedies to treat illnesses. Our house servants are very loyal and deeply appreciative of their special responsibilities. We've had the same cook and butler for over fifteen years and we are grateful for their loyalty and devotion to us.

I think your comparison of what you saw on board ship and our servants is not the same, as you contend. Those men that are enlisted to help run the ship are being paid for their work, in addition to being fed and quartered. They, too, are probably much better off than the lives they led living in flophouses on the waterfront. So I wouldn't waste much time feeling sorry for them.

Just as with our servants, they are assigned tasks and when they refuse to do them, punishment must be meted out. It works very well, in the infrequent instance where Sam has to discipline one of ours, the others seem to pick up the pace of the work and not causing any trouble for some time after the errant servant has been disciplined.

Servants are a vital part of our economic and social way here in the South. Without them, we would not be able to successfully run our plantations nor maintain our standard of life. They are as much a part of our tradition as our family structure and customs and will remain so as long as the South remains free.

I am extremely proud of what you have become, especially the very honorable appointment to serve aboard The Great Eastern *as an observer. Through your observations and participation you are learning more about the ship but you also have another role. To the British, you represent the South and your actions and behavior reflect that background. The British may be inclined to look favorably or unfavorably on us because of the way you conduct yourself. You are an unofficial ambassador for all of us. You can be sure your Uncle, who has already distinguished himself and looks to be one of the major military leaders under the now-General Lee, is also proud of you and has the same great expectations for you as I do. Forget your concern for those who are destined to do the hard work that makes our country run. They know their place, even those deckhands, and must respect those who are responsible for their actions.*

My dearest love to you. Mother also sends her love.

Father

3.

While the presence of *The Great Eastern* was widely known in New York City, few in town were aware of the presence of another lady, standing alone on the deck of the ship on this warm June morning. Harriet Lane, a tall, strikingly beautiful woman and the niece of former President James Buchanan, was on her way to London at the request of a friend. Her uncle, beaten out of the nomination for President by Stephen Douglas, retreated to the politically friendly Lancaster countryside and his farm, Wheatlands. But Harriet Lane was not about to give up her network of influential friends and connections.

Before his election to the Presidency, Old Buck had been the head of the United States mission to England, and his niece, at 21, had become the darling of London society and more particularly The Court of St. James. She was in the full bloom of young womanhood: beautiful, flippant and flirtatious.

As a guest of Queen Victoria's, she frequently danced with the Queen's husband Prince Albert at numerous royal balls. Her widespread popularity was highlighted at a ceremony at Oxford University where her uncle and the poet, Alfred Lord Tennyson, were to receive honorary degrees. The students paid only polite attention to her uncle and the poet but hooted and whistled their approval of Hal Lane.

Her subtle ways of influence enabled her to persuade some of the world's most important people into doing things that her friends requested. With a reputation for getting her own way, she demonstrated a knack for Washington politics and foreign courts. Never an obvious manipulator, Hal Lane had a way of always being owed a favor by those she wished to act on her behalf. And now she had been asked by one of her better-known friends for an audience with the world's most powerful ruler: Queen Georgiana Augusta Alexandrina Victoria.

George Trenholm had sent Hal Lane a telegram urgently requesting her presence in England to arrange a meeting with the Queen. She was not sure what he wanted from the Monarchy but her increasing distaste for Abraham Lincoln and his policies struck a responsive and sympathetic chord in her. She reached in her bag and pulled out the crumpled piece of paper that was the telegram.

DEAR HAL, I HAVE NOT SPOKEN WITH YOU SINCE THE INCIDENT AT FORT SUMTER BACK IN APRIL SO IM NOT SURE YOURE WILLING TO TALK TO A COMMITTED SECESSIONIST STOP I HAVE A SITUATION THAT INVOLVES THE BRITISH GOVERNMENT AND SOME INDUSTRIALISTS THAT IM SURE YOU AND YOUR CLOSENESS TO THE QUEEN COULD HELP ME UNRAVEL STOP I NEED YOU TO COME TO LONDON ON THE FIRST AVAILABLE SHIP TO HELP ME ARRANGE A MEETING WITH HER MAJESTY STOP THE PROBLEM COULD INVOLVE THE VERY SURVIVAL OF THE CONFEDERACY STOP I ASK YOU TO PUT ASIDE FOR THE MOMENT ANY NEGATIVE FEELINGS YOU MAY HAVE ABOUT THE SECESSIONIST MOVEMENT AND HOPE THAT OUR LONG AND DEEP FRIENDSHIP WILL TRANSCEND ANY OF THOSE FEELINGS STOP PLEASE REPLY AS SOON AS POSSIBLE STOP YOUR FRIEND GEORGE TRENHOLM

She was unaware that the subject of the telegram was the very ship on whose deck she was now standing and was the focus of a series of intense and on-going negotiations which could indeed affect the outcome of the war.

Two decks below, Allan Pinkerton was unpacking his valise, thinking over what had happened to him in the last few years. From his humble beginnings in Scotland, the barrel cooper-turned-detective had managed to convert a curiosity for detective work into a very important business, protecting railroad property for George McClellan, who had resigned his commission in the Army for a position as a Vice President of the Illinois Central Railroad. He performed so well that General McClellan, now back in the Army and in charge of Washington defenses, summoned him to Washington for an even more important job: forming the first Secret Service organization to protect something more important than railroad property: the President of the United States.

General George Brinton McClellan was about to assume command of The Army of the Potomac next month and had plenty of other assignments for the detective's burgeoning agency.

McClellan also wanted Pinkerton to head up an organization of spies and infiltrators to spread out over Virginia and learn of troop and supply movements. This information would be developed to help formulate a battle plan and keep track of what the Confederates were doing.

It was just another assignment added to the list of many that the Secret Service agent had already been given. First, there was the duty of organizing and implementing the Secret Service. Then there was *The Great Eastern,* where she was going, and who was trying to negotiate a charter: his first reason for being on the ship today. And the Eddings woman, now clearly working for Rose Greenhow but under the watchful eye of Percy, his best agent. Susannah Eddings was also to be aboard and was the second reason for his presence here. Mulling all this over in his Washington office last month, he had wondered how he would juggle all these activities and produce the desired results. Suddenly, Percy had surprised him with a suggestion that made it possible for him to make this trip. The spy volunteered to recruit this new group of spies and infiltrators himself, claiming he had a lot of acquaintances in the Baltimore area who were eager to make a contribution to the war on the side of the Union. It did not hurt that many of them spoke with a soft drawl, something that would help them infiltrate the Virginia countryside. Without the responsibility of supervising the comings and goings of Susannah Eddings, Percy would be free to organize this spy network while Pinkerton, in a reverse role, could arrange to meet Rose Greenhow's protege and her young lieutenant-lover.

For now, and for the next few weeks, he would be concentrating on learning all he could about this ship and her mission. But he would also be pretending that he was someone else; Major E. J. Allen, a businessman on his way to London, in search of wartime contracts, and. . .keeping an eye on Susannah Eddings.

Several levels below Pinkerton's cabin, in the paddlewheel engine room of the ship, another Scotsman was preparing the vessel for its voyage. Alexander McLennan, the chief paddle engineer and an old friend of shipbuilder Isambard Brunel's had been asked by

Brunel to serve him again. Possessing a sizable girth, large hands and a ruddy complexion, he epitomized the typical British vessel's version of the Scottish Chief Engineer. A man of few words, McLennan nonetheless was a capable and competent engineer who governed his hot sweaty environment and immigrant workforce with a firm hand.

McLennan's main ward was the engine that drove the gigantic paddlewheels on each side of the ship. The huge machine had four steam cylinders in groups of two forward and two aft. Each cylinder was over six feet in diameter and, with its cover, piston and connecting rod, weighed over 38 tons. No engine or ship this large had ever been built before. Likewise, no engineer took his job as seriously as Alexander McLennan.

4.

John Beauregard was nearly late for his watch. He had stopped to help one of the sailors up off the deck after a bullying boatswain kicked the deckhand so hard that the unsuspecting sailor was thrown to the deck. It was punishment for not moving out of the boatswain's way fast enough.

He had witnessed several more beatings of the illiterate Welsh and Irish sailors, many times occurring because the difference in dialects between them and the harsh and often cruel non-commissioned officers of *The Great Eastern* were not clearly understood by either person. What appeared to be insolence was often just a difference in language.

The inhuman nature and brutality that one group of men was inflicting on another continued to bother the young officer. What right did they have to impose their will on these poor wretched souls? After all, they had been captured and imprisoned against their will, forced to work long hard hours; their only place of rest, a damp, smelly canvas hammock.

One day their wretched existence was dramatically demonstrated to him. He had mistakenly made a wrong turn into the crew's mess and saw what they were fed. Simmering in a large caldron was a watery soup, laced with a few pieces of rice and slivers of meat. On a metal tray next to the pot lay a pile of biscuits, crawling with white worms. He touched one, only to find it rock-hard.

"How could the hands chew something like this, with so many of them missing teeth?" he asked the cook. "Some 'uv 'em don't eat much," was the reply.

John Beauregard remembered how the slaves on his father's plantation couldn't chew food very well either because of their missing teeth. The punishment was another matter. He could not remember seeing beatings of any of the Negroes the few times he saw them as severe as he had seen on the ship.

Suddenly, the whole matter came into sharp focus in a grim parallel. Both groups were enslaved, bonded peoples. To John Beauregard, the consummate Southern gentleman, any form of enslavement suddenly became unacceptable. As he hurried down the ladder to the engine room, he wondered how he would feel about it back home on the plantation.

His father's letter had only hardened his feelings about the way the deckhands and the slaves on his father's plantation were treated. All that talk in the letter about how they were "being taken care of", as his father said, simply sidestepped the issue that both groups were being held in bondage, against their will. He wondered what Susannah thought about this.

The deep bass voice of *The Great Eastern* sounded, the whistle that told the crew, captain, passengers, in fact most of New York City that the ship was pulling up anchor and setting sail for London. The noise was deafening and its onset jarred John Beauregard back to reality.

Deep in the South, the Confederacy began to mount its naval offensive.

5.

Captain Rafael Semmes thought it appropriate to name the Confederate nation's first raider in honor of the South's first military victory, Sumter. *And though the little 520-ton ship was slow, underpowered and could only cruise for six days because of a limited coal supply, she more than made up for her deficiencies with her performance under her captain's skillful guidance.*

Using every seafaring tactic Semmes knew, the former Havana-to-New Orleans passenger steamer became the terror of the Caribbean. In just one month's steaming she captured ten federal merchantmen, burning many of them to the waterline.

Semmes was not a man without compassion. Each of the doomed ships' crew was permitted to board the lifeboats, given a few days' provisions, and allowed to leave the scene of the seizure. As a matter of honor, it was only the vessel that was destroyed, not the crew.

Before she was sold in Spain the following January, the Sumter *went on to destroy eight more ships. Raiding had become a formidable factor in the naval war and an appropriate form of retaliation, especially in the hands of so artful a seaman such as Semmes.*

Sumter *continued to serve her country honorably. George Trenholm's trading firm, Fraser Trenholm, eventually acquired her, renamed her the* Gibraltar, *and put her to work as a blockade runner, delivering badly needed Confederate field artillery to armies and garrisons throughout the South.*

It was past four o'clock and James Bulloch was late for his next meeting in New Orleans. His luncheon with Louis Beauregard had produced some new surprises. First was the revelation that Louis' son, John, along with Ensign William Slater, another Naval

Academy graduate, were already aboard *The Great Eastern* as observers. Having two Americans aboard the vessel would be invaluable in the forthcoming negotiations with the British government, since the Americans would have more of a stake in the success of the mission.

The second surprise was that cotton planters had already doubled their crop plantings, based on the price cotton was bringing. That would ensure an adequate supply as well as more revenue to pay for the war. The immediate task facing him was to arrange a purchase of the South's first merchant ship raider.

His surrey pulled up to the offices of the owners of the *Habana*, the vessel that was undergoing the necessary modifications. Lt. Rafael Semmes, one of the first of the new Confederate Navy officers to promote the value of commerce raiding, had identified the vessel as seaworthy and suited to the task; it was up to Bulloch to complete the contractual part with the owners.

James Bulloch knocked on the door and was admitted by a small, frail man who introduced himself as Henry Porter, representing the ship's owners. Bulloch shook Porter's hand and introduced himself. The two men walked to the rear of the main office where a private office was located. Porter gestured for the Confederate agent to go in.

Lt. Semmes stood up to greet Bulloch. A tall man with an intense look in his eyes, the Confederate navy's first commander looked every inch the part. A meticulously waxed mustache followed the contour of the wide set mouth.

"James Bulloch, Lieutenant. I'm very happy to meet such a close friend of Secretary Mallory's."

"I, too, am pleased to meet you. I most admire your act of returning the *Bienville* to her owners. Obviously, so did President Davis." Semmes fidgeted nervously with his cap. "Can we get on with the negotiations?"

Semmes' impatience irritated Bulloch but he decided to ignore it. Porter and Bulloch reviewed details of when the Confederates could take possession of the ship and how much the owners wanted. Once the agreement was reached, Bulloch presented his letters of credit from the Confederacy, signed by President Davis.

There seemed little else to do. Bulloch stood up and shook hands with Porter and Semmes. But Semmes spoke out of turn again.

"Mr. Bulloch, may I speak with you before you leave?" The young lieutenant had a look of anxiety on this face.

Bulloch ignored his question. "Mr. Porter, I assume you have everything you need from me. Where is the ship right now?"

"Tied up about a mile down the river sir. She's close to the dock where she'll be refitted. Lt. Semmes has already been down there to begin the work. Would you like to see her?"

"No sir, I've got to leave for London tomorrow and I still haven't finished what I came down here to accomplish. With your leave sir, I'll be on my way."

Bulloch left the office with Semmes following him so closely he almost bumped into him. Outside, the normally good-natured agent turned and faced the young lieutenant.

"I appreciate your enthusiasm Lieutenant, but I don't appreciate your rudeness and overbearing attitude. In the interest of getting that contract signed and you your ship, I held my tongue in front of Mr. Porter. In the future I demand your respect, and your courtesy. I'll simply write off your attitude as tension and pressure. I've only met you today; I'm sure your reputation precedes your abrasive personality. Now let's just forget what happened in front of Henry Porter."

The young lieutenant bristled with anger at the dressing down. But he managed to suppress it and even managed an apology.

"I have not slept well for several weeks," he began. "I think it's the climate here. Once I get to sea I'm sure I'll be better. Please forgive me."

The two men shook hands, realizing their petty differences would have to be put aside for the good of the new nation.

"Good luck on your trip to England."

"Good hunting on the high seas."

6.

The offices of The Great Ship Company, owners of *The Great Eastern,* were located on Cannon Street in London just off the Thames and a few blocks from London Bridge. George Trenholm had met Daniel Gooch and some of the other directors of the company at a joint British-American trading committee meeting before the outbreak of the war. He found Gooch to be a somewhat colorless, emotionless, stiff British businessman.

He had not yet met Colonel Baker, the chairman of the organization, but this meeting between himself and Gooch was to include the chairman. The subject was a possible two-year charter of *The Great Eastern* to the Confederacy. On board the train to London, Trenholm had gone over possible obstacles for effecting the charter. The owners might object to taking *The Great Eastern* out of transatlantic service for any period of time. They certainly would be concerned about her operating in a war zone. And there was the possibility that the British government, and especially Lord Palmerston, would object, saying that they would be favoring the cause of the Confederates, and therefore angering Lincoln and American public opinion.

On the other hand, Trenholm mused, there was an immense amount of money to be made from the charter. British exports to the Confederates would result in substantial profits for a good segment of the British economy. The return voyage to England would bring vast amounts of cotton to keep the British mills humming, assuring further profits for the cotton mill owners. And the plantation owners could continue to grow cotton, knowing they had the means to get it to market.

But there was the possibility the ship could come under fire. Trenholm worried how he would protect such a huge target, should the U. S. Navy be able to bottle her up as she was unloading supplies or taking on cotton. The blockade was beginning to become effective, although Port Royal Sound in

South Carolina and the twin forts of Beauregard and Walker guarding the two-mile-wide bay had not yet been attacked or threatened.

His musings ended as the train pulled into Victoria station. He would have to hurry if he was to make the three o'clock meeting with the ship's owners. But at least he had a plan. Now all he had to do was sell it to the owners. Bulloch was right, he thought. This operation will have something for everyone. It was indeed an idea that was so right. Trenholm remembered those were Bulloch's exact words.

Outside the station he hailed a hansom cab and directed its driver to the Cannon Street office. Entering the office, he nodded a greeting to the doorman. "Please be seated sir," the doorman announced, "and I'll let Mr. Gooch and the Colonel know you've arrived." Trenholm sank down in one of the huge wing chairs that flanked the fireplace, rubbing his hands together rapidly to try and warm them.

Not much later, Daniel Gooch appeared in the doorway. Trenholm had forgotten that the engineer's nose was his most prominent facial feature. His heavy eyebrows were bobbing up and down as he extended his hand to greet the American.

"So glad to see you again," Gooch remarked "It's been awhile hasn't it?" Trenholm agreed, as the two men ascended a flight of stairs to the second story of the building. "The Colonel's been most eager to meet a genuine American Southerner," Gooch added. "You'll hear some curiosity about the South."

They reached the landing and turned left into the anteroom of the Colonel's office. Through the open door, Trenholm could see the huge bulk that was Colonel Baker, laboriously pushing his chair back from the desk, preparing to meet his visitor. As he stood up, George Trenholm estimated that the chairman of the company weighed at least 300 pounds. A pudgy hand came across the desk. George Trenholm grasped it firmly, but was surprised at how limp it was.

"Safe journey from Liverpool?" was the chairman's first question.

"Yes, thank you sir. I simply marvel at how efficient your railways are compared to ours."

"Well, you can thank Brunel for that, as well as *The Great Eastern*," the overweight Baker remarked, "The man was an absolute transportation genius. It's too bad the ship killed him."

It was the first mention of the subject of this meeting. Well, Trenholm thought to himself, at least they have been talking about my offer. What was not known was what their reaction would be and what they'd want for the proposed two year charter of the vessel.

"What part of the South are you from, Mr. Trenholm?" the Colonel inquired, motioning for the men to sit down.

"My family's mainly from South Carolina, Colonel, and we gradually all gravitated to Charleston. My firm has its headquarters there, too."

"Ah, the cradle of the conflict, Charleston," the Colonel observed.

"You must visit the city after the war, Colonel. You'd find it quite charming," Trenholm responded.

The trader leaned forward in his chair. "Colonel, you know my mission here in England. Our President Davis has empowered me and others to secure a continuing supply of materials for the Confederate war effort. Our problem will not be in their availability, since so many British companies are cooperating magnificently."

He stood up and walked to the window. "The major hurdle will be getting those guns, that ammunition, those uniforms, into the hands of General Johnson's men in the quickest time possible," Trenholm continued, turning to face Colonel Baker.

"If we can equip our armies before the end of the year and establish a reliable supply line before the enemy blockade becomes effective, President Davis, myself, and most of the Confederate government think we can defeat them."

He continued, pacing slowly around the room, directing his comments to the Colonel. "On the other hand, England's supply of good cotton fiber from our cotton fields is also being hampered by the blockade. I think I have a way around all this. Your ship, *The Great Eastern*." The trader was back in his chair, now alternating his gaze between Daniel Gooch and Colonel Baker.

"Tell me more Mr. Trenholm," the Colonel continued while delicately balancing a pen in his fat fingers. "Are you proposing some kind of charter?"

George Trenholm leaned forward again. "That's exactly what I'm proposing, Colonel. *The Great Eastern* as the principle supply vessel to the Confederate army. *The Great Eastern* as the largest ship afloat, carrying almost a third of the year's cotton fiber requirements of the English mills in one return voyage. *The Great Eastern* turning an immense profit for her owners at last. In fact, the ship could probably recoup the cost of itself and then some on the first voyage alone." He emphasized each point with his fingers.

Gooch broke his long silence. "How much would the Confederacy be willing to pay to effectively put our ship into the war, with all the inherent risks? And what of the political overtones? I'm not sure Lord Palmerston or the Queen herself wants this brazen an endorsement of the South."

"I'm prepared to offer you a million and a half dollars for the bare charter for the first two years. We are willing also to negotiate a percentage of the profits from the shipping fees as well. We will also pay for the necessary alterations to the ship, and contribute to her restoration after we have won the war."

He eased back into his chair.

The Colonel swiveled around and stared out the window at the London dock scene. It was beginning to get dark outside, so there wasn't much to see. But he did not want his facial expression to show his excitement.

He composed himself and turned to face the trader. "When do you need an answer, Mr. Trenholm?" the Colonel queried.

A frown formed on George Trenholm's face. "I'm afraid, that we need one very soon. Each day we delay gives the enemy a better chance to get organized, conscript and train men for their armies, and tighten the blockade. I'd like an answer before I return to Liverpool tomorrow evening. Is that possible?"

"Well, we'll give it a try. I will have to put this in front of the Board tomorrow afternoon, if I can convene a meeting in that short space of time. Can you stay an extra day if necessary?

"For an important decision like this, I certainly will," Trenholm commented.

7.

Like a latter-day Jean Laffite, Captain Raphael Semmes lay in wait at Pass a' Outer, a scant 40 miles from where the 18th-century buccaneer had his base of operations. Semmes' mission was to destroy and disrupt Federal merchant ships. The difference between Semmes and the pirate was that Captain Semmes was doing this for his country, not himself.

His crew and the newly outfitted raider *Sumter* had been waiting anxiously in the tall reeds at the mouth of the Mississippi for almost two weeks, waiting for the chance to elude the two big Union frigates, the sloop-of-war *Brooklyn* and the sidewheeler *Powhatan,* that stood guard out about one-half mile in the Gulf of Mexico.

The two seamen on watch in the rigging talked in whispers, not wanting to incur the wrath of their strict disciplinarian captain, who was below deck, performing his brief, Sunday morning solitary prayer session. They squinted at the horizon in the early light, searching for some sight of the blockaders.

"When d'ya think we'll be sprung?" He slapped his arm, and another dead mosquito fluttered down to the water.

The other seaman turned from his position. "When 'Ol Beeswax feels we can get past them cruisers, that's when." He gestured with his head towards the hatch leading to the captain's cabin.

The first seaman sighed and wiped his brow. "Jesus, another day in this hell-hole. Gawd, man, looks like another scorcher. Wonder if we'll get a bit of rain."

"You see any clouds? Betcha' we're still here tomorrow."

The first seaman turned to look down towards the rear of the ship. Out of the corner of his eye he saw the door to the captain's cabin open. "Look lively, here he comes."

Captain Rafael Semmes strode onto the main deck, mentally refreshed and recharged from his Sunday morning session with the Almighty at the small shrine in his cabin. Extending the brass tubes of his spyglass, he stared at the same spot on the horizon where the two lookouts in the rigging had been watching.

"I don't see the *Brooklyn*, Mr. Kell," he commented to his first officer. "Has she gone off station?"

"No reports from the lookouts, sir." He glanced up at the crow's nest. "O'Reilly, Nelson. You up there on watch! Have you gone to sleep? Or is the *Brooklyn* still on station?" The shouts could barely be heard as the *Sumter's* safety valve let off steam with a loud hiss. "Sir, we haven't seen her since the sunset last night."

They did not explain why this observation had gone unreported. On the other hand, the long-awaited chance to escape looked to be at hand.

Raphael Semmes lost no time in reacting. "Mr. Kell, get ready to cast off! Trip the anchor! Let's get going!"

Within minutes the raider was underway. Four miles down the channel the outline of the *Powhatan* appeared. But the *Brooklyn* was nowhere to be seen. Had she slipped away during the night? Had the lookouts fallen asleep? Or was it possible the *Sumter* had slipped her anchorage?

"Mr. Kell, oyster boat approaching the starboard side. Someone in the bow is waving for us to heave to," one of the lookouts was shouting from the crow's nest.

Semmes hurried to the railing next to the boarding ladder. "Mr. Kell, lower the boarding ladder. Give the order to stop the ship." Within minutes the ship's momentum had slowed to a crawl and the oysterman had lashed his boat to the side of the *Sumter*. He groped his way up the perilously swaying rope ladder.

Once on deck he saluted the captain and first officer. He was obviously very excited and his dialect hard to understand.

"Captain, the *Brooklyn* leff 'bout an hour ago! I, I wuz out beyond the bar, when I saw black smoke pourin' outa' her stacks. With the fog it was hard to see where she wuz goin.' But I saw her go out of sight."

70

Semmes lost no time in resuming his escape. "Mr. Kell, ahead full speed!" He thanked the fisherman for this vital piece of information and saw him to the boarding ladder. All the same, the mystery of why they had drifted four miles upstream still remained unanswered.

First Officer John Kell acknowledged the captain's order and also offered an explanation as to their being so far off station. "Captain, best I can figure, we slipped our mooring last night and the lookouts couldn't see where we drifted because of the fog."

But Rafael Semmes had already forgotten the unreported shift in their position. He was focusing on evading the *Powhatan*'s guns.

8.

"Dispatch from the Port of New Orleans Commander, sir." It was Gustavus Fox, the energetic young naval assistant Gideon Welles had appointed to help him reorganize the structure of the Union's Navy, who now handed the Secretary the piece of paper.

Welles' face compressed into a frown. "Did you read this?" he muttered.

"Yes, sir. It looks like Semmes is becoming a real menace. Eight ships burned to the waterline in less than one month. And that's only what's been reported."

The Secretary stood up and walked over to the open window of his office, hoping to catch a breeze to stem the rising July morning heat. "It says he's last been sighted sailing to South America. We'll never catch him down there. Too much ocean."

"Is it worthwhile to send one of the frigates after him? The *Sumter*'s a slow ship and has little coal capacity." Along with his high energy level, Gustavus Fox continually injected a note of optimism.

"We'll wait him out." Welles took out his handkerchief and wiped the perspiration from his face. "About all he'll find down there are a few ships coming back from California. Unless they're carrying gold, he won't find much of value in them. He'll be back in a couple of months. Then we'll get him."

But it was more bad news, coming on the heels of the defeat at Bull Run, the loss of the Gosport Navy Yard and all the other triumphs the Confederacy seemed to be pulling off.

9.

While Raphael Semmes was busy embarrassing the United States Navy at the mouth of the Mississippi, Susannah Eddings was enduring the last hour of the train ride from Washington. It had been a very tiring journey, involving five separate trains and at least as many stage transfers. And the July heat made it even more uncomfortable. But she knew it was worth it; tonight she would see John. Her mouth went dry just anticipating it. The irony of it all was it was Percy she had to thank for this trip.

She had had another meeting with the hated agent and he was just as obnoxious and offensive as always. After the usual questions about her contacts and whereabouts, he surprised her with a new assignment.

Percy had summoned her to his tiny cottage in the Rock Creek woods three months to the day after he had confronted her in the railroad station. He was angry that she hadn't found anything out about the ship. The message had been delivered to Rose Greenhow's mansion where Susannah had been staying.

She explained that there hadn't been enough time. At Martha Peyton's dinner party, he had to leave early; a sailor had arrived from the naval station to summon him back for some meeting. But now Percy had another request.

"I want you to sail on *The Great Eastern* for your coming voyage to London," he had said. "That way you can ask your navy lieutenant friend to take you on a tour of the ship and tell you all about it."

The tall agent was now standing in back of Susannah's chair, unable to see the frown forming on her face.

"And if I refuse?"

"I'll have you arrested immediately and tried as a spy against the United States of America. May I remind you what they do with spies? They HANG them, Miss Eddings. HANG them." Percy's deep voice resonated loudly at the word "hang." He had walked around to the front of Susannah's chair and bent down, his face not two inches in front of hers. She felt the same terror well up in her throat as that day in the railroad station.

He stood up and backed away from the chair. She stared at him, the hate shooting out of her eyes. Suddenly she started sobbing.

He spoke again, this time in his normal tone of voice. "You'll do this because I know you want to live, and not be disgraced by my exposing you." He went on to describe exactly what she was to learn about the ship. When she got to London, she was to telegraph the information back to him immediately. Only after posting that telegraph could she return to America.

Susannah stopped crying and managed to compose herself. She spoke slowly and deliberately. "When the South has finally beaten your hordes and won the war, I will come looking for you. I'll find you; you won't be able to hide from me. Then it will be my turn to expose you and this whole sorry business."

Susannah stood up and pulled her wrap about her shoulders. Percy grabbed her arm for one last remark.

"I suggest you book passage early. I'll be checking with the Great Eastern Company's ticket office in the next few weeks to make sure you've booked passage. If you don't, I'll be looking for YOU, and you know what happens after I find you."

Susannah ran out the door, barely hearing the threat. But she knew he meant it. During the carriage ride back to Rose Greenhow's, it suddenly occurred to her that she would have all that time with John. They could resume their intense love and perhaps make plans for after the War. There would be some good in this after all. A sudden lurch of the train ended her daydream.

She looked out the grimy train window at the desolate marshes that lay just west of the Hudson River. In a little while she would be on board the ship and she could enjoy surprising him with her arrival. She wondered if he looked any different.

10.

At last, the *The Great Eastern* was ready to leave New York Harbor. John Beauregard glanced at the steam gauge mounted high on the engine room bulkhead. It showed 22 pounds per square inch, not what could be called a full head of steam, but by the time they cleared Sandy Hook, the boilers of the vessel would be at full pressure.

They had brought 3,000 British troops and their horses from England to Quebec; a precautionary measure by the Queen to make sure the American insurrection did not spread north into Canada.

The young lieutenant was glad to see the troops and their smelly horses leave the ship in Quebec. Although their officers had kept the soldiers largely out of sight on the trip over, they had occupied almost the entire inside of the ship. Some of the officers had been billeted next door to his cabin and their loud voices, late-night card games and general rowdiness kept him from getting much sleep.

On top of that, the young captain engaged by the ship's owners for this one trip kept the ship at full steam for the entire voyage, an act that severely strained the crew and the ship as well. It was the first time the vessel had been put to the test of a high speed sustained run. Although there had been no mishaps, John Beauregard felt she should have been thoroughly checked for normal wear and tear after she docked in New York City. But no such order was issued. Instead, the crew cleaned the ship and made her ready for the journey back to England.

It had taken only eight days and six hours to cross from Liverpool to Quebec, a new speed record. The young naval officer thought of the implications of such speed and turnaround times in terms of a warship. He knew of none that either had the speed, or the ability to sustain it for days at a time, or coal capacity for such a distance. During his stint aboard the *Rhode Island*, loading coal was the one task that often consumed excessive time—time that kept a warship out of battle and vulnerable to attack.

Another incident had occurred involving some of the conscripted sailors, upsetting him and shaking his confidence in the young Captain Kennedy and his gang of non-commissioned officers. It happened the first morning out of Liverpool, when the sailors and some of the regular crew refused to scrub down the decks. A mutiny was declared and Kennedy went to the military man in command of the troops and borrowed a company of them to enforce the orders. When they again refused to obey, he sent them up the masts and onto the yards at bayonet point. There they stayed, for a full day, aloft in the smoke of the five funnels, which was heavy enough to turn the sails black. When they climbed down the next morning, the men looked as though they had just emerged from the mines of Wales.

Many of them were coughing uncontrollably, and some collapsed on the deck. Prodded again by the bayonets, they began to scour the deck. Those that could not get up by themselves were carried below by their fellow crewmen. John Beaureagard heard the commotion and came on deck, as he was not on watch. It had been another very disturbing experience.

The voice from the speaking tube interrupted his thinking. "Prepare for departure. Mr. Beauregard and Mr. McLennan, I want all engines ahead one-eighth. We're heading a course south south east down the bay to Sandy Hook."

The order brought life to the screw engine room crew. Men scurried around opening valves and closing others. Steam hissed from escape valves and the noise from the bilge pumps brought a sort of steady rhythm to the activity. The seven-foot cylinders slowly began their thrust and the driving rods their four-foot throw. The vessel was underway.

The motion of the pistons reminded John of his passionate lovemaking with Susannah. As he stared down at one of the polished connecting rods slowly pushing the propeller shaft, he suddenly realized why he was so drawn to Susannah. Like the ship's powerful screw engine that was his ward, in fact, like the entire legend that The Great Eastern had become, Susannah was, at once, unpredictable, strong, difficult to control, beautiful, and just a little dangerous.

11.

Susannah Eddings' body twitched, jarring her dream and awakening her. Tired from her long train ride from Washington, she had boarded the ship, was shown to her cabin and collapsed on her bunk, her unpacked bags laying in a heap by the cabin door. She had fallen asleep, missing all of the ship's festive departure activities from New York Harbor.

The dream was another one of those dreams where she felt she was seeing someone she knew, but couldn't speak to the person. This time it was someone on a horse, a tall gentleman with a top hat on. He looked gigantic and Susannah realized she must be much smaller, as she could not see the stranger's face. Yet she could hear him talking, in a soft, assuring tone, saying something like he would only be gone for two weeks, and to make a wish as to what she wanted him to bring back from his trip for her. He waved to her and she waved back, wanting to say goodbye but not having the breath or voice to do so.

Then the mysterious rider slowly turned his horse around and disappeared in the swirling marsh fog.

She sat up, rubbed her eyes, and noticed a small white envelope lying half under the door. She saw her name on it, below the fine line engraving of the ship and the handwritten words, "Captain James Kennedy." She picked up the envelope, opened it and drew out the engraved card.

"Dear Miss Eddings:

"Your honor and presence is requested at a reception and dinner in my cabin this evening, June 30, 1861 at six-thirty p.m. to celebrate our departure from New York. Dress is black tie and for the ladies, evening attire. You will have the chance to meet my officers and enjoy an evening with some of the better-known people on board this voyage.

Regrets only, please. I will send one of my officers to escort you a few minutes before the reception is to start. I look forward to meeting you.

Yours, etc.

James Kennedy
Captain"

Susannah hurriedly stuffed the invitation into the envelope and looked frantically through her luggage for her carriage clock. In one of the valises, she found it and turned its face to see what time it was.

Five o'clock already! Barely enough time to get ready. She opened her wardrobe, and ran her hand down the gowns she had brought with her. She stopped at the bright red strapless one that was one of her favorites. She remembered the last time she had worn it. It was at a reception at George Trenholm's house in Charleston, over a year ago and Raphael Semmes had been her escort, but she had left the party with John.

John! My god, would he find out I'd been invited to the Captain's reception tonight, she thought? Would he be my escort? Her heart began to pound wildly; her body felt a warm glow.

She began to undress, unfolded the top of the settee to reveal the bathtub, and began to draw herself a hot bath.

The warm water relaxed her. How much had happened in the last few months! Three separate events occurred that would forever change her life: she had decided she was finished with Peter Jenkins, she met John Beauregard, and she had been introduced to the famous Washington socialite Rose Greenhow.

12.

William Mervine's naval career could well be over. Sitting in a straight-backed chair outside Gideon Welles' office, the Flag Officer of the Southern Blockade Squadron was expecting the worst. He had to deliver an unfavorable report, and the sometimes crusty, offtimes short-fused Secretary of the Navy was known to react badly to such news.

It was the Raphael Semmes incident, and as the escape had happened in his area of responsibility and on his watch, he was accountable.

Now Mervine had to explain this mishap to his boss. Footsteps, followed by the appearance of a page, told him the time was here.

"Captain Mervine, the Secretary will see you now." The page led the officer down the hall to Welles' office. The Secretary was already on his feet as Mervine entered.

"Sit down, sit down," an obviously irritated Gideon Welles barked. "What the hell happened? How could you let that egotistical son-of-a-bitch slip through our fingers? Where were your men on watch—sleeping in their hammocks?" His full beard, intense eyes and wild hair gave him the appearance of some biblical patriarch. Indeed, Lincoln's nickname for him was Old Noah.

William Mervine sat down slowly before speaking. He looked directly at the Secretary, carefully choosing his words.

"Sir, the *Brooklyn* was chasing an unknown bark that had tried to enter the channel. Somehow the *Sumter* got by the *Powhatan*. After the *Brooklyn's* crew identified the bark as the British ship *Augusta Jessie*, my commanding officer Charles Poor hove-to and began pursuit of Semmes. We lost him after a three hour chase."

Welles frown deepened. "Didn't the British ship answer Poor's colors? Wasn't she flying the British flag? Couldn't he see that with his telescope? Do you realize what the *Sumter*'s mission is? She's a raider...." Gideon Welles' questions were like a fusillade of cannon shells.

Mervine gently interrupted his superior. "Sir, it couldn't be helped. Lt. Semmes was obviously waiting for a chance and somehow got tipped off that the *Brooklyn* was off on another chase. We were afraid to come in after him because the water's so shallow there at the Pass."

Welles sat down and let out a big sigh of exasperation. He stared out the window, for a time saying nothing. Finally, he spoke in a low voice, almost a monotone. "I'm citing you for incompetence, Captain. I hope this is sufficient incentive for you to lead your command in a more aggressive way. The American people deserve better vigilance. As of now, no more privateers must be permitted to make their way into the Gulf. Is that clear?"

"Yes sir." Welles stood up, a signal the meeting was over. He did not offer a handshake. That gesture alone did not bode well for William Mervine's career.

13.

The Great Eastern had been underway almost an hour. She had just dropped off the three New York harbor pilots at the Sandy Hook departure point. Most ships could make do with just one pilot, but the size of this vessel made it necessary to post a pilot on each of the paddlewheel housings as well as astern at the wheel.

Hal Lane had already been up on the bridge to meet the Captain. She found him young and exciting, and was flattered when he invited her to his cabin for dinner. She thought it was a bit impudent, since she hardly knew him, until he mentioned that he was having a small dinner party for the "better-known people", as he called them, of which she certainly qualified. A reception would begin at six-thirty, he had said. He would send one of his officers to her cabin to escort her to his suite for the event.

She had decided to retire for a short nap before dressing for dinner. She lay on her bunk, unable to sleep, enjoying the quiet and seclusion of her cabin, and looking forward to an evening of socializing and shipboard camaraderie.

Hal Lane was no stranger to *The Great Eastern*. She had been invited, along with her Uncle to visit the ship when it had been docked in Annapolis last summer. She remembered the event, and especially the luncheon where the ship's representative suggested to her uncle that the ship might serve the United States well, in the event of a conflict.

Hal Lane stood up and walked to the porthole in her cabin. Outside, the constant swarm of seagulls was nowhere to be seen; a sure sign the ship was headed out to sea. She remembered the elaborate tour and luncheon the ship owners had staged for her uncle.

She took a deep breath of ocean air. She couldn't remember whether her uncle had ever brought up a charter of *The Great*

Eastern with his cabinet or Congress. In all likelihood, she thought to herself, he probably forgot about it as the coming elections had become a more important issue.

14.

John Beauregard hurried down the stairway on his way to her cabin. Dressed in his crisp dress whites, white gloves, and ceremonial sword, he was careful to avoid the sooty ledges and dusty newel posts on the stairwells. His heart was beating wildly, the adrenalin in his system almost intoxicating him.

As one of the officers of the ship, he had been summoned to the captain's cabin earlier to plan the reception and review the invited guest list. He was astounded to see that Susannah Eddings ("Charleston, South Carolina and Washington, D.C.," the list had read) was in Cabin 2-F.

He had immediately volunteered to escort her to the Captain's reception as well as a "Harriet Lane," whose name was vaguely familiar to him.

But for now he could only think of his beloved Susannah, remembering the ecstasy of their last passionate embrace. He stopped to catch his breath and to inspect himself in one of the mirrors that were in each of the stairway vestibules. He liked what he saw; his white uniform set off his dark, recently grown beard, and the red sash that was part of the full dress regalia provided an appropriate splash of color. The gold buttons and trim on his hat and saber blade only served to provide a dash of elegance. And more than one woman had fallen for his green-blue eyes.

He wondered if Susannah would see it that way. He longed to kiss her once again. Well, there was no need to think about it; she was less than 100 feet from him and he was closing that distance rapidly.

The mahogany door was clearly labeled 2-F in silver letters. He knocked on the door itself, deciding not to use the somewhat dainty silver knocker that was provided for just that purpose.

Her voice, although muffled by the door between them, was clearly hers "Who is it?" He loved the silkiness of her voice.

"It's John, Susannah. I'm your escort." He tried to hide the joy that was welling up in his throat.

She flung open the door, radiant and beautiful in the low-cut red dress. Her hair was now almost waist length, her dark brown color with subtle henna highlights set off by her beautiful cream colored shoulders. Her magnificent breasts looked tantalizing from the red fabric covering them. But most of all, her full lips were parted in a smile that was the loveliest sight John had seen since they separated months before.

She was in his arms in a flash, the two of them melding as one, their mouths hungrily pressed tightly against each other. He could feel her chest pressing against him and his hot desire to have her. He reached to cup one of her breasts in his hand but she gently brushed it off.

"Darling, you will be with me later." They looked into each other's eyes and kissed again, this time a deep passionate embrace that confirmed their love for each other.

He gently ran his hand up her back feeling the soft skin that was not covered by her dress. His fingers caressed the long dark hair and she too felt limp with desire. But then, remembering Percy's ugly threats and menacing face, she broke away.

"I want you so much, John. . .but we have almost two weeks to enjoy each other, darling. If we do it now, we'll miss the entire reception because I won't be able to stop. . . . Let's wait just a few more hours."

He reluctantly stopped caressing her and instead pulled her body to his.

"I never realized how intensely I love you until now," he said, "and I don't ever want to be separated from you this long again. Your last letter said nothing about your coming to England, much less aboard my ship. I was overwhelmed when I saw your name on the passenger list. I had to fight off two other officers to get to escort you tonight."

She sidestepped his comment about the letter by slipping out of his arms gently, and back into her cabin to freshen up her makeup.

She kept reaching for one of his hands, as if she thought he would slip away with her back turned. A few seconds later, she was back in his embrace. By now he had forgotten that she had not told him she would be on the ship.

"Are you ready—let me look at you!" Susannah stepped back in the passageway to get a good look at her handsome naval officer.

"You look like an admiral, John! I'm so proud of you!" She slipped into his arms again and they kissed each other tenderly.

He spoke. "We'd better go now darling—Captain Kennedy is very punctual. Six-thirty means just that; not a minute later."

Climbing the two flights to the main deck, John and Susannah stepped out into a cool sea breeze and a sky full of stars. They stopped briefly to take in the magnificent sight of the moon, ducking in and out of the clouds, illuminating the sea each time it appeared, with the ship's lights dancing on the water. It was almost as if the moon were racing along, lighting the way for the ship.

The magic of the celestial display delighted them both and they embraced again, this time clinging to each other, as though the forces of nature, war and even the ship itself would somehow conspire to pull them apart.

Finally the couple turned and walked aft towards the captain's caboose, each with an arm around the other.

Susannah was ecstatic, feeling completely under his control. For the first time in her life she was ready to surrender herself to a man; before she had always wanted to have some control over her emotions. But her mission, her precarious role as a double agent, the spy Percy and her Southern loyalties were swirling around her, threatening her life, her security. And here was John, a strong handsome naval officer who made her feel secure, almost as if he would protect her from anything. It was the same feeling her father had given her when she was a little girl.

But she had to hold back something. She hadn't yet told him the fabricated story she had planned about why she was headed for England. Since he hadn't asked directly yet, she decided to take the initiative.

Pulling him close to her side she looked up at him. "Bet you can't guess why I'm going to England."

"That was my next question."

"The Committee has asked me to act as an unofficial emissary to talk about our Cause all over England. It was George Trenholm's idea to have a Southern lady talk to some of the people at a lower level—you know the merchants, the shopkeepers, the gilds, even the church congregations if they'll have me."

There was an element of truth in what she was saying. George Trenholm had mentioned the desire to show another side to the English, and had even suggested Susannah might be the perfect unofficial "ambassadress." She hoped John wouldn't ask her about what she did in Washington, but knew it would come up sooner or later. She hoped it would be later.

Once inside the captain's caboose, Susannah noticed several small groups of male officers in evening clothes, and two or three women were congregated around the room. One particularly tall officer left one of the groups and walked over to where John and Susannah were standing.

"Miss Eddings, I believe? I'm John Kennedy." He kissed her hand as Susannah curtsied.

"Thank you for the thoughtful invitation, Captain. It's so nice to feel welcome in a strange place."

"May I take you around and introduce you to our group? John has one more person to escort to my cabin. I promise you, he'll be back before I've finished the introductions." He looked at John, with almost a twinkle.

"That's very thoughtful of you, Captain." Susannah turned and squeezed John's hand and her eyes melted in his, saying *I'll be waiting. . .hurry back.*

The Captain offered Susannah his arm and they slowly walked away from John. He could not help admiring how every man in the room stared at her.

15.

Cabin 2-Q was on the other side of the ship from Susannah's cabin. As John Beauregard made his way along the passageway in that direction, he tried to think who Harriet Lane was. He vaguely remembered some association with the U. S. Presidency, but decided to wait and see how she introduced herself. Coming up to the cabin door, he again avoided the dainty knocker and knocked on the door itself.

An elegant, decidedly beautiful woman opened the door. Her appearance radiated refinement and upbringing. Her golden-blonde hair was done up in a bouffant, complimenting her lovely, ivory-toned skin. A perfectly-proportioned nose, bow-shaped mouth and well-defined chin completed the picture. Her full-length, peach-colored gown, trimmed with lace, brought out the best of her trim figure.

Admiring all this, John Beauregard found himself momentarily without a voice. He quickly recovered. "Miss Lane, I'm Lieutenant John Beauregard, here to escort you to the Captain's reception."

"Thank you, lieutenant. I'm pleased to meet you. And thank you for coming for me. Is it a British custom, when the Captain has a function, for him to send his officers to escort the ladies?" She was pulling the cabin door shut.

"I don't know ma'am. I'm from South Carolina, serving as an American observer and apprenticing my specialty in steam propulsion."

He offered her his arm and they began to walk down the passageway.

Hal Lane paused, turning to face the young lieutenant. "South Carolina, hmmm. What part, may I ask?"

"The Sea Islands, St. Helena's, to be specific, Miss Lane."

They resumed walking. "Please call me Hal. May I call you John?" He was somewhat surprised at her request for informality.

"Please do." He still could not place just who she was. "Please pardon my ignorance, Miss Lane-er-er Hal. I believe I've heard about you but my memory has completely failed me for me to give you your proper due."

Hal Lane smiled her gracious but warm, disarming smile. "It's nothing, John. If you didn't live in Washington, you might never have heard of me. My uncle is the former President, James Buchanan."

Suddenly the connection clicked. Uncle Pierre had mentioned her name in connection with the Buchanan family. He couldn't resist citing the curious coincidence.

"What a coincidence! It seems we both have famous uncles. Mine is General Beauregard, who commanded the Confederate forces that took Fort Sumter. We're very proud of him and think he will be one of the outstanding generals of the war." He blurted out the remark before he even thought of the reaction it might have on the niece of a former United States President.

"That *is* very coincidental," she remarked, somewhat detached.

They had reached the stairwell. She again stopped and turned to face him again. A look of concern was on her face.

"I certainly hope the South wins the war. Or at least its freedom. I think some of Lincoln's policies are simply terrible. And I speak from some experience."

The remark took the young lieutenant completely off guard. As they walked up the narrow stairs, single-file, it seemed strange for her to make blasphemous remarks against the Union. But he decided not to prod her further about it as they were just steps from the door of the Captain's caboose.

16.

The seating arrangement at the banquet table had been meticulously planned. Captain Kennedy had been careful to spread the few young ladies among the overwhelming number of his officers and male guests. Counting Susannah Eddings and Harriet Lane, there were only six women to the 20 officers of the ship invited to the event.

John Beauregard was surprised that Susannah and Hal Lane knew each other. When he had brought Hal into the Captain's parlor, Susannah had broken her conversation with one of the ship's officers to rush across the room and greet her. The two women embraced each other warmly, as though they had known each other for years. Susannah later explained to John that she had met Hal Lane at a reception at Rose Greenhow's house and seen her at other social functions in Washington.

John started to assess Hal Lane's political sympathies. She had already surprised him with her outspoken feelings about Lincoln on their way to the reception. Now, an association with Rose Greenhow and Susannah seemed to confirm that she was sympathetic to the South.

John also was comparing Susannah to Hal Lane. Both were beautiful women. Both talked and moved easily through the small groups, each showing an upper-class upbringing. But there the similarities ended. Susannah radiated sexual attraction, sensual feelings and had a loud earthy laugh, which could be heard, throughout the cabin, even over the small group of chamber musicians' music.

Hal Lane's laugh was much more female, higher in pitch, no less discernable than Susannah's, but somehow more refined. When talking to a group of men, she kept her hands to herself. She seemed to have a bit of reserve, although she was not shy about flirting. John had caught her eye several times during the reception and also during dinner and several times she managed a quick wink. John was surprised the first time; when she did it the second time he managed a broad smile.

Susannah quickly got over her initial reserve and began to enjoy herself and was stared at by all the men in the room. She, too, ever mindful of John's presence, also did her share of flirting and being coquettish. Knowing he was never more than a few feet from her side gave her a feeling of security.

The stewards had begun to clear the dishes from the main course from the table. John Kennedy, lighting a cigar, turned to Hal Lane.

"Tell me Hal, what brings you back to our country? Another proposal of marriage? Or are you rekindling your friendship with the Queen and Prince Albert?"

Hal Lane laughed her distinctive, high-pitched laugh. The dinner guests laughed politely. She turned to the captain, her head slightly lowered, her eyelashes fluttering.

"Now Captain, why would I journey to England to accept a marriage proposal? Isn't the gentleman supposed to go to his chosen fiancée wherever she is and make the proposal there?"

The guests laughed louder. It had been a typical Hal Lane response—a put-down handled with polish and humor. She continued.

"Actually, I'm going to see an old Southern friend, George Trenholm. He's asked me for some help, and I'm going to see what I can do."

Susannah perked up at the mention of the trader's name. After all, it was his idea of spreading the word about the South around the English countryside that had purportedly put her on board this ship. And he was also responsible for introducing her to Rose Greenhow.

She looked around the table at some of the other dinner guests. She was fascinated with the Scottish engineer Alexander McLennan, especially his accent and straightforwardness. His ruddy complexion, big hands, and constant twinkle in his eye when he talked to her endeared him to her right away. He was all male and she could feel him respond to her earthy beauty even though it was tempered with traditional Scottish reserve.

Then there was the mysterious man, only introduced as a Major E. J. Allen, a man who said little but seemed to listen to everything everyone else had to say. He had been seated next to McLennan, and Major Allen was soon talking more with the engineer than anyone else. Susannah overheard the word "Glasgow" mentioned several times and believed that the stranger was from Scotland.

There was an aura of danger around this Major Allen. As if sensing her uneasiness, Susannah felt John Beauregard's hand slip into hers, under the table. How did he know, she thought? The reassuring grip, the squeeze, made her heart jump and immediately relaxed her tension. Nevertheless, she decided to avoid any conversation with the stranger until she could find out why she was afraid of him.

The musicians had started playing again. John turned to Susannah.

"Would you like to waltz with this humble Confederate naval officer?" he asked.

"I'd *love* to," she said, using the same inflection she'd used when he first asked her to take a walk with him that first night in Beaufort. He stood up, and gently pulled her chair from the table. Captain John Kennedy was doing precisely the same thing with Hal Lane's chair. Several of the other officers were inviting the remaining ladies to dance.

Susannah looked up at John, who had been staring at her. They smiled at each other and he pulled her a little closer to him. She began to think of what was to happen after the reception, and her pulse quickened as their eyes once again embraced.

John was totally swept up with her. She was easily the most beautiful woman present. He, too, began to think about what would happen later. A hand on his shoulder interrupted his thoughts, a gesture that meant someone wanted to dance with his Southern belle. He turned to see the ruddy complexion and broad smile of his superior, Alexander McLennan.

"Come on, me lad, you can't have her all to yourself." His good nature made the task of giving up the dance with Susannah almost effortless.

He winked at her. "I will be back. Don't let this Scotsman tell you too many false stories about me."

For such a big man, Alexander McLennan was surprisingly graceful. He spoke first. "In case no one has said so, Miss, welcome aboard *The Great Eastern*. We've not had such a pretty lass on this iron maiden as you. In fact, you and Miss Lane both add a new dimension to ocean sailing."

"Thank you, Mr. McLennan. I must say I've been made to feel right at home with all the hospitality." Then a thought occurred to her. Perhaps he would tell her who the mysterious man was and what he was doing on the ship. She decided to give it a try.

"I noticed you and Major Allen were talking about Scotland. Is he from there?" She tried to make the question sound casual.

"Yes ma'am. He's from Glasgow, just like me. But he left when he was 23 and came to your country. I'm not sure what he does; he only mentioned that he was going to London on some business for the American government. Do you know anything about him?"

Susannah looked into the engineer's kindly twinkling eyes. "No, I don't. He seems to be here for a reason though, and I'm not sure what it is." And as her eyes met his, they showed her suspicious fear of the mysterious Mr. Allen.

The Scotsman held the same suspicion, but didn't want to alarm Susannah. Still, he felt she had a strong people sense, that she intuitively knew something wasn't right, sort of a street sense such as he had learned growing up in the slums of Glasgow. He wondered how someone with such obvious class and upbringing could know about such things. He decided to share his doubts.

"He's hiding something. I don't know what. It's just a feeling. You know, we've had all kinds of strange people on this ship going to and from America, especially since the war started. Maybe he's a spy. I'd stay away from him."

The irony of his use of the word "spy" was not lost on Susannah.

The musicians were in the final bars of the tune and Alexander and Susannah ended the dance with a little twirl.

"Thank you, Alexander. You're a grand dancer!"

The engineer kissed her hand. "Perhaps we can do it again."

Several dance sets later, the party began to break up. Susannah and John paid their respects to Captain Kennedy, who had practically monopolized Hal Lane. John Beauregard guessed that he would not be needed to escort her back to her cabin. Hand in hand, the two southerners walked out into the warm June night.

17.

John Beauregard carefully made his way down the narrow catwalk of the paddlewheel engine room. He was tired, and the heat had already begun to bother him, yet it was only the beginning of his noon-to-four watch.

He dreamily recalled the night in Susannah's cabin; their passion for each other masking the growing conflicts each was being forced to face.

Alexander McLennan was standing at the mid-point of the catwalk, directly between the two shafts that drove the gigantic paddlewheels. He motioned for John to follow him to the aft end of the catwalk. Once there, he turned and shouted to the young lieutenant.

"Have a minute? Got something I want to share with you."

"Sure."

They reached the platform at the end of the catwalk, where the noise level almost allowed normal conversation. The Scotsman's normally jovial personality seemed troubled. A deep crease lined his forehead.

"Has Major Allen visited you down here?"

The young lieutenant looked directly at the Scotsman. "Yes, he's been back in the screw engine room asking all kinds of questions about the machinery and the ship."

"Well, he just left here a few minutes ago. He's been here several times, also asking about the ship. I think he's a spy."

"Yes, Susannah told me you had doubts about him. Who do you think he's working for?"

"Well, my lad, if he was working for the South, wouldn't he tell you?"

John Beauregard rebuked himself for such an obvious thing. "I never thought of that, Mr. McLennan. He certainly is odd."

Alexander McLennan nodded his head and drew a deep puff on his pipe.

John Beauregard turned and disappeared into the boiler room passage.

But the rest of the voyage turned up nothing new about the stranger, except more suspicion. He was careful to keep to himself even after Alexander McLennan began asking pointed questions about why he was so interested in the ship and her engines. The Chief Engineer did not know that Allan Pinkerton had already been over most of the vessel, making detailed sketches and descriptions of how the ship was built, and how she ran.

And Susannah Eddings, who continued to suspect his intentions, made no attempt to engage him in conversation, even though she saw him alone on deck, leaning out over the railing and taking notes. Susannah had her own agenda, and it did not include any pointed questions on what her mission in London was to be.

The ship arrived in London on the morning of July 10, 1861.

18.

George Trenholm received Hal Lane's reply just three days after he had sent his telegram to her.

......IM LOOKING FORWARD TO SEEING YOU AGAIN MR. TRENHOLM. STOP OF COURSE ILL HELP IN ANY WAY I CAN STOP. IM SAILING ON THE GREAT EASTERN; THERE IS SOME TALK SHE TOOK SOME BRITISH SOLDIERS TO CANADA TO SUPPORT THE CANADIAN ARMY AND MAY BE TAKING SOME MORE STOP ITS ALL VERY MUCH UP IN THE AIR STOP ILL TRY TO FIND OUT MORE ON BOARD.

YOURS IN FRIENDSHIP

HAL LANE

The irony of Hal Lane on board the very subject of her trip was almost too much for even the sophisticated Southerner to comprehend. More importantly—what was this about embarking soldiers? Was this why the ship's owners turned him down? Had the British Government made some deal with the Union?

He and James Bulloch met her at her hotel and wasted no time in leaving for the Queen's summer residence. On the train, she detailed her long friendship with Prince Albert and the respect and trust the Queen had for her. She also related how much closer she had moved in sympathy to the South, because of her growing dislike of Lincoln and his mounting aggression against the South. She cited the blockade and what it was doing to the economy as an example.

They were sitting in the first class compartment he had hired for privacy. She was watching the greenery of Southern England slide by the window. George Trenholm was convinced that she was sincere. He proceeded to outline what the South's ultimate plan to answer the Union blockade was; the employment of *The Great Eastern.*

"How ironic, George. Here I was traveling on the very vessel you're trying to obtain for the War. What has been the position of the owners?" Hal Lane was remarkably composed for such a twist.

George Trenholm leaned forward in the swivel chair. Hal had turned from the window after she posed the question. "They turned us down, citing that they don't want to risk the ship in a war zone. We've offered them a good deal of money, a share of the profits, and the promise to fix the ship back to her original configuration at the end of the charter."

Hal Lane leaned back in her seat. "I'm surprised. I told the Queen in a telegram that I wanted her to meet some important people representing business interests here and in the South. I also told her of yours and Mr. Bulloch's mission of getting armament and supplies for your armies—I hope you don't mind—but I wanted no room for speculation or a feeling of deception on her part. I knew you had interest in chartering some British vessels, but until now I had no idea it was *The Great Eastern.* That will have to be explained to Her Majesty clearly."

James Bulloch spoke words of assurance. "Of course we will disclose everything. We will try to show her that everyone can benefit from it. The ship's perfect for the role, Miss Lane. We can arm most all of our armed forces in about four voyages, while bringing the entire cotton crop on each of the return trips to the mills of Manchester."

The train was slowing for the station at Southampton. Further discussion would only be speculation. No one knew what the Queen would say.

The Royal yacht *Victoria and Albert II* was anchored in the bay at Southampton. Her masts clearly showed the presence of the Royal family aboard; the ensign flapped incessantly at the top of the mainmast. A fresh breeze off the English Channel made the early July morning seem more like spring than early summer.

The Royal tender *Elphin* gently bumped the public dock at Southampton where George Trenholm, James Bulloch and Hal Lane boarded and got underway to the royal yacht.

The entire upper deck area of the ship was sheltered from the sun by enormous white canvas shrouds. The only thing whiter was the hull of the ship itself, contrasted against the dark green waters of Southampton harbor. At the ship's side, the Americans made their way up the boarding ladder, just aft of the port paddle box. The fresh breeze caused the canvas overhead to flap up and down like the wings of some giant bird.

Captain Denman and his first officer greeted the visitors as they stepped on deck.

"Welcome aboard Her Majesty's ship the *Victoria and Albert*. The Queen is hosting tea in the aft teahouse and asked me to escort you there."

Hal Lane smiled and curtsied for the ship's commander and the crew who were standing at attention nearby. Trenholm and Bulloch shook the captain's hand and followed him towards the stern of the ship.

Inside the teahouse, Queen Victoria was sitting in a captain's chair at the far end of the room. Her long dark hair was severely parted in the middle and hung down the back of the chair. She wore an expression of concern, as she chatted with one of her aides. The aide noticed the presence of the Americans and he and the Queen quickly stopped the whispered conversation. They both looked across the room at the group. The look of concern gradually melted into a gentle smile as Captain Denham bowed towards the Queen and spoke.

"Your Majesty, may I present Mr. George Trenholm and Mr. James Bulloch of the Confederate States. I believe you already know Miss Harriet Lane."

"Welcome aboard the *Victoria and Albert*," repeated the Queen. The gentle smile became a wider one. "Miss Lane, it's been awhile hasn't it? We've invited Albert to join us—we know he'll be happy to see you."

As if on cue, the Prince came through the glass door, past the bowing Court attendant. He immediately went to Hal Lane who offered Albert her hand, while punctuating the gesture with a curtsy.

"So good to see you Your Majesty. I'd like to introduce Mr. George Trenholm and Mr. James Bulloch from the Confederate States of America." The two Americans bowed to the Royalty. The Prince sat down, followed by Hal Lane and James Bulloch.

George Trenholm, still standing, addressed the Queen, explaining to her what the South wanted with *The Great Eastern*. He stressed the non-involvement of the British government, since the vessel was privately owned. He also mentioned the economic factors of cotton and munitions and what they meant to British industry. The whole explanation took about twenty minutes. He sat down and there was a deep silence.

The Queen finally spoke. "Gentlemen, you are asking for our intervention on a matter which does not really fall under our jurisdiction. We had heard that you attempted to charter the ship to bring cotton from the southern United States and to deliver munitions, armament, and clothing to your organization's army. We also understand the vessel's owners have declined the charter, citing their concern about the ship entering a war theater."

The Queen continued. "That reason is not entirely true. They neglected to tell you about the British government charter. We have arranged for the ship to ferry some of our Royal Artillery, and others to Montreal, as a protection against your war spreading to the North. We told the owners to hold the ship in reserve for just such a purpose. We have no further plans to use the vessel after this charter, which will end this month, and have so notified the owners yesterday."

She took a sip of her tea and continued. "Great Britain does not wish to antagonize the United States by taking sides with your organization. On the other hand, we certainly can make use of your cotton, as we're sure your military can make use of the supplies from England. We view this as a strictly commercial venture, with no involvement of our government in any part."

George Trenholm breathed a silent sigh. "Your Majesty, Mr. Bulloch and I are here as agents of the Confederate States of America and receive our authority directly from President Jefferson Davis. I am sure if he could be here, he would be most grateful."

The Queen set down her teacup. Servants promptly refilled it.

Her tone became more concerned.

"We certainly hope your President and the entire organization, for that matter, know how serious war can be. Our agents tell me you believe you can win it and win it quickly. That remains to be seen. If *The Great Eastern* can shorten the war, we support its use as a supply vessel."

It was Bulloch's turn to speak. "Your Majesty, there is little doubt in my mind or Mr. Trenholm's that the use of the ship will shorten the war and cut the number of casualties. When she is adequately refitted for her new role, she will be well prepared to defend herself."

The Queen stood up, signaling the end of the meeting. "Gentlemen, we wish you Godspeed. We suggest you try another approach with the ship's owners. Knowing they don't have a charter from the British government any longer may make them receptive to another offer from you."

"Miss Lane, we hope you will visit us soon and stay longer next time." It was the first time anything had been personalized in the meeting. The Prince rose and walked to Hal Lane's side where he embraced her lightly. She smiled and embraced him as well. Trenholm and Bulloch bowed to the Queen, and the Prince, and followed the Captain out of the teahouse.

But a subsequent meeting with the ship's owners, Gooch and Colonel Baker with both Trenholm and Bulloch, failed again to budge the owners. The ship, they said, was beginning to enjoy full or nearly full bookings on the transatlantic run. To take her out of service now would cause them to lose even more money. No, they could not approve a charter.

It looked like the matter was settled.

George Trenholm and James Bulloch began to entertain alternative methods of getting the cotton out of the South and getting supplies in to the Confederate army.

19.

Susannah returned to Washington after a whirlwind week with John in London. They had been together constantly, both on the ship and the brief time his ship had laid over in London. Business seemed to be picking up for the beleaguered vessel; she was booked with more than three hundred passengers for the return trip to New York. He was gone in less than a week; she lingered in London, had dinner with George Trenholm who was lukewarm to her idea of trying to explain the South to the largely neutral English people.

He did take time to explain to her that some very important negotiations were going on behalf of the Confederacy and that her presence and rhetoric might send the wrong message at this time because the whole situation was so sensitive. She agreed, and booked passage on the next ship to New York. But she had left London with only part of what Percy had asked her to find out.

Now Susannah was getting ready for another meeting with the agent, something she learned from a note Percy had left her at Rose Greenhow's mansion while she was gone. She was a little nervous about the meeting because it was to be held at an address in Alexandria, not at the agent's tiny cottage near Pierce Mill. She wondered why there was a change; he had always stressed the private location of his house as perfect for their transactions.

Now, on her way to the address Percy left for her, she was worried what he might do. The August heat made her perspire; she could feel the moisture running down her back.

The carriage pulled up in front of a drab townhouse on St. Asaph Street. A sign in front said "Rooms for Rent." The sign itself was badly in need of a coat of paint. She paid for the ride, and walked to the front door. Inside, Percy was waiting for her on one of the shabby chairs in the sitting room.

He stood up and greeted her as if they were old friends and not adversaries.

"I have someone I want you to meet; he's upstairs in a room I've rented." He guided her to the stairs.

Upstairs, Percy opened the door to the room. When Susannah saw who was looking out the dingy window, she let out a little cry. It was Major E.J. Allen, the now not so mysterious Scotsman on board the ship. But Percy was introducing him as Allan Pinkerton.

Pinkerton motioned for her to sit down. He smiled gently as he began to speak.

"I know you must be puzzled why I was on the ship under another name. Please forgive me for not identifying who I was and for ignoring you. Let's just say it would have been inopportune for me to socialize with you."

He continued. "Percy tells me you have information on whether the ship's under charter to the Confederacy. What's the situation?"

Susannah sat down and crossed her legs. "Mr. Pinkerton, nothing's been finalized as far as I could find out." She went on to describe her dinner conversation with George Trenholm; the information about "delicate negotiations."

Percy stared at her, his face wrinkled into a frown. The geniality was gone, replaced by the Percy she hated.

"What about the details of the ship that you were supposed to get from your lieutenant friend? That was part of the deal!" Percy's deep voice filled the tiny room. "Are you hiding that information from us? What was your idea. . ."

Pinkerton interrupted his agent. "I took care of that, George." He pointed to his valise on the bed. "It's all there. I don't think Miss Eddings could have gotten the amount of detail I did without her friend and the others getting suspicious."

Percy sat down on the sagging mattress, making the bed sag even more than before.

Allan Pinkerton walked across the room. "I don't think we should detain Miss Eddings any further, George." He was standing in front of her, his perfect-triangle face focused on hers. "Miss Eddings, our business is still unfinished. I want you to keep in touch with Mr. Percy. If you have to leave Washington, I want you to tell him where you're going. I also want you to keep your ear to the ground about the status of the ship. We want to know as soon as possible just when the ship is chartered by the Confederacy. Once that happens, it's likely we'll ask you to perform another assignment. In the meantime, don't forget just who you are. You must continue to get information to your committee to avoid raising their suspicion. But don't be too clever. George will be keeping his eye on you."

George Percy stood up, his tall lanky frame lurking over Susannah, his glare menacing. "I'll be in touch, Miss Eddings." His tone had dropped; the deep voice carrying as much of a threat as his stare. Allan Pinkerton opened the door to the hall: Susannah couldn't leave fast enough.

On the carriage ride back to Washington, she realized she must get word to the Committee about what the Union now knew about the ship. She also realized the further danger she was in. Knowing who Major Allen really was and what his role on the voyage over to England was, and how he had performed a detailed survey of *The Great Eastern,* was all information she should immediately transmit to the Committee. She decided to use one of Rose Greenhow's couriers to send the information.

But how could she have discovered his identity? She knew from talking with John in London that he and Alexander McLennan had been unsuccessful in unmasking the stranger's identity. Once the ship had arrived, Major Allen disappeared into the London streets and was not seen again.

Somehow, she thought, I must look past my personal safety, and protect my countrymen. At once she realized that her role as a double agent was a two-edged sword which could be wielded either way. It was slowly becoming apparent to her that here was the elusive thing that she could make a mark on the world with: the world would know that Susannah Eddings had done this. In spite of her coerced spying for the North, she was privy to what they had discovered about the ship. That knowledge would be of great help in the Confederate strategy of protecting its cargo and supplying the army.

But she decided to postpone any disclosure until she was sure the ship was under charter to the South. That way she could protect herself and devise a plan to keep her out of the hands of Pinkerton and his henchman.

She felt dirty, soiled, after the visit to the dingy rooming house. She directed the carriage driver to go back to Rose Greenhouse's house to change her clothes and freshen up. As her carriage slowed to make the turn into Lafayette Square, she noticed the mansion had several Union soldiers guarding the entrance.

Telling the driver to slow down, she saw that the guards were stopping anyone who walked by, and examining their identity papers. She decided not to stop, but to try and contact Hal Lane to see what had happened. Without Rose Greenhow's front, she would have no base of operations in the Capital, and no source of information or place to meet people, other than the contacts she had made in the Department of the Navy. She began to be afraid of just how vulnerable she had become.

She decided to chance a meeting with the former "First Lady" and directed the driver to take her to Georgetown, where Hal Lane owned a townhouse. Thirty minutes later, the carriage pulled up in front of the small brick dwelling on Dumbarton Street. Telling the driver to wait, she stepped down to the cobblestones and walked up to the small picket fence gate. Carefully opening the latch, she walked through the gate, up the two stairs, and knocked on the door. A black servant answered.

"May I help you, ma'am?"

"Yes. I'm Susannah Eddings, a friend of Miss Lane's. Is she at home?"

The servant motioned for her to come in. Susannah had only been in Hal Lane's house once before, for a reception. The beautiful antiques and the furniture that she had collected from living in London served to reinforce her image as a woman of taste and breeding.

"Susannah! What a surprise! When did you get back?" Hal Lane was on the landing and, even at home in her own house she was impeccably dressed, her makeup perfect.

The two embraced and walked into the parlor. They sat down on the loveseat. Susannah lowered her voice to almost a whisper. "Actually, I arrived late last night. I was staying at Rose

Greenhow's mansion but this morning, after I had business in Alexandria, I came back and found her house, surrounded by Union soldiers, checking everyone's identification. Not knowing who or what they were looking for, I took a chance and came directly here. Now it seems I don't seem to have a place to stay." The two women walked into the parlor.

Hal Lane quickly responded. "Of course you do. You're welcome to stay here as long as you want here. I have two extra bedrooms upstairs and I insist you stay with me. We've got lots to catch up on. I'm having a party tonight for some of the War Department. Of course, you're invited; we could use a little Southern beauty to spice up some of these boring bureaucrats."

Susannah voiced concern over what she had seen at the mansion earlier. "What has happened to Rose Greenhow?

Hal Lane noticed the look on her friend's face. Taking Susannah's hand in hers she also spoke in lowered tones.

"Allan Pinkerton's been threatening to put her under house arrest for spying. Between you and me, nothing's slowing down much. She's still being fed information and is somehow getting it into the hands of the Confederates. "

Susannah let out a sigh of relief. "Thank God. I've got some information I've got to get to the Committee—I can channel it through her." They stopped talking, as the servant was standing in the doorway.

"'S'cuse me Miz Lane. The driver wants to know if you need him anymore."

Susannah fumbled in her purse for some coins, giving them to the servant to pay the driver. The thought of Rose Greenhow's imprisonment just hit her. Pinkerton hadn't said a word to her about this and he knew she was Susannah's front. Was he doing this to further put her in danger of being discovered? Fortunately he did not know of Hal Lane's southern sympathies nor of Susannah's friendship with her or Hal's ties with Rose Greenhow. Susannah felt faint and sat down on the sofa. She realized she hadn't had anything for breakfast and it was well past lunchtime. "Are you all right?" Hal Lane asked, noticing Susannah's face was slightly flushed.

"Yes. I suddenly realized I haven't eaten since last night on the train. I'll be all right."

"Nonsense. I'll have Clarissa fix you something cool."

After the brief and belated lunch, Susannah explained she wanted to rest after her long journey. Hal showed her to her room. Susannah immediately lay down on the bed, exhausted, not even bothering to take off her dress.

But she couldn't get to sleep. Was Pinkerton planning to expose her now that he had arrested Rose Greenhow? What were his plans for her? Would he have Percy kill her and dispose of her body near his house in the woods? Would he leak word to the South that she was a spy for the North? She wished John were there to comfort her and protect her.

The sweetness of sleep began to relax her body. Soon it blotted out the doubts and fears which had kept her awake.

Over the next few days Hal Lane introduced Susannah to a whole new circle of people. She entertained two or three times a week and Susannah assumed the role of co-hostess at many of the parties. The two complimented each other: Susannah, the passionate, worldly, vivacious crusader for the South; Hal Lane the cool, gracious Washington socialite quietly straddling the delicate line of official Unionism to her evolving but still largely clandestine support of the South.

The two women often sat up after the last guest had left, having a sherry and discussing the war. Susannah found Hal Lane was far more outspoken about her feelings in private. Susannah learned of her tutelage also at the hands of Rose Greenhow during her uncle's presidency and things began to fall into place. It didn't surprise her to hear the niece of the former President expound on her support of slavery as an economic necessity. Lincoln wasn't supporting the Constitution; he was strangling the South and would likely bankrupt its whole economy the way he was going.

They shared some secrets about each other's love lives. Susannah told Hal she wanted to marry John and have a family, but also thought she would like to go into politics. She was careful to avoid any further discussion about Pinkerton and the whole Rose Greenhow affair, as she feared she might slip, and Hal would then begin to suspect her.

20.

"The President will see you now." Sitting in the row of chairs was Allan Pinkerton and his boss, General George McClellan. They were quietly ushered into the President's office.

Lincoln stood up and came around his desk to offer a warm welcome to the spy and to his new commander of the Army of the Potomac. Both had just completed two very difficult assignments successfully; Pinkerton with his clandestine survey of *The Great Eastern*; McClellan with turning the Army of the Potomac into an effective fighting force after the defeat at Bull Run.

"Sit down, gentlemen, please sit down." The President seemed relaxed, even jovial in the face of so many defeats for the Union in these early months of the war.

"Mr. Pinkerton, I've read your report about the ship. A very thorough job. Tell me again how the ship poses such a threat as you described her."

The spy leaned forward in his chair. "Sir, she's built with a double hull, with bulkheads dividing the ship that reach all the way to the deck. She'd be almost impossible to sink, with the shells we have available."

He continued. "She's got two sets of engines; one for the paddlewheels and one for the propeller. Together they can push her speed beyond 15 knots, without hoisting the canvas. If the paddlewheels got damaged, she could still navigate with her propeller alone."

Lincoln listened carefully. "Is she armed, Mr. Pinkerton?'

"Just four Dalhgrens was all I could find, sir. She had an armory but I don't think it had anything more than a few rifles; it just wasn't big enough."

George McClellan listened to the conversation intently. Although it didn't affect him directly, the presence of such a ship could certainly mean some kind of massive supply effort was afoot, and that would mean a longer and probably bloodier war.

The President stood up behind his desk, his size dwarfing the two other men. He turned and looked out the window at the warm September afternoon. "We're working on some surprises, too. I'm getting proposals for building an armored ship with a revolving turret, armed with two cannon. I'm told she can be ready in about three months. Her armor is to be four inches thick, almost four times that of *The Great Eastern* hull. I have also been told the South is rebuilding the *Merrimack* into an armored warship. It looks like the days of wooden warships are finished."

McClellan spoke. "The armed ship—that's wonderful news, Mr. President. I'm sure it will prove very valuable in protecting our fleet as well as adding another dimension to naval offensives."

"That may be, General." Lincoln turned to sit down. "The trouble is we just don't have anything as big as that huge monster." He punctuated his statement by slowly sinking into his chair.

BLOCKADE RUNNER
BOOK 3

1.

The crew of the lighter *Samuel Pepys* crowded the bow section of the small harbor workboat. What lay in front of them, the hulk of *The Great Eastern*, was a sorry imitation of the ship that had only made her gala maiden voyage little more than two years earlier. Partially dismasted, the deck was littered with all manner of baggage and ship's stores, many skylights were shattered and the badly scarred hull of the vessel looked like she had participated in one of the early naval battles across the ocean in America.

But the most startling thing was the absence of the paddlewheels. Approaching the ship's port side, the entire paddlewheel assembly, including most of the protective cage that surrounded it had been ripped away, right down to the huge shaft that disappeared into the hull. Great scratches and gashes marred the side of the hull where the whole mechanism must have banged against the ship, as whatever it was, wrenched the assembly from the vessel. The only piece left was part of the outer walkway, hanging sickly from the front section of the ship.

The ship had experienced a bout with gale force winds and waves. One of those huge waves managed to wrench the entire paddlewheel assembly loose from the ship. Several successive waves completed the job. In order to prevent damage to the hull from the still-turning starboard paddlewheel, the captain was forced to cut power entirely from the paddlewheel. The ship broached sideways, exposing the rudder to the full force of the waves. The strain was too much for the rudder and she was soon parted from the rudderpost on the stern of the ship. The captain then cut power to the propeller in order to prevent damage to the rudder. Right after that, another big wave managed to wrench the starboard paddlewheel assembly from the side of the ship. The crew managed to immobilize the rudder so that the captain was able to restart the propeller engine and steer the vessel by the propeller alone. A tow from the small coaster *Advice* enabled the stricken liner to be pulled into Queenstowne harbor.

"Come starboard ten degrees," the captain of the *Samuel Pepys* told the helmsman. The vessel heeled slightly to the right as the ship's commander maneuvered his boat closer to *The Great Eastern*. He had been assigned to offload all the four hundred passengers who ten days earlier boarded the ship in Liverpool for the voyage to New York. In order for him to do this, he had to approach the ship's starboard side, where the passenger gangway was located. As the lighter rounded the stern of the ship, another strange sight presented itself. Hanging from the deck, was a random mass of chains, pulleys and ropes lashed to various hawser posts and culminating around the steering shaft attached to the rudder. The huge rudder itself hung at an odd angle. The lighter captain wondered how the ship had made it into Queenstowne without assistance.

When the starboard side came into view, the startled crew saw that the starboard paddlewheel assembly had also been stripped from the ship. There were only two lifeboats in their davits where there should have been ten. Nothing remained of the paddlewheel, its housing, or the guardrail. The starboard side of the ship was as badly scarred as the port side.

The captain eased his craft up to the gangway where anxious passengers, crowding the boarding stairs, eagerly awaited the chance to disembark the badly damaged vessel. *The Great Eastern* had now experienced another colossal piece of bad luck.

The news reached Daniel Gooch and the other directors just as the ship had arrived off Queensland. It could not have come at a worse time. Transatlantic passage on the vessel had finally become profitable and it seemed the ship was shaking off all its old bad habits and reputation. Everywhere she went, she could be counted on to attract thousands who simply wanted to board her (for a fee, of course) and roam through her cavernous insides.

And now she was out of commission. Not only would the owners lose money because she was out of service, they would have to pay for some very extensive repairs to the ship's most important parts: her paddlewheels and rudder. Even at the cost of borrowing more money to pay for the repairs, the ship would not earn any revenue until she was repaired and put back into service. While the owners and directors of the ship debated over how they would pay for the repairs, they ordered her towed out into the Atlantic from Queenstowne, across to Milford Haven in Wales, where the engineers could get the repairs started.

While it was obvious that both paddlewheels had to be replaced and the entire rudder structure and steering apparatus rebuilt, some not-so-obvious and extensive damage had occurred to the paddlewheel shafts, bearings, and the gargantuan engine so favored by her first engineer Alexander McLennan. There was also some damage to the hull from the pounding and wrenching she took during the storm. The bill was $750,000, far more than the ship's company had in the treasury. The money would have to be borrowed, at a time when the world's financial community looked anxiously at the war raging in America.

The loss in income during the six months the ship would be laid up plus the repairs would exceed a million dollars.

2.

With her husband's physical condition rapidly deteriorating, Queen Victoria wanted to make him as comfortable as possible. Their summer residence, Osborn, on the Isle of Wight on the southern coast of England was the perfect retreat for Albert.

On this chilly September day, her staff was making preparations for another visit from the two Confederate agents-Bulloch and Trenholm. The Queen herself had distanced herself from her government's enthusiastic support of the rebels. She knew the support was coming largely from the textile mill owners who were totally dependent on Sea Island cotton; in fact, all of the cotton grown in the South. She was also aware of why the armament and steel mill owners supported the cause because they stood to profit from sales of their products.

The American entourage included young ensign John Beauregard. Trenholm and Bulloch felt his knowledge of the cotton economy as well as the coastal areas of the United States would help influence the Queen's decision on *The Great Eastern*. Of course, the young Beauregard's experience on the ship was equally important to insure the ship's proper operation.

The young naval officer's views on enforced labor aboard the British ships had not yet reached the ears of George Trenholm. Several times the young lieutenant had confronted non-commissioned officers of *The Great Eastern* while they were beating the sailors. Sometimes his intervention successfully prevented further injury. Captain Walker chose to lightly rebuke John Beauregard and told him to "kindly refrain from further interference with the non-commissioned officers of this ship and their duties."

The note had been served on Beauregard by Alexander McLennan, who played down its meaning. In his fatherly way he advised the Confederate to turn the other way when he was about to be a witness to some punishment to the sailors. Beauregard listened to his superior but said nothing. But it served to put John Beauregard on notice that his feelings towards the sailors and their plight were to be hidden.

He continued to have no sympathetic ear from his countryman, William Slater. And in her letters, Susannah reminded him of his heritage and that he had been raised affluently and educated because his father's plantation had flourished, due in no small part through the employment of slaves. But the resentment in him smoldered. Would the slavery issue in him result in some similar personal catastrophe like the national catastrophe exploding in America?

The forthcoming meeting was nearly at hand. Aboard the train on its way to Southampton James Bulloch outlined their progress in the negotiations. "I'm meeting with Daniel Gooch and Colonel Baker next week to try and finalize our relationship. With the ship in such a state of disrepair, I think they'll be much more receptive to our offer. The only thing we haven't defined is just where the British government stands with respect to the charter at this point. I hope this visit with the Queen and Palmerston is positive and that the Queen hasn't changed her mind."

George Trenholm responded. "Well, I certainly hope the Prince is feeling better; he's a big supporter of improved armament and a very innovative individual. Thank goodness for Hal Lane. I don't think we'd have gotten this far with the Queen without her help."

The train lurched and Bulloch grabbed the large brass handle on the compartment door. "John, I'm not sure the Queen is familiar with your stint on the ship. I want you to be sure and bring it up. I'm positive she will have more confidence in the venture if she knows your background."

The high pitch of the locomotive's whistle and a gradual slowing of the train signaled their arrival at Southampton Station. Met by representatives of Palmerston's cabinet and an envoy from the Queen, they were driven to the docks where they boarded the tender *Fairy* to journey to the Isle of Wight and Osborn.

It was the first time John Beauregard had seen the Queen. Seated in a large overstuffed chair, her small frame and stature seemed to directly contrast with her reputation as a strong ruler. One by one,

George Trenholm, James Bulloch, and then Beauregard approached Her Majesty, bowed, and kissed her proffered hand.

"Please sit down gentlemen. We are honored to have you here. We're expecting Lord Palmerston and the Prince to join us any moment. Would you kindly join us in some tea?"

The servants poured tea and offered dainty tea sandwiches containing cucumbers and other distinctly British fillings. The formality of the activity was shattered as Prince Albert entered the room.

George Trenholm was shocked at his appearance. In just three months he had become paunchy, balding and pale, and looked more like a man of sixty rather than one approaching forty. His breath came in short gasps and his voice was faint. One of the Queen's footmen assisted him into the chair next to the Queen's.

The Prime Minister, Lord Palmerston, also entered the room, acknowledged the Queen's and Prince Albert's presence, and introduced himself to the American entourage.

The Queen spoke first. "Mr. Bulloch and Mr. Trenholm, you must try and understand our ambivalent feelings towards your organization." The Queen carefully avoided reference to "nation" or "confederacy." "As an economic entity we support your thrust. But as a nation, we must remain neutral. We are anxious to hear what your final proposal is first hand."

Bulloch took up the gauntlet. He explained the purpose of the ship's charter once again and what it would involve.

"And you may not know this, Your Majesty, but Lt. Beauregard has already spent six months on *The Great Eastern* as an observer. His continued presence would be invaluable in dealing with the Southern armed forces. We are proposing that he and William Slater, the other American naval engineer continue to be aboard as observers, both be part of the crew and participate in the refitting of the ship as an armed merchant ship."

"What kind of modifications will be made to the ship?" The frail voice of Prince Albert could barely be heard.

Bulloch outlined the changes and ordnance additions. He took particular time to explain the addition of the new Ericson-Coles revolving gun turrets and their strategic and tactical value which would go a long way in protecting the great ship from a successful assault by Union vessels.

The turrets were the combined invention of two men: Henry Cowper Coles and the Swedish engineer John Ericsson, widely known for his invention of the first successful ship's propeller. Mounting them at the front and rear of a vessel would add an entirely new dimension to naval battles. For the first time, ships could continue to fire at their opponents as the vessel is maneuvered to avoid the other's bombardment. The attacking ship can continue to fire when its least vulnerable silhouette-bow on or stern on- is showing, lessening the ability of the other ship to get a hit. But navies had been slow to accept the effectiveness of this new technology.

Palmerston spoke up. "We rejected those untried devices when we built the *Warrior* last year. They're just a lot of mechanical nonsense. No one has successfully employed them yet. Our engineers think they're unreliable and not battle proven."

The Prince's voice could be barely heard. Yet everyone heard what he had to say. "If we support this charter, why don't we try them out on the ship? They're not costing us anything and we'll get a first-hand observation of how well they work in battle. What have we to lose?"

His short plea was followed by a fit of horrible coughing, so intense that he had to be helped from the room by one of the footmen. The Queen broke the silence that followed his exit.

"If you can assure us that the ship will not be used in any offensive action and will only fire when fired upon, then we give our tentative approval of her charter. This is conditional upon total restoration of the ship to her original status."

Palmerston remained silent, unwilling to try and split the Queen from her beloved Albert.

Bulloch slowly stood up. "Your Majesty, we will do our utmost to keep the ship out of an active battle. We think this decision reaches far beyond the confines of this room and has worldwide implications. You will continue to receive cotton for the Lancashire mills; we will be able to outfit our growing army. I, Mr. Trenholm, Lt. Beauregard, and most importantly, the entire

Confederate States of America and its president, Jefferson Davis, thank you for this vote of help."

The Americans stood up and said goodbye to the Queen and her prime minister.

"I certainly hope the Prince is feeling better soon," the Southern trader offered.

"Well, we've got him here where he seems to be most happy. We only wish the doctors could agree on a diagnosis and proceed with the right treatment." The Queen's eyes were staring out the window, focused elsewhere.

In a month or so of continued advances in securing *The Great Eastern,* another event confirmed George Trenholm and James Bulloch's theory of how to get around the Union blockade.

3.

She was as unlikely a candidate as any to be the first to go. But she could carry a lot of cargo and because she was fast, the recently constructed Bermuda was chosen to try and make the first blockade run to the South.

She belonged to George Trenholm's British trading arm in Liverpool. Her master was Eugene L. Tessier who had commanded another Fraser-Trenholm vessel before the War. Someone described him as a "determined little man." That made him the perfect captain to take the fully loaded vessel through the Union blockade.

In just one month, the Bermuda arrived off the mouth of the Savannah River. Although Union blockaders were reported to be in the area, Tessier saw none, and boldly sailed up the river to the port city of the same name. The cargo was quickly claimed and distributed.

Oddly enough, for such an obvious triumph, there was no mention of its arrival, or departure one month later in any of the local newspapers. Her destination was England and she carried over two thousand bales of Southern cotton in her holds.

The trial run had been a complete success.

4.

The pleasant September weather in Washington could not mask the unfortunate losses suffered by Union forces. First, there was the humiliating defeat at Bull Run in July and the equally embarrassing loss of the Navy's huge Gosport Yard in Norfolk. The Confederate raider *Sumter* was wreaking havoc with Federal merchant ships around the Caribbean area. In August the Union lost another battle, the biggest one ever fought in Missouri. General Nathaniel Lyon's forces were beaten at Wilson's Creek near Springfield by a Confederate force nearly twice its size. Some 11,600 rebels defeated 5,400 Union soldiers.

And in Kentucky, long a bastion of neutrality, the Confederacy ended that tradition by successfully occupying the fortress at Columbia, just south of the Federal Base at Cairo, Illinois on September 3. It was another major loss for the Union.

The blockade had so many holes in it that the Confederates were easily able to slip supplies into almost any port they wanted. The *Bermuda* had boldly delivered her cargo of 24,000 blankets, 50,000 pairs of shoes, 18 rifled field pieces, four heavy seacoast guns, 6,500 Enfield rifles and 20,000 cartridges upriver September 18 th on the docks of Savannah. The success of the journey, both strategically and economically, was telegraphed to London to George Trenholm, who knew now that he and the Confederacy were on the right path.

It was clear Lincoln needed to make some changes in both his tactics and his strategy. He began to listen seriously to some of the radical proposals that were proliferating, proposals that often used unorthodox and unconventional methods and technology to achieve results.

One of those proposals had come from a most unlikely source.

Cornelius Bushnell was the founder of a successful wholesale food distributorship in New Haven, Connecticut. His knowledge of naval architecture was limited to a short stint as a fifteen-year-old captain aboard a sixty-ton schooner. The success of his business, however, allowed him to return to his first love-designing and building ships.

His first design, submitted to the Navy and named the *Galena*, had serious design flaws and was turned down by the U.S. Navy's examining board. She was too heavy and the board had doubts about her armor plating. After several meetings with the Swedish inventor John Ericsson, modifications were made and the design for the *Ericsson*, later to be named the *Monitor*, was submitted to the board for review.

Lincoln received a letter of introduction to Bushnell from Secretary of State Seward, and subsequently consulted with fellow-Connecticutian Navy Secretary Gideon Welles. The President decided to take a look at the former food distributor's latest proposal and summoned him to Washington.

A hot and dusty train trip down from New York by Bushnell was followed by a restful night in the Willard hotel. Now, Bushnell found himself sitting outside the President's Office, fifteen minutes early for his appointment.

"Mr. Bushnell, please come in. I've been expecting you." The President of the United States was tall, lean and had dark sunken eyes. Bushnell expected a deeper voice from the over six-foot frame but the voice rang with conviction and authority nevertheless.

"Welles tells me you've got a design for an ironclad with a powered gun turret. Sounds interesting. Let's see it."

Bushnell undid the brass locks holding the cover of the case with the model inside. The President stared at the curious-looking vessel.

"I've been working with John Ericsson on this design, Mr. President. He's certain it will be successful."

The President was silent. He had heard of Ericsson's high opinion of himself and the difficulty of working with him. But this man seemed reasonable. Bushnell stood up and walked to the mahogany table at the far side of the office where he began to unfurl the plans. The President joined him.

Bushnell pointed to the model. "The ship actually has two hulls: the armored part and the lower part is wooden. The upper hull is longer and wider which prevents another ship from ramming and sinking her."

"The turret sits on a brass ring when the ship is underway. During battle, the turret is elevated slightly to allow her to turn. She is powered by a small steam engine. As you can see, there is plenty of room for the Dalhgrens. If you look over here, you can see the shutters that cover the gun openings in the turret when she's not firing. That's to protect the crew." The President's eyes followed Bushnell's index finger as it pointed out the various design and safety features of the vessel.

"Her engines are aft of the crew's quarters. Propulsion is by a four bladed screw....."

".....of Mr. Ericsson's design, of course." The President finished Bushnell's sentence.

"Why, yes sir."

The President returned to his desk. "How soon could she be built?"

"I've met with John Griswold and John Winslow who own foundries in Troy, New York. They feel it could be built in about three or four months."

"Let's meet with the Navy tomorrow. I'll arrange it. Can you come back at eleven?"

"I would be most pleased to, Mr. President."

But it took two more meetings with the board and a personal appearance from the Swedish inventor himself before the board, the President and Navy Secretary approved the construction of the first Union ironclad, the U.S.S. *Monitor.*

5.

As Rose Greenhouse was now under house arrest, Hal Lane's Georgetown townhouse had taken over as the place to see and be seen, in the hierarchy of official and social Washington. In this peculiar war it was often difficult to separate what was official and what was societal. But the haziness made it easy for the seamier parts of the opposing sides to obtain information and make sure it got to the right people.

These gatherings were a study in deviousness and gossip. People working for Allan Pinkerton stood side by side in Hal Lane's parlor, sharing gossip with members of the Committee, represented by Susannah Eddings and, somewhat more subtly, Hal Lane herself. The glitter and gloss that was the pretense of Washington society was merely an attractive coating for an ugly and dangerous business.

Even though Rose Greenhow was now under the watchful eye of Allan Pinkerton, her network continued to function even after her arrest and confinement in her house on Lafayette Square, as Hal Lane had confided to Susannah Eddings, just a month ago. Susannah continued to visit her and act as a conduit for requests.

The most recent request, code-marked "Urgent," concerned obtaining information on a military device known as the Cowper-Ericsson gun turret. Plans were believed to be circulating throughout the Naval Architecture Department to be used in a warship the Union was going to build. Susannah was asked to make acquiring those plans her highest priority.

This warm September night found the gathering at Hal Lane's with some new faces, including the businessman Cornelius Bushnell. Navy Secretary Gideon Welles had also been invited but declined Hal Lane's invitation, citing important war business. Bushnell had been meeting with Naval officials for two days from what Susannah had heard, and apparently the subject was something very important. Perhaps it was relative to the information she had been requested to obtain.

She moved around the room from group to group, her earthy laughter and beauty charming the largely male contingent.

"What part of Connecticut are you from Mr. Bushnell?" Susannah had her hand gently on the arm of the visitor. She always seemed to have an opening comment that was relative to the person she wanted to meet.

Bushnell was flattered by the attention of this striking woman. After two days in the company of the stiffly formal Navy architects and military staff, her attention was refreshing, to say the least.

"Well, ma'am, I was born in Madison but my company is located in New Haven. Are you from there?"

"No sir, I'm from Charleston, South Carolina, but I attended school in Greenwich. I loved the countryside but it got awfully cold in the winter. I couldn't get used to that. What, may I ask, is your business?" Susannah took a sip from her glass of sherry. She began to suspect this man represented some special information, just as she had heard.

"You might say I'm in the shipping business with a side interest in naval architecture." His somewhat incomplete answer alerted her sixth sense that he was hiding something. Susannah bit her lip.

Hal Lane joined the group. "Thank you for coming to my reception, Mr. Bushnell. I trust Susannah is taking good care of you."

"Thank you, Miss Lane. We were just discussing Connecticut."

Susannah excused herself, promising to return later. After talking to several other people in the room, including a young naval attaché whom she knew wanted to get to know her better, she was able to piece together what Bushnell was doing in town. He had indeed brought plans for a new armored vessel, radically different from what the Navy currently had. It had the Cowper-Ericcson armored turret, the one that was Susannah's priority assignment. This was indeed important news, and she began to plot how she could get it to the Committee.

But she was worried that one of Percy's men was also privy to the information and would make sure he knew about it. She knew if Percy found out he would assume Susannah also knew and would probably attempt to stop her from disclosing it to her contacts.

She decided to leave for Charleston immediately. The couriers would take too long. But first she had to lay her hands on a set of those plans so they could be delivered to George Trenholm.

6.

Susannah slowly opened her eyes. The heavy drapes of the hotel room had been drawn tightly shut the night before to prevent prying eyes from seeing just who Cornelius Bushnell had invited to his room at the Willard Hotel. As her eyes became more accustomed to the semi-darkness, she looked over on the other side of the bed and noticed it was empty. She wondered where he had gone and how long she had been alone in his room.

She threw back the covers, quickly reached for her dressing gown and stood up. She crossed the room to the washstand and noticed an envelope leaning against the bowl with one word written on it: "Susannah."

She picked it up, opened the flap and took out the note inside:

My dear. I truly enjoyed being with you last night. Thank you for a most unforgettable evening. I am concerned that someone will see us together as I am on an important mission, expecting to meet once again with the President tomorrow. It would not be good for him to find out I had been entertaining a lovely lady from Charleston!

I'm sure you will understand. I am going downstairs to the restaurant for breakfast and then onto some more appointments in the Navy department. I won't return until after lunch. That should give you plenty of time to bathe, freshen up and enjoy some breakfast yourself.

Thank you again. Maybe after this craziness between the North and South is over, we can once again enjoy each other's company, without the need for such secrecy.

Fondly,

Cornelius

124

She felt soiled, dirty, discarded. Cornelius Bushnell had used Susannah and thrown her away, like some unwanted piece of china. It had not been like this with Jordan or some of the others. And she never felt like this after making love to John. There was always a deep inner glow after it was over; a sense of belonging; of being wanted. And always exciting to dream about the next wonderful time with John. She put the note down on the washstand. Tiptoeing over to the tightly drawn curtains, she pulled them aside a tiny crack. Two delivery wagons stood in front of the hotel, no doubt purveyors to the hotel's restaurant. A couple of horses were tied up to the iron railing. Few people were out on the Pennsylvania Avenue. She concluded it was still fairly early.

No time to waste, she decided.

It was time to complete her mission. She must find where Cornelius had hidden the large round leather container that contained the turret plans. That would be the easy part. Getting them out of the hotel, on board the train to Charleston and into the hands of the Committee would be a dangerous undertaking. Suppose she was stopped and searched? Worse yet, suppose Percy intercepted her and found out what she was carrying? It would take too long to take them to the Committee; she had been told to get them into the hands of George Trenholm's shipping firm just as soon as possible.

She decided to take the plans directly to England, as she had heard at Hal Lane's party that the negotiations for the chartering of *The Great Eastern* were nearly concluded. She knew the ship had been badly damaged and was laid up somewhere on the coast of Wales. No doubt the vessel was in some shipyard, being readied for its mission as a blockade-runner.

I'll take the next train to Savannah and catch a return trip on one of the active blockade runners, she thought to herself. *They won't ask to see what she was carrying onboard the ship, she thought, especially when I tell the captain where I'm headed and who I am working for!*

She quickly washed up, put on her clothes, and opened the curtains slightly so she could see around the bedroom. Cornelius Bushnell's valises were stacked neatly in the corner. She walked across the semi-dark room to look more closely for the cylindrical leather case. It was not among his luggage.

Quickly, she crossed the room, back to the bed and knelt down to peek under the bed itself. It was dark and felt very dusty as her hand felt around under the bedspread. Nothing.

She lay down on the carpet, determined to thoroughly search the entire area under the bed. She reached up under the heavy headboard and felt something. It was the case. He had hidden it upright behind the headboard, not under the bed as she thought. She stood on her feet and reached around the corner of the headboard. The case was surprisingly heavy. She wondered if she should try and take the whole case, or just look through it and try to pick out just the plans for the turret.

Sitting down on the floor with the case flat on the carpet next to her, she undid the leather thong that held the tube's end piece. It came off easily. She reached inside and tried to pull the heavy rolls of drawing paper out of the case. They wouldn't budge. That settled it. She would have to carry the entire case to Savannah on board the train and then to England.

She closed up the case, gathered up her belongings and picked up the heavy leather cylinder by its handle. Opening the door slightly, she looked up and down the hall for signs of anyone. Quickly exiting the room and pulling the door shut quietly behind her, she walked quickly to the end of the hall to the door marked "Service Stairway," the same stairway she and Cornelius Bushnell had used the night before to come upstairs to his room. She knew it connected directly to the alleyway next to the hotel, a route she could use to get away from the hotel unnoticed.

7.

With the tacit approval of the British monarchy, there remained just one more step to get *The Great Eastern* under charter.

The rain was coming down hard, wet, and cold. At times, one could hardly see for more than ten or twelve feet. James Bulloch's hansom gingerly made its way down towards Cannon Street and the offices of the Great Ship Company.

It was getting dark, which made vision even harder. Bulloch leaned forward in the cab to see if he could see the Westminster Bridge. It shouldn't be difficult. The bridge had recently been wired for electric lights and should shine like a beacon in this rainstorm. Sure enough, off in the distance, Bulloch could see the dark towers silhouetted by the eerie bluish glow of the powerful graphite arc lamps. It was almost as if the great structure was bathed in a halo. The arc lamp's heat turned the cold rain into steam, as the drops hit the metal covering the arcs themselves, further adding a mysterious fog to the scene.

The cab turned into Cannon Street and stopped at the company's office. Bulloch grabbed his bag and jumped down to the cobblestones, handed the driver his carfare and ran for the front doorway of the building. He stepped into the reception area where the small cheerful fireplace glowed with its accustomed warmth.

The long letter that Bulloch had written to Colonel Baker outlined the new terms and conditions, now that the ship had been heavily damaged. Essentially, it suggested that the cost of repairs might be underwritten by the Confederate government if the directors of the company would reconsider the offer made last spring to charter the ship to the Confederates. During the repairs to the paddlewheels and the rudder, the ship would be reconfigured to an armed all-cargo vessel in preparation for her role of carrying arms and war supplies to the South, and the valued cotton crop of the area back to the English mills. George Trenholm and James Bulloch calculated that the cost of the conversion would be considerably less, since the ship was already in a state of disrepair.

Several structural alterations were proposed. Among them was the addition of two Ericsson's revolving gun turrets, one at each end of the ship. Each of the turrets would be steam-powered to facilitate their quick deployment and insure accurate alignment on any target selected.

Each turret would contain a pair of 110-pound, breech-loading cannon. While meant only to defend the huge vessel in the event she was challenged by the Union Navy, together with the four Dahlgrens she already carried, the addition of these Armstrong cannon would give *The Great Eastern* more effective firepower than many British men-of-war. But, in accordance with British law, the guns would have to be fitted once the vessel was at sea. The plans for the turrets would be obtained through the Confederate spy network.

"Mr. Bulloch, sir, good to see you again." Daniel Gooch walked across the room to the fireplace where Bulloch was trying to dry out. "Let me have your coat—I won't ask how you like our famous London rain and fog."

Gooch's mutton-chop beard appeared grayer than before; his hairline had receded slightly and there were streaks of gray through the almost black strands.

"Since you didn't ask how I like London rain and fog, then I won't tell you how unpleasant it can make one feel," Bulloch remarked, "but then the heat and humidity in Charleston in the summer can be just as unpleasant," he added.

Gooch was already hanging the Southerner's coat on the coat tree in the corner of the room. He joined Bulloch back in front of the fireplace and they shook hands.

"Let's meet the Colonel upstairs. We've saved you a spot of tea to help warm you up."

Upstairs, Colonel Baker opened the door to his office himself. The enormous man's bulk filled the doorway and the fat pudgy hand extended to Bulloch's in a symbol of friendship.

"Come in, come in, Mr. Bulloch. Please sit down," Baker urged as he slowly shuffled his enormous body across the Oriental rug to his equally immense desk. "It's good to see you."

Daniel Gooch began to pour afternoon tea at the sideboard. Colonel Baker produced a bottle of French cognac and three glasses from one of the drawers of his cavernous desk.

"I've got some good news for you Mr. Bulloch. The Board of Directors of the Company has voted to accept your proposal in its entirety, with one provision. We must obtain permission from Lord Palmerston, and quite likely the Queen herself, before we can commit the ship to any hostile action. I've already bounced the idea off some of the cabinet members, stressing of course the usefulness of employing the ship to bring cotton back to the British mills. I also cited the boost to the British arms and munitions factories. I don't think we're going to get much resistance."

"Neither do I," Bulloch responded. "George Trenholm and I already have the Queen's and Palmerston's agreement." Bulloch reached in his valise and handed the document signed by the Queen to the Colonel.

Baker pulled a portfolio out of one of the drawers and opened it, revealing the contract. It was a scene worthy of a painting: the meticulously calligraphed parchment contract, laying on the green leather of the portfolio, carefully placed on the Colonel's rich brown mahogany desk. Baker poured the pale golden brown cognac into the Waterford brandy snifters.

"I'm at once relieved and elated," Bulloch said," and I'm anxious to convey the news to President Davis and George Trenholm as well," he continued. He picked up the document and began to review its contents. "I'll need an extra day to have our lawyers review it; I've already prepared them as to the urgency of the matter. Is the ship still in Queenstown? And are the dockyard facilities adequate for repairs and refitting or will we have to tow her to Liverpool?"

"My dear Mr. Bulloch, the ship is already in Milford Haven, ready to be outfitted and awaiting the opportunity to serve the Confederacy. We will of course honor your request to review it with your counsel. Now let's toast our agreement and an early victory for the Confederate States of America." The men clinked their snifters together and the unmistakable clear ring of Waterford lead crystal was like a clarion call for the Confederacy.

Bulloch swallowed the mellow liquid, savoring the exquisite bouquet. "Colonel Baker, we will be engaging two of our Naval construction and engineering people in the modifications to the ship. In my telegraph to President Davis I'm going to ask that they take the first fast ship over here."

The Confederate agent finished his cognac and rose from his chair. "Gentlemen, I will be in touch with you within the next two days for the contract signing. Thank you for everything."

8.

Susannah took a deep breath of the fresh ocean air. The weather had been beautiful and the Atlantic Ocean surprisingly docile since they had left Savannah yesterday. The telegram from George Trenholm had been waiting for her in the railroad's telegraph office after her long, tiring journey from Washington. She delivered it directly to the ship's captain, Eugene Tessier. It read:

SUSANNAH:

YOU WILL SAIL TO LONDON ON THE SHIP BERMUDA. STOP SHE WILL STOP FIRST IN MILFORD HAVEN SO YOU MAY DELIVER THE PACKAGE STOP PLEASE INTRODUCE YOURSELF TO CAPTAIN EUGENE TESSIER AND SHOW HIM THIS TELEGRAM. STOP

CAPTAIN TESSIER: CONGRATULATIONS ON YOUR SUCCESSFUL VOYAGE TO SAVANNAH! STOP THE YOUNG LADY BEARING THIS TELEGRAM IS MISS SUSANNAH EDDINGS OF CHARLESTON. SHE IS WORKING FOR ME ON AN EXTREMELY IMPORTANT MISSION STOP PLEASE ARRANGE TO MAKE AN INTERIM PORT VISIT AT MILFORD HAVEN OFF THE ST. GEORGES CHANNEL SO THAT SHE MAY DELIVER SOME IMPORTANT DOCUMENTS TO THE SHIPYARD THERE STOP THANK YOU FOR YOUR HELP STOP GOOD SAILING!

GEORGE TRENHOLM

Susannah introduced herself and stood quietly in the captain's cabin while he read it. She found him to be a gracious and kind man.

"Please sit down, Miss Eddings. We will, of course comply with Mr. Trenholm's instructions, remaining long enough in Milford

Haven for you to accomplish your mission. Then we will continue our voyage to London. May I offer you some tea?"

Susannah crossed her legs. "No thank you, Captain. I have not slept in a bed for several days now, since I left Washington. The train trip from Washington was very tiring. I would appreciate being shown to my cabin so that I may rest."

The Captain looked at her. She was a stunning beauty, but the lines under her eyes showed her fatigue. "Of course, my dear. I should have anticipated that you would be very tired."

He stood up from behind his small desk and walked across the cabin to the speaking tube that connected directly to the bridge.

"First Officer George, please direct one of the midshipmen to my cabin to escort Ms. Eddings to her stateroom. Her luggage is here also."

The response from the bridge was prompt. "First Officer George here, sir. He's on his way."

9.

The trip to Milford Haven went smoothly, with just two days of rough sailing and Susannah remaining in her cabin for safety. The Captain thoughtfully had her meals sent to her cabin.

They arrived at the shipyard just eleven days after leaving Savannah. Susannah was totally unprepared for what she was about to see.

The Great Eastern lay on the mud bank of the harbor, resting slightly at an angle, completely stripped of her paddlewheels. Scaffolding had been erected to allow shipworkers to begin the process of making her into an armed merchantman. She looked forlorn to Susannah in the early morning light; like some impotent creature, unable to sit up straight or even appear as if she could even cross the waters of the harbor, much less the Atlantic Ocean.

Yet, on the lighters and small ships surrounding the silent hulk, she could see a high level of activity. Several large cranes were aboard the vessel's hull and she could see they were already at work in spite of the early hour.

She delivered the large leather case that she had removed from Cornelius Bushnell's hotel room to the ship's engineering office, located on the dock behind the ship's hull. No one asked where or how she had gotten it. The engineers who took the heavy drawings out of the case and unfurled them on the tables in the shipyard's engineering offices expressed amazement at the design of the Union vessel, the *Monitor*. But they were especially impressed with the ship's revolving gun turret, the key piece in the defense of *The Great Eastern*. They set about immediately to adapt the mechanism to fit aboard the merchantman.

The *Bermuda's* skiff took her back across the harbor, where the blockade runner awaited the completion of her journey. As the small boat approached the dock Susannah was surprised to see John waving to her from the head of the boarding stairs.

133

She ran up the stairs and into his arms. They embraced passionately.

"Darling, how did you know I was aboard?" Susannah was so excited she could hardly get the words out.

"Mr. Trenholm got word to me two or three days ago that you would be delivering some important documents that the shipbuilders needed. Everyone involved with this rebuilding is grateful to you and very proud of your efforts." John Beauregard drew her closer to him for another passionate kiss.

He looked into her eyes. "Darling, I am so proud of you. You have courage and bravery I could never hope to have. Captain Tessier arranged to have me picked up and brought here, but also told me we could only spend a few moments together. He's due in London in a few days and wants to get underway."

She looked longingly at him. "It was nothing, John. I wouldn't want to have to do it again, but I'm glad I did. Darling, you look wonderful! I wish we could spend more time together. . ."

He interrupted her, gently putting his finger across the lovely full lips. "After the rebuilding is complete, we'll be coming to London to take on our cargo. We'll be there for a few days and we can spend time together then."

Out of the corner of her eye, Susannah saw Eugene Tessier walking across the deck towards them. She kissed John lightly on the lips and turned to meet the captain. He looked at the couple.

"I'm glad you two had the chance to see each other. But I telegraphed Mr. Trenholm that we would be in London in three days, which means we have to set sail in just a few minutes."

John Beauregard extended his hand to the Captain.

"Mr. Tessier, say no more. I'm deeply grateful for this chance to see Susannah and tell her how proud of her I am. "

They shook hands warmly. Eugene Tessier bowed, turned and walked back to the ship's bridge.

John and Susannah embraced again but this time Susannah started to cry.

"Every time we say goodbye, I'm scared to death it'll be the last time," she sobbed. John Beauregard took a handkerchief out of his pocket and dabbed at the tears now cascading down her beautiful cheeks.

"But we always do manage to see each other, don't we?" His smile, loving gaze and strong arms reassured her, as they always did. "It won't be long, darling. Just a few days. I'll look you up when the ship docks in London."

Her sobs stopped. She composed herself, not wanting to appear weak. "I'm sorry, darling. I just love you so much." Lurking in the back of her mind was the terrible truth of what she had to do. It almost caused her to start sobbing again. But she bit her lip firmly to hold back the tears. They embraced once more and he turned and walked to the boarding stairs. She waved feebly as he turned to descend the stairs. He waved back. Once again she had managed to avoid having him know just what her real mission was. The act of stealing the *Monitor's* plans had succeeded in restoring her credibility.

10.

While negotiations to secure *The Great Eastern* had been successfully concluded on the other side of the Atlantic, the Confederacy continued its offensive in waters south of the mainland.

In the Gulf of Mexico, a fall hurricane was in its last fury. The winds had subsided but the sizable swells kept Captain Raphael Semmes' little raider, *Sumter,* bobbing around the choppy waters of the Gulf of Mexico. Holding course had gotten easier, with the lessened gale and Semmes had joined the crew on the bridge, unable to sleep because of the rough weather. Daylight was faintly beginning to show, an odd yellow tint through the black and grey clouds that hurried endlessly across the bow of his ship.

The last few weeks had not been good ones. After his very successful raids in July and August, the *Sumter*'s machinery had deteriorated badly and needed overhauling. The boiler was unable to supply steam at full pressure because of leaks. These were patched as best his carpenters could manage, but the ship was only able to steam at about half-speed.

His reputation as a commerce raider was well-known throughout the entire Caribbean and officials in the ports where he attempted to buy coal and supplies were less than cordial with him, only allowing him brief stays to purchase what he needed. A longer layover, to fix the leaky boiler and perform some other necessary maintenance, was not permitted in any of the ports where he stopped. So he returned to Brazilian waters, hoping to find a more favorable diplomatic reception as well as capture vessels sailing from California. But in both cases he came up short; Brazilian port officials were no more anxious to violate international law than their Caribbean counterparts. Likewise, the merchant ship pickings were thin. By the first part of October he had seized only two ships. Faced with a crippled vessel, he decided to risk a return to

New Orleans to repair the ship and reprovision. Both he and the crew were due for some shore time anyway.

His first officer joined him on the bridge, fresh from a visit below to the engine room. "Mr. Kell, set a course for the Pass a'l'Outre. We should be there by nightfall. I don't want to chance a run in daylight. We were lucky before; perhaps our luck will hold and let us slip through to New Orleans."

John Kell looked at Semmes, an expression of concern on his face. "I just chatted with Jamie and he says we can only make about six knots, maybe seven if necessary. If we get chased, I don't know that we'll be able to outrun anyone. The Union hasn't done much to increase the patrol around the Mississippi, so maybe we can sneak by. Since the builders at the shipyard know this ship's machinery very well we should get in and out with a minimum amount of time."

Semmes stroked his long, waxed handlebar mustache. "We don't have much choice. But the element of surprise is with us. Welles and the Navy think we're still prowling around the Atlantic, looking for more prey. Before we left I made sure the officials in Brazil would think that was our next destination."

John Kell looked up at the mainmast, noticing that the wind had become more manageable. "Mr. Semmes, why don't we shut down the engine and rig for sail? That will ease the load on the boiler, in case we do have to make a run for it."

"Good idea, Mr. Kell. Tell the crew to start rigging."

After twelve hours of sailing, they dropped anchor two miles off the Pass. A thorough sweep of Semmes' spyglass in the twilight showed no blockaders guarding the channel. Semmes ordered steam up, but kept his crew ready at the sails just in case they had to run. The *Sumter* quickly slipped through the mouth of the river, arriving in the port several hours later. Tied up safely at the shipyard, Semmes called his men on deck and ordered them to return to the ship in seventy two hours, the time the shipyard had told him it would take to repair the machinery. It would also give his first mate time to purchase provisions.

In the shipyard office, using his code, Semmes telegraphed Secretary Mallory to report his whereabouts and the condition of the ship. He returned to his cabin on the vessel for some needed rest and had finally settled down when one of the shipyard hands knocked on his cabin door.

"Telegram for you, Captain." Semmes opened the door, thanked the worker, and turned to his oil lamp on his desk, raising the wick so he could read the message. The message was in code. He reached into the drawer of his desk for the cipher book.

CAPTAIN, EFFECT ALL NECESSARY REPAIRS TO HAVE YOUR SHIP IN CONDITION FOR BATTLE STOP CANNOT DISCUSS FURTHER AS DETAILS STILL SKETCHY BUT BE PREPARED TO SAIL FOR PORT ROYAL SOUND IN TWO WEEKS FOR POSSIBLE ENGAGEMENT WITH UNION NAVAL FORCES STOP YOU WILL PLAY A SUPPORT ROLE STOP OTHERS WILL BEAR THE BRUNT OF THE BATTLE. MORE LATER STOP

MALLORY

He had heard about the plans to charter *The Great Eastern* as a confederate blockade runner, but knew little of the outcome. Because *Sumter* was a small, lightly armed vessel, he wondered what support he could offer in the face of the heavily armed, Union frigates. Drawing out his charts of the Port Royal Sound area, he noted there were several shallower inlets where he might hide and surprise one or more of the enemy, who would have their gun crews on the opposite side of the vessel, firing at *The Great Eastern* and who knows what else.

Surprise. That was what had made him so successful as a commerce raider. That's how he was able to elude the Union when he left New Orleans three months ago and during this last run through the Pass. Perhaps now he could use that same element in what appeared to be looming as a very crucial battle.

11.

Louis Beauregard stopped his horse at the railroad crossing. He was tired from the long ride up from the plantation. Dusk had already begun to fall and he still had to find the encampment where the shipments of cotton were to be delivered, in preparation for loading aboard ships to go back to the British mills.

It would also be the railhead for the outgoing shipment of arms and supplies, bought from England aboard those same ships. He had been called into duty to help supervise what would be one of the most important pieces of logistics; getting the war materiel out of *The Great Eastern* to waiting railroad freight trains and quickly loading the heavy cotton bales aboard the ship before the Union Navy could amass enough ships and soldiers to destroy the mission.

To help supervise the large number of slaves who were hired by the Confederacy from the surrounding plantations, he had brought his overseer, Sam, and two of his slave drivers. The four men urged their horses across the tracks and stopped to look down the track.

"I don't remember the track going this way. Useta' go straight into town from this crossing." Sam had been into Coosawatchie on errands many times. Indeed, where the rail line crossed the road coming from the river, a switch had been built, dividing the line in two. The left side of the turnout disappeared into the scrub pine, while the right side continued down the old right of way.

Louis Beauregard offered an explanation. "That's probably where the track goes into the new yards they built. We should probably go there first. I'm supposed to look for Colonel Shackelford who is in charge of the military garrison here." The fall dampness and gradually darkening skies chilled the air. Fog had begun to cut visibility in the swampy area.

The high-pitched whistle of an approaching train caused the horses to stir. The four men coaxed their mounts down the road, away from the crossing.

The whistle behind them now grew very loud and the locomotive and first few flatcars slowly made their way down the track towards Beauregard and his men. The horses now became very skittish and it took every bit of concentration to keep them under control.

The brakeman jumped from the locomotive cab and walked towards the switch. The cars were heavily loaded with cotton bales, some of them sagging in the middle from the weight.

The train wheezed by Beauregard and continued into the scrub forest. The group returned to the track and began to follow the train into the yards.

Louis Beauregard could now see how the tracks split into eight separate sidings, each with wooden platforms between them. The group crossed over the yard tracks to the left and headed for a group of tents pitched about three hundred feet from the outermost track of the yard. A flagpole with the newly designed Confederate flag flying confirmed the presence of infantry headquarters.

Squatting on the siding directly opposite the encampment was a strange looking engine with eight driving wheels instead of the usual four. Unlike most of the engines Beauregard had seen, this one had no engineer's cab in back of the boiler. Instead, directly behind the diamond-shaped smokestack was a covered cab, sitting directly on top of the boiler. Two narrow ladderlike stairways attached to the rear of the cab ended in a platform which backed up to the tender. As Beauregard got closer, he could see the firebox door between the two stairways. Just as they were turning to head towards the tents, the black locomotive shrieked its whistle to warn everyone that it would soon start backing out of the yard.

The group stopped to watch. With a loud hiss, a plume of very black smoke, and a loud clank, the engine began to back up. The men waved to the engineer as the locomotive eased its way out of the yard. The fireman was too busy to acknowledge the greeting but the brakeman, riding on the cowcatcher managed to wave back along with the engineer. The men turned their horses toward the camp and began to move towards the headquarters tent.

"I've been told to ask for Colonel David Shackelford." Beauregard was addressing a lanky sentry, the only one guarding the small encampment. He wore no Confederate uniform, but an infantryman's cap confirmed he was a soldier.

"Sorry suh, he ain't heah right now. Gone down the line towards Savannah. Should be back 'fo dark. Wanna' speak to his aide-Copral Anderson instead?"

Beauregard identified himself, and pulled an envelope from his saddlebags. In the envelope was the letter from his brother, now a full General, sharing leadership of the Confederate forces in Virginia with General Joe Johnston. He leaned down to hand the letter to the sentry.

"Sorry suh, Ah cain't read. You kin show it to Copral Anderson when he come out."

The sentry did a smart about-face and disappeared between the rows of tents. The planter and his group dismounted and led their horses to the hitching rail.

"Corporal Sam Anderson at your service, sir." Louis Beauregard stepped forward, extended his hand and handed him the letter. The infantryman dropped his salute and warmly grasped Beauregard's hand.

"So glad to see you, Mr. Beauregard. And such an honor to have the brother of our hero of Bull Run! Colonel Shackelford told me to expect you and to fix you up a place to stay. I've secured a tent for you where you can establish your headquarters. Colonel Shackelford is down the line at Ridgeland, negotiating for some more lumber from the sawmill for those platforms and the log road that's to be built down to the creek."

"How many trains do you think we can process at one time, Corporal?"

"I'd say between twelve and fourteen. We plan to alternate incoming and outgoing on separate tracks so the cotton can be unloaded on one platform and the military stores loaded from the opposite side. Colonel Shackelford has this all drawn up in a plan which he will want to show you. He's very grateful for you and the others; he's not really a quartermaster and will appreciate all the assistance and leadership you can contribute."

After showing the rest of the group their separate area where they would sleep and eat, Corporal Anderson escorted Louis Beauregard to the Officer's tent where he would stay.

"Chow in about an hour, sir. Colonel Shackelford should be here by then." With a salute, Anderson left Louis Beauregard to himself.

He sat down on the cot and tried to think through the fatigue. The job at hand; 12,000 tons of cotton to be unloaded from the trains onto wagons, manhandled down the steep path to be reloaded aboard flatboats, moved out into the Sound, to again be unloaded and stacked on a barge to await the ships. All of this in less than a month.

The task looked impossible. He decided to lie down. Perhaps he could think clearer after a short nap.

12.

At the other end of the long supply line, agents were trying to reconcile what was to be put aboard *The Great Eastern* to be shipped to the Confederates.

For now, there seemed to be a shortage of boxes of rifle cartridges. Duncan Hanson, George Trenholm's overseer and his two agents had counted fifteen thousand crates as they were unloaded from the last boxcars. He had already signed the manifest from the manufacturer for twenty thousand cartons, which meant that the Confederacy would have to pay for five thousand more boxes of cartridges than it would receive.

The cold mist of late afternoon enshrouded the enormous piles of wooden boxes and bales that lined the dockside. It was not a place for the fainthearted. The frenzy of unloading one freight train after another with the dockside cranes, the constant movement of the tiny but powerful dockside railroad engines, horses and horse drawn carts and carriages, made standing still in one place very risky.

Hanson heard the whistle of the locomotive toot, meaning it would be moving the empty freight cars that had brought the cargo of cartridges to the dock. He decided to ask the conductor to look through the goods wagons one more time. Hurrying along the length of the train towards the engine, he found the conductor talking with one of the brakemen, both of them about two cars back from the noisy smoky locomotive.

"Excuse me sir, we seem to be short some boxes." Hanson was careful not to mention their contents. The whole shipment might be impounded if anyone on the dock knew what the boxes contained or where they were going.

The conductor turned from his discussion with his brakeman. "Mr. 'Anson, I presume, sir. What was it you're missing?"

"I wonder if I might ask your men to check the wagons one more time. I signed for twenty thousand boxes but only counted fifteen thousand. Perhaps one of the wagons wasn't fully unloaded. I'll be happy to help."

Hanson showed the conductor the document indicating he had signed for twenty thousand boxes. The conductor swung his lantern up to see the document. Sure enough the neatly lettered number under the column "Quantity" was twenty thousand. He also noted the boxes' content—"Carpenter's hammer heads." That would explain why they were so heavy, the conductor thought to himself.

"Bert, you and Billy there, open them car doors and make sure them wagons are unloaded." The conductor now turned and swung his lantern back and forth towards the engine, signaling the engineer not to move the train. "Now Mr. 'Anson, let's have a look-see at them boxcars."

The four men walked towards the rear of the train, the two brakemen on one side and the overseer and conductor on the other side. It was a narrow passageway between the boxes waiting to be loaded aboard the ship and the goods wagons.

The brakemen had already reached the last car, slid open the door and were inside the car. Hanson and the conductor hadn't reached the car yet.

"Jesus Christ, Bert, here's a box that broke open. I'll eat my Aunt Nellie's fish cakes if them ain't gun cartridges." The brakeman lifted his lantern over the shattered wooden lid. Apparently something had broken one of the slats.

"Maybe that's why they weren't unloaded. This here's supposed to have come from some tool company in Sheffield."

"Yea, but the boxes look the same as the ones the guys unloaded before."

"Maybe we ought to look at all of 'em."

"Henry 'd kill us, doin' the jobs of the dock hands. Let's just nail the goddam thing shut and get the guys back here to finish unloading."

Not wanting to anger the conductor, the two men hastily nailed the crate back shut with their mallets they used to couple and uncouple the link and pin couplers of the railroad cars.

They finished just as Henry the conductor and the American pulled themselves up into the freight car.

Hanson pointed his lantern at the half of the freight car that was still full. He noticed the one box on the floor, and bent down to read the number on the top of the box. It matched the shipment number on his manifest.

Henry was watching him, too tired to bend over and look for himself. He had been on this train since six o'clock this morning.

"What's it say guvna? Are they your boxes?"

"Yes sir, they appear to be. Can we get them unloaded with the rest? They're supposed to be loaded early tomorrow"

"I'll have to speak to the yardmaster. Most of the workers went home about a half an hour ago."

Hanson had been through this before. He motioned for the conductor to join him outside. The two men jumped down to the wooden dock.

Hanson reached in his pocket for the coins he knew would help get the boxes unloaded. "Would these help get the boxes unloaded tonight?" He emptied the coins into the already outstretched hand of the conductor.

The conductor quickly pocketed the money, out of sight of the brakemen.

"I'll see what I can do, guvna'. We should be able to get 'em out. If I need to, I'll get me men to help. We ain't supposed to be back in the freight yard for awhile."

Hanson extended his hand and the conductor shook it. "Your name?"

"'Enery, sir. I go off at eight. I'll be in the freightmasters office until this gets done. Then I check out in the engineer's dispatch office. It's right at the end of this dock. We can meet here just before I go off duty, if you want."

145

"Thanks, Henry, that's a good idea. See you here about half past seven." Hanson started to walk towards the head of the train. He tipped his hat to the brakemen as he passed. Soon he was past the engine and a good ways down the track.

The conductor had joined the brakemen. One of them was frowning.

"'Enery, you know what's in them boxes?"

"No, and I don't give a damn. They were supposed to be unloaded with the rest. The gen-ul-man looked at the numbers and they matched the shipment number. The dockhands fouled up."

"Yea, well one of them boxes broke open. We saw bullets inside. Them ain't no goddam tools from Sheffield."

The conductor felt the coins in his pocket. "I don't care. They're supposed to be unloaded; they'll be unloaded. Wait here—I'm going to get the dockmaster to round up another crew. They got to be unloaded tonight."

Darkness had begun to fall. The two men cursed, as they knew the conductor would have to fight with the dockmaster to get any men at all, this late in the day. They knew they would end up breaking their backs themselves, getting the heavy boxes unloaded.

13.

"More tea, ma'am?" The waiter was leaning over Susannah's chair. She glanced at George Trenholm's face. They had just concluded dinner in her hotel's dining room.

"Please do. Susannah. I'm so happy to see you and renew our friendship. I've time if you do. Would you enjoy a cognac also?"

"Please. Oh, that would be lovely." She blotted her mouth with her napkin.

George Trenholm leaned forward. "I know you risked your life to get those plans of the Union Monitor's turret to the shipbuilders. I want you to know I am personally grateful, but your country will also thank you. The addition of those turrets to the ship will help insure the delivery of its cargo." He spoke in a low voice, his eyes seemingly staring at the sideboard across the dining room.

Susannah smiled weakly. She avoided looking directly at the trader, instead, directing her gaze at her hands, now folded and resting on the table. "Thank you Mr. Trenholm. It was a mission I'd not want to have to do again. There were times when I had to do things I really didn't want to do."

"Well, now that you've done it, perhaps you'd like to do something a little less risky for your country." He sat up straight in his chair, his voice resuming a normal tone. "I think England is ready to hear a little more about what this Cause is all about. Especially what it will do for their economy. I heard from President Davis and he's encouraged me to also take on the role of presenting our case to the British people. I know you had great success visiting some of the more prominent families in the South in the past few months and getting them to open their purses for contributions."

The waiter had returned and was now filling their teacups. He also placed snifters half filled with cognac in front of Susannah and George Trenholm.

Susannah gently squeezed the lemon into her tea.

He continued, "I've some contacts outside of London, folks who are supplying some of the things that will be loaded aboard the ship. Many of them are well known in the countryside; heads of companies who employ some of the people in their towns and villages. I have already written to a few of them and asked if they would host a meeting of some of the townspeople and hear from one of us just what this trade means. I assumed you would be that person, since we already talked of this before."

She still avoided looking directly at him, instead, lowering her eyes again. "Of course, I would be happy to do that. Perhaps tomorrow we could get together and decide what points you think I should make in these meetings. And also, where you want me to go." They each sipped from the elegant Waterford snifters. It was all Susannah could do to maintain her composure.

While the mission for the Confederacy was complete, she still had unfinished business to get done for George Percy. It was getting harder for her to maintain her countenance as a loyal Southerner. She had experienced a certain triumph each time she succeeded in one of these tasks. It was almost a physical excitement, living so close to danger and intrigue. But living the double life was exhausting.

George Trenholm lifted his brandy snifter again, nodding to Susannah to do the same with hers. "Let me propose a toast; for two reasons, Susannah. One, the successful completion of your mission. Two, the upcoming campaign to present our case to the English."

She smiled, this time looking at him in a sweet, yet seductive way. "To our success," she added, taking another sip of the aromatic drink.

The trader switched subjects. "Did you see any of John at the shipyard? How is he?" His question reflected some concern.

She changed her shy continence for a full, joyful smile. "He looks wonderful. I think his role in the war suits him very well. I hope to see him before he departs. Do you know if he will be onshore at all? Should I ask the ship's office or would the Navy know?"

A look of concern crossed the trader's face. "I would try the ship's office at the dock first. But I wouldn't go there alone. If you can wait until tomorrow morning, I'll be glad to send one of my men with you. It's very dangerous down there now, particularly with the war and war material that's going through there."

Susannah pressed the issue further. "Do you know when the ship is going to sail? I really want to see John before he goes." George Trenholm looked directly at Susannah's eyes. The question seemed a little odd.

"I don't know the exact date. She's due to start loading tomorrow. Probably in a couple of days. She's picking up another load in Southampton before she heads for the U.S."

"What are they shipping, rifles and bullets? Things like that? I'll bet the ship can hold a lot."

The comment seemed out of place. He was certain Rose Greenhow had told her to be extremely discreet about what she discussed with whom. The contents of the ship were known only to a very few key people. He was one of them. James Bulloch was another. Even the Queen didn't know what the manifest was. He decided to sidestep the question.

"I can't tell you anything about the ship Susannah," he said, "and I would advise you not to discuss it with John either. There are people all around here who would pay dearly for that information. Your life would be in grave danger if someone knew that you had information about the cargo."

George Trenholm was staring intensely at Susannah. She is beautiful, he thought to himself, but awfully naive.

She glanced at him with a coquettish look. It was almost as if a father were admonishing his daughter for coming home too late the night before.

"I will be careful. And I will take you up on your offer of an escort. Can we do it about ten tomorrow morning?

They had finished their cognacs. Susannah excused herself to retire to the ladies room to freshen up. They would meet at the front of the hotel dining room.

While in the ladies room, Susannah thought about George Trenholm's warning. If she waited until tomorrow morning to visit the dock, she would have an escort, someone who would be at her side wherever she wanted to look; someone who might hear any conversation she might start, while trying to find out more about the ship. No, she must go tonight, look around, ask a few questions if she could and then, tomorrow, try and fill in the missing information about the ship's cargo and destination. How dangerous could it be, riding in a closed hansom cab?

After bidding goodbye in the hotel lobby Susannah dawdled until George Trenholm had had a chance to catch a cab back to his residence. She wandered around the lobby, looking at some of the paintings. After a few minutes she pulled her cloak around her and stepped outside.

The cold London mist swirled around the streetlamps. She walked to a waiting hansom, being careful to gather her full skirt and cloak before attempting the high step into the vehicle. "Whereto, mum?" The cabdriver, perched at the rear of the cab had leaned down and opened the small window.

"The docks. I want to go where *The Great Eastern* is to be berthed tomorrow. Can you find her berth?"

"I'll do m'best, mum." The driver shut the door, clucked to the horse, and headed for the docks. Even though her cloak was made of wool, she still shivered in the cold. She reached back and pulled the hood of the cloak over her head, carefully trying to avoid disturbing her hairdo. If she <u>did</u> see John, she wanted to look her best.

The hansom cab jounced along the cobblestones, its lone passenger trying to maintain her balance, in spite of the bouncy ride. Outside the cab window Susannah could barely see the tall masts of the ships tied up at the wharf. The smell of fish, tar, and hemp permeated the air. They were almost there. The street they were on ran right down to the dock, and the sound of wood underfoot confirmed their arrival. The driver stopped under a streetlamp where a small huddle of rough-looking men, stood outside one of the many dockside pubs.

"Say, guvna', 'happen to know where *The Great Eastern* is gonna tie up?"

"The what?" A voice came out of the small knot of men, but the driver couldn't tell who was speaking. Susannah settled back in the shadows, not wanting the men to see her.

"Ya' know the <u>big</u> ship. Five smokestacks. A monster."

"Oh that one. She ain't gonna tie up; too big. She'll likely anchor midstream. I'd say about there." The driver squinted through the fog at the small group and faintly saw an arm gesturing down the dock. A cloud of pipe smoke wafted up from the men.

"Thanks, guvna'."

The driver clucked to his horse and the hansom lurched forward, past the men and into the strange culture of the London docks. They had gone about one hundred yards down the dock, past a three masted schooner, and some piles of coal. Susannah saw a fight take place between two obviously drunk sailors at the ship's gangplank. The driver slowed his cab to a stop in front of a little shack next to a warehouse. Susannah slowly sat up to see why they had stopped.

A man in a long blue coat was waving a lantern, signaling the driver.

"Can't go in there mister. Place's been roped off."

Susannah reached up and unhinged the glass window of the cab. Another man was now approaching the cab. He had evidently been watching from the little shack.

The man spoke. "Can't go in there. Mr. Trenholm's orders. Who's in that cab?"

Susannah answered.

"I'm just wondering when *The Great Eastern's* expected. I have a relative on board and I need to get word to him as soon as possible."

The man walked over to the side of the cab and hoisted his lamp up to the open window. He was startled by the presence of such a beautiful woman in this dangerous and unfriendly place.

"Ma'am, the best thing you can do is leave this place right now. It's just not safe here. For your own well-being, please leave now."

The conductor's face and beard were both a ruddy red, but his eyes seemed honest and caring. "Who would you be lookin' for, ma'am?"

Susannah weighed the risks of telling this man who she was and possibly the word getting back to George Trenholm that she had come directly here, rather than waiting until morning for his offer of an escort.

"Actually, all I need to know is where *The Great Eastern* is dropping anchor." Her voice had a slight quiver in it.

The conductor waived his lantern down the dock. "See them piles of boxes and bundles and bales? That's where she's tying up." Susannah leaned out the window and squinted through the mist ahead. As far as she could see, neat rows of boxes and bales were piled as high as the eaves of the warehouses to the right of the railroad tracks that ran straight down the middle of the dock. She had never seen so much cargo in one place. Directly behind the boxes were some strange shaped objects, shrouded in canvas covers.

She decided not to arouse suspicion. "I'll come back tomorrow. What time's she due in?"

"She'll be here before dawn. She's sailing up from Milford Haven."

"Thank you very much. By the way, what's your name?"

"'Enery, ma'am. I work for the railway company." Another hansom clattered up behind Susannah's. A gentleman with a top hat and dark overcoat jumped out and yelled something to his driver.

"Henry, can we take a last look at the railway car to make sure it's been unloaded? I need to report back to Mr. Trenholm."

The man did not see Susannah Eddings face at first, as he walked towards the conductor.

"Oh excuse me, ma'am. Didn't know you were talking to Henry. Name's Hanson. Can I help?"

She quickly ducked back into the cab, not wanting him to see her face.

"No thank you, sir. I found out what I needed. Good evening to you." She tapped the roof of the cab to signal the driver to get underway. He pulled sharply on the reins and the horse slowly turned and headed off the dock. Susannah stayed in the shadows, hoping Hanson hadn't seen her face. That would surely get back to George Trenholm.

Hanson and the conductor watched the dim red lantern of the hansom fade into the swirling fog.

"What was she asking you, Henry?"

"She wanted to know where the ship was puttin' in. She was also starin' at them cargo piles."

"Did she leave a name?"

"Nope. Just said she had some relative on board that she had to get word to"

The two were walking down the dock towards the huge piles of cargo.

"Certainly seems strange, some good-lookin' bird down here this time of night."

"Did you get a good look at her face Henry?"

"Yep. Dark hair. Dark eyes. It was a beautiful face. I'd not forget it."

"Was she British?"

"Gawd, no. Had a strange accent, kind of a drawl. Maybe American?"

They had reached the site where the train had been unloading. More boxes lay on the dock, but the train was nowhere to be found. Hanson bent down with his lamp and began to identify and count the boxes.

"Where's the train?"

"Had to send the engineer and brakemen back after they'd finished. Don't want to pay 'em anymore that we have to."

It took Duncan Hanson about half an hour to count the missing boxes. He reached in his pocket and handed the conductor an envelope.

"There's a five pound note in there. See that your men get some of it. They deserve it, too."

The conductor stopped and put down his lamp. He opened the envelope and took out the note.

"Thank you, Mr. Hanson. I takes care of me men." He offered his hand to the overseer. As they shook, Hanson could feel how rough and calloused the conductor's hand was.

"We've got more goods coming into the docks for loading aboard the ship. I'd appreciate you're keepin' an eye on things Henry. There's plenty more where that came from." His eyes fell to the conductor's hand, still clutching the five-pound note. "If you see that girl again, try to get her name and then tell me."

Hanson pulled on his gloves as the two men returned to the overseer's cab. Henry said goodnight and hurried into the warmth of the engineer's dispatch office.

On his way back to his hotel, George Trenholm mused over a piece of information Susannah had disclosed during dinner. She said that the Union warship, now named the *Monitor* was expected to be completed around the first week in December of this year and that the New York shipyard where she was being built was working around the clock to get the revolutionary vessel complete. George Trenholm feared that she would be used against his main supply link. The *Monitor*'s four-inch armor plate and two cannon could wreak all kinds of damage to *The Great Eastern's* thinner iron plate.

14.

Back in her hotel room, Susannah shivered, undressed and crawled under the comforter. It was past midnight and she was exhausted; the long dinner with George Trenholm, the guise of traveling to the wharf to learn more about the ship; the near-discovery of her identity had all combined to weigh heavily on her.

Because she was overly tired, she found it difficult to concentrate and this interfered with her reasoning. She began to feel sad. It was apparent that being a double agent was becoming an ever-increasingly dangerous role. The awful, undeniable truth was that she would probably never have a life with John Beauregard; she would be lucky to spend her life in some Union prison. She knew she could even be executed by her own countrymen. There was no escape. She began to drift off to sleep.

She thought of John; his strength, devotion; his tenderness during their lovemaking. She imagined his large, animated brown eyes staring at her.

Suddenly, it was as if he were in the room, at the foot of her bed, his face a study in sorrow and hurt, his arms outstretched towards her. She couldn't hear what he was saying, yet his lips seemed to be moving. Slowly he lowered his arms, putting his face in his hands. Was he crying?

Just as suddenly, the image vanished.

She twitched violently, waking her up from the dream. She began to cry; first some small sniffles, than real deep sobs, finally an almost uncontrollable series of retches. She sat up, trying to get some control over herself. She wanted John there in her arms; to confess her unfaithfulness, her perfidy to her country and have him tell her it would be all right. Maybe he could sneak her aboard the ship; hide her in his cabin! Then, when they got back to America she could slip off *The Great Eastern* and disappear into the South Carolina marshes until the war was over.

She blew her nose, and it was if the whole terrible dream had never happened. She climbed out of bed and shuffled over to the washbasin, letting the cool water she splashed on her face calm her down. She blotted the water off and walked back to the bed and slid under the covers.

No, I must do what is expected of me, she said matter-of-factly to herself. *Tomorrow I will get up early and be the first at the telegraph office. If I do what Percy asks, perhaps the Union will spare my life; even treat me as a decent human being who has worked to save American lives by preventing the South from continuing the war.*

Yet John's image, standing at the foot of her bed, his head in his hands in sorrow for her and their love for each other, flashed through her mind again, even as the fatigue finally overwhelmed the emotion.

15.

Shake, shake, shake. What now? His watch in the paddlewheel engine room of the ship was over. It seemed like he had just fallen asleep. John Beauregard had been so tired that he had just fallen onto his bunk, still clothed in his grimy uniform.

The cabin boy continued to shake the sleepy lieutenant.

"Breakfast, Sir. Captain's requested you be there for briefing."

"What time is it?" The young lieutenant's voice was hoarse from fatigue.

"'Bout five."

"But I just came off watch an hour ago."

"Sorry, sir. Captain's orders. Something about loading cargo. He expects you in twenty minutes."

The cabin boy closed the door to the cabin. John Beauregard slowly swung his legs over the side of the bunk and rubbed his eyes. A quick bath, he thought, would help wake him up. He pulled off the dirty uniform, socks and underwear, and threw them into his laundry bag. Lifting the fake settee cover up, he reached for the hot and cold water faucet and immediately began to fill the bathtub.

Minutes later, he was dressed in a crisp, clean uniform, combing his hair and what was becoming a full beard. He had decided to grow one until the voyage was over for good luck.

He closed the door of his cabin and made his way down the passageway towards the Captain's cabin. They had gotten underway last night after dark, with some of the workmen staying on board for the voyage to London, finishing up some of the last-minute details of the ship's renovation. There had been no time to see what had been done.

But now he had five minutes before the meeting so he decided to take a quick look up on deck to see what the refitting had done to *The Great Eastern's* appearance. A shortcut across the Grand Saloon, or the space that it used to occupy would get him there sooner. He pulled open the heavy mahogany door.

The room had been stripped bare. Where a column of mirrors had once hid the funnel that passed through the center of the huge area, now there was just a protective wooden railing, standing about four feet high, surrounding the metal tube. That would protect anyone from touching the hot metal, he thought to himself.

The vast open space was almost a half an acre in square footage. The room was almost three stories high, not including the two skylights, and a huge area for stowing cargo had been created. At least as much room had also been made by removing most of the staterooms. The ship had been transformed into a heavily armed cargo ship—not exactly the original plan of the designer.

He reached the opposite side of the cavernous room and exited out into the passageway. He found himself at the foot of the grand stairway, which had also been stripped. The elegant mirrors and panels were gone. The silver-oxide railing had been removed and a black utilitarian wrought iron one substituted in its place. He hurried up the metal uncarpeted stairs and through the doors onto the vastness of the ship's deck.

Even that had disappeared. With the installation of the two Ericcson revolving gun turrets and the machinery necessary for their operation, space fore and aft had been cut by almost twenty percent. New hatchways had been cut to facilitate the transfer of ammunition and supplies. Most of the cabooses had been removed and, like the skylights, became locations for huge hatchways to make loading and unloading the ship a fast proposition. Three steam-powered hoists had been added, one forward of the ship's paddlewheels, and two aft. They, too, would contribute to the ship's ability to take on and discharge her cargo speedily.

The young lieutenant stopped by the port turret to peek inside. The powerful 110-pound Armstrong breech-loading cannon were retracted inside the turret, their muzzles shrouded by the canvas covers to protect them from the corrosive salt spray. A seaman was busy cleaning the floor, although even with the dim light of dawn barely affording any light, John Beauregard could see the deck was immaculate. Above the turret, a lookout position covered with a canvas roof afforded a place for the Morse lamp system that, in conjunction with other similar positions on the other turrets and a command position on the bridge, would constitute the fire control system for the ship's guns. This was a clever innovation devised by his Naval Academy classmate William Slater, the designated fire control officer. It overcame the great distances that commands had to be shouted, the way navigation commands had formerly traveled from the bridge some three hundred feet aft to the helm. The Morse lamps would provide a much more responsive and accurate way of relaying firing directions as well as directing the ship's movements.

Firing adjustments would be ordered from the Captain's bridge. Lookouts, stationed in the crow's nest on masts Tuesday and Thursday, would provide Slater with the appropriate corrections. Slater, in turn, would relay by Morse lamp changes in direction, elevation, and projectile loading to the appropriate turret. In theory, it would make the devastating firepower of the turrets deadly accurate and powerful. In practice, the system had not been tried, and would have to wait until the vessel had put to sea fully loaded.

The breakfast bugle was blowing. Beauregard glanced down at the brass ring the turret revolved on when she was in battle. When the ship was underway, an elevating mechanism enabled the turret to be lifted off her bearings to quickly clean out the waste that accumulates during battle. If necessary, during battle, the turret could be raised in an emergency to allow quick evacuation of the gun crew, since the gap would be almost eighteen inches.

Alexander McLennan appeared on the other side of the turret as the American began to walk forward to the Captain's caboose, where the officers were to meet for breakfast and the Captain's briefing.

"'Mornin', Mr. McLennan." John Beauregard managed a snappy salute. Since the Chief Paddlewheel Engineer was, for the duration of the voyage, Beauregard's commanding officer, he still liked the formality of using "Mr." The young lieutenant guessed that it also came from his Scottish background.

McLennan returned the salute and replied with a broad grin. He too had changed into a fresh uniform, although he was not scheduled for a watch until eight o'clock. "Ready for the docks at London, young man?"

Beauregard slowed his pace to allow his superior to catch up.

"Yessir, I understand it'll take us two days to load the ship. I'm hoping to get some time to see Susannah. She's here as part of an envoy from the South to meet with some of the British women and explain the South's cause." He omitted the other reason for her visit, as she had requested that George Trenholm be the one to tell the ship's captain about the menace of the Federal *Monitor*. "Why don't you bring her aboard and introduce her to the new captain? He's probably never met a, what do you call them, Southern Belle. I'm sure he and the rest of the officers, especially the new ones, would love to meet her." McLennan reached for the brass handle of the door leading into the Captain's caboose.

"I'm sure she'd be thrilled. I'll ask the Captain after the briefing. I understand it's about the loading process." John Beauregard entered first, at the engineer's urging.

16.

The office of The British Telegraph Company was barely large enough to hold three people in front of the counter. Susannah Eddings was first in line, filling out the piece of paper that would begin the process of the betrayal to her country and her beau.

She had gotten up that morning with the resolve to carry out what she was in London to do for Allan Pinkerton and George Percy. There was the war to think about and then there was Susannah. She shut her mind to her feelings for John Beauregard, knowing that to think of the consequences of what she was doing could make her stop. To do so would jeopardize her life. She decided that John had a better chance of surviving than she, even with the act of treachery she was about to begin.

SHIP UNDER CHARTER TO CSA, she wrote in the code Percy had given her,

SAW LARGE CONTINGENT OF SUPPLIES O N DOCK. MEETING WITH CREWMEMBER T ONIGHT TO LEARN MORE STOP

S.

She folded the form and handed it to the clerk.

"Two pounds, ma'am," the clerk said after he counted the letters.

Susannah reached into her purse and fished out two one-pound notes and handed them to the clerk.

"How soon will that be sent?"

"Your party will get it in about six hours. Is he expecting it?"

"He goes by the telegraph office every morning. I'm sure he'll get it."

She thanked him and left the closeness of the tiny office, hurrying down the street, as it was almost ten, the time she was to be at

George Trenholm's office. It was still chilly and damp and seemed like it would always be that way. She pulled her cloak tighter around her body to ward off the chill.

The reception area in the London offices of Fraser Trenholm glowed from the warmth of the little coal stove located in the corner of the room. Susannah had given her name to the receptionist and seated herself next to the stove to warm up. She loosened her cloak to take advantage of the heat radiating from the ceramic front of the stove.

"Good morning, Susannah." George Trenholm entered the room, followed by two men in overcoats, who seemed to be in a hurry. Susannah stood up but quickly turned away as if to sneeze, as she recognized one of the men as the one who had been on the dock last night. The men hurried by her, paying little attention. The third man, a tall well-dressed handsome gentleman, joined the trader as he was kissing Susannah's hand.

"I'd like you to meet Thad Howard, one of my overseers. He'll take you down to the dock so you can learn when and where you'll be able to meet John. Please stay close to Thad as the dock's not a place for a beautiful young woman to be, even in daylight and with an escort." George Trenholm spoke with the kindly affection usually reserved for a daughter.

Susannah extended her hand. The young overseer grasped it and bowed. "Nice to meet ya', Miss Eddings," he said, adding, "Mr. Trenholm, I'll be back as soon as I can, sir."

The sun was trying very hard to shine as they made their way through the London traffic to the docks. From the windows of Fraser Trenholm's carriage, Susannah could clearly see the tall masts and five smokestacks of *The Great Eastern*. The ship was anchored in the midst of the Thames, just as the dockworker had said. As they rounded the corner of the street that led directly to the dock, she could also see the long black hull and the large flotilla of small boats that was shuttling the cargo out to the vessel.

She was stunned at the change in the ship's appearance. Gone were the graceful lines and vast decks. The armored gun turrets created an odd top-heavy appearance to the once beautiful hull. Streaked with rust, the ship looked like some unkempt hodgepodge of odd angles and shapes. As the carriage approached the dock, the traffic of other carriages, wagons and horses became very heavy. As they got closer, traffic was stopped altogether at intervals to allow the passage of the small dockside locomotives pulling loaded freight and flatcars.

Thad Howard tapped on the front window of the carriage and signaled the driver to stop. "We'll do better walking to the warehouse. I'm sure our supervisor will know which officers are aboard the ship and when they're coming ashore. We can leave a note for your friend if you like."

He helped Susannah down from the carriage and they began to thread their way towards the warehouse. The shadows of night had obscured the filth and chaos that was so much a part of the dockside scene during the day. Sidestepping the piles of horse dung and other garbage only added more obstacles to the short walk. Finally, they reached the warehouse. Inside, was more chaos. Loaded wagons were now being brought out directly onto small lighters that went to the center of the river, to the side of the ship. Susannah noticed that the huge piles of cargo that had lined the edge of the quay last night were considerably smaller. They headed for the supervisor's office, up a flight of wooden stairs on a little platform.

The door at the top of the stairs opened before they reached the top, and two men emerged. One of them was Duncan Hanson. He immediately spotted Susannah and tipped his hat. "Mornin', ma'am. Glad to see ya' got home safely."

"Thank you." Susannah did not wish to start a conversation and hurried past the overseer and his companion. She hoped Thad Howard would not ask any questions.

She reached the platform and stopped to wait for her escort. He had also stopped on the stairs and was talking with Duncan Hanson and the other man. She strongly suspected it was about her nocturnal visit to the dock last night. Duncan glanced at her several times during the interchange but Thad Howard did not. At last the little group broke up and her escort bounded up the stairs and opened the door to the supervisor's office.

"Company business, please forgive me for keeping you waiting."

She instinctively knew what business he meant.

A short conversation with the supervisor disclosed that none of the crew had come ashore and stopped by his office, although that was supposed to be the first place they went. Susannah jotted down the name of the hotel and when she would be there and handed it to the supervisor, who promised to get it into John Beauregard's hands before noon, if he was aboard the ship.

17.

The Captain said during the breakfast meeting that he wanted all hands back on the ship after the farewell party that evening in London. The officers would spell the boatswains and cargo handler supervisors in overseeing of the loading the vessel. To John Beauregard, now on his way to the dock aboard one of *The Great Eastern's* steam launches, it seemed like one day was melding into the next, with no rest in sight.

He was still tired from being aroused just one hour after he had come off watch. Nevertheless, he looked forward to the next few hours; a few hours away from the ship. A few hours when he didn't have to watch the abuses the boatswains heaped on the sailors and hide his feelings about the beatings. And only a few hours to be in Susannah's arms.

The launch bumped against the dock as the mates secured her to the piling. The young lieutenant grabbed his seabag and jumped onto the dock. They had landed just steps from the dockside freight office of Fraser Trenholm and he walked quickly across the traffic-clogged pier, mounted the steps and walked into the office.

"Do you have a note for me?" He was addressing the burly supervisor who was looking over some papers.

"Name?"

"John Beauregard. The note would be from a Susannah Eddings."

The supervisor winked at the young lieutenant. "Got yourself a real good looker, Yank. She dropped this off this morning." The supervisor handed him the small note with his name neatly written on the envelope. He decided to ignore the nickname the supervisor had given him, sensing that trying to explain the geography of the United States and that "Yank" was short for "Yankee" or anyone north of the Mason-Dixon line might just take too long.

"Thanks, Mister. If anyone's looking for me, here's where they can find me." He pointed to the address of Susannah's hotel that was on the carefully folded note inside the envelope.

A short cab ride and he was in the lobby of Susannah's hotel and racing up the stairs to her room.

"Susannah!" John said, excitedly, as he knocked on her door. She opened the door and John nearly flew into her arms, embracing her passionately. Both fell into the bed—their eyes searing each other's soul. Susannah loved his muscular body and long legs, but most of all his intense, maddeningly blue-green eyes.

They made love again and again and again. And although Susannah was flushed with their consummated love, John noted that the strain of the past few weeks showed on Susannah's face. Dark circles lay under her eyes and lines of fatigue showed in her forehead and also around the corners of her eyes. He took his hand and gently brushed the dark hair out of her face.

"You look tired, darling. Has there been no rest in these gatherings of the Committee other than just now?"

She wanted to tell him why she was so tired, why everything was tormenting her. She thought of the dream last night and the urge to cry was almost uncontrollable. But she quickly composed herself, thinking about her web of survival.

"I have been traveling to the countryside, and I think it's the travel that's doing it." She rolled over in bed, facing him. "But enough about me. Let me look at you."

His beard had filled in and he looked much older to her now.

"You look like a Captain now instead of just a lieutenant. I adore your beard."

He kissed her once more and sat up on the edge of the bed. Under the covers, he found one of her hands and squeezed it tightly.

"We've been invited to a farewell party tonight. It's at The Lion's Head at eight. Just for the captain and officers on board *The Great Eastern* and a few of George Trenholm's British contacts. It's almost five now. Why don't I go back to the ship, get cleaned up and change, and you can do the same. I'll pick you up at seven thirty." She smiled at the thought of going to a party with this handsome naval officer. All the fear and doubt she felt last night seemed to disappear.

"I'd love to go with you, John. You always look so distinguished when you're in full dress and I can only imagine you in. . .no dress. Not to mention how I feel about you."

"And how's that?" He was kissing her forehead.

"As if I can never get enough of you. As if I start missing you the moment you leave."

He was staring into her dark brown eyes. They were full of devotion.

"I love you, John."

He knew she meant it. "And I love you Susannah." They kissed again, this time the deep passionate kiss that they had showered on each other during the afternoon's lovemaking.

He sat up, got off the bed, and began to pull on his longjohns. She lay on the bed, one breast exposed, one half hidden under the comforter.

As he buttoned his tunic, he leaned over the bed and lightly kissed her full lips.

"See you at seven thirty, darling."

He was gone and she was already missing him.

18.

John and Susannah held each other's hands tightly for the entire carriage ride to *The Lion's Head* tavern. It was as though some invisible force was trying to pry them apart. Now it was John 's fatigue that was making him feel insecure. Would Susannah ever be his? Would the treacherous voyage back to America be successful? Would he be able to continue suppressing his feelings about the enslaved seamen?

Arriving at the tavern, John paid the carriage driver as Susannah stepped down and hurried into the shelter of the tavern's roof overhang. A light rain was falling. John opened the door and they walked up the stairs to the private room, still clutching each other's hand tightly and occasionally looking dreamily at each other.

Inside the mood was festive. A large banner stretched across the room, emblazoned with the British flag at both ends. In the middle, were the words "Godspeed, Great Eastern! Britannia Rule the Waves!"

In the far corner of the room, a chamber quartet quietly played Mozart. Tables around the room were festively decorated with deep blue tablecloths, white napkins and bouquets of brilliant red carnations and chrysanthemums. The candelabra blazed brilliantly from the light of the dozens of candles. A servant took Susannah's cape and the young naval officer's coat while a waiter handed each a glass of champagne.

Susannah's beauty radiated like a beacon. She had chosen a dark green strapless gown that accentuated her creamy white shoulders and magnificent chest. Her dark hair hung loosely at shoulder length and made a marked contrast to her shoulders. With her impeccable makeup, pearl necklace and earrings, and a single gold bracelet, she was stunning.

But John Beauregard noticed something strange, something different about Susannah this evening. Usually very outgoing and vivacious, she had alternated between clinging to John's hand, to being aloof and, at times, even uncommunicative. It reminded him of the night in the garden, when she told him how she felt about marrying Peter Jennings. Even then, though he didn't know her very well, he felt she was holding something back. While she had held nothing back during their lovemaking this past afternoon, she was definitely bothered by something this evening.

The officers of *The Great Eastern*, dressed in their full winter dress were also elegant, their colorful campaign ribbons accenting the dark wool tunics. Each of them also had their dress swords buckled tightly around their waists. Even George Trenholm, ever the patrician Southerner, had dressed for the occasion in a full cutaway, complete with a frilly shirt with ruffles. A stranger would not be aware that many of these men were about to risk their lives on an extremely risky and dangerous voyage. There was little talk of the event or the ship itself. It was as though no one wanted to create another jinx for the beleaguered vessel.

Susannah was very careful not to show her interest when the topic came up, even as infrequently as it did. Percy's last instruction to her was very specific: get as much information on the cargo, and the ship's departure date and time but don't appear too inquisitive.

She wondered what else the agent expected her to find out about the ship. After all, hadn't Allan Pinkerton gone over *The Great Eastern* thoroughly when he sailed on it earlier in the summer?

But Percy had sent her a letter also telling her that it was crucial she get as much information as she could on the ship's cargo manifest. Most importantly was the vessel's final destination in the United States. Until her return to America, he had written, he was going to hold her to her word and strongly reminded her that he would not hesitate to reveal her identity to both the Union and Confederacy. And now she also harbored the terrible secret of just who Major E.J. Allen really was.

She found herself enmeshed in a web, which could ensnare her at any time without warning. To further complicate matters, she was now very sure she loved John and scared to death of what would happen if he ever found out the true nature of who she was. She knew he was fiercely loyal to the Confederate cause and would never allow anything to compromise it—even her.

His wasn't the only trust she was violating. There was his uncle, General Pierre Gustave Toutan-Beauregard, emerging as one of the most important Confederate generals of the war, second only to Robert E. Lee. And, of course, George Trenholm, the ship and its crew, including the friendly and earthy chief engineer Alexander McLennan; all stood to fall if she did what Percy told her to do.

As they circulated around the room they came to a group with Daniel Gooch and his wife chatting. John recognized him immediately, with his mutton-chop mustache bobbing up and down as he spoke. He shook the ship owner's hand. Gooch introduced his wife.

"Nice to meet you, Madame Gooch. And good to see you sir. I'd like to introduce my friend Susannah Eddings. She's from my part of the South—St. Helena's Island, in South Carolina." Turning to the ship's Captain, also a member of the group, he continued the introductions. "Captain Paton, this is Susannah Eddings."

"Nice to meet such a pretty Southern—what do you call them— Belle?" The new Captain of the ship had taken over after her disaster during the September storm and her subsequent refitting as an armed merchantman. For all her moodiness, the Captain's compliment made Susannah blush. She smiled her broadest smile. "I'm just a loyal Southerner, sir," she said softly, accenting it with a small curtsy.

Across the room, Susannah spotted Alexander McLennan. Their eyes crossed and the engineer winked. The ruddy-faced Scotsman had dressed for the occasion as a true Scotsman, in a kilt. His plaid, a rich criss-cross pattern of bright reds, forest greens and black background added another brilliant touch of color to the room. He excused himself from the group he stood talking with and came across the room to join Susannah and the others. He bowed and reached for Susannah's hand, kissing it with a flourish.

"How have you been since that last voyage? You look stunning," he commented.

She felt the glow of another blush spreading to her head. "I've been fine, sir. Thank you for the compliment."

McLennan turned toward John Beauregard. "Have you extended an invitation to Susannah for a last visit and tour of our ship yet?" The Chief Engineer had a smile on his face and the wrinkles around his eyes compressed.

The young lieutenant turned to Susannah, feeling somewhat embarrassed. "I completely forgot...Captain Paton and Mr. McLennan asked if you would like to see the ship before she sails tomorrow night." It was the first mention of her sailing time. "Can you break away tomorrow and join us for lunch and a tour? I can't promise everything will be in order because of our mission but I think you'd enjoy it."

Susannah had wondered how she would finish finding out what Percy expected of her. Getting near the ship would have been a problem. Uncannily, it was now being handed to her openly.

"We'd look upon it as an honor to have you on board, ma'am." Susannah was flattered by the personable remark of the ship's stocky captain.

"I, too, would be honored to visit your ship, sir."

"We'll expect you around noon, then."

The conversation drifted to Susannah's reason for being in England. Mrs. Gooch mentioned that she had heard of the Committee's work but had not attended one of the meetings but would like to.

Susannah spoke up. "I hosted one just yesterday morning outside London. Had I known, I would have been happy to have invited you. They're usually quite lively, especially since your countrymen are so politically knowledgeable."

George Trenholm, circulating among his guests, overheard the remark about the purported meeting. He wondered what Susannah was trying to hide, since he knew she had been in the company of his overseer on the docks most of the morning. He decided to ignore it but to keep an eye on her activities while she was in London.

BLOCKADE RUNNER
BOOK 4

1.

As shocked as she had been at the sight of *The Great Eastern's* transformation into an armed merchantman, Susannah was totally unprepared for the chaos and apparent disarray she saw when she came on board for the farewell luncheon.

There were boxes, crates and shrouded objects scattered about the decks. Men were running around barking orders at other men to move this or that; to carry that package below to hold number two; or to watch out for the steam crane lowering that load of boxes. It was quite unlike her first trip over from America, the romantic nights under the stars on deck with John; the gentle roll of the ship underway, and an excitement that she was going to England.

As vast as the ship's decks were, they had not been designed to accommodate the two 33-foot-wide iron turrets, and the crates of military materiel that were not to be loaded in the holds. Nevertheless, as Susannah made her way across the deck behind John, Chief Engineer McLennan, and Captain Walter Paton, the ship was still an impressive sight.

She had been royally entertained in the Captain's caboose. The meal had been sumptuous, and she was feeling a little tipsy from the champagne and brandy that had been served, along with fresh oysters, roast pheasant, leg of lamb, and bread and pastries baked especially in her honor.

"Our Last Supper" the Captain had named it. He was referring to the transition and conversion of the ship to one capable of waging war; it would not be appropriate to eat in this manner when men were in imminent danger of losing their lives.

She had only seen a portion of the cargo since areas like the Grand Saloon were floor-to-ceiling, wall-to-wall packed with all manner of crates, boxes and bales. With some discreet questions directed at her friend Alexander McLennan and couched in her most innocent way, she concluded there was enough material to outfit an army of 100,000 to 150,000 men and enough arms and artillery to support an army half again as big.

William Slater had joined the elegant meal, having missed the reception at George Trenholm's the night before because of watch duty. Susannah was glad to see another countryman and spent much time talking with him about life on his plantation.

They reached the gangway stairs, to the rear of the port paddlewheel housing. Susannah stopped and turned to face her hosts. "Thank you, Captain, and you as well, Mr. McLennan. And you too, William. This is going to give the Yankees a bad scare."

We hope it's a great deal more than a scare, Susannah," William Slater emphasized.

The Captain and the Chief Engineer kissed Susannah's hand, said their goodbyes, and left her with her two countrymen. Slater, recognizing that his presence made John and Susannah's goodbyes awkward, hugged Susannah and wished her well.

"When will you be back?" the engineer asked.

"I hope in the next month. I'll try to book passage on the next ship bound for the South. There aren't many doing that since the blockade started."

"Well, have a safe trip." Slater waved a goodbye and disappeared behind the paddlewheel housing.

John put his arms around Susannah's shoulders and drew her close to him. They kissed passionately and longingly. She wondered what it would be like without him.

"Darling, I want you to promise me you won't flirt with danger."

"I'll be four decks below any firing. My biggest problem will be staying clear of the machinery."

They both laughed. She stood on her tiptoes and lightly kissed his lips. They clasped each other tightly, and she sensed it was time for her to leave. She felt the tears welling up in her eyes as she turned for one last look.

He looked magnificent in his uniform and his now full-grown beard. Against the background òf the paddlewheel housing, Mast Tuesday, and the wisps of black smoke from the ship's funnel, he looked like the captain of the ship, ready for anything. Her heart pounded at the thought that she might not ever see him again.

She ran the few steps into his arms and they embraced again. He felt the moist tears against his face.

"Don't worry darling, I'll be back to marry you, if you'll have me. Please wait for me."

She swallowed hard but the lump in her throat wouldn't go away.

"I will. I love you." Her voice was small and choked with tears.

"I love you too, Susannah."

She turned, picked up her skirts and started down the long stairs to the dory waiting to take her back to the London docks. She had managed to avoid having him find out the terrible truth of her real mission in London. Now that she knew when the ship was leaving, where she was heading and what she was carrying, it was time for the ultimate act of betrayal. She wept silently, hiding her face from the sailors.

It was now almost four o'clock. Percy had told her to send the information about the ship's departure at least six hours before it happened. She hired a hansom cab as soon as she arrived ashore at the now nearly deserted dock area. The afternoon breeze that was always there chilled her and she pulled her cloak tightly around her body to ward off the cold.

She arrived at the telegraph office, still sobbing as she stepped out of the cab. An image of the unkempt Percy and Rose Greenhow gave a short pause to the sobs. She was betraying everything to save her own skin. There would be no John; he might not survive what might come.

But the awful fate that would await her when she returned to Washington if she didn't send the information could be worse. A trial, humiliation to herself, her family, John, if he survived. The hangman's noose. Death. She had to do it.

With a six-hour time differential, and the ship departing at ten, she would have to send the telegram right now. Percy no doubt would stop by the military telegraph office before he went home. She knew the security officer rarely left the Capital before nine. That would be perfect timing.

The telegraph office was crowded as usual. Susannah kept the message short, including the new thing she had learned; the destination of the ship and her cargo was Port Royal Sound, between Hilton Head and St. Helena's islands, right in her backyard. Of course, she later reasoned, the water's very deep there and they will be able to unload her cargo and load the cotton a lot easier and faster.

She paid for the telegram and got into the cab, but failed to see the figure peeking out the door of the pub across the street from the telegraph office. At George Trenholm's request, Duncan Hanson, who had told the trader about his strange encounter with the beautiful woman late at night on the dock, and then her appearance the next day at the warehouse, had followed her from the hotel, to the dock, and now to the telegraph office.

He had discreetly dismissed his cab and ducked into the pub across the street to observe her movements.

It was almost time for the telegraph office to close. Hanson watched the movements in the office until he saw the last customer leave. Donning his coat and pork-pie hat, he ran across the street and into the office.

The telegrapher was making preparations to close the office. "I'm sorry, sir, we're closed. . ."

Slightly out of breath, Duncan Hanson interrupted him. "That woman that was just in here, did she send a telegram to America?" The clerk seemed surprised at the question.

Hanson continued. "I'm with Fraser Trenholm, and they're supposed to get a telegram from her in Charleston. Is that where she sent it?"

The clerk walked to the wire basket where telegrams to be sent were piled up. He flipped through the pile until he came to the one with the feminine handwriting. Pausing, he mused over the request.

He walked to the counter. There was no one else in the office. Hanson had folded a five-pound note in his hand and now offered it to the telegrapher.

"Split it with the clerk. May I see it please?"

"Don't know if I should do this, guvna'." The telegrapher hesitated, then handed the folded paper to Hanson, taking the note with the other hand.

Hanson opened the folded sheet and almost dropped it as he read the words describing the ship, her cargo, and destination. The addressee, a Mr. Percy in the Washington D.C. Military Telegraph Office, left no doubt as to what Susannah was doing.

"Has this been sent yet?"

"Why yessir, we send 'em just as soon as we can. The lines were clear, so we took advantage of that. They ain't always usable, you know."

The overseer paused and handed the telegram back to the clerk. Duncan Hanson somehow had to get to the ship before she left. But first he had to tell George Trenholm what he had found out.

2.

Departure was imminent, judging by the chaos on The Great Eastern. On the bridge, the decision to depart four hours early was made because the ship was drawing more than thirty-two feet of water with her cargo. If they waited until ten, she might not make it over the bar at the mouth of the Thames. They had to leave while the tide was high. A cold gray sun had set an hour earlier and it was nearly dark. The two arc lights on Masts Tuesday and Thursday, similar to the ones on Westminster Bridge, cast an eerie bluish glow of light across the ship's deck. The lights had been installed at the request of the Confederate marine engineers to allow loading and unloading at night.

Below deck, in the screw engine room, the order had just been given for departure. Steam had been up for over two hours to accommodate any changes in departure time. John Beauregard walked the catwalk directly over the engine. He would have the six to ten p.m. shift, to be spelled by his countryman William Slater. The young lieutenant had had a long day and was looking forward to a hot bath and some rest. He had not found the opportunity to take Susannah to his cabin when she was visiting the ship, so the fantasy of making love to her in his bunk would have to remain just that.

The voice of Captain Paton could be heard through the speaking tube. John Beauregard picked up the odd-shaped horn and put it to his ear.

"...to get underway. Prepare to get underway. This is Captain Paton. Stern engine in idle. Main engines ahead one third. Acknowledge."

"Beauregard, stern engine, aye aye, Sir." He could not hear the reply from the main engine room.

The ship began to rock very slowly, a sure sign that the paddlewheels had started her forward.

John looked at the clock on the wall next to the steam pressure gauge. It said five minutes after six.

3.

"Go wake the President. Tell him I have information he needs to hear. And tell him I think we should call a cabinet meeting."

Gideon Welles was addressing one of the pages outside his office. Beside him stood the unshaven Percy, who had removed his hat exposing his shiny bald spot.

"And for Christ's sake don't dawdle. It's goddam important that you get to the President immediately."

It took the young teen carrying the important news just fifteen minutes to ride his horse from New Jersey Avenue to the famous Pennsylvania Avenue address. At the gate he was challenged by the sentry and showed him his special pass. In the front door of the White House he dismounted and ran up the stairs. A negro, dressed in a tuxedo answered the door.

"Urgent message from Mr. Welles at the Secretary's office. Says for you to wake up the President and have him come to the Secretary's office immediately. Says he thinks the President should call a cabinet meeting."

The older man sighed at the youth's impatience. "Mr. Lincoln hasn't retired yet. What's your name?"

"Robert. I work for Mr. Secretary Welles. The President knows my name."

"Wait here." The servant opened the door wide enough to admit the page and disappeared down the hall. After a short wait he returned. "Mr. Lincoln says you are to go back to Mr. Welles and have him send for the other cabinet members. He will be there in about twenty minutes."

Half an hour later Welles, Percy, the President, and Secretaries Seward, Cameron of the War Department, and Chase of the Treasury were crowded around Welles' desk. The President was scrutinizing the handwritten telegraph copy. It was from a woman whom he had never heard of before, a person who merely signed the telegram "S."

Welles interpreted. "She's an agent, working for Percy. I can vouch for her, Mr. President. She's from a plantation owner's family out of Charleston. She'd been working exclusively for Rose Greenhow until Percy compromised her. She's also been working for us for about a year now. I met her at a party at Rose's last summer."

The President was silent. He had been told that something big was about to happen, that the cotton picking had been proceeding at a furious pace. He had even heard about a special rail yard under construction somewhere between Charleston and Savannah. Now the picture was clear. Guns for cotton. A whole shipload of military materiel for the fledgling army he was having so much difficulty trying to suppress. *If those supplies ever get through, we're in for a long war*, he mused.

Lincoln turned and stared out the window. The street was deserted. "Has Captain Du Pont gotten underway yet? Get word to him that his orders have changed. He's to intercept *The Great Eastern* and prevent her from getting to her destination."

Welles looked with disbelief at the President. "You mean try and sink her?"

Seward spoke. "I don't think the Queen or Palmerston would like that. They're already sympathetic to some of the Southern causes."

For once, it seemed he and Gideon Welles agreed on something.

The question hung in the air. But the President was already ahead of them, at least tactically. "Where's Farragut and the *Hartford*?"

Welles spoke. "She's due in Philadelphia in two weeks. That should put her about a thousand miles out to sea."

Abraham Lincoln's mind was moving faster than his ability to issue orders. "Get word to Farragut that I want him involved also. It's going to take everything we've got to stop that ship. I've been told that she's undergone substantial renovation, including additional cannon. I thought the Queen was only building the *Warrior*. I guess she decided two iron warships would be better than one."

Welles quickly sensed the urgency of the situation. "I'll telegraph Captain Du Pont right now. Hopefully he's ashore. They're not due to leave for three more days," he said, dipping his pen into the inkwell. "The *Rhode Island's* due to put into Wilmington. I'll get word to have her intercept Farragut. She's the fastest we've got. Lieutenant Trenchard ought to be able to catch her."

It was eleven thirty in the evening. More bad news was in the making, several hundred miles south of the nation's capital. Only this time it involved a couple of misfits, one of them a ship.

4.

She seemed to be a naval misfit the day she was put into service. One year after she was commissioned, the San Jacinto's *entire drive train had to be replaced. Her propeller shaft was off center, causing unacceptable vibrations when underway and preventing her from getting up to full speed. And her engines were also deemed unacceptable; they were not reliable. In 1854, after a complete refit, she rejoined her peers in the United States Navy.*

She was destined early on to clash with Southern principles. In 1860, while on patrol off the mouth of the Congo River, she captured the brig Storm King, *loaded with 619 slaves and purportedly bound for the Southern United States.*

She was a favorite with her crew, so much so that they nicknamed her Saucy Jack. Formidably armed, she carried one eleven-in. and ten nine-in Dalhgrens and one twelve-pounder Parrot rifle gun.

But she had the bad luck to be commanded by another misfit, someone who would manage to give her worldwide notoriety.

5.

Captain Charles Wilkes was looking for some information on the whereabouts of Rafael Semmes and the *Sumter*. He knew the raider and its clever captain were somewhere in the vicinity; now that she had returned from South America. Nothing could please him more than to catch the slower ship and sink her. But knowing where the raider was operating and capturing the ship that had already sacked sixteen Federal vessels were two entirely different matters.

Each new bar and flophouse he visited along the Havana waterfront could offer little more new information. A lean man in his early sixties, Wilkes was the captain of the *San Jacinto,* or, as her crew had nicknamed her, *Saucy Jack.* The Union screw frigate was on patrol for the Union in the Straits of Florida. Wilkes had been designated commander of the frigate *Merrimack* before the ship was scuttled to prevent her from falling into rebel hands at Gosport, early last summer. *Saucy Jack* was Wilkes' consolation prize.

Wilkes had already had his share of misfortune. His ship had just survived a collision with the French brigantine *Jules at Marie* off the Cuban coast, a consequence of misunderstood commands and navigational ineptness. Although he had earned fame for mapping some sixteen hundred miles of forbidding Antarctica coastline twenty years ago, his reputation for harsh discipline eventually cost him. He was court-martialed for mistreating his crewmen. Gideon Welles thought him "ambitious, self-conceited and self-willed." He had written that Wilkes "has abilities but not sound judgment and is not always subordinate though he is himself severe and exacting towards his subordinates."

After this long disappointing evening Charles Wilkes decided to stop for a nightcap in the last bar on the wharf where his ship's dory was tied up.

"Any news of the raider *Sumter*?" Wilkes asked the bartender, as he sipped his beer. The bartender shook his head, but a short man with a black beard and black bowler looked up at the tall American from the end of the bar.

"Would you be lookin' for rebels?" the stranger inquired.

"Have you seen any?" Charles Wilkes responded, knowing the presence of Confederates might mean the presence of Confederate naval ships.

"For a couple of beers, I might have," the stranger commented. Nodding to the bartender to give the man what he wanted, Wilkes turned to the end of the bar.

The man took a long sip from one of the tankards. "Well, I heard two of 'em got aboard the *Trent* at sunset. Someone said they were a couple of Southern agents, goin' to England on business," the stranger remarked.

His companion, who was smoking a pipe and seated next to him spoke up. "It was someone called James Mason. The other one's last name was Slidell. Can't remember his first name."

Wilkes was astounded. "*Senator* Slidell, from Louisiana? Are you sure?" Captain Wilkes addressed the pipe-smoking man.

"Saw 'em board myself, right off this wharf. Looks like they was gonna be away for awhile, judging by the amount of baggage they had."

"When did they leave?" Wilkes tone was impatient.

The man drew on his pipe thoughtfully before answering. "No more than two hours ago."

"Where was the ship headed?"

"I think back to London."

Wilkes signaled the bartender. "Buy this gentlemen another round on me. I'll be back to settle up in a day or two."

Saucy Jack's captain quickly drained his beer and hurried out into the early evening. His ship was about one-quarter mile out in Havana harbor and he would have to hurry if he was to catch the *Trent* before sundown.

He found his dory, woke up the two sleeping sailors who manned the oars, and jumped in. "Shake a leg men, we're in hot pursuit of a couple of renegades."

One of the sailors reached up and unfastened the line attached to the dock. Soon they were well underway, out into the bay.

Captain Wilkes finished the explanation of what they were about to do. "We're going after two rebels on the *Trent*. They're carrying Confederate dispatches and we've got a right to seize them."

"Stop an English ship, sir?" The sailor was incredulous, his voice filled with fear.

"According to the law, if we suspect she's harboring enemy information, we can stop and search her." Wilkes seemed to know the law.

They were just a short distance from *Saucy Jack*. The captain stood up in the stern, cupped his hands and began shouting in the direction of the ship.

"Officer of the deck this is Wilkes. Get steam up and prepare for departure. We're in pursuit of some rebels."

Even in the growing darkness Wilkes could see his command had set the ship into action. Several sailors and officers could be seen scurrying around on deck. One crew was assembling in order to hoist the anchor chain; another had begun to ascend the masts to unfurl the sails.

The captain's dory reached the ship and Wilkes hurried up the ladder. On board there was organized chaos, as the ship prepared to get underway. "Let's see what *Saucy Jack* can do with a full head of steam and all her sails trimmed," he announced.

Wilkes was on the bridge as the man-o-war's single stack belched black smoke and the ship began to vibrate from the revolving propeller. The vessel swung out into the Bahamas channel and Wilkes already had his spyglass out, searching for the telltale wisp of smoke. After about an hour of hard steaming he found what he was looking for.

"British ship off to port, Cap'n," The lookout saw him first and sounded the alarm. Wilkes scanned the mast of the ship, confirming its nationality by seeing the British ensign. He signaled the helmsman and the engine room to close in on the ship.

The men Wilkes was after were two of the most influential politicians in the South. Contrasted with James Bulloch and George Trenholm, who were the logistics element behind the South's war effort, James Mason and John Slidell were the political element on their way to Europe, to attempt to gain recognition for the fledgling government. John Slidell, who had been influential in gaining admittance to Annapolis for his nephew John Beauregard, had run the Yankee blockade to Havana along with Mason aboard one of George Trenholm's blockade runners, the *Gordon*, now renamed the *Theodora*. Slidell and Mason were now continuing their journey to England and France from Havana.

"Battery one, commence fire across bow of the British ship when in range."

Four of the ship's nine-inch Dahlgrens fired the challenge. Wilkes dipped his signal flags to demand the right to board, citing the presence of belligerents. The captain of the *Trent*, wanting no bloodshed and having nothing with which to defend himself, hove to, and agreed to allow a boarding party.

Wilkes ordered his first officer to form a boarding detail, emphasizing the need for using the biggest and strongest of his men. Six were selected, enough to put the prisoners into shackles and leg irons and overcome any resistance. All were given pistols which, with their scabbards, assured the success of the mission.

The dory which Charles Wilkes had used to go ashore in Havana still hung loosely from the ship's davits. The boarding party climbed into the small vessel as the crew assisted in lowering the boat into the water.

"Watch the clearance!" Wilkes was back on the bridge, supervising the launch, his first officer in command of the excursion. "I want those men alive." But the dory was out of earshot of the captain's last command.

One hour later the party was back on board, prisoners successfully captured and put in leg irons. Both were angry and protested their capture. Wilkes ordered them locked up below, deciding he would interview them after they got underway. In the meantime, he ordered the ship back to Havana to provision coal and supplies for the trip to Boston, the ship's homeport.

6.

Duncan Hanson managed to reach the offices of Fraser Trenholm in less than twenty minutes. He hurriedly paid the cabdriver and rushed inside, past the receptionist, past the accountants, directly into George Trenholm's office. He knocked on the trader's office door but did not wait for an acknowledgment to go in.

"Mr. Trenholm, we've got to get word to the ship! The Eddings girl's a spy for the Yankees! She's already telegraphed its destination and cargo to Washington!"

"Are you certain?" A frown had already formed on the trader's patrician face.

"I followed her to the telegraph office, waited until she left, went in and bribed the clerk to let me see the message. Yes sir, I'm certain."

George Trenholm swiveled his chair around to gaze out the window at the London evening. He felt a sinking feeling in his groin. "If we could get a telegram to Southampton, hire one of our associate's coastal steamers to intercept the ship, perhaps we could warn her before she gets too far out to sea."

"The telegraph office is closed sir. They shut down right after I left." Hanson was perched on the edge of one of the wingback chairs flanking the fireplace.

"We'll have to send someone by train to catch her. Is Thad still here?" Trenholm was already on his feet, coming around the corner of his desk.

"I haven't seen him." Hanson was also now on his feet, following the trader out of his office, into the accounting area. Trenholm saw Thad Howard bent over his desk, reviewing some records. He looked up to see the trader motioning for him to come into his office.

"Sit down, Thad. I want you to do something important for me. It's more for the Confederacy than for me. You remember that lovely lady you took down to the docks to leave a note for her beaux aboard *The Great Eastern?*"

"Who could forget her? She was gorgeous."

"Well, behind that beauty lies a brand of treachery that's about as bad as I've ever seen. The woman's a spy for the Yankees and has sent a telegram to the government in Washington, telling them the ship's destination and her cargo."

George Trenholm continued. "I want you to take the next train to Southampton, hire a ship and try to intercept the *Great Eastern* before she gets too far out to sea. We can't have her get caught unprepared by the enemy forces." He sat down and quickly scrawled a letter of authorization on company stationery, something the young overseer would need to charter a vessel. He quickly folded the letter, sealed it with beeswax and stamped the wax with the imprint of the firm. "Here's the necessary documentation you'll need to charter a ship. Draw some cash from the safe and get going. When you get there try to let me know what's happening."

The trader sat down with a heavy sigh. It was the first time Duncan Hanson had ever seen him so distraught. A breach of honor was, to this Southerner, an act worse than treason. It was an attack with a weapon, only instead of a knife or a gun it had been a beautiful woman.

The overseer stood in the door of the trader's office. "Do you think he can beat the ship, sir?"

"Well, the train is about twice as fast as the ship. If he can get one right away, I think we've got a chance." George Trenholm drew in a deep breath and slowly let it out.

7.

William Seward hurried down the hall towards the President's office, the official communiqué in his hand. A messenger from the British Embassy had just delivered the official reaction of the British government to the *Trent* boarding, from the Queen herself.

Lincoln was standing in the door of his office speaking to one of his male secretaries. He looked at the worried brow of his Secretary of State. They walked into his office and Seward closed the door. The situation was clearly very tense. Nobody sat down. Seward spoke.

"Mr. President, one of our ships intercepted the British mailship *Trent* and boarded her, taking two rebel diplomats prisoners. The Queen has demanded an apology and retribution or she will declare war on our shipping interests." He handed the President the communiqué.

The dark circles under the deep-set eyes of Abraham Lincoln were now matched by a darker frown. He had not had much sleep since the midnight cabinet meeting about *The Great Eastern* nine days ago. He read the carefully lettered words.

". . .and we consider this a serious breach of British sovereignty. We are dispatching several warships to the North Atlantic in anticipation of a state of war. Among them is the iron frigate *Warrior*."

Lincoln slowly sat down behind his desk. The Union could shortly be fighting the most powerful Navy in the world, besides waging its conflict with the South. He looked up at his Secretary of State, a deep frown on his forehead.

"I'll wager the *Warrior* will join forces with *The Great Eastern* and we'll end up fighting two heavily armed iron ships with our wooden ones. Better get Welles in here quickly," he said to Seward.

Within the hour, the President and his two cabinet officers drafted an apology to the Queen, not admitting any guilt but offering to release the two men when the *San Jacinto* reached Boston. It was dispatched to both the embassy and by telegram to the Queen herself.

By the time the apology reached the Queen, the warships had already gotten underway.

And the operations of assembling Southern cotton to be loaded aboard *The Great Eastern* upon her arrival on the South Carolina coast were nearing their conclusion.

8.

The staging area for the bales of cotton had been in operation for just two weeks. The heavy bales had been stacked off the loading platforms, awaiting transfer by wagon to the flatboats which would carry them out to the loading barges in Port Royal Sound. The slaves were laboring fourteen to sixteen hours a day unloading the heavy, unwieldy cotton bales.

Unloading the cargo was dangerous and tiring work. Each bale averaged 350 pounds apiece and it took three slaves to move them off the rough floorboards of the flatcars and freight cars onto the wagons waiting on the platforms. From there, it was but a few hundred feet down the steep embankment to the Coosawatchie and the flatboats.

More than one careless slave got an arm or leg crushed by the heavy bales. Several ended up in the cold waters of the river when they lost their balance or one of the bales pushed them overboard.

Then there was the movement of the trains themselves. The conductors, brakemen, and locomotive engineers were mostly from other areas of the South. Most of the slaves knew nothing of railroading, indeed, for many of them, their introduction to steam locomotives had been right in this yard. They soon learned that two toots of the engine whistle meant movement. They also learned not to stand between a stationary car and a moving train as they were likely to be crushed.

For Louis Beauregard, supervising the movement of the bales from railcar to barge meant long days and nights. The trains arrived when they arrived whether it was ten at night or four in the morning and had to be unloaded to free up the tracks for more trains and to send the empty cars back up the line for more cotton. At one point all eight tracks were in use and there were two more trains waiting on the siding outside the yard.

Colonel David Shackelford had helped the planters organize the slaves into shifts or watches, as he called them, of eight hours duration. Each watch was made up of forty to fifty slaves, overseen by a driver. Each watch also had a plantation owner and a military non-commissioned officer in charge. The planters rotated their shifts so no one had to do the midnight to eight watch every day.

But this meant that a watch sometimes had to do double duty; two watches in a row, and then two off. And it was always near the end of the second watch that accidents happened and lives and limbs were lost.

Louis Beauregard had just finished a double watch—it was now four in the afternoon. He was now free until eight the next morning, barring any serious accidents or calamities. Before he could rest, there was the accounting for what had been unloaded. The planter kept his records on foolscap, which he kept in a leather pouch for protection from the cold rain.

The cacophony of noise in the rail yard was now just a familiar din. Occasionally it would be punctuated by a scream—from someone getting hurt. The planter made his way across the tracks to the Colonel's headquarters tent where he would turn in his record of the night's transfers; whom the bales belonged to and how many had been transferred.

The sentinel saluted Beauregard and pulled the tent flap aside.

Inside, the Colonel's orderly had a fire blazing in the pot-bellied stove. The Colonel was at his table, reconciling the records of the preceding watch.

"Have a seat, Louis. Like a drink?" Even though he was a military commander, David Shackelford had relaxed the rules in this unusual union of military and civilian personnel.

"Thanks, Dave. What have you got?" Louis Beauregard managed a slight smile at the thought of a colonel pouring him a drink in his headquarters.

"One of my detachments came back from Beaufort with what was supposed to be the last case of Tennessee bourbon. Here, let me pour you a shot."

The planter sat down on one of the folding campstools and unhooked his tin cup from his belt and put it and his pouch on the Colonel's table. Shackelford produced his cup and the nearly full bottle with the black label with the big number seven on it.

"I've tested it, as you can see by the level in the bottle and certify it as thoroughly drinkable." Shackelford winked at the planter as he poured. Beauregard found the Army officer was one of the first he had met with a good sense of humor.

"To the Confederacy, *The Great Eastern*, our friends in England." The two Southerners touched their cups together and drank the toast. Shackelford quickly refilled them.

"Let's see how much cotton we moved." Beauregard was undoing the thong on the flap of the pouch. He pulled the foolscap pad out and handed it to Shackelford.

"I counted ten five-car trains the first shift and six three-car trains during the second shift. They were mostly flatcars, so that tallies up to sixty-eight cars. With each flatcar holding nine bales, I calculate we moved at least six hundred twelve bales since four o'clock yesterday afternoon. But here's the exact tally." Beauregard pointed to the figures on the paper.

"Not a bad watch, Louis." The Colonel took another sip of bourbon. "At this rate, we'll have everything unloaded before the ship gets here."

"How many more loads do they expect?"

"We should see the last of it in about a week, just about the time the ship arrives. Not having to haul the cotton down there at the same time we haul the munitions and ordnance up here will speed the unloading of the ship by making more wagons and flatboats available."

Louis Beauregard took the last sip of bourbon left in his cup.

"A refill?"

"Thanks. Just one more. It'll help me sleep." The planter drained his cup, hooked in his belt and stood up to leave. Shackelford handed him his pad of foolscap.

"Would you send someone to wake me in time for supper, Dave?" The fatigue and bourbon were conspiring to slur the planter's words.

"Is about an hour enough time?" The army officer looked at the planter's tired face.

Suddenly, a combination of train whistles blowing, bells clanging loudly and men shouting interrupted their conversation. The flap of Colonel Shackelford's tent was yanked open.

"Colonel, Colonel, come quickly! Some of the cotton bales caught fire!" It was Corporal Anderson excitedly waving his arms around. Louis Beauregard noticed he did not have his weapon at the ready.

The three men rushed out into the railroad yard to witness a column of white smoke boiling up from one of the platforms. Both slaves and army personnel alike were running around with canvas buckets, forming a line down to the Coosawatchie River to begin to pour water on the burning mass.

David Shackelford started barking orders. "You there," he pointed at a slave who was trying to bring a panicky team of horses under control, "take that wagon and team and get them away from the fire!"

Then, to a pair of soldiers running towards the supply shack. "Get as many of those buckets as you can carry and give them to everyone you see!"

Louis Beauregard noticed that the blaze had so far been confined to one or two flatcars and the platform. Fortunately, the cool night air was still, not fanning the flames.

"Dave, let's see if we can get that train backed out and separate the fire on the platform from the one on the cars. If we can back the train over the bridge at the head of the yard, maybe we can push the burning bales into the river. Then we'll only have to deal with the platform fire."

The last train to arrive in the yard was still being attended to by the locomotive engineer, who was in the process of banking the engine's coal fire. With David Shackelford nodding his agreement, Louis Beauregard sprinted across the tracks to the still-hissing locomotive.

"Engineer please get steam up! We need to switch those burning cars out over the river bridge and push the burning bales into the river! I'll get some help and meet you at the siding where the fire is!"

The engineer had already climbed into the cab of the locomotive. From out of nowhere another man was seen climbing into the other side of the cab. Louis Beauregard assumed it was the fireman. Good, he thought, now all we need to do is get a few slaves to get out by the bridge to help push the bales into the river.

The combined effects of the bourbon and extreme fatigue were working hard on Louis Beauregard. He turned to see what was being done about getting the slaves down out on the bridge's narrow catwalk to help push the burning bales into the river.. His feet felt like lead weights and as he walked towards the bridge he noticed he had no feeling in his feet. Once there, he saw that Dave Shackelford had things under control, having gathered a dozen or so slaves at the point where the track connects to the bridge. Each slave held a large pole, ready to leverage the bales off the flatcars and into the river.

He waved to the infantry colonel just as the train of flatcars backed onto the bridge. "Dave, if you don't need me anymore, I'm going to go lie down," he shouted over the din of the moving train.

An acknowledging wave from Dave Shackelford told him the infantry colonel had things under control. Wearily, Louis Beauregard turned and headed for his tent.

9.

Susannah lay partially undressed on the bed in her hotel room. It had been an extremely long and emotional day for her, starting with the last meal aboard *The Great Eastern* and her tearful and heartbreaking goodbyes with John Beauregard. As she sent the telegram to Percy disclosing the ship's contents and its destination, however, the emotion became a grim feeling for self-survival, becoming more determined with each word she wrote. All she could remember were Percy's threats for turning her in and his blunt description of what happens to a person's neck when the hangman's noose closes suddenly around it, cutting off air to the lungs and even snapping the windpipe in a last excruciating thrust of pain.

Now, trying to fall asleep and plan her next move, getting back to America and disappearing into the confusion of the wartime South, her emotions, successfully suppressed until now, began to burst up to the surface of her already-fragile state of mind. She began to bite her lip.

The room seemed unusually warm to her, so she got up off the bed and began to undress completely, throwing her underclothes in a heap on the foot of the bed.

John Beaureagard had looked absolutely magnificent in his uniform and full beard. She remembered the long, loving kiss he gave her as they said goodbye on the ship and how strong his arms were as he embraced her. She began to cry, collapsing in a naked curled heap on the bed's comforter. The cries became sobs and retching, almost uncontrolled.

She had probably sent John to his death, occurring in the certain battle that would be waged once *The Great Eastern* reached her destination. Along with John, she had put the caring and fatherly Alexander McLennan into grave danger. The sobs continued as she thought of the man she had finally been able to commit her life to, who would now only be a memory and one that would constantly remind of her perfidy.

The fatigue soon gave way to sleep, a restless series of twitches eventually blotting out her memory. She floated off, amongst mixed images of John, the ship, Alexander McLennan and his kindness and obvious affection.

Suddenly she saw John's image at the foot of her bed, the same blurry image she had seen just a few days before. This time his arms were not outstretched but folded across his chest. He was standing very rigidly and she could see a frown on his face. She started to cry, to tell the image how sorry she was and how she would turn herself into George Trenholm tomorrow morning and face whatever punishment would be given her. Anything ANYTHING, she screamed, *ANYTHING, I'll do anything to save you, John!*

Her screaming woke her up, and with it the image dissolved. The room still seemed hot and the comforter she had thrown over herself as she fell asleep was now tossed back in a heap, as she lay on the bed perspiring profusely. She lay there in a state of semi-consciousness, her mind at last a blank, with no tormenting images of the hell she was experiencing. With that silence, fatigue once again overcame her and she fell fitfully asleep.

She floated off again, in a dreamless drifting mode, virtually unconscious.

A harsh grip on her arm suddenly awoke her and she opened her eyes into the glare of two lanterns shining directly in her face. The comforter only partially hid her nakedness and, with her free arm, she snatched it up to cover her breasts.

"Susannah Eddings?" the voice queried her. "You're under arrest for betraying the United States of America." She saw the flash of a gun barrel pointed directly at her.

The terror welled up in her throat almost stifling her from saying anything. When it came out, her reply was in a high-pitched wail.

"Who are you? What are you talking about? I'm a citizen of the Confederate States of America and I'll have you arrested for barging in here like this..."

The deep male voice cut her off. The gun moved menacingly closer to her face.

"Get up," the voice barked, releasing his grip on her arm, "and put some traveling clothes on. You're going back to the United States to stand trial for treason. And make it snappy. You ship's leaving in just a couple of hours."

The two lanterns were set down on the nightstand and Susannah could at last see whom her accusers were. One was a tall man dressed in a heavy overcoat. The other, the one with the gun, still pointed at her, was short and stocky, dressed like someone who worked on the docks.

She wrapped the comforter around herself and swung her legs off the bed, stood up and walked behind the dressing screen in the corner of the hotel room.

"Could you please put my undergarments and that dress that are on the bed on the screen here so I can get dressed?" Her voice was still high pitched and stressed. "And while you're doing that, please tell me what grounds you have for arresting me?"

"Saw the telegram you sent to the Mr. Percy in the U.S. Military Office in Washington, telling him all about *The Great Eastern.* Mr. Trenholm took steps to warn the ship's captain, but it's probably too late."

"And who are you?" Susannah began to get ahold of herself.

"Name's Thad Howard. I work for Mr. Trenholm. You'll be in my custody aboard the *Bermuda* on the trip to Charleston. Now hurry it up, Miss. We won't miss that ship, even if I have to tie you up and carry you there myself."

"Do I have chance to send a note to Mr. Trenholm?" Susannah thought perhaps contacting the trader with a personal appeal for clemency, citing their friendship, might at least delay the process.

"No. Mr. Trenholm's seen enough of you and your treachery. He's too busy trying to undo the harm and danger you've put the ship and its crew under. Now hurry up and get dressed."

She started to cry and then stopped, sensing that this would be a sign of weakness and guilt. She finished dressing and came out from behind the screen to confront her captors.

"What about my clothes and baggage. Can I bring those along?"

"No. We'll have the hotel pack them up and send them along to the ship. If they get there before the ship sails, you'll have them. But you WILL be aboard the ship!" Thad Howard's deep voice resonated throughout the room.

Susannah laced up her boots quickly, sensing that the two men meant business and that she'd rather walk out of the hotel than be carried out like some trussed-up animal.

10.

Although the coaling schooners had left Norfolk a week ago, the fleet of ships assembled by Captain Samuel Francis Du Pont was not due to depart until today. The slower colliers would eventually space themselves out over the length of the east coast of the United States, ready to disgorge their cargo to satisfy the voracious appetites of the steam frigates.

There were more than fifty vessels in this fleet, and they had been assembled to overwhelm Forts Walker and Beauregard that flanked Port Royal sound. The objective was to capture the body of water and the area surrounding it to provide a safe deep-south port for the blockading fleet. Its location would increase the time a given ship could stay on station and put more pressure on the burgeoning Confederate blockade-running activity.

The fleet had barely gotten underway when Captain Du Pont, on the bridge counting the vessels that were still in the channel, noticed a harbor tug following his flagship, the *Wabash*. She was belching thick black smoke, a sure sign that she was trying to catch up to his warship.

"Signal the vessel aft that we're heaving to, to let her catch us." Captain Du Pont grabbed the engine room speaking tube. "Mr. Taft, I want all engines stopped."

Slowing a 3000-ton vessel, loaded for a long trip and a prolonged battle was not done quickly. The *Wabash* continued to drift down the channel at five knots. Captain Du Pont could now see the tiny Morse light flashing off the bow of the lighter.

HAVE URGENT MESSAGE FROM WASHING TON FOR

CAPTAIN DUPONT

Captain Du Pont read the signal, wondering what sort of news might be coming from the Capital. He turned to the duty officer. "Signal confirmation of the message."

The gap between the vessels had now narrowed to less than one hundred yards. Within minutes, the smaller ship was alongside the steam frigate, and her first officer was scurrying up the boarding ladder and escorted to the bridge.

First Lieutenant Robert Smith saluted the admiral handsomely, punctuating it with a click of his heels. Captain Du Pont returned the salute slowly and accepted the sealed envelope.

He ripped open the envelope, noticing the wax seal bore the stamp of the Commander of the United States Naval Base. He opened the sheet of paper. The first thing he saw was the signatory: "Welles." He began to frown.

"Thank you, Lieutenant. Please inform the Commandant that you have accomplished your mission." Smith saluted again, and turned to leave the ship.

Captain Du Pont slowly reread the message from his boss. They were to steam directly southeast to intercept a chartered British vessel, *The Great Eastern*, a ship Captain Du Pont had heard about but never seen. She was underway with contraband for the Confederacy and was to be treated as any other blockade runner-contraband seized or destroyed, crew imprisoned, ship destroyed. That was Welles' order, to the letter.

"Destroy *The Great Eastern*? Why she's made of iron. Has the Secretary lost his head? She'll likely destroy us before we can get to her." The incredulous voice came from the officer on a duty, a redheaded first lieutenant named Jefferson, who was reacting to what Captain Du Pont had just told him.

"Let's get this ship underway again, Mr. Jefferson," the admiral ordered, "then I want you to convene a meeting in the wardroom of all the officers. We will have to change our strategy, and inform the rest of the fleet of the changes in plans. We've got a lot to get done in a very short space of time."

Captain Du Pont had already left the bridge to stop off at his cabin to consult his copy of **The Record of American and Foreign Shipping**, the thick registry published in New York that listed every ship, its dimensions, and all other vital statistics, for insurance purposes. He reminded himself to question his officers about the ship, in case one of them had ever been on board.

11.

Lieutenant Stephen Trenchard steadied himself against the rolls the *Hartford* was making as she wallowed through the heavy swells of the South Atlantic. He was on his way down the narrow passageway to the Captain's quarters in the rear of the ship.

The trip down from Wilmington had strained his crew and the *Rhode Island* as well. Steaming at full power for two days put all kinds of strain on the wooden vessel and her iron engine. Gaskets leaked faster under the constant pressure of steam, mechanical parts broke more frequently in the power train, and the men themselves were dead tired from long watches and fitful sleep. It was quite a different matter to travel in the open ocean under full steam as opposed to chasing blockade-runners in the quiet waters closer to the coast.

Trenchard removed his hat and gently knocked on the door. From inside he heard the deep voice of Captain David Farragut.

"Yes, who is it?"

"Lieutenant Stephen Trenchard of the *Rhode Island*, sir, bearing an urgent message from Secretary Welles."

The door opened and Trenchard shifted his hat to his left hand so he could salute Farragut. He was impressed by the erect posture and strong gaze.

"Come in, come in, Commander. Welcome aboard the *Hartford*. What the hell's so urgent that Secretary Welles sent you chasing me over half the ocean?"

"Don't know, sir. Dispatch is marked for your attention and sealed with the Commandant's seal."

"Well, let's see what our commander wants. I hope its not bad news— that we have to do any more fighting. This ship has been halfway around the world and needs repairs." Farragut was ripping the envelope open.

"Please sit down, Commander."

Trenchard pulled out a chair and sat at the small table in the Captain's cabin that was used when Farragut ate in his cabin or had small meetings with his officers.

He looked up at the face of the fleet commander. It was like a cloud had passed over the sun. Farragut's brow furrowed. "Have you ever heard of *The Great Eastern*, Commander?"

Farragut was staring at Trenchard.

"Yessir, she's that huge iron white elephant ship of the British. Why do you ask?"

Farragut proceeded to disclose the contents of the message to the young commander. "We should intercept her in a couple of days Commander. What were your orders after you were told to deliver this to me?"

"To put myself and my ship at your disposal."

"Excellent. Consider it done. I'll have the order drawn up immediately. Like a drink?" The Admiral was reaching into his locker. He placed a bottle of rum and two glasses on the table.

"Thank you, sir." Farragut filled the two tumblers halfway and set the bottle down.

"To the Union." The two men touched glasses and swallowed half the contents.

"How's your ship—her condition, I mean?" The Admiral looked at his subordinate.

"She's in fair shape. Needs a few minor things. Those days under full steam put a strain on everything. A couple of normal duty days ought to have her back to her old self."

"How are your gunnery skills? Men pretty sharp when it comes to shooting?"

"Yessir." Trenchard swallowed the rest of the fiery liquid. "We've had a lot of practice chasing those fast blockade-runners. We've been able to capture two of them."

"Good. I want you to stay aboard for a meeting with my officers. I'll have my men signal your ship that you'll be here overnight." Farragut grabbed his speaking tube to the bridge.

"Send my steward down immediately."

Stephen Trenchard wondered how heavily armed *The Great Eastern* was. David Farragut suppressed his feelings that they were being sent to their death. His wooden ships were no match for the British iron ones. He would have to stop the ship by superior maneuvers and tactics. Both men knew they were facing a formidable foe.

12.

From the dockworkers to the shipowners in Liverpool, the blockade-runner *Bermuda* was a renegade hero. Even though the British government was ambivalent about the recognition of the Confederacy, popular sentiment was overwhelmingly sympathetic to the South. When word got out that British sovereignty had been violated in the *Trent* boarding, reaction became even more outspoken. News that the Queen had dispatched the new iron frigate *Warrior* to protect British shipping interests only intensified and provoked verbal and printed expressions of support for the rebels.

Having made the first successful penetration of the blockade back in August, the British-built *Bermuda* had originally been constructed for George Trenholm's trading company and was now loading arms, munitions, and luxuries for another run, this time to Charleston.

On the chilly dock, Susannah Eddings sat on her trunk, her wrists bound tightly together. Standing in back of her, watching the ship load her cargo was Thad Howard. Susannah felt totally mortified from her exposure—it had been more humiliating than she imagined. Her face was red as she remembered trying desperately to persuade her captor to let her send a note to George Trenholm. She cringed, knowing he would get word to John and eventually his uncle would also find out. Her family would never forgive her; her mother would be humiliated but would probably continue to love her. And now she was to return to the United States for certain imprisonment and possible death, ironically aboard the very ship that had brought her and the stolen plans for the U.S.S. *Monitor* triumphantly to England.

George Trenholm had given Thad the unpleasant duty of taking Susannah into his custody after discovering her perfidy. He had already notified the Confederate authorities of her treason and requested that she be arrested and tried as a traitor.

The thick black smoke that was coming out of the stack of the blockade-runner indicated the engine room was getting up steam and was ready to leave.

Thad nudged his prisoner and Susannah got up and walked towards the gangplank. Susannah looked up at the figure of Captain Eugene Tessier. She became terrified.

"Captain Tessier, this is the prisoner Mr. Trenholm mentioned. She's to be quartered by herself, under lock and key. I'm responsible to see she's handed over to the authorities when we get to Charleston. She's to be under armed escort when it's necessary for her to leave her cabin."

The captain stood over the stooped shoulders, the head hanging in shame. "I totally misjudged you, Miss Eddings. Instead of being a heroine, you're a heel. No better than some of the strumpets that hang around this wharf." The now-famous captain of the now-famous blockade-runner looked quizzically at the beautiful young woman being remanded to him for custody in his ship. Susannah stared at the dock, thoroughly shamed.

"What have you to say for yourself?" The captain's voice had the tone of a judge and jury who had just found the defendant guilty.

She raised her eyes to those of her inquisitor. They were beginning to fill with tears.

"I'm so sorry." It was all she could think of to say.

"Well, you'll get no favored treatment from me or any of my crew. You're lucky to have an armed escort, 'cause I'm sure one of my men would likely kill you as soon as we got to sea. Take her out of my sight, Mr. Howard. She's in Cabin 3A. It's two decks down in the bow of the ship."

Cabin 3A was indeed in the bow of the ship, sharing the area with the ship's brig. The accommodations were not much better; a far cry from the stateroom she was accorded on the trip over. A single porthole was the only source of light and ventilation. A small coal stove did little to remove the dampness of a cabin so close to the water and the bilge of the ship. There was barely enough room for Susannah's trunk in the crowded room. Her bed was a canvas sling.

"I'll be down to check on you in the morning before the midday meal and in the evening before dinner. No one else will be authorized to let you out of your cabin."

He reached for Susannah's bound wrists and undid the leather thong that had bound them. He noticed the red welts on her arms, the result of being tied up. He could not but help to notice the long shapely fingers and the tapered nails, broken and torn from her being arrested and bound. She looked like a fallen angel: her hair had not been brushed since her capture two days before. It was now a mass of tangles.

He went out into the passageway and turned for a last look at this striking woman who had fallen into disgrace. She had her back to him and she, too, slowly turned to look at the handsome overseer.

"God help you, ma'am." The words were almost a damnation.

He pulled the narrow door shut and turned the lock. As he walked away, he could hear her sobs, even over the shrill whistle of the ship as began to get underway.

13.

While conditions aboard *The Great Eastern* were uncomfortable, they were almost unbearable aboard the *Bermuda*. She was crossing the ocean on a more northerly route than the larger vessel and was encountering the same storm that was battering the heavily laden ship.

Susannah had been seasick all night and was lying partially unclothed in her canvas hammock. The airless room retained the sour odor from her sickness and she had been too ill to even try and open the tiny porthole.

Thad Howard had been down to look into Susannah's condition but each time she had been asleep. He was beginning to feel sorry for this outcast woman, who now was only wanted by the hangman. He wished there was some way he could help her but realized that any help or sympathy he showed her would be misconstrued as disloyalty to George Trenholm.

While on this visit, he had decided to change the washbasin where she had been sick. That was just human decency. He slid the key into the lock, knocked gently on the door and opened it slowly. The fetid, foul air made him gag. Susannah was slumped in a heap on the canvas hammock. One of her breasts was partly exposed, and for a moment Thad forgot about the odor and what fate was to befall her. He saw her partial nudity and the desire to have her overwhelmed him temporarily.

He set the clean washbasin and chamberpot and reached under the hammock and brought the soiled ones out, standing up to set them out in the passageway. Crossing over to the porthole he reached up and gave it a yank. It squeaked open and a rush of cold damp air came in. He stared at the beautiful face, now streaked with dried tears, dirt and matted hair. *God she's beautiful*, he thought, wanting to get a cloth and clean up the mess so the beauty would radiate again. The cool fresh air caused her to stir, and she rolled over and opened her eyes.

"I brought you a clean washbasin and chamberpot, as well as some bread and fresh water. I thought you might need it."

"Thank you. I'm feeling a little better now. She quickly pulled her blouse around the partially exposed breast. "How long have you been standing there?"

"Oh... about five minutes," he stuttered, somewhat embarrassed. "I'm not supposed to let you out but I could probably arrange for you to take a quick bath before dinner."

Susannah looked at her filthy clothes. "I would really appreciate that. I haven't had a real bath since I was in the hotel a week ago." Her voice was hoarse from the vomiting but the thought of a bath clearly perked her up.

He was glad to see her feeling better. "I'll be back in about a half an hour. I'll sneak you into the captain's quarters; he's got the only tub." He pulled the door shut and turned the lock.

With her stomach quieting down, Susannah could better think about her desperate situation. Could she somehow escape when the ship got closer to Charleston? This kindness on Thad's part, could she coax it into something more? If she slept with him would he help her escape? Who would know—he was the only one with access to her cabin. Perhaps he could slip her overboard on one of the ship's lifeboats as they got closer to Charleston and the two of them could row to safety.

Maybe the idea was too preposterous. Wasn't this another betrayal to John? Her self-survival came back.

Yes, she rationalized, *but then I could see him again, explain everything, get my life straightened out and live someplace in hiding until the war is over. We could get married and have everything we wanted.* Her disillusionment of her plight was complete. There were too many chances at getting caught. She overlooked almost all of them.

She heard the key in the lock and the soft knock. "What did you find out?" she asked.

He closed the door behind him. "We'll have to hurry. The watches are due to change in another hour. Nobody's there. Here's a towel and my soap. I'll stand guard in the passageway."

"Can I wash out some clothes after I'm finished bathing?" She had noticed how disgusting they were. Grabbing her robe, she looked up at him.

"Sure, but let's hurry."

They tiptoed down the passageway towards the middle of the ship, Thad checking to make sure no one saw them.

After the quick bath in cold sea water, she rinsed out her mouth and scrubbed the clothes in the soapy bathwater. She threw on a robe, carrying her wet clothes and dress under her arm. They hurried along the passageway, at last arriving at Cabin 3A. He opened the door and noticed for the first time she wasn't wearing anything but the robe. Her hair was wet but had regained its sparkling henna luster he remembered that morning when he took her to the dock. She turned and smiled at him. Her ruby full lips parted to show her sparkling teeth.

"Thank you for your kindness." She stood on her tiptoes and lightly kissed him. His mustache tickled her nose.

The kiss surprised him but he smiled back at her. "You know, another time, another place and I'd kiss you back. There's too much at stake, Susannah."

"There's no obligation. I just wanted to thank you." She had turned and was hanging the wet clothes on the short rope that stretched across the tiny cabin.

He was standing in the doorway, watching her reach up as the robe clung to her still damp body. She closed the porthole and seductively smiled at him with her intense inviting brown eyes.

"I'll bring your dinner up in about an hour," he stuttered again, his total arousal affecting his speech. He closed the door, turned the lock and withdrew the key.

14.

The huge crash woke John Beauregard out of his fitful sleep. Something had broken loose on the deck above and it was only a matter of the next roll to starboard that would bring whatever-it-was to the opposite side of the ship.

The Great Eastern had been running in heavy seas for two days. They were astride the Gulf Stream and experiencing the vicissitudes of that current's strength. The ship had been battened down and two of the crewmen had already been washed overboard. John had not had a square meal for almost three days, his watches crowded with keeping steam up and the machinery in the aft engine room functioning.

The strain on the ship's powerplants was beginning to tell. They had already had to replace the bearings in the propeller shaft, a job that entailed not only shutting down the engine while underway but rigging a small hoist to lift the heavy shaft out of her housing so the worn bearings could be replaced. One of the Welsh crewmen lost his footing in the narrow slippery shaft passage and had it pinned under the heavy shaft as it was being lowered into place. Before they could lift it high enough, the shaft crushed his entire lower leg, the remains leaving a slimy mess of crushed pink bone, white muscle and red blood hanging from the shaft. Someone had the good sense to grab a fire axe from the engine room bulkhead and separate the man from his limb before they lifted the shaft off the crushed leg.

John had never heard a scream of pain like the one that came out this man's mouth. He had passed out, the pain mercifully providing unconsciousness. They carried the man off to the dispensary, where the surgeon would finish the amputation. Someone scraped the flesh and bone off the shaft so it wouldn't interfere with the rotation of the long cylindrical object which connected the engine to the ship's propeller. John watched the bloody mess slither down towards the rear of the ship, sloshing around in the brackish water of the bilge.

Bang! Bang! Bang! The loose missive on the deck had indeed careened across to the other side.

Whatever it is that is loose needs someone to tie it down before it destroys something, the young lieutenant mused. He decided to get up, although it was just three-thirty in the morning, a full thirty minutes before he was to relieve William Slater. He caught himself falling as the ship pitched steeply to starboard. He pulled on his tunic and trousers, shoved his feet into the cold boots that had been soaking up the cold from the iron deck since he had tried to go to sleep almost three hours ago, and threw his oilskins on, knowing that within five minutes on deck he would be soaked to the skin. *Well, I'll be able to get dry in the engine room,* he thought to himself.

The journey from his cabin down the ship's passageway and up the ladders was a perilous one. He opened the hatch to the deck, and the wind ferociously tore it out of his hands. The ship was in the middle of a gale and John could see that the cold rain and sea spray were being driven almost vertically. There was ice everywhere. A lifeline forward to the bridge was the only secure way to the ship's command post.

He gingerly made his way down the deck towards the bridge, narrowly avoiding getting hit by some wooden boxes that had broken loose and now slid from side to side of the ship as she rolled like a lazy walrus in the current. He could not see the bridge, even though it was only about one hundred fifty feet from the passageway hatch, so bad was the storm. Then, in the darkness, he saw a shapeless mass sliding towards him on the icy deck. As it slid across the deck it bumped into the stanchions and mast bases. John Beauregard recognized the noise although it was not the amplified banging he had heard in his cabin. As it slid by him, he could make out the markings of an armament factory in Sheffield and the numbers 1861 on the canvas cover.

A human shape emerged from the rain as the mass collided with the railing, the front part of it lodging between the stanchions, immobilizing it, at least for the time being. The human shape turned out to be Captain Paton who stopped and cupped his one free hand to his mouth. The other held tight to the lifeline.

"Get below! This is no place for anyone who doesn't have to be here!" He motioned for the young lieutenant to go back to the hatch. They slowly made their way back to the safety of the bowels of the ship. Beauregard wrestled with the heavy hatchway, finally pulling it shut with the help of the Captain.

"The barometer's starting to rise so I think we've been through the worst of it." The captain had taken his oilskin hat off and was shaking the water off of it.

"Any damage to the ship sir?"

"Minor, from cargo breaking loose. One of the lookouts didn't report back after his watch. I guess he's gone. A couple of the lifeboats came loose but we managed to save 'em before they got battered up. You due on watch?"

The casual reference to the abandonment of a crewmember showed how callous even Walter Paton could be about the immigrant sailors. John Beauregard decided to take everyone's advice and bury his feelings for the time being.

"Yes sir, I couldn't sleep with all the noise and rolling around. When will we be there?"

"We should sight the coast in about twelve hours. These damn seas have cut our speed in half. Have you checked the new bearings on the shaft to see if they've seated themselves?"

"No sir, that's not due to be done until this evening. I was told to let them run for forty-eight hours before I make any adjustments."

"I want you to check them and give me a report after you come off watch. Please make sure the job gets done properly." The inference was that the captain didn't trust anyone on the watch beside he and William Slater. A small prideful feeling welled up in the young lieutenant's chest, temporarily replacing his ill feelings towards his commanding officer.

The two made their way down the hatch, stopping at the first level, the level of the Captains quarters. Beauregard saluted his commanding officer. He had quickly learned why the ship's owners had picked this man to shepard the vessel on so important and potentially profitable voyage.

Walter Paton, like John Beauregard and William Slater, understood steam engines, something his predecessors did not. He was preoccupied with maintenance and proper adjustments in pressure, heat and all of the mechanical joints which translated the mysterious vapor into such awesome power. There were so few men who had the experience because the technology applied to such a large ship was basically still in its infancy.

John turned and made his way down the ladder to the comparative warm comfort of the ship's screw engine room.

15.

A soft knock woke Susannah up. She had been asleep the better part of two days and two nights, now that the ship was in calmer waters.

"Who is it?" She knew it would be Thad.

The key turned in the lock and the handsome young overseer stepped quickly into the cabin and shut the door. From a cloth bag, he produced a small bottle of wine and two tin cups. "We'll be in Charleston tomorrow morning. I thought you might enjoy this before...before tomorrow."

She swung her legs seductively over the side of the hammock. "How thoughtful of you, Thad." The full lips parted in a wide smile. "You have really looked after me on this trip. Why? You told me you thought what I did was despicable, and, indeed, all I have for that is sorrow and remorse. If I could tell you the reason I did it you would understand better. But there are too many people involved and they'd be hurt."

He had set the two cups down on Susannah's trunk and was extracting the cork from the bottle. After a brief struggle, it popped out.

"I have been interested in you since Mr. Trenholm asked me to escort you to the docks. Whatever you have done, you'll have to live with. I feel sorry for you and would like to do something to help save your life. I know about John Beauregard but doubt you'll ever see him again."

They each took a sip of the wine. He was infatuated with her deep brown eyes, her dark hair and her magnificent body. She put down her cup and took his hand in hers. Very gently she brought it towards her and gazed provocatively into his eyes.

"If there was some way I could thank you, I would do it." She had placed his hand on her lips.

He put down his cup and stood up. In an instant he was at her side, sitting on the hammock. He put his arm around her shoulder and she tilted her face to his.

"There is something." He was now kissing the full mouth, finding it as soft and exciting as he had anticipated. He pulled her closer, simultaneously taking off most of her clothes as quickly as he could. His lust overcame him as he continued to kiss her passionately, almost tumbling as he fell over on the hammock. His face was flushed as he forced himself into her roughly. Susannah pretended John was in bed with her, remembering how his passion was tempered by his love.

When he was finished, he raised himself off the hammock and began to dress. She sat up and pulled her clothes back on. They had not even gotten fully undressed. Susannah remembered a similar event with John in the park in Charleston where they had remained partially dressed. But that time it had seemed much more intense, much more overwhelming and tempered by love.

She maintained her countenance of caring. "Thad, you said you'd like to spare my life. Would you help me escape if we could think of a way to not disgrace you in front of Mr. Trenholm?"

He stared at her, his face a mixture of expressions. The one she saw was mild disbelief.

"Escape? To where?"

She laid out her plan: a midnight escape in one of the lifeboats. He would assist her in lowering the boat and provide her with enough food and water for a day. They would do this when they were less than an hour from the mouth of Charleston harbor, at night of course.

He thought it would be very difficult to accomplish.

"I have to go and eat now and bring you your supper. I'll think about it and look over the logistic possibilities. I'll be back in about an hour with an answer. What about your things?"

"I'll leave them. Perhaps you can send them to me after the war."

He had finished buttoning his coat. "I'll see you later."

John would have kissed her goodbye. She felt unclean, the same way she felt after she had made love with the Union officers and

Cornelius Bushnell in Washington. She closed the door of the cabin, hearing him turn the key in the lock. She wondered if she had given herself to him for nothing.

The wind on deck seemed to have shifted. Instead of blowing perpendicular to the ship's course, it now seemed that they were headed into the wind. Thad Howard decided to seek out the Captain to see if they had changed course in the last few hours.

"Yep," was the terse answer from Captain Tessier, who was on the bridge in the waning daylight, his spyglass sweeping the horizon for signs of Union warships. "We're headed for Beaufort or Port Royal. There's less chance that we'll get shot at. Last time I came out of Charleston, I really had a run of it."

"When do you expect we'll sight land?" Thad Howard began to get concerned.

"I'm puttin' in close to shore as soon as it's dark. That ought to be within the hour. By the way, how's your prisoner? In good health, I hope. She'll get hers when we get ashore."

He resumed his horizon sweeps with his spyglass.

Thad decided he would help Susannah escape as soon as the watch changed after midnight.

16.

The issue of the conscripted sailors had been suppressed, at least as far as John Beauregard's feelings were concerned. Not so for some of the crew of *The Great Eastern.*

John Beauregard was totally unprepared for the attack. The blows seemed to come from everywhere; on the back of his head and neck, into his groin and even over his wildly flailing arms and hands.

There were at least three attackers that he could see in the semi-darkness of *The Great Eastern's* lower deck passageway. While all of them had some sort of club to deliver the bruising blows, John Beauregard had nothing but his fists to defend himself.

He had just finished the midnight watch in the screw engine room. It had been a hard shift; the screw shaft had been vibrating for the last twenty-four hours in a very uncharacteristic way. He had suggested a shutdown of the propulsion system to check out how the bearings were seated, but had been overruled by the first officer, citing the loss of speed and subsequent danger to the ship and its cargo. John Beauregard had gone so far as to invoke the Captain's name, citing the request made to the young officer by Captain Paton just hours earlier to check how the new bearings were wearing in, but since the Captain was asleep, the first officer was in charge and his command stood.

There had been words between the two officers. The first officer on duty, an up-from-the-ranks British sailor who had been at sea for over twenty years, resented the younger officer's superior knowledge of the powerful steam engine that was his ward. If that wasn't bad enough, John Beauregard's interference with the constant beatings of the uncooperative crew struck the officer as insubordination, something that should receive some sort of discipline. But it was John Beauregard's status as an observer on board the ship, an observer from a country with an entirely different culture that rankled the officer the most.

For now, John Beauregard was fighting for his life. When one of his attackers went for his groin again, he grabbed the club away from the burly seaman and quickly whirled around with it, knocking his assailant off balance, onto the hard metal deck of the passageway.

"I'll 'ave your 'ead for that!" One of the other two managed to grab John Beauregard around the neck, temporarily immobilizing the officer, and giving the third seaman a chance to deliver a deadly blow to the Confederate's nose. But the ship suddenly took a sharp roll to starboard, causing all three of them to collapse in a heap, falling on top of the already-prone seaman.

One of the three managed to leap to his feet, steadying himself by holding onto the bulkhead. Temporarily disarmed, their clubs rolling around on the passageway floor, the other two flung themselves on John Beauregard, pummeling him with their fists.

His nose began to ooze blood and the young officer could feel pain in his groin and his chest. But now all three of the sailors were punching his face, his head, his chest; any exposed part of his body that he could not cover with his now-swollen hands.. He was dizzy from all the blows and unable to protect himself from the assault. One of the assailants was picking up one of the clubs and prepared to bring it down on the young officer's body when one of the other sailors stopped him.

"Let 'im be," the sailor said. "I thinks he knows to not mess with the crew no more."

The other sailor got up and the three of them stared at the now-still body of John Beauregard.

"In case ya' don't get it, mate,"the spokesman for the group warned, "this is to tell ya' to stop gettin' in the way of the crew gettin' punished. It's none of yur damn business, so stay away! Ya" hear me?"

John Beauregard, unconscious by now, was unable to answer. The three sailors picked up their clubs and staggered down the passageway.

BLOCKADE RUNNER
BOOK 5

1.

An eerie yellow color, diffused by the cold mist hanging over the water, had begun to intensify. The sun was making a feeble attempt to show that she could still radiate light and some limited warmth, in spite of the early morning October chill.

The morning watch on the parapets of Fort Walker stared in fascination as the frenzy of activity increased, about one thousand feet from where they stood. Everyone knew about the cotton, and that some ship was coming to pick it up and unload much needed military supplies. But it was the first time they had ever seen such a concentration of cotton bales, steamships, pontoon boats and activity in a body of water that was normally just a peaceful sound, alive with waterfowl and vegetation.

A barge was anchored in the middle of the deepest part of the sound, packed with the stacked bales. Some of the guards guessed the stacks were over twenty feet high. The small flotillas of longboats, barges and pontoon boats, towed by small steam coasters, were still arriving from up the river, themselves loaded to the gunwales.

For Thomas Chaplain, it was just the beginning of another weary day. Thomas had the unthankful role of overseeing the slaves as they unloaded the bales from the small boats. Using both brute force and two steam-powered cranes, his workforce stacked the bales carefully to conserve space on the huge barge.

They were almost at capacity, the unloading and stacking process having gone on for almost three weeks. Chaplain had passed word up the river to the railhead that they would be out of storage space within a couple of days. If *The Great Eastern* didn't arrive by then, the whole process of unloading the railcars, loading the

223

boats, floating or towing them down the river to the barge, and stacking them up to await the British vessel's arrival, would have to be stopped.

Chaplain, like Louis Beauregard had been enlisted by the military to supervise the crews. But he was on the opposite side of the supply chain. He watched careless slaves lose their footing on the slippery barge and fall into the chilly dark water. Most of them had never learned to swim, so by the time someone was able to throw them something to cling to, they drowned. He witnessed one of the crane operators lose an arm when he had reached into the machinery of one of the cranes to try and untangle the mechanism. The machine, for some reason, unsnarled itself and the heavy gears grabbed the man's jacket, and, before someone could throw a lever to stop it, the machine crushed the man's hand and most of his forearm into a bloody pulp.

Chaplain was one of the first to reach the scene of the accident. There was blood everywhere, and the remains of the man's arm hung off one of the winch's gears. He gently lifted the man's body off the machinery, and laid him on the wooden deck of the barge. The operator had fainted from the pain and Chaplain had shouted to the crew of a nearly unloaded boat that they should get the man's mangled remains upriver to the army doctors.

That was over three days ago. Last night, Chaplain learned the man had died from bleeding, before he had even been delivered to the doctors. He wondered if things wouldn't be better without all this machinery.

He slowly walked down to the end of the barge to greet another set of pontoon boats, strung out behind the tiny steam launch that was their towboat.

Things were a little different, half a mile out in the Atlantic. The ironclad *Columbia* was doing her best to stay on course. But it was a difficult task. The men who designed and built her had never intended it to be put to sea. It was designed for river duty, and, as such, became unstable in the ocean current. It's heavy iron bulwarks, low freeboard, and an engine that was not made to fight strong ocean currents contributed to its handling difficulty.

The crew of the ship had been braving the five-foot swells for the past two days, waiting on station for signs of *The Great Eastern*.

Columbia was to be the pilot ship, guiding the larger ship into the safety of the natural harbor. Once there, she would return to her station offshore to guard the precious logistical undertaking that would shortly be taking place in the Sound.

Captain Bryan Griffith had gotten up before dawn, tired from being unable to sleep soundly in the pitching vessel. He went up to the bridge, his spyglass immediately scanning the horizon for telltale smoke. The eerie yellow of the earlier sunrise had been replaced with a whitish grey glow, with the sun a round white disc, trying to pierce the clouds, but not succeeding.

"Mr. Smith, run up the signal flags. I see smoke on the horizon."

The *Columbia,* wallowed in the trough of a swell, making it almost impossible to see above the top of the waves. In the next instant, the ironclad rose to the crest of the swell and the cloud of black smoke, larger than Griffith had ever seen, became a long dark shape. He counted six masts and what he thought were five funnels.

"Sir, smoke on the horizon!" The starboard lookout had also spotted the ship.

The mass was immense. The closer she got, the bigger she got. The off duty and on duty crewmen crowded the decks of the small gunboat to catch a glimpse of the world's biggest ship. They were not disappointed.

"Captain, another ship off the port side!" The fascination at watching the British merchantman-turned-man-o'-war obscured the arrival of the *Sumter,* Rafael Semmes' raider. Griffith walked across the bridge to view the arrival of the Confederate vessel. The layup and repairs accomplished in New Orleans had rendered the vessel fit for the coming conflict.

The players were beginning to arrive for the game.

2.

William Slater stood outside the doorway of the small infirmary on the second deck of *The Great Eastern*. The ship had just crossed the Gulf Stream and the constant pitching and rolling that had characterized the journey of the past few days had subsided. He was therefore able to stand without holding onto anything, although his second instincts still had him in a wide stance; his "sea legs."

He had stumbled into the unconscious body of John Beauregard as he had come off watch and had seen a pool of blood next to John Beauregard's head. When he bent down to look at his face, he saw it was a mass of dried blood, and raw pink tissue. John Beauregard's nose had been severely deformed and both eyes had dark circles around them. Slater had quickly grasped his limp wrist to see if there was a pulse and breathed a sigh of relief to find there was. After summoning two seamen, the three of them managed to drag the body to the dispensary. While the two seamen wrestled the young lieutenant's body onto the bunk, William Slater decided to wake up the ship's surgeon. Concerned for his countryman's safety, he told the seaman to stay with John Beauregard until he returned.

After seeing John Beauregard's injured face, the surgeon sent the two seaman to notify Captain Paton and Alexander McLennan of John Beauregard's condition. Meanwhile, John Beauregard began to regain consciousness.

Captain Paton and Alexander McLennan lost no time in getting to the dispensary. The Captain gently knocked on the door and the surgeon, a Scotsman named McGuinness, opened it. The Captain ordered one of the two seamen to stand guard outside the dispensary door,

Until those responsible for the beating of this officer were identified and appropriately charged, Captain Paton did not want to take any chances.

"Yessir!" The seaman, armed with an Enfield rifle, snapped his heels together, holding the weapon at port arms.

The Captain and Alexander McLennan stepped into the small room. Dr. McGuinness had resumed cleaning John Beauregard's wounds, although he was moaning from the pain.

"I've given him morphine, so he'll be out of pain soon. His nose is broken, although just across the bridge. After the morphine takes effect, I'll put it in a splint. His eyes are okay, just bruised, as are his arms and legs. I don't think he's had any internal injuries, but I still haven't given him a complete examination. While he's still conscious, I thought you might like to talk to him. But please be brief. I'll be back in ten minutes."

William Slater stepped to the side of the bunk and gently grabbed the young lieutenant's hand. He was surprised when the hand squeezed him back.

"Took a bit of a beating eh, John? The doc says outside of a broken nose, the rest of you seems all right. Do you know who did it?"

The young officer could barely talk. His breath was coming in short gasps. "I just asked him if he knew who was responsible for the beating, Captain," William Slater said.

Slowly, word by painful word, John Beauregard unfolded the tale of the noisy propeller shaft bearing, it's subsequent vibration and his disagreement with the first officer on duty for his watch.

The Captain thought a moment. "That would be Pearson. Why he's one of my most capable men!" the Captain exclaimed. "Did you tell him I had specifically requested that you monitor the condition of that bearing?"

John Beauregard nodded feebly. He sputtered, started to say something and instead, let out a deep sigh. William Slater turned to Alexander McLennan. "Isn't Pearson the officer who reported John Beauregard's helping one of the seaman who had been beaten after the voyage began?"

The engineer stroked his beard for a moment. "Why, yes, I believe he's the one. But Captain Paton's right: he's damned capable. Been at sea almost as long as I have."

Slater turned to the Captain. "Captain, do I have your permission to interview this officer?"

"No need, Mr. Slater. I think this whole matter deserves a formal hearing. I want it resolved before we reach South Carolina. While you and Mr. Beauregard are not members of our Navy, you both have full rights as officers, especially since you are part of the crew, here with the full support of Her Majesty."

"I must get back to the bridge," he continued. "I'll arrange for the hearing in the next few hours. In the meantime, let's get ready for the unloading phase." He turned and left the dispensary.

William Slater was still holding onto John Beauregard's hand, when it suddenly squeezed his again. He turned to see the young lieutenant's bloodshot eyes wide open. He sputtered again, only this time the words came out.

". . .it, it was Pearson, I'm, I'm sure. The three men. . .who beat me. . .told me not. . .to. . .interfere anymore. . ." He stopped, trying to regain some strength to finish the sentence, ". . .not to interfere with disciplining. . .the sailors." John Beauregard, exhausted at the effort, let out a deep sigh and closed his eyes.

William Slater turned to Alexander McLennan, a dark shadow crossing his face. "I don't know how you feel about all these beatings of these men who don't often understand what they're being told to do. . ."

The chief engineer interrupted the American. "Mr. Slater, as you know, I run my engine room without the beatings. The work is hard enough, without making the men afraid they'll get a beating if they don't do what they're told. I don't like to see anyone beaten either."

The two men started out the door of the dispensary. Slater turned to the engineer. "You know, Mr. McLennan, this whole war my country is fighting involves this very issue. People are dying so they can retain the right to enslave other people. This incident puts a whole new light on it for me. At one time I was at odds with

228

Lieutenant Beauregard and his beliefs about your men. Now I understand why he felt and acted the way he did."

The two men filed down the passageway.

3.

The five-foot swells off the coast had little effect on *The Great Eastern*'s stability. Her six hundred twenty-foot length effectively canceled out any significant motion. For the next few moments this would be important.

They had come to a critical phase of the voyage: entering the narrow channel of Port Royal Sound, dropping anchor and unloading the precious cargo of arms and supplies. Since *The Great Eastern* drew over thirty feet of water fully loaded, as she was now, the vessel would require a pilot to assist in navigating the ship into the deepwater channel of the Sound. Marker buoys, already left in place, helped Captain Paton align the ship properly.

John Beauregard was still recovering from his assault, keeping much to his cabin, as it was still painful for him to walk. His nose had been healing nicely, according to the ship's surgeon. But his legs had absorbed a lot of punishment during the beating and the act of continuously balancing oneself as the ship moved through the swells and rocked from side to side was very uncomfortable. He was excused from this upcoming navigation exercise. Alexander McLennan would supervise the crews in both engine rooms.

First Officer Pearson had been found guilty of the assault by the hearing committee and had been remanded to the ship's brig until they returned to London, where he and the three seamen, also confined, would be turned over to British authorities.

Activity on the ship's decks had increased markedly as the ship neared her destination. "Lower the boarding ladder." Captain Walter Paton was on the bridge, issuing orders in preparation for the arrival of the pilot. "All engines stop. Mr. Slater, see to the arrival of the pilot; Mr. McLennan, stand by. I may need you to also use the aft engine to help turn the ship."

Paton had seen the signal flags of the ironclad raised, indicating she would be sending a harbor pilot to help him guide the huge ship into the Sound. He's from the ironclad *Columbia*, out of Savannah, and will be our pilot. He did not have accurate charts in his cabin that showed the contour of the bottom of the Sound, so he would have to trust the knowledge of the pilot and the accuracy of the soundings taken as the basis for guiding the ship into the harbor.

A small cortege was coming up the steps to the bridge. It was made up of Slater, the pilot, and two crewmen. Slater made the introductions.

"Captain Paton, this is Lieutenant Joseph Fripp, CSN. He's from the *Columbia* and will be our pilot. More importantly, he's a local, and grew up on the Sound. I know him personally sir, and he's the man for the job."

"Welcome aboard, Lieutenant. So you know these waters?"

The short young navy officer saluted Paton. "Yessir, I've sailed them most of my life. Most recently as the captain of the *Nashville*. The channels are only tricky when there's a fog or a gale. Port Royal's channel's about three hundred feet wide and narrows to about one hundred-fifty feet where the barge is anchored. How wide's the ship?"

"She's twenty-five meters, or about eighty-three feet. That's cutting it pretty close. How wide's the barge, Lieutenant?"

"She's about sixty-five feet, sir, but she only draws about twelve feet of water. If we have to move her over, we can do that."

The young naval officer had a set of rolled-up charts under his arm. "Would you like to see what I mean, Captain?"

"Yes, let's get out of this infernal chilly breeze and go look at them in my caboose. Mr. Slater, would you take command and keep the ship headed into the wind while we go below." He grabbed the speaking tube to the aft engine room. "Mr. McLennan slow ahead one third. Mr. Slater's in charge until I'm back on the bridge."

They descended the ladder to the main deck and walked to the caboose. Inside, Paton stared intensely, as the young Fripp traced their proposed course, pointing out the island where he had grown up that now bore the family name. Fripp paused a moment to explain the defensive set-up.

Pointing to a space representing a distance of about 2,000 yards, he began to outline the defensive posture. "We'll have at least two small frigates and my ship, the *Columbia,* stationed outside the harbor. We've been told to expect the federal frigates *Hartford* and *Wabash.* The *Wabash* is bringing a huge flotilla with her; they were supposed to take Forts Beauregard and Walker but first they'll have to deal with us. We've also word that the British are coming, aboard some big frigate called the *Warrior* to also protect your ship. All told, I think we'll give 'em a run for their money."

Fripp handed the captain a sheaf of papers about the federal ships that were arriving shortly. The captain looked at the young Confederate.

"The *Warrior* huh? The Queen's dispatched the best we have in the fleet. Are any of the federal vessels made of iron?"

"No sir, and none of them have the Ericsson turrets. If we get into it, I have no doubts as to who will win."

They rolled up the charts and walked out into the November chill. Walter Paton suddenly became very grave. "What you must realize, Lieutenant, is that we must not 'get into it' as you say. The Queen gave me specific orders to avoid an engagement at all costs. We are to unload the cargo and take on the cotton as quickly as possible and try to get to sea just as quickly as possible and use our superior speed to outrun any of the Union warships. The presence of the *Warrior* and whatever else is with her will be to protect our flank. If fired upon, she will respond first."

They were back on the bridge. "Mr. Slater, have the ship set a course in accordance with Mr. Fripp's commands. As the official pilot, he will have command of the direction and speed of the vessel. Any deviations will need my approval."

Fripp called out his course, Slater relayed it to the Morse operator, who passed it via the Morse lamp-signaling system to the bridge and simultaneously to the helmsmen at the rear of the ship.

4.

The noon watch at Fort Beauregard crowded together on top of the parapet and was astonished at the gigantic black and rust-streaked mass that was slowly entering the Sound. It was taller than anything they had ever seen, indeed, it dwarfed everything within sight. The small coasters looked like toys beside the ship. The black turrets at the front and back of the ship gave the vessel a warship-like appearance. Her paddlewheels turned very slowly, so slowly the soldiers could almost count the individual splashes of water cascading down as the wheel reached the top of its cycle.

The guards went through the ritual of the change of watch, and the relieved contingent as well as the group that had just come on duty flocked to the parapet to stare at the monster. She had stopped and the soldiers could hear the clanking of the anchor chains as the ship prepared to unload her precious cargo and take on the equally precious one that was stacked on the adjacent barge.

What had appeared to be tall stacks of cotton bales on the barge were now dwarfed by the sixty-foot iron wall. There was no longer a clear view across the Sound to Fort Walker as the way was now blocked by *The Great Eastern*. The noon sun had managed a weak break through the clouds and caught the brilliant blues, reds and whites of the British ensign, high atop mast Saturday. Most of the soldiers had never seen a British ship before, much less an iron one this large.

Already the ship had begun to unload her military cargo. They could see the cranes beginning to hoist the bundles, boxes and strange, canvas-shrouded shapes that lined the deck of the ship. Over at Fort Walker on the other side of the Sound, the soldiers watched as the ship's winch lowered its line to the barge to pick up the first bales of South Carolina cotton.

Up on the deck, in the captain's caboose, Captain Paton prepared to meet Colonel Shackelford and the rest of the contingent from the Confederate army. Paton had been told to expect to receive a high ranking general as well as senior members of Fraser Trenholm, who, along with a small group of clerks and bookkeepers, would account for all the material that had been shipped by English manufacturers as well as just how much cotton was actually loaded aboard the ship.

The caboose door opened and a British officer made the announcement.

"Confederate ironclad emerging from Skull Creek, sir. They're approaching the ship."

Captain Paton responded. "Thank you, Mr. Smythe. Gentlemen, let's proceed to the boarding platform. Mr. Smythe would you find Messrs. Beauregard and Slater and tell them to meet us there? Should Mr. Beauregard require any assistance on the ladders, please help him or detail a seaman to assist him."

"Yessir." The officer saluted smartly and left the caboose.

Paton and his officers departed for the platform. On deck, organized chaos had again taken the place of an orderly state of the ship. Men were everywhere, moving the pieces of cargo close to the winches for unloading. The group stopped to watch the first cotton bales land on the deck of the ship. They would have to be stacked just as they had been on the loading barge until all the stores had been unloaded from the ship's holds. That way, if she had to get underway, the cargo would already be on board and they could load it while the ship was escaping.

As they approached the top of the boarding stairs, John Beauregard and William Slater joined them and together they formed a reception line for the visitors. Beauregard was gripping the left arm of Lieutenant Smythe. Walter Paton leaned over the railing and saw that his visitors had disembarked and were coming up the long stairway. He turned to one of the crewmen.

"Sound the ship's whistle three times. And make it fast." The Confederates reached the platform, turned and saluted the captain and his officers.

"Request permission to come aboard." The voice was that of Colonel David Shackelford, commander of the loading/unloading detail at Coosawatchie Yard.

"Permission granted. I'm Captain Paton, and these are my officers. These two fine American officers have assisted me in the voyage. You may know or have heard of them."

John Beauregard was watching the Captain's face and was totally unprepared for what was about to happen. Rising above the railing, as he ascended the last few steps of the boarding stairs was the unmistakable hat of a Confederate general, and the young lieutenant turned to see who it might be.

". . .I'd like to also present my commanding officer, General Pierre Gustave Teutont Beauregard, Confederate States of America and hero of Manassas."

It was Uncle Pierre! Tears of joy welled up in the young lieutenant's eyes as he saw his uncle step onto the deck.

"John! What a surprise!" The usually serious face showed a wide grin. But the grin suddenly became a concerned frown. "What has happened to you! Has the Union already engaged the ship? Or did you. . ."

The Captain interrupted the General. "Lieutenant Beauregard has shown himself to be an exemplary officer on this ship. Unfortunately, some of the regular crew harbored a resentment about his abilities and beliefs and tried to make him see things their way. They are all in confinement now and will be turned over to the authorities when we return to Great Britain. Meanwhile, Lt. Beauregard has been recovering satisfactorily according to our surgeon."

Both groups broke ranks for the two. John released his grip on Lieutenant Smythe's arm and slowly walked to his uncle. They embraced passionately.

The normally reserved general returned the embrace. The two broke apart, each with an arm around the other.

"Excuse me, Captain, for my bad manners. I haven't seen my nephew for almost a year. I had no idea he had been in a fight. Thank you for making sure he received the appropriate medical care. And thank you also for disciplining those who are responsible. His father's on his way here to the ship—he's been supervising the cotton transfer at the railhead. You'll soon be surrounded by Beauregards."

The Captain saluted. "I'll be honored. As I said, your nephew and Mr. Slater are both to be commended for their conduct and performance as naval officers. They have taken over the running of the ship's engines, under the guidance of my chief engineer, and have relieved me of a lot of anxiety and worry because of their competence."

His comments were interrupted by three blasts of the ship's whistle.

Pointing at the ship's whistle atop the third smokestack, Captain Paton explained, "Your formal welcome, General and Colonel. Shall we adjourn for some lunch in my caboose? What time do you expect your brother?"

"Before dark. Mr. Shackelford, what time did he say he'd leave Coosawatchie?"

"He may have already left."

"Mr. Smythe, please to it that General Beauregard's brother is escorted to my caboose as soon as he arrives."

The group had reached the hatch of the Captain's caboose and filed inside.

5.

The last train had been ushered into the yards. Louis Beauregard mounted his horse at the edge of the camp and slowly made his way across the tracks to supervise it's unloading. He noticed how rapidly the tracks had become worn, how the rails were loose in their tieplates, creating a wavy, uneven pattern, as the eye followed them away, unlike the straight parallel lines they had been when they were first laid down.

The tracks, like everything and everyone else, were just plain tired. They had been at this unloading process for nearly a month, through the cold rain, the dark moonless nights, and the sunless days. Because most of the area surrounding the Coosawatchie River was swamp, the cold air seemed even colder because of the dampness.

Louis Beauregard buttoned the two top buttons of his jacket to try and keep warm. It was about an hour before his watch ended, and he would be able to sleep straight through, knowing that tomorrow they could probably rest for a day until the first load of military supplies made it's way up the Sound for loading and shipment to the various armies.

The strange-looking locomotive with the eight driving wheels and the little cab right over the boiler had brought this last load all the way from Florence. She had ten flatcars behind her, each loaded with nine bales of cotton, the majority of this load coming from plantations near Camden and Columbia. The engineer was inspecting the driving rods as the planter rode by.

"How was the ride down?" Louis Beauregard stopped his horse by the grimy engine-driver, marveling at the raw power of the eight wheels, and welcoming the heat that radiated from the coal fire under the boiler.

"Not much happened. We heard about some Union troops over in east Tennessee, but didn't see nuthin'. When do the guns arrive?"

237

"In a day or so. Your train is the last load of cotton for this trip. After this, you'll be dispatched anywhere the hardware's needed. By the way, my name is Louis Beauregard. I own a plantation over on the Sea Islands."

"Name's Joe Kane. I'm from Baltimore, so's my engine." The engineer had removed his oily glove and reached up to shake Louis Beauregard's hand. "Ain't she a beauty? We stole her from the B & O yards before the Yankees seized her."

"Why is she built that way? The other locomotives have only four driving wheels and four wheels in front of them."

"Power. She's a freight engine, known as a Camel. She's a bear on hills, going up or coming down. Those eight wheels provide a lot of power and also help slow down a train."

The planter stared at the odd cab arrangement on top of the boiler. "Don't you get a lot of smoke in that cab?"

Joe Kane had put his glove back on and was busy squirting oil into the oilcups on the driving rods. "If the wind's just right, it makes it hard to see. But for the most part it ain't too bad."

Ben, Louis Beauregard's other foreman, appeared from behind a pile of unloaded bales."

"Suh, we needs you to show us where to put the bales from deze cars. There ain't much room."

The foreman had turned and was walking around the pile of bales. The planter tipped his hat at the engineer. "Nice talking to you, Joe." The engineer nodded and went back to his oiling.

A loud whoosh escaped and the Camel let go with a shower of steam and sparks. Beauregard's horse reared up. It took all the planter had to bring the animal under control. He noticed that some of the sparks had landed on the first few bales of the flatcar behind the locomotive. Smoke had started to appear; it looked like a small fire had started.

"Ben! Ben!" The planter cantered down the platform in the direction of his foreman. Ben turned at the sound of his name.

"Get a bucket brigade started. There's a fire on the first car." Ben turned and ran towards the group at the rear of the train.

"Fire! Fire! Get the buckets from the toolhouse," he yelled. "Start a line from the water tower. Hurry!"

Louis Beauregard turned his horse around and galloped back towards the locomotive. A Confederate corporal was running towards him, also in the direction of the fire. It was now in full blaze, creating a shower of sparks all its own.

Joe Kane was already up in the cab of the engine and pulled the whistle cord twice to signal he was moving the train. Two shrill long blasts, and he moved the huge levers that let steam into the cylinders.

WHAP, WHAP, WHAP, WHAPWHAPWHAPWHAPWHAP WHAP. The engine's driving wheels spun hopelessly in place as too much power had been applied too suddenly. The fire continued unchecked and had now spread to the rest of the bales on the flatcar. Smaller columns of smoke on some of the bales on the platform indicated they were on fire, too.

WHAP. WHAP. WHAP. WHAP. The train slowly eased in reverse and backed past Louis Beauregard. The corporal had caught up with the planter. It was the same lanky corporal that the planter first met when he arrived in camp.

"Engineer's gonna back her out of the yard. You take charge of the train, sir. I'll muster some men to put the fire out on the platform."

"Corporal Anderson, make sure you get it all. Some embers could smolder for hours and we'd never know there was a fire." Beauregard turned his horse in the direction of the retreating train. The fire had gotten some assistance from the motion of the train and it appeared that the locomotive herself was engulfed in flames.

The train slowed to a stop next to the water tower. By coincidence, the track where the train had been standing happened to be the same one where the water tower was located. In the light of the fire, the planter could see someone was already lowering the huge spout that was normally used to fill the engine's water barrels or tank.

Joe Kane eased back on the throttle to position the car on fire under the spout. He stopped the train as he and the fireman scurried down the ramp at the back of the engine and jumped to the ground, just missing the hot flames.

A loud hiss and a huge cloud of steam and the fire was out, the amount of water coming out of the spout creating what amounted to an instant end to the danger. The steam continued to rise, as an active chain of slaves and soldiers formed, each passing canvas buckets full of water along the platform to the bales that had been set ablaze by the train fire.

Joe Kane surveyed the damage to his engine. Outside of a little blackening of the cab roof, everything else seemed intact. Already the charred bales on the first car were being pushed off onto the ground by the slaves. The flatcar itself was also slightly charred, but appeared structurally sound. The ground around the area was saturated with water from the fire and Louis Beauregard's horse splashed its way slowly towards the train. Once there, Beauregard dismounted and headed for the engineer.

"Joe, you saved us from a disaster. That was a great idea to back the train up under the water tower. Losing the cotton bales would have been a catastrophe. We probably would have lost the entire yard." They were watching the bucket brigades mop up the remaining smoldering bales and wetting down the surrounding ones, just in case.

"Better get back to unloading the rest of the bales. We're expecting the first of the military supplies sometime tomorrow morning. I was supposed to be joining my brother and son aboard the ship for dinner tonight. Doesn't look like I'm going to make it."

The weary planter turned his horse back towards the platforms. Joe Kane had already swung himself back into the engine cab and was whistling for the tracks to clear.

6.

The midnight watch on the deck of the Columbia first spotted the U.S. armada. There were so many ships and mast lights that he stopped counting at twenty. The wallowing that the unbalanced ironclad experienced in the swells made an accurate observation almost impossible.

"Enemy ships off the port side. At least twenty."

"Beat the men to quarters. Port battery prepare to fire. Notify the *Sumter*." Bryan Griffith issued his orders as he buttoned his oilskins. There was a slight drizzle coming down.

WHOOOOOOOSH! A Drummond light, fired from one of the federal vessels soared in the sky and cast a harsh glare on the flotilla.

". . .thirty-one, thirty-two. Captain, there's over thirty-two vessels in the fleet." The midshipman on watch squinted through the drizzle.

"Captain, Commander Semmes is going to cut across our bow and attack the lead ship."

"Acknowledge the message. Tell him we will be firing our port battery first."

Griffith squinted through his spyglass, presently trained on the big steam frigate that was fourth or fifth in the column. It was the *Wabash*, flagship of Captain Du Pont. He wondered why there were so many ships in the fleet.

The flash of gunfire from the lead Union vessel followed by a deep boom signaled the battle's beginning. The *Sumter*, only a couple of hundred yards from the attacking vessel, answered the volley.

"Maybe they won't see us until the last moment, because we're so low in the water." Walter Smith, *Columbia's* first officer had joined the Captain on the bridge. "Port battery ready to fire, Sir."

Two more Drummond lights went off. The *Wabash* was now less than a thousand feet from the *Columbia*. In between, was the former mail ship given back to the Union by James Bulloch, the *Bienville*. She was less than three hundred feet off the port side of the ironclad.

"Port battery, FIRE when she's in range!"

BOOM! BOOM! BOOM! The nine thirty-two pounders of the *Columbia* fired, almost in perfect unison, causing the ship to lurch back on its starboard side from the guns' recoil.

Through the smoke, Griffith could detect no explosions, and in fact, saw a couple of rounds plop harmlessly into the water, short of hitting the vessel.

"Port battery, check your charges! We had some short rounds!"

A huge blast from the *Wabash* signaled her entry into the battle. She missed the *Sumter*, as Semmes was adroit at guessing where his opponents would fire next. The battle for control of Port Royal Sound was underway. But the whole reason for the imminent conflict was still busy upstream, unloading her cargo and loading cotton.

7.

"Message from Little Rhody, sir. She's sighted Drummond lights and gunfire approximately ten miles ahead."

Captain David Farragut strained his eyes but the only thing he could see over the horizon was a reddish glow, occasionally enhanced by a whiter one."

"Acknowledge Trenchard. Ask him if he knows any of the ships."

"Aye, Aye, Sir."

A dark image was beginning to blot out the glow on the horizon. It was a ship's hull, and Farragut had no idea who the ship might be. She certainly couldn't be *The Great Eastern*. Surely she hadn't left the Sound yet.

"Sir, HMS *Warrior* requests identification."

"The *Warrior*? What the hell's she doing here? Signal Trenchard that he might be in danger."

"Sir, *The Great Eastern's* a British vessel. Perhaps she's an escort."

Farragut vaguely remembered his conversation with Stephen Trenchard in his cabin. Trenchard had mentioned something about a British mailship being stopped and boarded by armed Union Navy officers. Great Britain had protested vigorously, Trenchard had said, and threatened military action if the Confederates captured were not set free. Trenchard did not know what the United States reply was. Perhaps the *Warrior's* presence was Great Britain's response. The Admiral decided to proceed cautiously.

"Signal identity to the *Warrior*."

A Drummond light soared from the deck of the British warship. It was punctuated by a single cannon firing directly across the bow of the American warship.

"Sir, she's serious. She's asked us to halt. Her commanding officer would like you to come on board and state your destination and mission."

"She's asked for an immediate reply."

David Farragut knew he was no match for the armored ship, in spite of his firepower. His ship and crew were both tired from their long engagement in the Far East. He couldn't run, as that would admit guilt. So he decided to simply tell the *Warrior*'s captain that he was on his way to Norfolk and was to stop to re-coal at one of the blockade colliers off Port Royal Sound.

"Tell the *Warrior* we are on our way and mean no hostile action."

As he climbed down the boarding ladder of the *Hartford* David Farragut noticed the glow on the horizon was getting brighter.

8.

"Beaufort? Port Royal? My God, we're liable to be blown out of the water! Doesn't he know what's going on?"

Susannah turned to Thad Howard, her face contorted in disbelief and fear.

"Perhaps you'd like me to tell him, Susannah." The overseer had come to tell his prisoner how much more danger she would be in trying to escape here. But it was apparent by her reaction to this latest nautical maneuver by the Captain that he would be putting the whole ship in grave danger.

She stood up and took the three steps to the small porthole, turned and looked at him.

Her voice trembled. "You said you saw the message I sent to Washington. Do you remember what it said? About *The Great Eastern*? About where she was going? About what she was carrying?"

Thad grabbed onto the bunk as the ship took a sudden roll to starboard "Why should she be a danger? She was chartered by Mr. Trenholm. She's a friendly vessel." Leaning toward her, his tone became menacing. "What aren't you telling me?"

Susannah just stared at him. Suddenly it was clear to him why she had sent the message: to alert the Union Navy. No wonder she was upset. Not only would they have to avoid the already-present blockade vessels, they would probably be confronted by everything the Navy could muster here to stop *The Great Eastern* from leaving the United States with her cargo since they had left England.

"I've got to tell Captain Tessier." He stopped in the doorway. "I have a better idea. *You* tell him. It would give you a chance to save yourself and I wouldn't have to be involved."

Susannah stepped around her trunk and stood in front of the overseer. Her disbelief had given way to surprise.

"What makes you think he'd believe me? You heard what he said to me."

Thad's tone became more conciliatory. "Susannah, I came to tell you I would help you escape. I really care about you but I know I can never have you the way I want. The next best thing is to do anything I can to help you save yourself. This might be one of those ways."

She continued to stare at him in disbelief. But his eyes softened more and he moved toward her, his arms outstretched. At first, she stepped towards him, but, thinking about the urgency, paused.

"There's no time for that now, Thad." Susannah gazed at him with a look that said later. "I have to tell the Captain before we get blown away by some Union warship." She began to see a way out for herself.

She quickly brushed her hair, put a little rouge on her cheeks. She turned and faced him again.

"How do I look? Contrite enough?" She managed a little sarcasm.

"Don't be so saucy, Susannah. I'll have to tie your wrists again," he smiled mischievously.

Once outside the cabin, they started down the passageway and up the narrow iron stairway to the deck. As they ascended the stairs, they could see that dawn was approaching. The captain wasn't on the bridge but they did find him in his cabin. He had been resting after an all-night watch for blockaders.

Eugene Tessier was a shrewd man. He listened to Susannah's information but remained skeptical of her motives. Why shouldn't she come forward? She's got everything to lose. There was no way for him to check her story except to simply keep on the course until he ran into this supposed Union flotilla.

"Thad, take her back to her cabin and lock her up. Then come back here. I need to talk with you."

After taking Susannah back to her cabin, Thad hurried up to the deck and the Captain's cabin. He tried to answer a barrage of questions about the beautiful woman who was his prisoner. How well did he know her? How long had he known her? How long had George Trenholm known her? What was she doing in London? Did he trust her?

"Captain, I saw the telegram after it was sent. It was addressed to someone in the Federal government."

A loud knock interrupted the conversation.

"Sir, Union vessels on the horizon." It was Isaac Gaston, the first officer. Eugene Tessier opened the door.

"How many, how far?" The captain began pulling on his coat.

"Looks like five or six, Sir. But there may be more. I ordered the ship to stop all engines until you came on the bridge to see for yourself."

The three of them hurried down the deck and climbed the ladder to the bridge. In the early dawn, they could clearly see more than one ship. It looked like a whole armada. On the horizon, it appeared as though a naval battle had just begun. With the engines at rest and the screw not turning, Eugene Tessier thought he could hear cannon fire as well. The armada dramatically confirmed at least part of Susannah's story. But he wasn't sure they were after *The Great Eastern*.

"If *The Great Eastern*'s where this lady says it is, we ought to try and get near her for protection. We'll set a course up St. Helena Sound, circle around Beaufort and come back down the Broad River. That should put us right under the protection of the ship's guns." He began issuing orders. "Engines ahead one third. Helmsman, come about one hundred-eighty degrees. Set a course for the lee side of Hunting Island."

9.

It was now dusk, and John Beauregard slowly climbed up the ladder to the bridge to get a more commanding view of the apparent chaos that was taking place in the fading light on deck and below on the barge. Just a few minutes ago, his father and uncle had hastily left the ship; Louis on his way back to the railhead to supervise the dispatching of the all-important war materials and Pierre, to organize defenses of the railhead and its precious contents.

His father had the same reaction to his battered appearance as his uncle, but upon hearing the details of the attack directly from the captain, expressed his gratitude to the Captain and sympathies to his son. He couldn't help feeling a little surge of pride at his son's bravery.

The celebration in the Captain's caboose was becoming a dim memory. A joyous reunion had taken place, with John, his father, and his uncle sharing perhaps their last meal together as a family. There were toasts, pledges, and restated alliances to the Confederacy. The young lieutenant remembered something Captain Paton had said about never thinking the Americans had the courage of their convictions. It reminded him of the callousness the Captain demonstrated at the loss of one of the ship's lookouts during the storm.

But the remark had been one of admiration, not criticism. John had felt a tremendous burst of pride at being a Southerner; even his usually-serious uncle's face with the sad eyes had brightened at the Captain's remarks. On the face of it, Walter Paton appeared to have become a passionate witness to Southern conviction.

The celebration was cut short by news that a flotilla of Federal ships, lead by the steam frigate *Wabash*, had been sighted under full steam and sail off Charleston. It meant they would be here in less than twelve hours, ready to attack. The reunion quickly broke up, father and son hugging each other and not knowing when they would see each other again; brother embracing brother, each wishing the other well in their roles, the struggle; finally, General Beauregard saluting his nephew and urging him to make the whole Beauregard family even prouder of him as the second-in-command of the *The Great Eastern's* screw engine room.

The decks were now stacked with cotton bales, replacing the more orderly piles of wooden boxes since off-loaded to the barge. They were being loaded into the open hatch, where the former skylight for the grand saloon had been located. The front holds were still a little less than half full of military supplies; the Captain had estimated they would be unloaded before dawn. The last of the cotton had arrived from Coosawatchie late this afternoon.

Some good news and some more bad news had become known. The *Warrior* had also been sighted off Charleston; this led to guesses on whether she was there to show the British flag or whether she would take on the entire American fleet. Captain Paton had said he was glad for the reinforcements. Even though *The Great Eastern* was heavily armed she would undoubtedly have a tough time with multiple targets, despite the distinct advantage of the Ericsson turrets.

The bad news was the rumored arrival of a smaller but still very dangerous group of Union ships, this one led by the steam frigate the *Hartford*. John Beauregard had heard that his former duty-ship, the *Rhode Island*, was part of this flotilla. How ironic! Fighting his own former commander!

But how sad, too. He would be fighting former teacher, friend, man of deep religious and moral convictions, Captain and very capable seaman, Stephen Trenchard. Trenchard had been responsible for the glowing report on the then-young ensign's performance aboard Little Rhody. Now there was the possibility they might face each other in battle.

"Hostile warships in sight, five thousand yards to the starboard." John Beauregard followed the blinking Morse as she signaled the arrival of one or both the flotillas. Heavy cannon fire could already be heard and an orange flash, together with a bluish glow had begun to appear on the horizon.

Captain Paton suddenly appeared on the bridge. "Mr. Beauregard, are you fit enough to resume your duties in the screw engine room? I'll need your skills and experience to help get us safely out of here. Can you stay on duty?"

John Beauregard straightened up, standing at attention. "Yes sir. I'm ready to resume my post. I'm still in pain, especially when the ship pitches and rolls, but I promise not to fail you."

The Captain shook his hand. "Good lad. Having met your uncle and father I can see where you get your mettle." He quickly resumed his role as the ship's commanding officer. "Where is Mr. Fripp? We need to prepare to get underway. I don't want to get bottled up here and have no room to maneuver." He waved to the cabin boy who had followed him onto the bridge to go find the harbor pilot. That done, he turned to the young lieutenant.

"Mr. Beauregard, get the boilers fired up for maximum pressure." The layover had given the engine room some time to perform some badly needed maintenance.

"Sir, you know numbers four and five are still being cleaned. I was told that process was speeded up but even if the men are finished the boilers need about six hours for full steam."

"Can you raise full pressure on the other eight? We've taken on quite a load and we'll need all the speed we can muster."

"Sir, I'll ask Mr. McLennan and get back to you in ten minutes over the speaking tube." John Beauregard saluted the captain and made his way down the ladder to the main deck.

The cabin boy suddenly appeared on the ladder, preceded by Lieutenant Joseph Fripp, who was still buttoning his coat.

"Get Mr. Slater on deck. I want all turrets operational." Captain Paton again motioned the cabin boy into action.

"Mr. Fripp, I want you to plot two courses out of here. That means we'll have to see what comes once we clear the sound before deciding which one to follow. I have no idea what's there except I know one armada's headed by the *Wabash*. I respect that ship."

Fripp finished buttoning his coat and looked at the Captain. "Sir, less than a thousand feet astern, the shelf drops off to forty-five feet and the channel widens to fifteen hundred feet. That's enough room to turn her around. I'll signal a couple of the smaller steam tugs that've been towing the flatboats from Coosawatchie to stand off where the channel gets shallow."

"Report back to me with your recommended courses in fifteen minutes."

"Aye, Aye, Sir."

Paton aimed his spyglass out into the darkness. The deep thunder of cannon fire was continuous now and it was obviously getting closer. He could see the harsh glare of the Drummond lights as they exploded overhead, although a good cloud cover had cut their usefulness.

The ship's arc lights on masts Tuesday and Thursday continued to burn. Captain Paton wondered how long he dared keep them on, as he knew the dangers of trying to load and unload the ship in the dark. He decided to leave them on until they had turned the ship around in the channel. Even without them lighted, it would not be difficult to see a vessel this size.

Again, Captain Paton dispatched the cabin boy. "See if Mr. Chaplin can join me on the bridge. Tell him I need an immediate status on the remaining cargo on the barge. Also ask Mr. Russell to delegate his duties of loading the cotton and unloading the supplies and join me here on the bridge with Mr. Chaplin. I feel we ought to be underway within the hour."

The British midshipman, who also acted as cabinboy and messenger for the Captain, briskly saluted and disappeared down the bridge ladder.

"Sir, Beauregard here." The voice was coming from the aft engine room speaking tube. "Mr. McLennan and I think we can give you a little over twelve knots without the two boilers."

"And what of the two being cleaned?"

"I suspended work on them as they still had another day's scraping before we could use them. I made the decision, along with Mr. McLennan to fill them with water and stoke the fires underneath, so you'll have near-full power in a few hours."

"Thank you, Mr. Beauregard. I concur with your and Mr. McLennan's decision."

William Slater appeared, the man responsible for the defense of the ship. "Sir, we're having a bit of trouble with the mechanism on turret three."

"What kind of trouble?"

"She won't do the full one hundred twenty degree rotation. I've got two of the carpenter's mates on it right now."

"Everything else ready, Mr. Slater?"

"Yessir. Each turret's got thirty rounds and enough charges. We're prepared for anything, chainshot, hot shots, explosive shells, or straight cannon. The Morse lamps are manned and communicating. If you don't mind sir, I'd like to join the lookout on Mast Tuesday. It's the best place to direct the firepower, rather than here on the bridge."

"Permission granted. Have your signalman clear firing orders through the bridge."

"Aye, Aye, Sir."

10.

The noise inside the *Columbia* was deafening. She was under the full firepower of the *Wabash* and the *Bienville*. And, while not suffering any serious damage, she was not able to move fast enough to avoid taking hits.

"Mr. Smith, I want explosive shells in the next starboard broadside. Those cannon balls are ineffective against the *Wabash's* sheet chain armor."

Captain Bryan Griffith was the first to notice the ineffectiveness of his bombardment against the disguised armor of the big frigate. The Union carpenters had apparently covered over the net-like armor of chain links with wood planks but the continuing shelling managed to penetrate the planking and expose the armor. A few rounds of explosive charges ought to blow a hole in it.

Shellfire sounded behind the *Wabash*. It was the *Sumter*, on the opposite side of the big frigate. Griffith climbed up into the tiny navigation pilothouse that barely allowed two people to stand. The *Sumter* and the *Bienville* were going at each other with fusillade after fusillade. Suddenly, a loud explosion indicated a magazine had been hit. No one could see which ship had taken the hit.

"Mr. Smith are we ready?"

"Not quite, Sir. We've had to change the ball out for the shells, per your orders."

"Hurry it up, Mr. Smith. We'll be out of position soon."

The stern of the *Wabash* slid by and slowly revealed the source of the fire. It was the *Bienville's* magazine ablaze, a direct hit from the *Sumter*.

"Fire, Mr. Smith. It's our last chance."

The explosions from the cannon were overridden by the noise of the shells exploding on the sheet chain armor of the *Wabash*.

"Two hits, Sir!"

"I see them, Mr. Smith. Can you put some more in there before she gets out of range?"

"I'll give it a try, Sir."

Suddenly, a loud explosion at the stern gun position announced a direct hit from the stern gun of the *Wabash*. The gun crew, stunned by the concussion, lay sprawled over the rear gundeck of the ship. Cries of pain could be heard as well as moans from men who had lost a limb, or whose limbs were partially severed, and were bleeding to death. The noise could even be heard over the explosions from the loose shells lying close to the destroyed cannon. Fire was lapping around its wooden base. Blood and human limbs were everywhere.

"Smith, organize the fire brigade! Get those men to safety! Get the ship's surgeon! Helmsman, I want a starboard broadside on the *Wabash* Prepare to come about one hundred eighty degrees! Engine room full ahead one-third!"

But the ironclad had taken some heavy damage. It was questionable if she and the *Sumter* would be able to deflect the Union armada from a chance at *The Great Eastern*.

11.

The two American officers bounded up the boarding ladder of the 9,400 ton British warship, *Warrior*. They had no desire to arouse British suspicion as to why they had suddenly changed course from heading towards Philadelphia to laying off the coast of South Carolina. They wanted to get through this inquiry as soon as possible.

They reached the top of the boarding ladder, saluted the deck officer, and asked the traditional maritime question.

"Captain David Farragut, U.S.N., and Lieutenant Stephen Trenchard, U.S.N., request permission to come aboard." Even though it was pitch black, the two officers could see that more than just the midnight watch was active on the ship. They could hear the preparations on the gundeck below for a confrontation.

"Permission granted. Vice Admiral Earl Paul requests you join him in his cabin. Please follow me."

Earl Paul looked every bit the flag-rank Admiral that he was, although his uniform reminded David Farragut of his own early in his career. Attired in full-dress uniform, Admiral Paul looked like someone who was reincarnated from the War of 1812. He stood up from behind his oversized desk and walked across the elegant Oriental rug which covered the highly polished teak deck of his cabin.

"Welcome aboard the *Warrior*, gentlemen. Please help yourself to some tea."

After the chill of a journey in an open boat in the Atlantic in the middle of November, both men readily accepted. They sat down in two of the wooden chairs that were lined in front of the desk.

"I'm charged with the protection of *The Great Eastern* from hostile attack. I'm sure you gentlemen are aware of the violation created by your ship, the *San Jacinto*. In case you're not, she illegally detained a British ship, the *Trent,* and removed two Southern gentlemen. The Queen has asked me to protect the interests of the British government and ensure that you do not try the same thing with *The Great Eastern.*" The Admiral moved closer to the two American officers.

"May I ask what you are doing in such close proximity to her?"

Earl Paul had a magnificent handlebar mustache and huge bushy eyebrows. The effect only reinforced his appearance as a British naval officer.

David Farragut explained his ship's return from the east and that he was low on coal. His orders had been to recoal from the colliers that made up part of the Union blockade.

Earl Paul was silent for a moment. "And you, Captain Trenchard, your orders?"

Stephen Trenchard looked straight at the eyes overshadowed by the bushy eyebrows. "I'm on patrol for blockade runners, sir."

Earl Paul paused, slowly folding his hands behind him as he turned to go back behind his desk. "I believe both of you. Her majesty's government has no desire to get involved in your internal affairs; however, as I said, it is my duty to protect the British ship now lying in Port Royal Sound, taking on cargo. Until she clears the area. I'm afraid I'm going to have to detain your departure. You are not prisoners, as were the two gentlemen removed from the *Trent*; I'll give you the run of the ship for the next twenty-four hours. You will not be confined to your cabins as long as you don't try to escape or interfere with the operations of this ship. Perhaps you'd like to see a bit more of Her Majesty's newest naval weapon." His tone was authoritative, yet chatty, much like an Englishman would describe a routine matter.

"I have instructed the officer of the deck to deny boarding, under arms if necessary, to anyone from either of your ships who tries to forcibly come on board. I'm sure you'll understand the circumstances."

Farragut was already on his feet, livid with anger. Trenchard stood up and stared at the comical- looking Vice Admiral. David Farragut's deep voice resonated throughout the cabin.

"Admiral, I vehemently protest this illegal detainment. I realize you have provocation and your orders to follow but what you are doing is no better than what those men of the *San Jacinto* did. I intend to register a full..."

"...And you'll have your day in court, Captain, as soon as *The Great Eastern* is out of potential danger.

"Please make yourselves comfortable. I'll have someone show you to your cabins. I'll also make sure you have something dry to wear. We'll be having breakfast in the wardroom shortly. Please join us when you hear the boatswain's whistle. I would suggest you draft up a message to the commands of your ships, telling them about this. I'll see that they're sent promptly. After you've changed, please give the message to the midshipman."

The interview over, the door to the captain's quarters opened and a midshipman appeared, ready to show the detained Americans their home for the next twenty-four hours.

Back on the main deck, the officers could see the mast lights of their two ships. But in the opposite direction, on the horizon, they could see and hear a gun battle had already begun. Both knew their first officers would take command if they didn't return to their ships. Both also hoped that neither of their subordinate commanders would attempt any hostile action.

BLOCKADE RUNNER
BOOK 6

1.

John Beauregard acknowledged Walter Paton's command for an "all reverse one-eighth" speed setting on his screw engine. He looked up at the steam gauge and noted its full pressure of twenty-five pounds. The mates had already let steam into the engine's chambers by turning the valve wheel, and below the catwalk, the clanking of the connecting rods announced the engine's start.

Beauregard began to painfully climb down the ladder for another shaft bearing inspection. So far, the mid-ocean repair of the shaft seemed to have been satisfactory although she had yet to be tried under a sustained high-speed run. He likened the condition of the bearing to his own physical condition: functioning, but not yet tested under stress. Without warning a loud metallic thud reverberated throughout the engine room. The ship had struck something.

Or something had struck the ship. The young lieutenant rushed as fast as he could back up the ladder to the speaking tube fastened to the railing next to the steam valve.

"Captain Paton! The ship's struck something or been hit. Loud noise on the port side!"

Up on the bridge, Paton had been issuing commands to back the ship down the channel where he could turn her around when the loud explosion, partially muffled by the water, attracted his attention.

"Ask Mr. Slater to investigate what that explosion was!"

The Morse lamps were frantically flashing messages back and forth to each other. It appeared the ship was under attack by some kind of unseen or underwater vessel.

"Captain, Mr. Slater reports enemy torpedo ship wallowing off the port side. Claims she's sinking."

"I want a damage assessment immediately. Mr. Beauregard and Mr. McLennan, stop all engines. Lower a boarding ladder."

Within minutes the event had been reconstructed. Apparently, during the night a small Union torpedo boat, it's lethal charge of powder encased in a waterproof copper can and mounted on a thirty-foot pole in the bow of the ship, had remained in close proximity in the shadow of the huge hull, under the bow. Hidden from view and out of the glare of the harsh arc lights, she waited her chance and struck when the crew's attention was focused on getting the ship underway. Swaying from the bottom of the boarding ladder, Midshipman Reginald Sheffield could see some twisted metal about two feet below the waterline. The hole was about eight to ten feet long and no more than three feet wide. Beauregard and McLennan had reported no abnormal water in the bilge. The ship's double hull and compartmentalization averted a disaster.

Slater hurried up the ladder to join Walter Paton on the bridge. He found the Captain discussing the incident with Midshipman Sheffield.

The Captain turned to face the Confederate. "Mr. Slater, this ship never ceases to surprise me. We are seaworthy, with only minor damage to the outer hull. The worst that may have happened is the torn iron plates may slow us down a bit. Mr. Brunel is to be congratulated for his forethought in building the ship with a double hull, although he's probably turning in his grave at the thought of her in naval combat."

"Sir, I checked with all the other lookouts and there are no more surprises. The torpedo boat sank by the bow and we have the three crewmen in custody."

"Have them questioned and bring your findings to me."

"Yes, sir. I'm resuming my post on Mast Tuesday sir. The smoke from the battle seems to be moving upriver towards us and I don't want us to get caught unprepared."

Walter Paton turned to the sailor standing behind him, awaiting his next order. "Boatswain, beat the men to quarters on the remaining batteries. Prepare the ship for battle. Mr. Beauregard, Mr. McLennan, slow astern, one-third. Mr. Sheffield, I want you astern to supervise the lookout. I don't want to put this ship on a sandbar and have her a sitting duck for some Union gunnery barrage."

The slow slap-slap-slap of the paddlewheels signaled that the ship was once again underway. On deck, loading the cotton bales into the holds continued. At times, some of the piles obscured a clear firing line or navigation fix.

"Mr. McGarrity, I want those piles of bales down to no more than two high in case we have to use the turret guns." The Irish midshipman who had been appointed the ship's cargo master acknowledged the captain's shouted command with a wave. But something else caught his eye—smoke coming out of the main hold. It was not a swirl of smoke from the ship's funnel; this smoke was whitish in color and billowing out in dense clouds.

"Fire in the main hold!" McGarrity was hurrying towards the clouds of smoke now engulfing the entire midships deck. At the edge of the hold, he had to cover his mouth because the smoke was so thick.

"Get a firehose over here! Tell the engine room to turn on the water pump!" McGarrity ran to the base of the port turret and shouted a command to the Morse signalman.

"Signal the Captain we've got a major fire in the hold. Tell him I need some men to help put it out!"

The deckhands stopped the loading process and were beginning to assemble a second hose brigade. The Captain signaled back that he would dispatch additional help from the loading crews forward of the bridge. Walter Paton tried to think what had started the fire. He remembered a conversation at the farewell luncheon with the Beauregards, a comment made by Louis Beauregard about a fire in the cotton bales at Coosawatchie started by sparks from one of the locomotives. The blaze had probably started in a bale that had been smoldering for the entire journey to the ship.

By now at least one hundred men were battling the blaze. Huge white clouds of smoke and steam poured out of the hold, rivaling the black smoke belching out of the five funnels and making navigation down the narrow channel even more difficult. At the risk of getting stranded, Paton decided once again to stop the ship.

"Mr. Beauregard and Mr. McLennan, stop all engines. We've got a fire in one of the holds that must be brought under control before we move this ship any further."

The Captain climbed down the ladder and hurried astern to the main hold. The fire hoses were showering water into the hold. Paton began to worry about the pumps keeping up with the water now accumulating in the hold and the bowels of the ship.

"Sir, possible enemy ships approaching the mouth of the sound. Distance about two thousand yards. Commander Slater wishes permission to commence firing from the stern turret and batteries." The old shouted-order-by-relay routine had resumed because no one could see the Morse lamps.

"Tell him only to return fire. I don't want us to assume an offensive posture." Another shouted order.

"Sir, Ensign Slater says the *Warrior* may be part of the group but needs confirmation of the ship."

"Tell him I'll be there in about five minutes."

The fire was stubborn and continued to blaze, barely being contained by the hoses.

"Mr. Sheffield, I want a detail to take a hose down into the hold. We'll have to attack the fire at its source. I think it started in the bales that were part of the fire in the rail yard at Coosawatchie. Report to me at the watch at Mast Tuesday when you've surveyed the situation in the hold and gotten some water on it."

It seemed like the ship was restating its reputation as a jinxed vessel. Paton remembered what his predecessor said about the ship: She'll make you think she's headed for a major catastrophe but she always vindicates herself. He remembered the recent incident with the torpedo explosion: a ship with a single hull might have now been lying on the bottom of Port Royal Sound. *The Great Eastern's* double hull had indeed vindicated her.

Paton hurried forward to the base of Mast Tuesday. Thirty feet up, on the watch platform, between smoke billows, he could see Slater squinting through his spyglass, his arms coiled around the mast.

"Mr. Slater, if she has three masts and two funnels forward of the middle mast, she's probably the *Warrior*. Hold your fire." Paton strained to see the hazy black image that appeared to be the British frigate. But she was headed at them, bow on, and this made identification even tougher.

"Captain, can barely read her Morse lamp. Something about the *Wabash.... Hartford* flotilla.....*Warrior*. It's her, Sir."

Another anxious voice interrupted. "Sir, there's quite a fire in the hold. I don't know that one crew can put it out. Can you get us some more men and firehoses?" Midshipman Sheffield, standing at attention, was black with soot from head to toe. He looked like a part of the black gang, the firemen who stoked the fires under the giant boilers in the boiler room.

"Mr. Sheffield, go tell which officer is on the bridge that I want you to get all the help you need. Tell him it's an order; tell him if I have to use every person I've got, I will. I want this fire out and soon."

"Sir, the *Warrior's* stopped. She's turning around. I guess she means to protect us from the *Wabash* and the *Hartford* ."

Walter Paton barely heard the comment. He was concerned this fire could get out of control and reach the unprotected magazines, the temporary little wooden shacks that had been erected behind each turret so that powder and shells could be quickly accessed by each gun turret crew. In the grand scheme of things, Isambard Brunel, the shipbuilder, could never have foreseen his ship as a multi-turreted warship, loaded with explosive materials and shells.

2.

The view from the bridge of the *Bermuda* was anything but encouraging. Marsh grass and cat o' nine tails grew right down to the edge of the channel, the vegetation sometimes growing high enough to obscure any long-distance sighting. It appeared that the channel was narrowing, which could mean that it was also getting shallower. Since the ship was drawing over eleven feet of water, there was real danger of proceeding any further.

Eugene Tessier was in a dilemma. To expose his ship to the kind of Union firepower that the Eddings woman described as steaming off Port Royal Sound and its environs would surely mean the ship and its cargo's destruction. The cargo was probably more valuable than the ship, and of course the rewards in commissions and fees to the Captain would be quite substantial, once it was safely landed.

The sun was sinking lower in the sky, meaning a nighttime navigation through the narrowing channel. He had to make a decision.

Even with the tide rising, Eugene Tessier knew there would be a substantial risk to his ship and its cargo if he attempted to sail the narrowing and darkened channel. In spite of the charts showing a distance of about seven miles, he could not rule out his ship running aground. He decided to weigh anchor in St. Helena Sound and wait out the emergence of *The Great Eastern* from Port Royal Sound. At that point he would attempt to catch up to her, signal his identity and ask for her protection until they were off Charleston harbor. He turned to issue orders to his officers and engineer.

"Mr. McGuire, I want lookouts posted on the bow, port and starboard sides of the ship. Please bring the ship about so her bow is facing the Atlantic Ocean and then drop anchor. When *The Great Eastern* appears to be coming out of the harbor we'll pull up the anchor and get underway to catch up with her. We'll attempt to stay within the protection of her guns as we sail up towards Charleston Harbor."

3.

The fire continued to smolder but departure could no longer be delayed. The *Warrior* could be seen firing her guns at some target out of sight. The smoke often obscured the British frigate, but it was apparent she was under attack. Damage assessment to *The Great Eastern* showed no structural harm to her hull from the fire. But the ship had taken on more water from the fire hoses and the helmsmen complained that the vessel appeared sluggish during course changes.

Walter Paton ordered the pumps to run at top speed to rid the ship of the excess water before she got to sea. He did not want to create any additional instability: the weight of the turrets, the nature of the cargo, and the hole in the side of the ship could make an unmanageable situation, especially in the stormy North Atlantic in winter.

"Stop all engines. Mr. McLennan, we are going to execute a stern port maneuver. That will require a port-paddlewheel-only engagement at slow ahead one-eighth. The two tugs that marked the channel are going to give us a shove. Helmsmen, I want a rudder position of one nine zero. When she straightens out, I'll issue new course commands. I want to see what's out there waiting for us. Mr Beauregard, stand by. We'll not be needing you until she's turned around."

The lookouts at Fort Walker had watched the arrival of another big black ship, and were surprised that she, too, flew the British ensign. They were even more surprised to see her engaged in combat with two of the Union's most powerful warships: the *Wabash* and the *Hartford*.

It had been an inconclusive battle; the Union ships could not inflict damage on the first all-iron warship. Now, bearing down on them from the mouth of the Broad River was the giant that had gone upriver just a few days ago. The sight of the two monstrous vessels in the same body of water at the same time was a sight the soldiers would never forget.

Back on the bridge, Walter Paton prepared his transformed ship for battle.

"Mr. Slater, I want the forward turret firing forward. The stern turret should be positioned to fire to the port side. I think that's where the Union ships and the *Warrior* are. No one, I repeat, no one is to fire unless this ship is fired on first." The Morse signalman was having difficulty keeping up with the Captain's rapid-fire order. Finally he stopped.

"Mr. Slater, do your gunnery sergeants understand the order?"

William Slater signaled back that they had all acknowledged the Captain's order.

The tugs had finished turning the huge hull around.

"All engines stop. Mr. McLennan, you may engage the starboard paddlewheel again. All engines ahead one-third." The delicate turn in midstream had been accomplished without a grounding.

"Sir, unknown vessel sighted astern, about four thousand yards. Looks like a Federal gunboat. She's under full steam—looks like she's trying to catch us."

Walter Paton asked to have the message retransmitted as smoke from the funnels and the still-smoldering cotton bales had obscured parts of it.

Could some Federal ship have been hiding in one of the many little rivers that fed this broad estuary? Why would a ship one-third the size of his want to take her on?

"Stern lookout, request further identity. Mr. Slater, I want the stern turret to be ready to fire."

Ahead, Walter Paton could see the *Warrior* directly in front of him, blocking the path upriver to the Federal Armada. In the dense smoke and mist, he thought he could make out at least six Union gunboats. The *Warrior* partially hid the two powerful Union frigates, the *Wabash* and the *Hartford*. There was a lot of cannon fire, but the *Warrior* appeared to be holding them at a distance. That's one for an iron hull, the Captain muttered to himself.

Slater's Morse lamp was flashing a message. "*Warrior*, dead ahead three thousand yards. *Wabash*, *Bienville*, to port five thousand yards. *Columbia* steaming out from Fort Walker. Another frigate, probably the *Hartford* off to starboard six thousand yards. *Columbia* headed for her."

The lamp stopped momentarily.

"Receiving message from HMS *Warrior*. She says to stay on her port flank, about one thousand yards astern. She will issue further orders after we've taken up position. Signed, Vice Admiral Earl Paul."

The steersmen's lamp was now messaging again. "Ship sighted astern still unidentified. Suggest a warning round be fired."

Why doesn't she identify, Paton thought to himself. *Time is running out.* He knew that in very little time the stern turret's inability to fire at anything closer than one hundred feet would place the ship in possible danger.

"Stern turret, prepare to fire ONE warning round."

But the Morse signalman atop the stern turret could not read how many rounds the message had said to fire. The smoke had made it impossible to see the message, yet the unknown vessel was closing on the ship's stern fast.

4.

Eugene Tessier could not seem to make the signalman aboard *The Great Eastern* understand his signal flags. Neither he nor his mate knew Morse code nor did he carry a Morse lantern, so his signaling knowledge was confined to signal flags and semaphore signaling. Apparently, *The Great Eastern's* signalman did not know semaphore, as the message he kept sending requested identification.

It had been a very tense night, waiting for *The Great Eastern* to leave Port Royal Sound. But it was not difficult to know when she was underway. The armada of Union ships surrounding the entrance to the Harbor began a relentless bombardment of the vessel and her escorts and Eugene Tessier had plenty of warning to weigh anchor and get the *Bermuda* underway.

His plan, once he was able to communicate with the ship, was to ask her protection, as a sister ship belonging to Fraser Trenholm. He would ask her to escort him up to the safety of Charleston harbor. It should not noticeably deter the bigger ship from her course for England.

Since Susannah had given him the information about the Union Navy's ships and *The Great Eastern*, he had allowed her to use his cabin to bathe and wash her clothes, not knowing she had already done so.

Susannah returned to her cabin. Thad had tried again to make love to her but she discouraged him. When she found out she would be within a stone's throw of John's ship within a short while, she once again thought of being with him.

But John had no idea where she was or of her treachery that now threatened the safety of *The Great Eastern*, it's cargo, and the lives of the crew, including his own. No one on board the ship had any knowledge of how the Union found out about the ship or her mission. Everyone just assumed that because of the size of the operation and the vessel that had been chartered to carry it out, somehow the Yankees would find out.

Captain Tessier watched the strange-looking turret high above on the stern of the ship he was trying to reach. It was slowly turning around, bringing the two oval openings in the turret's side to bear on his ship. Suddenly, two puffs of smoke appeared, simultaneously with two loud explosions Two plumes of water erupted not twenty feet in front of the *Bermuda*. The spray drenched her bow.

5.

"Sir, the stern turret has begun firing on the unknown vessel following us."

Walter Paton had heard the explosions. He took careful note of the content of the message just relayed to him.

"Get Mr. Sheffield up here on the bridge. I think you'll find him still supervising the firefighters."

Midshipman Sheffield quickly appeared, still as grimy as he had been when the fire started. Already another set of explosions from the stern was heard, indicating the turret gunnery crew had been given the wrong command.

"Mr. Sheffield, I want you to PERSONALLY convey this message to the stern gun crew. CEASE FIRE UNTIL THAT VESSEL IDENTIFIES HERSELF." Walter Paton found himself shouting the order both because there was so much other noise, and the level of frustration at his order having been disobeyed. Reginald Sheffield hurried down the bridge ladder to the deck, bearing the shouted command.

6.

The latest salvo from the stern turret had hit the bridge of the *Bermuda*, knocking Eugene Tessier clear down to the deck, ten feet below. A fire had started in the wooden superstructure, and the captain had been temporarily blinded by the blast. He lay on the deck, unable to move.

Thad Howard and Susannah Eddings had felt and heard the blast and now hurried on deck to witness the chaos. Some of the sailors were trying to put out the fire, but the pumps couldn't seem to get any water to the hose. Someone brought a stack of nested canvas buckets on deck and Thad and Susannah each grabbed one. Someone else managed to open another tap that had not been damaged by the explosion, and seawater gushed out. Soon the bucket brigade was starting work.

Thad looked around to see who was running the ship. The bridge itself was almost destroyed, which meant the ship would have to be steered from the stern position. Someone had the good sense to tell the engine room to stop the screw turning, and the ship was now wallowing in the swells and the wake of the monstrous ship in front of her.

7.

"The Captain orders you to CEASE FIRE NOW UNTIL THAT SHIP IS IDENTIFIED!" Reginald Sheffield was shouting the order at the top of his lungs to the signalman atop the stern turret. The acrid smoke and the smell of burnt powder burned the young midshipman's eyes. But he could clearly see that the ship's guns had inflicted mortal damage on the unidentified vessel. He watched the signalman bend over and relay the orders through the hatch to the gun crew.

William Slater now joined the crewmen staring at the sinking ship off the stern. "Where is the signalman who was responsible for the identification of that ship?"

It was the first time in anyone's memory that Slater had raised his voice in anger and was speaking with accusatory tones.

The signalman climbed down the ladder on the side of the turret and hurried over to Slater.

"Sir, Seaman Keith O'Donnell. I was on duty and tried to get the ship to identify. Someone with flags was trying to tell me but I don't know semaphore."

Slater stared hard at the frightened sailor. "What were your orders, seaman?"

"To commence firing on the ship because she was closing on us. Sir, I couldn't really see the bridge light, there was so much smoke blowing around."

"Your orders were to fire one round at the ship, to stop her, not to sink her!"

The seaman looked down at the deck. Slater could see his hands were shaking. An explosion from the sinking vessel astern momentarily stopped the interrogation. It was the doomed vessel's last gasp. All that could be seen that remained was the last third of the hull. The surrounding water was full of debris, boxes, bails of material, and a lot of unidentifiable flotsam and jetsam. Some persons could be seen floundering in the chilling waters.

"Report to me when we get out to sea. I want the captain to hear your full explanation, seaman. Resume your duties."

"Midshipman Sheffield, get a detail together to pick up any survivors. I must get back to the supervising the turrets. We're about to be fired upon ourselves."

On his way back to Mast Tuesday, William Slater decided to stop at the bridge and brief the Captain on the mixed-up signals and subsequent tragedy. He found Walter Paton very preoccupied and concerned about the coming confrontation.

"And we still don't know the ship's identity?" The tone of the captain's question bordered on the incredulous.

"No sir. But she didn't appear to be heavily armed. Judging by the stuff floating in the water I'd even venture to say she might have been a blockade-runner. I dispatched Midshipman Sheffield to form a detail and pick up any survivors."

Walter Paton was staring at the position of the *Warrior,* which had changed her position and now no longer blocked the channel. She lay off to the port side of *The Great Eastern*, about one thousand yards ahead. To her left, the *Wabash* and *Bienville*, together with about four smaller ships were forming an attack line, carefully avoiding getting too close to the potentially deadly armored ship. Off to starboard, Paton could see the *Hartford* being approached by the *Columbi*a. Semmes' *Sumter* could not be seen, although there was not a clear view from the bridge.

William Slater saluted his Commander-in-Chief and climbed down the ladder, heading for the lookout platform halfway up Mast Tuesday.

8.

Susannah could not believe how cold the water was. The second hit on the *Bermuda* had thrown her and most of the crew overboard. Thrashing about, she frantically looked for something to hang onto. A big wooden box, bound with rope floated by and she grabbed onto the rope.

She could see a log wall on the shore, which looked to be a quarter of a mile or so from where she was. The heavy wool cloak she had put on when the first explosion had brought her out on the *Bermuda's* deck was now soaked and heavy and made staying afloat difficult. With some effort, she unbuttoned the top button and wiggled out of it. She watched it float away with the rest of the debris.

Someone was crying for help. It was a man's voice and Susannah strained to see who it was. There weren't more than three or four other people in the water; the rest must have perished in the wreck. She wondered if Thad had survived.

The pleas got closer, and she could see the body struggling to hold onto a slippery barrel that was floating by. Susannah thought it was the captain, and although she could offer no more than the box she was clinging to, she began to paddle slowly in the direction of the cries.

It was Captain Tessier, holding on for his life with just one arm. He looked up and saw Susannah swimming towards him.

"My arm's broken. Please help me," his weak voice gasped.

She thought about how he had treated her on the London dock but could not bring herself to simply ignore his urgent cry for help. She noticed the barrel had a long rope attached to it, the loose end floating out from the barrel about ten feet.

"Hold still, Captain, I'll try and lash you to the barrel until help gets here."

She untied the sash around her waist and, knotting one end to the box and the other to her wrist, slipped off of it and swam over to the barrel. Reeling the rope in, she looped it around his body three times, under his good arm and under the broken one and tied it in a knot.

"That should hold you." She looked up at the side of *The Great Eastern* and saw the dangling ropes from the davits on the ship; it probably meant that a rescue party was on the way.

"Did anyone else make it?" The Captain's voice was very feeble; the icy water was sapping his strength.

"I think there were a couple of more that jumped off the stern after the last explosion." The brief exercise had warmed Susannah up but now she began to really feel the cold.

She reached the comparative safety of her box. It occurred to her that if she were picked up by the rescue craft that her imprisonment and trial would be resumed, once they could get her back to Charleston. On the other hand, she would possibly get to see John again. Her alternative, trying to swim to shore and disappear into the landscape, might save her—she could move elsewhere and start all over.

". . .Susannah." It was the Captain's voice. "Thank you for saving my life; I can probably save yours. Swim to the shore." The request was barely audible.

Susannah was surprised at the offer and the Captain's perception. He continued, "I can simply say you died in the explosion. I would do that for you, even though I know you should be tried for treason. You saved me; I think you must not have wanted to commit treason."

Susannah's whole body was shaking uncontrollably. "Thank you, Captain. That's very decent of you. I. . .I never wanted to betray my country. Right now I don't have much choice. I only hope I can survive."

Susannah started to paddle towards shore as she noticed the rows of long oars and the longboat headed in their direction. She hoped they could not see her.

But someone besides the Captain had also seen Susannah. A dazed and partially unconscious Thad lay sprawled across a wooden plank about one hundred feet from where she was now paddling.

9.

From his tiny perch halfway up Mast Tuesday, William Slater had the best overall view of the ongoing naval battle. To his left, about fifteen hundred yards was the sleek, black-hulled British frigate, the *Warrior*. She was heavily engaged with the converted mail steamer *Bienville* and the Union frigate *Wabash*. Both Federal ships had failed to effect much damage against the iron hull of the English warship. Through his glasses, Slater could see that the *Bienville* had had a fire on her afterdeck, the whole part of the ship blackened from the flames. Some smoke wafted from the burned area but the ship continued to fire on the *Warrior*. Slater also noticed that neither ship stayed within range of the iron ship's guns for very long; their captains knew their wooden hulls and rigging were vulnerable.

Off to starboard, he could see the *Hartford* and *Columbia* practically on top of each other, firing salvo after salvo. Although they, too, were at least two thousand yards away, through his glasses he could see both ships had suffered some damage.

Even with the smoke and haze of the battle, the Southerner could observe some of the differences between the two sets of ships. The *Warrior* had her guns below the main deck, protecting the crew in the event of a hit. The *Hartford*, although only two years older, still carried her guns on the main deck, exposing them and the gun crews to danger. The *Hartford* looked like a sailing ship with a funnel, as though adding a steam engine was more of an afterthought than a key element of the ship's design. Indeed, Slater observed, the Union frigate was employing her sails as help in maneuvering the ship during battle.

The *Warrior*, sat low in the water, her sails furled. Although both ships had three masts, the *Warrior*, with her twin funnels, looked like she had been designed as a steamship. She still carried the sailing vessel's trademark, the bowsprit, but it only seemed to add grace to the smooth black hull.

Behind the *Hartford's* hull another ship was emerging, this one smaller than the Union frigate. She was a side-wheeler and was positioning herself to bombard the other side of the *Columbia*.

The Fire Control Officer of *The Great Eastern* was unaware that both the *Hartford* and the other ship, the *Rhode Island*, were being commanded by their first officers, as both Stephen Trenchard and David Farragut were being held as prisoners aboard the *Warrior*.

"Captain Paton says hold your fire until we're fired upon." Slater's Morse operator was in the process of acknowledging the Captain's order.

"Tell Mr. Paton that we have another Union vessel to contend with, a side-wheeler. Looks like she might be the *Rhode Island.*"

The Great Eastern was now under full steam, her five funnels belching thick clouds of black acrid smoke. The fire in the hold seemed to have been extinguished, although smoke still wafted skyward from the still-uncovered cargo hatch. Fortunately for Slater, Mast Tuesday was in front of the first funnel so Slater did not have to contend with it. He did notice that the ship was closing fast on the *Warrior's* position.

"Tell Mr. Paton we'll be in the *Wabash's* gun range in about fifteen minutes. Ask him if he's going to try and outrun the Union ships."

The noise of the battle between the *Warrior*, the *Wabash*, and the *Bienville* was growing louder. The *Bienville* was now circling the bow of the British ship, apparently about to try the same strategy as the *Rhode Island* was doing with the *Columbia*. Suddenly, Slater saw a huge blast amidships, on the *Bienville*. The bow gun of the *Warrior* must have scored a hit. But at the course *The Great Eastern* was sailing, she would be within range in about five minutes.

"Order the forward turret to train their guns on the *Bienville*.

"Tell Mr. Paton we're closing on the *Bienville.*"

"Sir, Mr. Slater says we're closing on the *Bienville.*"

Walter Paton strained to see the *Bienville's* position but the smoke from the battle and his own ship's funnels made only a fleeting observation possible.

"Repeat the order, Mr. Slater, to only fire if we're fired upon."

Even as that message was being sent to the observation post, Slater could see the former mail ship was going to take a shot at the ship. Her course had changed and her bow was now pointed in the direction of *The Great Eastern.*

"Tell the bow turret to stand by to fire on the hostile ship. Get word to Mr. Paton the *Bienville*'s coming after us."

The Union ship was less than five hundred yards off the ship's bow, looking as though she would attack the port side. Slater watched her change course slightly so her starboard guns were now within range of *The Great Eastern.*

The *Bienville* fired first.

"Forward turret, commence firing!"

"Tell Mr. Paton we're under fire and are returning it." The Morse operator quickly swung his signal lamp the one hundred-eighty degrees to the rear of the bridge.

The two Dahlgrens in the forward turret answered the blasts from the *Bienville. The Great Eastern* had now assumed the role of a warship.

On the bridge, Reginald Sheffield, having changed his sooty uniform for a fresh one, saluted Walter Paton.

"Sir, the survivors of the ship have been rescued. She was the *Bermuda* sir. I'm sure you know who her owners are."

"Yes Mr. Sheffield. I'll be held accountable; but I can't worry about that right now. What about the survivors—who are they?"

"Sir, Mr. Slater says the *Bienville*'s getting closer."

"Tell Mr. Slater to engage the stern turret as well"

Walter Paton turned back to face Reginald Sheffield.

"A Mr. Eugene Tessier, who claims he's the Captain. Also a man who can't speak, who appears to have been hurt. Mr. Tessier's right arm is broken."

"Have them looked after and made as comfortable as possible. Tell Mr. Tessier I'll be down to see him as soon as possible. Convey my apologies."

A heavy metallic clank signified the iron hull of the ship had been hit.

"Get a detail to the starboard side of the ship to look for damage. The ship's been hit."

Both turrets fired, almost simultaneously. Slater trained his glasses on the *Bienville*. With a huge gush of water and a shower of sparks, wood planks and a dramatic burst of fire and smoke, the Union ship sustained major hits from *The Great Eastern*.

"Tell Mr. Paton we've scored a direct hit on the *Bienville*."

William Slater watched as the crippled ship attempted to get out of range, with a change of course to port. Too late, the starboard turret of the big ship simply swiveled a little further towards the aft section and fired another salvo. This time she hit one of the ship's paddlewheels, which went up in another dramatic shower of water, pieces of wood and metal and sparks, fire and smoke.

Had James Bulloch been on the scene, he would have felt vindicated. The ship he had returned honorably to its rightful owners at the beginning of the war had been converted by the Union into a vessel of destruction, it's current mission to help stop *The Great Eastern.*. It was a fitting ending to such a disgraceful act.

The severely crippled *Bienville* drifted slowly to a stop. *The Great Eastern* could finish her off if she wanted. But that was not her mission.

"Tell the bow turret to cease fire. The *Bienville*'s no longer a danger."

But in the interval, the *Wabash* had sailed in a wide arc away from the *Warrior* and now threatened *The Great Eastern*. William Slater focused his spyglass on the *Hartford* scene. Much to his chagrin, he observed the *Rhode Island* had broken engagement with the *Columbia* and was also headed for *The Great Eastern*. The *Warrior* was in hot pursuit of the *Wabash*.

"Tell Mr. Paton I recommend a course change thirty degrees to starboard." To Slater, it looked like the *Wabash* was trying to force *The Great Eastern* into range of the *Hartford*'s guns, where the two Union frigates would then join forces with the *Rhode*

Island to destroy the ship. The only thing that would prevent this would be the superior speed of the vessel.

"Sir, Mr. Slater recommends a course change, 30 degrees to starboard."

Walter Paton could see the coming together of the two Union frigates.

"Mr. McLennan and Mr. Beauregard, I want everything this ship can give. Are the two boilers that were being cleaned operational yet?"

But no voices came back through the engine room speaking tubes. Most probably they were not near them, attending to other duties.

"Mr. Sheffield, I want you to get Mr. McLennan and Mr. Beauregard up on the bridge as soon as possible. You go after Mr. Beauregard and send someone else after Mr. McLennan."

The burning and now motionless *Bienville* slowly drifted astern of *The Great Eastern*. William Slater and Walter Paton both watched the crew try and put out the flames. Some men could be seen jumping into the water.

John Beauregard appeared on the bridge first. His bandaged nose and still blackened eye sockets showed the stress he had already been through and his uniform was spattered with oil and coal dust, but he saluted smartly. Alexander McLennan wearily climbed the ladder to the bridge. He too appeared grimy and tired, but also managed a smart salute.

Walter Paton turned slowly from watching the *Bienville*. The look on his face was grave.

"Gentlemen, off to our port and closing fast is the U.S. warship the *Wabash*. Chasing her is the British ship, the *Warrior*. Off our starboard is the U.S. warship, the *Hartford*, together with the fast cutter *Rhode Island*. I believe you served on that ship Mr. Beauregard. How fast can she go?"

John Beauregard thought a moment.

"Well sir, we had her up to almost fourteen knots when I ran the engine room. But she was fairly new then. I understand they've been using her to chase blockade runners. That's a lot of high speed running. Unless she's had an overhaul in the last, let's say, six months, I doubt she could do fourteen knots."

"Mr. McLennan, can *we* do fourteen knots?"

The Scotsman drew a puff on his pipe before replying.

"Captain, we've still got a lot of water in the bilge from the fire. The pumps are working fine, but it'll be awhile before it's gone. A lot of those bales absorbed some of that water. I'd say we'd be very lucky to sustain even thirteen knots."

The Captain was staring again at the hulk of the *Bienville*. She had hoisted most of her sails and looked like she was heading for the shore.

"We are caught between of the two most powerful ships the U.S. Navy has. I'm sure the *Warrior* can handle one or perhaps even both of them. But that leaves the *Rhode Island*. We're going to have to fight, something I promised the Queen we wouldn't do. Unless we can outrun the *Rhode Island*, we will have a fight on our hands."

At the mention of his former ship, John Beauregard remembered how kind and brotherly its commander, Stephen Trenchard, had been. Always patient, always considerate, always looking after his junior officer's welfare, John Beauregard knew the captain of Little Rhody would put up a game fight. But, in the end, he knew that he would probably go down with his ship. For the first time, he wished he didn't have to fight this war.

"I want everything those two powerplants are capable of generating. We won't be able to use the sails as they would cut the vision of the gun crews. Besides, I don't think the crew's ever rigged all of them. Is everything clear?"

Both men answered in the affirmative. They saluted and hurriedly left the bridge.

The two engine room officers made their way down the iron ladders, into the gloom that was the heart of the vessel. Although the gas lamps provided some light, the smoke from the boiler rooms and the lingering cotton-bale fire made seeing more than twenty feet a chore. The place had taken on a decidedly strong odor of burned cotton fiber and burlap. Together, they made breathing difficult, and exertion painful. As John Beauregard passed through the boiler room on his way to his post, he could see the firemen were having to stop every few moments to catch their breath. He wondered how this would affect the ship's speed. He climbed the ladder to the catwalk astride the stern engine and motioned for the midshipman on duty to join him at the railing.

Midshipman Edward McKenzie had been recruited by another Scotsman, Alexander McLennan, to serve aboard the ship. He had been with her through the good times and the bad. The Scottish engineer had given him over to John Beauregard's command when the young lieutenant had first taken over his duties with the ship's propeller engine. McLennan had correctly figured the midshipman could help John Beauregard learn the ropes but also would not be afraid to ask help from his former leader.

John Beauregard cupped his hands around his mouth so what he was going to say could be better understood. "Mr. McKenzie, I want you to pass the word along. The next six hours will see this ship fighting for its life. We are going into battle against the best ships the U.S. Navy's got and we are going to try and outrun them. Here in the engine room we must keep up full steam and keep a watchful eye on all the machinery. I want bearings and oil cups checked hourly for signs of wear or lack of lubrication. I want all other mechanical joints checked similarly and a log kept, which I will review after each inspection. No one will go off watch until I say so. If the men are due to go off watch and their replacements arrive, the relief is to take over and the other men may relax but are not to leave the engine rooms. I will be in constant contact with Mr. McLennan to be sure he doesn't need help."

"I needn't say that the Captain, indeed Queen Victoria, are both looking to us to get out of this mess. I have no idea how the U.S. Navy found out about this operation, but after it's over I'm sure we'll be told."

"Dismissed."

A similar scene was taking place in the noisier, smokier paddle-wheel engine room. In his usual Scottish efficiency, Alexander McLennan kept his charge to his men to a couple of sentences. He added one more note of caution.

"With all this machinery going full speed, I would make sure of my footing. The ship is going out into the ocean and sure to start rolling and pitching again. We can't afford to lose any of you to carelessness."

A loud metallic clank reverberated throughout the ship The guns of the *Wabash* had spoken. One of the cannonballs had hit the hull of the ship. As before, a quick survey showed a small dent but no hull penetration.

The *Warrior* was now less than five hundred yards in front of *The Great Eastern*, her port side blazing at the U.S. frigate. She had scored several hits, one bringing down a considerable part of the center mast's rigging. But the crew of the Union vessel, under the seasoned command of Captain Du Pont, kept an evasive course, and managed to avoid taking all the shells the British frigate threw at her.

"Signal the forward turret to commence fire on the *Wabash*!"

Finally unfettered by the Captain's order not to fire until fired upon, the gunnery crews in the forward turret unleashed a deadly barrage from their protected positions. On their second salvo, they scored a direct hit on the ship's funnel and her middle mast. But she kept on coming, in spite of the withering fire from both the *Warrior* and *The Great Eastern*.

William Slater noticed that the *Rhode Island* had altered its course to stay out of the range of the *Warrior*'s and *The Great Eastern*'s guns. She was nearly parallel with the ship's course and Slater figured she would try an attack from the stern.

They were passing the bow of the *Wabash*, who now had several major fires to fight. She had temporarily ceased any major salvos; indeed only sporadic guns fired. If they got past the *Wabash* without incident, the *Warrior* could engage the threatening *Hartford*, and they only need worry about the *Rhode Island*.

So far *The Great Eastern* had escaped any major damage from the shelling. Now her speed would be put to the test, as Slater could see the *Rhode Island* coming about, to keep up with the ship and keep her under fire until the guns of the *Hartford* could be brought to bear.

"Mr. McLennan and Mr. Beauregard, keep up the steam." Walter Paton had noticed a marked increase in the ship's pitching and rolling, a sure sign they were out in the South Atlantic. He had not left the bridge to consult his navigation charts but estimated from the last fix of the cold afternoon sun that they were headed North North East at about twelve knots.

It looked like the *Wabash* had retired from the battle, wishing to save herself rather than risk total destruction at the hands of the two apparently indestructible iron ships. The *Warrior* had dropped astern of *The Great Eastern*, to protect her from a possible counterattack from the *Wabash*.

Straining to see through the lowering clouds, Walter Paton could barely see the *Hartford*, but estimated she was at 2,500 yards the starboard side of the bow and closing fast. Swiveling around to the rear of the ship, he could see the *Rhode Island* at about the same distance. She seemed to be closing a little faster.

"Tell Mr. Slater to alert the stern turret to be ready to fire.

The Morse signaling system devised by the ship's architects and the Americans had proved to be a very useful tool. Except for the mishap with the *Bermuda,* which could more properly be blamed on lack of training, the system had functioned well under fire. It worked day or night, and could, for the most part, function under the most adverse conditions.

Semmes' *Sumter* had not been seen recently. It was assumed she had taken on the *Hartford*, together with the *Columbia*.

But it was the *Rhode Island* that now menaced the ship. After a brief exchange of fire with the *Warrior*, the fast cutter had nearly drawn abreast of *The Great Eastern*, still keeping out of range of her deadly turrets. As Walter Paton trained his spyglass on the trim little ship, she suddenly swung her bow directly at the ship. Almost simultaneously, she began to fire.

She was lobbing explosive shells at the iron hull. Walter Paton wondered how the seven-eighths of an inch thick plate would hold up to such explosions if they were hits.

The Great Eastern returned fire. But the rounds fell short of their target.

Walter Paton heard two of the rounds from the *Rhode Island* whistle harmlessly overhead. The third round landed on deck, just aft of Mast Thursday and his own caboose. The explosion created a shower of wood, glass and flame. Some of the cotton bales which had not yet been loaded into the ship's hold caught fire. Screams of pain could be heard.

William Slater saw a dramatic explosion on the foredeck of the *Rhode Island. The Great Eastern* must have hit an ammunition store, as the explosions continued. He looked astern at the chaos on the deck of his own ship.

Fire seemed to be everywhere. Mast Thursday had most of its lower rigging and sails blown away or severely damaged. Spars hung down at crazy angles. The captain's caboose was shattered, it's glass windows completely blown out.

"Midshipman Sheffield! Take charge of damage control! Get that fire out! Find out how many men were injured! Mr. McLennan and Mr. Beauregard! Keep up steam!" Walter Paton took each item that needed attention and addressed it quickly.

Alexander McLennan was issuing an order to one of his oilers when an explosion ripped through the side of the hull, right next to the huge crankrods that turned the paddlewheels. An unlucky sailor performing maintenance duties was blown off the ladder as he was attempting to oil one of the huge joints. The explosion threw him in the path of the huge arm, and there would not be enough clearance for his body, the arm and the thirty-one ton shaft.

McLennan and the other men watched helplessly as the still form of the man slowly disappeared under the crushing weight of the arm. Mercifully the man was unconscious and never felt a thing. When the huge arm came back up again, the mashed mass of pink flesh, remnants of a blue uniform, and an immense amount of blood began to pour off the metal. As it swung higher, the whole mess, reacting to gravity, slipped off the arm and fell down into the bilges.

The ship had claimed another victim. The crew was stunned. It was up to their leader to galvanize them back to reality.

"He never felt a thing. Let's get back to our duties lads. Any damage to the engine?"

Alexander McLennan was shouting his orders. His men, still numbed by the horrible scene they had just witnessed began swarming over the mechanical parts, looking for something out of place. There appeared to be nothing; the rhythmical clanking continued.

The explosion had torn an eight-foot jagged hole in the hull of the ship. McLennan guessed it was about twenty-five feet above the waterline, based on its alignment with the shaft of the paddlewheel. He quickly ran to the speaker tube and delivered his report to Walter Paton, who lost no time ordering a repair.

"Rig a boatswain's chair for the carpenters. I want that hole patched up before we go any farther."

"But, Sir, those men will be under fire from the *Rhode Island*."

"We're almost out of her range. I don't want this ship in danger of taking on any water."

10.

With all the excitement of defending the ship, the crew of *The Great Eastern* had momentarily left the fighting of the fire in the hold to those who were not directly involved with running the ship or firing its guns. The very survival of the vessel depended on her being able to get underway, while fending off the numerous attempts to damage and destroy her.

But the fire had now spread to a second hold, while continuing to burn vigorously in the first. With the ship nearly out of range of the *Rhode Island* and the *Warrior* protecting her other flank, Walter Paton turned his attention to the out-of-control conflagration that was an entirely different threat to his ship.

On the bridge, watching the acrid smoke pore out of the second hold, he leaned over to the speaking tube. "Mr. Beauregard, please report to the bridge. Put Mr. McKenzie in command of the screw engine room for the time being. I need an officer to assume command of this bloody fire!"

The clouds of billowing smoke, fanned by the ship's gradual acceleration were getting worse. Reginald Sheffield, one of the few to have stayed with the fire during the ship's escape, now appeared on the bridge, wearily saluting the captain.

"Sir, the fire in number two hold is getting worse. We can't spare anyone of the number one hold fire as we're barely able to keep it under control." His words came out in gasps, attesting to the density of the smoke.

Without acknowledging the salute, Walter Paton wheeled around and again shouted into the screw engine room speaking tube.

"MR BEAUREGARD! MR. MCKENZIE! IS ANYONE ALIVE DOWN THERE? I NEED MR. BEAUREGARD ON THE BRIDGE IMMEDIATELY. MR. MCKENZIE, IF YOU CAN

HEAR THIS, HAVE MR. BEAUREGARD GET TO THE BRIDGE IMMEDIATELY WITH FOUR OF YOUR STOKERS!

This time there was an answer.

"Beauregard here, Sir! McKenzie's in charge. I'm rousing four of the off-duty stokers as you requested. We need everyone on duty to tend to the boilers as we get up speed. I'll be there momentarily."

The captain turned to the midshipman, rubbing his eyes, trying to get the sting out. "Mr. Sheffield, show Lieutenant Beauregard where the firefighting equipment is. Let's get the steam crane over number two hold fired up. Maybe we can lift some of those burning bales out of the holds and dump them overboard. Look lively, lad. I don't want any casualties"

A sooty John Beauregard slowly climbed the ladder to the bridge. He saluted the Captain who turned from speaking to the midshipman. Two of the four off-duty stokers also appeared on the bridge, saluting the Captain.

"Mr. Beauregard, I want you to oversee this entire firefighting exercise. Midshipman Sheffield doesn't have the resources to fight the fire in the second hold, much less contain the one he's already trying to put out. I think we should get the steam crane over the second hold fired up and try and get some of those burning bales out of the hold and overboard. Get that operation started while Midshipman Sheffield gets your detail outfitted and into the second hold.

The other two stokers appeared, somewhat disheveled. Reginald Sheffield was already herding them back down the ladder, together with the first two, and towards the second hold. John Beauregard hurried down the forward ladder, heading for the carpenter's shop. He'd need at least two of them to devise the rigging to lift the burning bales out of the hold.

A half-hour later, things had not improved. The steam crane had been activated, but no one could get close enough to the edge of the hold to supervise lowering the line, much less attaching it to one of the burning bales. John Beauregard, observing the operation had an idea.

"Mr. Sheffield, hose me down. I'll go down through hold number two where the fire's not so hot. When you see me appear, direct the water to the edge of the topmost bale. I'll try and attach the line to the bale's binding rope. Just remember to keep the water on the bale itself." He motioned to one of the carpenters to follow him.

Within minutes the young lieutenant was seen by the other ship's carpenters. He had climbed to the top of the pile of cotton bales and was motioning for the crane operator to lower the line. After a brief instance, the steam crane operator engaged the windlass and the smoldering bale slowly emerged from the hold. The smoke made it difficult to see, but the crane operator swung the boom out over the water. The other carpenter leaned out over the railing and with a single swing of his ax, cut the rope binding the cotton bale together. The rope from the crane's windlass, suddenly having nothing to hold onto, went shooting up into the air, releasing the bale.

Freed of their binding, the cotton bolls, some visibly on fire wafted up, back towards the ship But a strong downdraft soon had the loose ones and the tightly packed center of the bale rocket down to the water, splashing and hissing as they hit the surface.

Walter Paton had raced to the end of the bridge after seeing the crane had successfully removed the first bale on fire. He ran back to the center and instructed the Morse operator to aim his lamp at the starboard turret Morse station. "Tell them to pass the word to Lieutenant Beauregard to continue the operation. Tell them also to pass along to Lieutenant Beauregard my congratulations on the success of a dangerous mission."

The other two stokers appeared on the bridge, saluting the captain. "You hands get down into number two hold to assist Lieutenant Beauregard in getting those smoldering bales out." The two stokers saluted and disappeared down the bridge ladder.

11.

The captain's caboose, having sustained a direct hit from Union warships, was almost uninhabitable. Shards of glass littered the fine oriental carpet and furniture. The first officer and some of the deckhands not busy fighting the fire, running the ship or manning the four gun turrets had managed to clear a space in the captain's bedroom for Eugene Tessier and the as yet unidentified redheaded man found floating near Captain Tessier in the water.

Efforts to interview the man directly were fruitless, as he seemed to have lost his speech. Eugene Tessier, outside of his broken arm which was being attended to by the ship's surgeon, was quite lucid.

Standing over him was the first officer. "And so you and this other gentleman were the only survivors? "

"Yes, sir. That other gentleman is Thad Howard, from Fraser Trenholm. He was guarding the prisoner, the spy Susannah Eddings. I saw her floating face down in the water. She wasn't moving, so I assumed she perished in the blast."

"Who was she and why was she in your and Mr. Howard's custody? Was she caught spying on Union activities?"

Eugene Tessier proceeded to retell what he knew of Susannah's deeds and why he was following so closely behind *The Great Eastern.* "She was a traitor to the United States and the South as well. She telegraphed the destination and contents of *The Great Eastern* to military officials in Washington from London after the ship left. But she got hers, all right. Blasted right into the water. I tell you she wasn't moving when I caught sight of her body, still in the bright red coat she was wearing on deck when the ship exploded."

Thad Howard, still unable to speak, had suddenly sat up and was vigorously shaking his head from side to side, making noises like he was trying to say something. The first officer turned his attention to him.

"Did you see the prisoner alive, Mr. Howard?" Thad Howard was now nodding, just as vigorously as when he had been shaking his head earlier. The first officer continued. "Captain Tessier says he saw her floating face down in the water, apparently not moving. Is that what you saw?"

Once again, the head shook back and forth vigorously. Now he was flailing his arms in a crude effort to show some sort of swimming motion. "You saw her swimming away from the wreckage?"

Yes, yes, nodded Thad Howard. Suddenly he collapsed in a heap, either from exhaustion or simply from pain. The surgeon walked over to examine him.

"He's unconscious. I'm going to have him put in my cabin, where I can keep an eye on him. I don't know why he can't speak. He may have had some internal injuries. I'll examine him carefully." The surgeon motioned for two of the deckhands to pick Thad Howard up and move him gently to the surgeon's cabin.

The first officer turned back to the captain of the sunken *Bermuda.* "I think you're correct in your observation of the Eddings girl, Mr. Tessier. Our crew did a pretty thorough search of the wreckage and you were the only two people we could find who were alive. And I don't even know how you managed. There was nothing left of that ship by the time we reached her. Whoever aimed that cannon was right on target."

Eugene Tessier nodded wearily and leaned back against the wall. The surgeon spoke. "Mr. Tessier, I'll try and make you as comfortable as possible. I'll help you change into some dry clothes shortly. Please understand that Captain Paton was under great pressure to get the ship out of harm's way. I think you and Mr. Howard have given good accounts of yourselves and the *Bermuda,* and Captain Paton can explain why he destroyed your ship."

But the *Bermuda,* a Confederate hero herself, had gone to her graveyard, a tragic victim of botched signaling.

12.

Raphael Semmes had just given the order to break off engagement from the Federal frigate *Hartford*. His little raider was a shadow of its former self. The tiny bridge had taken a direct hit from the huge warship. Semmes and First Officer Kell had barely escaped with their lives and retreated temporarily to the rear, to better direct the fate of the small ship. There was a peculiar scraping sound on the hull whenever a course change was ordered. Another direct hit had almost toppled the main mast, causing the ship to lose some of its momentum. Sailors had been ordered quickly up into the rigging to patch the mainsail and its rigging so they could get back up to some semblance of normal speed.

"Mr. Kell, see to maintaining our course." The *Sumter*'s captain started forward, carefully avoiding the debris that littered the deck. "I'll begin a damage assessment."

The *Hartford*, successfully distracted from chasing *The Great Eastern* by Semmes, had also turned course to resume the chase. Semmes could only see part of her, so thick was the smoke from their brief battle.

Meanwhile, activity aboard the *Sumter* had settled down to normal. Midshipman Nelson, promoted from seaman during the action by Semmes for leading the gun crew now appeared from around the corner of the main cabin. He saluted his leader.

"Mr. Nelson, have you been able to assess damage to the vessel?"

"Yessir. We lost three men; two of them when the bridge blew up and one overboard during our evasive moves. Two men wounded; one lost a leg sir. We're still rigging the mainsail as the main spar was heavily damaged. It should be ready by nightfall. I asked the carpenters to work on it until it's fixed."

"How's the engine? Can we make it back to New Orleans for repairs? Do we have enough coal? Has Engineer Mackey given

294

you his report yet?" The captain's famous impatience was making its appearance again.

Midshipman Nelson, grateful for his new rank, was not about to test the captain's temper. "I was just on my way below to talk to him, Sir, when I met up with you. I'll get below right now."

"Good. Please also arrange for someone to took at the steering ropes and the rudder to see what's making that scraping sound. Meet me in the seaman's cabin when you know something. I'm going there to speak with the wounded and make sure they're comfortable."

"Yessir." Midshipman Nelson saluted the captain and hurried toward the aft hatch and the engine room. Semmes looked out at the place in the water where the *Hartford* had last been seen. The smoke and mist had begun to dissipate with the wind. In its place, a weak sun dimly illuminated the deep green of the Atlantic Ocean. But there was no sign of the frigate.

Semmes was glad to be free of his role as a decoy in the battle to spring *The Great Eastern* from Port Royal Sound. He much preferred having the odds in his favor when he was a raider, surprising his often unarmed prey into submission. Deep down, he was anxious to get back to that role.

He would not have to wait long. His next command was already under construction at Laird and Sons in Birkenhead, across from Liverpool on the Mercy River. After his meeting with James Bulloch in New Orleans last June to arrange purchase of the *Sumter*, the Confederate agent had promptly arranged to sail back to England and, unbeknownst to Semmes, arrange construction of the second-generation Confederate raider, the *Florida*. In August, while the *Sumter* was earning her reputation as the terror of the Caribbean, acting under the disguise of a private individual, he again visited the shipyard and signed contracts to begin construction of a vessel simply known as Hull 290. She would later become the famous raider *Alabama*. Semmes had already been picked to be her captain.

13.

The two stokers struggled with the badly burned body of John Beauregard. The young officer's early success at getting the burning cotton bales out of the ship's hull had been eclipsed by a sudden flare-up in hold number three, his planned exit route, since they were still fighting the fire in hold number two. In trying to outrun the flames, he had stumbled and fallen. In a matter of minutes, the fire cornered him and the intense heat started his uniform smoldering. Only the quick work of two stokers, aided by water from a hose held by a third, saved his life.

"Let him down gently. Try not to touch any more of his uniform than you have to. We must be careful not to disturb his skin."

John Beauregard had passed out from the shock of getting burned by the fire. His limp body lay still as the ship's surgeon delicately cut away the charred uniform from the confederate officer's legs, trunk and arms. The blackened skin had already started to ooze a yellowish fluid.

The two stokers, both poor conscripted Welshmen who had been shanghaied in a Liverpool flophouse, stood quietly by the surgeon. One of them spoke to the surgeon.

"'e saved my life, this officer. I was bein' beaten cuz I couldn't understand what the bosun was tellin' me to do. This man stopped the beatin' Thank gawd he's still alive."

The surgeon had cut away most of John Beauregard's uniform. It appeared that his leg had been burned the most. The rest of his body seemed relatively unscathed, including his torso and his head. While his uniform had been badly charred, it had protected his upper body from being burned.

The surgeon bent down and pulled a jar of salve from the cabinet under John Beauregard's couch. He turned to the Welshman who had spoken.

"You men did a very brave deed. I intend to notify the Captain of your bravery. In the meantime, let's pray that this young officer pulls through this." He turned and began to gently apply the ointment to the officer's legs.

14.

Utterly exhausted, waterlogged and shaking violently from the cold, Susannah slowly moved her feet in the water, propelling her and the wooden box which had literally been her life raft towards the shore of Port Royal Sound. The battle raging in the water; the noise and the acrid smoke from both cannon fire and burning ships were behind her, and she was virtually numb.

How much further, how much longer do I have to endure, she thought to herself. She could dimly see lights in the distance when she crested a wave. She had swallowed so much sea water that it was making her retch every few minutes. But now, even over the now-distant cannon fire, she could hear waves washing on a beach. It gave her renewed energy; she began to use her arms to hasten her landing.

Soon her feet were able to touch bottom and she abandoned the wooden box, gently sliding off of it into the icy water. She waded up on the beach and collapsed in a heap on the dune, still shivering violently. The physical exhaustion overwhelmed her fear of being captured and she dozed off, totally oblivious to the two Confederate pickets who were on patrol and had seen her lurch out of the water, across the beach and into the dune. They raced in her direction.

15.

Captain Paton was on the bridge, as the last light of dusk faded in the west. He looked out at the vast deck of his ship, at the chaos and disorder that had been created from having to fight a naval battle, get the vessel underway and extinguish a dangerous fire in three of the cargo holds.

The fresh sea breeze helped to dissipate the acrid odor left by the burning cotton. It was everywhere; in his uniform, his hair; throughout the ship.

He had ordered a general cleanup, after the all-clear had been sounded by the lookouts, still commanded by William Slater. He turned to his left, noticing the sleek shape of the *Warrior* about 1,000 yards astern, easily keeping pace with *The Great Eastern's* thirteen-knot speed.

The presence of the iron warship had undoubtedly saved *The Great Eastern* from considerable damage. Indeed, the size of the United States armada alone might possibly have prevented the ship from getting underway at all. After they had cleared the battle area, he signaled his thanks to Vice Admiral Earl Paul for his effective tactics and gunnery. The acknowledgment from Commander Paul included an invitation to visit the warship when things had returned to normal aboard *The Great Eastern.*

Judging by the appearance on deck and the number of hands involved in cleaning up the disorder, that would not be long. He wished it were so for his young Confederate officer who had been burned in trying to extinguish the cotton bale fire.

John Beauregard had stayed unconscious for almost a day. He had been carefully watched over by the ship's surgeon and his assistants, but the healing process for the officer's burned legs was slow in starting. The two Welsh seamen who had saved him had been honored in a brief ceremony.

None of the crew of *The Great Eastern* had been seriously injured in the battle. Both of the Ericsson turret gun crews had been able to fire their artillery successfully and manipulate the turrets to bring the guns on target. A few hits had even been scored, particularly on the disgraced *Bienville*. Even the swift gun ship, *Rhode Island,* had been hit.

The ship itself had survived several dangerous events. The cotton bale fire, even though it had spread to hold number three, had eventually succumbed to the fire hoses and the work of a determined crew. *The Great Eastern's* double iron hull had prevented the Union torpedo boat's deadly torpedo from sinking the ship. And the propeller shaft bearing that had been replaced on the journey from London had seated itself and was wearing evenly, thanks to the vigilance of young John Beauregard, who now lay on his bunk, semi-conscious from the morphine that the surgeon had been giving him.

Scabs had begun to form on the burned tissue; scabs that would eventually turn into possibly crippling scars when the skin finally regenerated itself. But the pain was subsiding, and the doctor had been decreasing the morphine dosages accordingly.

Alexander McLennan gently knocked on the door to John Beauregard's cabin. "McLennan here," he announced softly in anticipation of being asked who was knocking.

The voice from inside was weak and hoarse. "Please come in, sir." John Beauregard slowly, painfully, rolled his body over to face the bedside where his visitor would be standing.

The ruddy-faced engineer turned the brass knob in the door, swung it open slowly and entered the cabin. The room smelled of antiseptic and sickness. But there on the bed was his young assistant, his body mangled, but his blue-green eyes had a bit of a twinkle in them.

"Please, please come in and sit down, Mr. McLennan. I've not had many visitors lately; I guess everyone's been pretty busy getting the ship underway and the fires put out." Uttering the sentence in his weak and hoarse voice was obviously a difficult task for the young officer. He finished the sentence with a long sigh.

"You've been through enough strife for a lifetime, me lad." The Scotsman stood up and walked to John Beauregard's bedside. His oversized hand found that of his subordinate and squeezed it. The ruddy face softened as John Beauregard squeezed back. The blue-green eyes continued to sparkle.

"Did you know that one of the Welsh sailors that pulled me from the fire was the one I saved from a beating? Do you remember what you said to me about the whole incident?" He had managed to prop an elbow under his left side so he could talk more naturally.

Alexander McLennan smiled. "The captain didn't want to make a big thing about this. And he didn't want to implicate First Officer Pearson in anything that had been reported to him third-hand. I'm quite disappointed in Pearson, myself," the engineer was turning to go back to the small camp chair that was the only other seat in the cabin. "Been through a lot with him. Damned good seaman. Knows sailing and the rigging like the back of his hand. Guess this steam engine business is a bit of a blow to someone who only knows sail."

John Beauregard lay back down on the bunk, somewhat tired by the effort of propping himself up on his elbow. "What's to become of Pearson and his men? Does British Naval law have provisions for things like this?"

Alexander McLennan crossed his legs and folded his hands around his knee. "Pearson'll probably lose his license. He'll not likely get command of a ship for the rest of his career. And I think even the issue of forced conscription might get an airing, mostly for its denying a man his freedom."

John Beauregard breathed a deep sigh. "You know Mr. McLennan, I grew up with slaves. I just never thought of them as human beings. They were a necessary part of my father's plantation. Without them to do the work, we simply couldn't have grown cotton. When I saw these poor, basically helpless seamen being forced to do work they had not signed on to do, I saw the whole slavery issue in a different light. I've decided that when I get back home, I'm going to fight to get rid of slavery."

The last sentence had obviously been a pained effort for the young lieutenant. He closed his eyes.

Alexander McLennan stood up to leave. "I'll try to pay you a visit tomorrow, son. I'll be pretty busy watching over both engine rooms while you're recuperating. But we want you back, just as soon as you're able."

He grasped the handle of the door and turned to see the young officer had dozed off. As he stepped out into the passageway, he realized he had not delivered the message of Susannah's demise that he had been asked to do. Perhaps he would wait until the young Confederate lieutenant was feeling better.

16.

The ship's activities had settled down to the routine. They had now been at sea for almost twenty-four hours, and mercifully the weather had not yet turned for the worse as they headed for the North Atlantic.

Walter Paton was on the bridge, taking a final fix of the sun before nightfall while the first officer had gone below. He was not looking forward to informing his young American lieutenant about the drowning of Susannah Eddings. John Beauregard was healing well from his burns, although it would be some time before he could resume full command of the screw engine room. Suddenly, an idea came to him: he'd have Alexander McLennan disclose the tragedy. The Scotsman had seemed to take a fatherly role in not only training Beauregard; but after Beauregard had become badly injured, the engineer was visiting him between watches, looking after his needs and helping the surgeon attend to his burns.

He put down the sextant and approached the speaking tube. "Mr. McLennan, please report to me on the bridge immediately."

Alexander McLennan now appeared on the bridge, his uniform clean, but unaccustomedly wrinkled. "McLennan here, Sir. Sorry for the wrinkled uniform; everyone's been pretty busy including the lads in the officer's laundry."

"Stand easy Mr. McLennan. We've all been through hell. Please step over here," the Captain gestured to the opposite side of the bridge, "I have a personal favor to ask of you."

The two men now leaned over the railing. Walter Paton looked at the now inquisitive ruddy face of Alexander McLennan. "Mr. McLennan, I've appreciated the interest you've shown in Lt. Beauregard's well-being. I feel you're better in touch with his emotions right now and better able to tell him of his lady friend's drowning. That seems to be certain now, as the other man we rescued, Howard, I believe, is his name, has still not regained

303

consciousness. I know it will be a big blow to the lieutenant, but you're probably better fitted to the task than I. What's your feeling?"

Alexander McLennan took out his pipe and tobacco pouch and started to fill it. In almost no time he had lighted it and was now drawing on it, the smoke from his puffing quickly disappearing in the brisk wind. He turned his face to his commanding officer. His brow was furrowed.

"Sir, I don't think it will matter who gives the lad the bad news. It's heartbreaking, but perhaps we could spare the information about her being a traitor for some later time, when he's regained more of his strength. The only ones that know about it are the *Bermuda's* captain and you and I. I don't much like withholding information like that, but for his health, I think it's best. If that sounds right to you, I'll be glad to tell him about Susannah."

Walter Paton audibly let out a deep sigh. "Thank you, Mr. McLennan. I suggest we wait until Lt. Beauregard is able to resume some of his duties before we tell him of her deceit. That's all I was asking. Please return to your station. I'll leave it up to your discretion as to when to tell him."

As he expected, the young lieutenant took the news rather badly. Alexander McLennan broke it to him the next morning, the time of day when John Beauregard felt better. He had sobbed as the Scotsman told him he thought she was returning to America to wait for his return. He mentioned nothing of her perfidy. That would have to come later.

17.

Her short nap was interrupted by a hand shaking her shoulder. Between her still shivering body and the hand shaking her it was difficult to tell which was which. Her hair lay strewn in a swirled mass on the sand. Her dress, still soaked from the swim ashore, clung to her body; a faded and wrinkled garment that Susannah had once worn to a ball in Charleston. But try as hard as she could, she could not shake her fatigue.

Lemuel McCoy was now standing over the prone female who lay still on the beach. "Hey Jim, this one looks dead!" he shouted to James Pickens, his companion on guard duty.

"Geezuss Chrast, that's about the fifth corpse we seen on this beach in the last two hours." The other picket had joined his companion. "What the hell's going on out there in the bay. . .some kind of big naval battle?" The picket looked at Susannah's body. "She's still breathin'—look at her teets; they're movin'."

Private McCoy took the blanket from around his shoulders and gently laid it on Susannah's body.

"What d'ya think we should do with her? Turn her in?" He looked at Private Pickens, who was shaking his head.

McCoy kneeled on the sand and bent down further to look at the stranger's face. "Gawd she's a looker, Jim. What the hell's she doin' here?" He laid his hand one more time on Susannah's shoulder and shook it, this time a little more gently.

Susannah twitched and rolled over on her back. Her eyes slowly opened. She was still shivering, but the soldier's blanket was starting to warm her up. Quickly, she realized she had to regain her composure. She wiped the hair from her face and bit her lip. "I was a passenger on the *Bermuda*. We came over from London, headed for Charleston. We got involved in some kind of naval battle between the Union and us. The ship was destroyed. I was lucky to get away. Where am I?"

"Well, ma'am, this am the beach at Fort Beauregard."

The two pickets listened to her explanation. Judging by her appearance, it did indeed look as if she had survived some kind of disaster. In the lull, Susannah decided she could no longer be Susannah Eddings. She might already be known as a traitor. Instead, she would be Amanda Peyton, Martha Peyton's sister whom Martha had told her had died of smallpox several years ago.

Private Lemuel McCoy stood up and slung his rifle back on his shoulder. "Can you walk, Miss? We'll be glad to take you back to camp where's there a fire and maybe some dry clothing for ya'. May we ask yer name?" Private Pickens now bent down to help this beautiful but unkempt woman to her feet. Susannah continued to shiver.

"Who do I have to thank for this blanket?" she said with a little smile, looking at both of the Confederate soldiers as she stood unsteadily.

"That's Lem's, ma'am. We got more back at our camp. Y'all got a name, ma'am?"

As Susannah regained more of her composure she began to bite her lip. Now that she had thought of an alias, she must also have a history. "I'm Amanda Peyton from Charleston," she answered.

She knew the two soldiers would have no way to trace the information before she had a chance to leave the Confederate camp and begin her new life. Just where that new life would take Susannah Eddings would have to wait for another time.

THE END

About the Author
Ronald A. Zeitz

I started writing in 7th Grade whe was the Sports Editor for t school's magazine, I found out liked to write and was told by m English teacher that I was good a it. Having encouragement a something you do well at an early age can really make a difference.

In college, I found a way to escape my life on an isolated campus by more writing. Influenced by J.D. Salinger's character, Holden Caufield in *The Catcher in the Rye,* I reinvented myself into Chris Butler, another screw-up in his freshman year in college. I began to submit these "chapters" as Freshman English themes.

My professor praised my writing and characterization. At one point, he wrote in the margins of one episode ". . .I can't wait to see what happens next!" Once again, encouragement from a professor just made me want to write more.

The idea for this book stemmed from a series of articles on *The Great Eastern* in *The New Yorker Magazine*, published in the early 1950s. I have always been fascinated by large mechanical objects like ships and steam locomotives. The image of the ship lay dormant in my mind until it surfaced in the early 1990s when I sat down to write the book.

If you enjoyed following the characters of Susannah Eddings and John Beauregard, you'll also enjoy the follow-on to *Blockade Runner*, currently being written. It tracks both of them out West, where many Southerners fled after the South was devastated.

I live in the historic village of Harpers Ferry, West Virginia, which may have something to do with my writing historical fiction.